I0593763

Charles Dudley Warner

In the Levant

Charles Dudley Warner

In the Levant

ISBN/EAN: 9783337427375

Printed in Europe, USA, Canada, Australia, Japan

Cover: Foto ©Andreas Hilbeck / pixelio.de

More available books at **www.hansebooks.com**

IN THE LEVANT.

BY

CHARLES DUDLEY WARNER,

AUTHOR OF

"MY SUMMER IN A GARDEN," "BACK-LOG STUDIES," "SAUNTERINGS,"
"BADDECK, AND THAT SORT OF THING," "MY WINTER
ON THE NILE," ETC., ETC.

NINETEENTH EDITION.

BOSTON:
HOUGHTON, MIFFLIN AND COMPANY.
The Riverside Press, Cambridge.
1894

COPYRIGHT, 1876.
BY CHARLES DUDLEY WARNER.

TO

WILLIAM D. HOWELLS

THESE

𝔑𝔬𝔱𝔢𝔰 𝔬𝔣 𝔒𝔯𝔦𝔢𝔫𝔱𝔞𝔩 𝔗𝔯𝔞𝔳𝔢𝔩

ARE FRATERNALLY INSCRIBED.

PREFACE.

IN the winter and spring of 1875 the writer made the tour of Egypt and the Levant. The first portion of the journey is described in a volume published last summer, entitled "My Winter on the Nile, among Mummies and Moslems"; the second in the following pages. The notes of the journey were taken and the books were written before there were any signs of the present Oriental disturbances, and the observations made are therefore uncolored by any expectation of the existing state of affairs. Signs enough were visible of a transition period, extraordinary but hopeful; with the existence of poverty, oppression, superstition, and ignorance were mingling Occidental and Christian influences, the faint beginnings of a revival of learning and the stronger pulsations of awakening commercial and industrial life. The best hope of this revival was then, as it is now, in peace and not in war.

C. D. W.

HARTFORD, November 10, 1876.

CONTENTS.

IN THE LEVANT.

I.

FROM JAFFA TO JERUSALEM.

SINCE Jonah made his short and ignominious voyage along the Syrian coast, mariners have had the same difficulty in getting ashore that the sailors experienced who attempted to land the prophet; his tedious though safe method of disembarking was not followed by later navigators, and the landing at Jaffa has remained a vexatious and half the time an impossible achievement.

The town lies upon the open sea and has no harbor. It is only in favorable weather that vessels can anchor within a mile or so from shore, and the Mediterranean steamboats often pass the port without being able to land either freight or passengers. In the usual condition of the sea the big fish would have found it difficult to discharge Jonah without stranding itself, and it seems that it waited three days for the favorable moment. The best chance for landing nowadays is in the early morning, in that calm period when the winds and the waves alike await the movements of the sun. It was at that hour, on the 5th of April, 1875, that we arrived from Port Said on the French steamboat Erymanthe. The night had been pleasant and the sea tolerably smooth, but not to the apprehensions of some of the passengers, who always declare that they prefer, now, a real tempest to a deceitful groundswell. On a recent trip a party had been prevented from landing, owing to the deliberation of the ladies in making their toilet; by the time they had attired themselves in a proper manner to appear in Southern Palestine, the golden hour

had slipped away, and they were able only to look upon the land
which their beauty and clothes would have adorned. None of
us were caught in a like delinquency. At the moment the anchor
went down we were bargaining with a villain to take us ashore,
a bargain in which the yeasty and waxingly uneasy sea gave the
boatman all the advantage.

Our little company of four is guided by the philosopher and
dragoman Mohammed Abd-el-Atti, of Cairo, who has served us
during the long voyage of the Nile. He is assisted in his task
by the Abyssinian boy Ahman Abdallah, the brightest and most
faithful of servants. In making his first appearance in the Holy
Land he has donned over his gay Oriental costume a blue Frank
coat, and set his fez back upon his head at an angle exceeding
the slope of his forehead. His black face has an unusual lustre,
and his eyes dance with more than their ordinary merriment as
he points excitedly to the shore and cries, "Yâfa! Mist'r Dun-
ham."

The information is addressed to Madame, whom Ahman, utterly regardless of sex, invariably addresses by the name of one
of our travelling companions on the Nile.

"Yes, marm; you see him, Yâfa," interposed Abd-el-Atti,
coming forward with the air of brushing aside, as impertinent,
the geographical information of his subordinate; "not much, I
tink, but him bery old. Let us to go ashore."

Jaffa, or Yâfa, or Joppa, must have been a well-established
city, since it had maritime dealings with Tarshish, in that remote
period in which the quaint story of Jonah is set, — a piece of
Hebrew literature that bears internal evidence of great antiquity
in its extreme *naïveté*. Although the Canaanites did not come
into Palestine till about 2400 B. C., that is to say, about the
time of the twelfth dynasty in Egypt, yet there is a reasonable
tradition that Jaffa existed before the deluge. For ages it has
been the chief Mediterranean port of great Jerusalem. Here
Solomon landed his Lebanon timber for the temple. The town
swarmed more than once with the Roman legions on their way
to crush a Jewish insurrection. It displayed the banner of the
Saracen host a few years after the Hegira. And, later, when the

Crusaders erected the standard of the cross on its walls, it was the *dépôt* of supplies which Venice and Genoa and other rich cities contributed to the holy war. Great kingdoms and conquerors have possessed it in turn, and for thousands of years merchants have trusted their fortunes to its perilous roadstead. And yet no one has ever thought it worth while to give it a harbor by the construction of a mole, or a pier like that at Port Said. I should say that the first requisite in the industrial, to say nothing of the moral, regeneration of Palestine is a harbor at Jaffa.

The city is a cluster of irregular, flat-roofed houses, and looks from the sea like a brown bowl turned bottom up; the roofs are terraces on which the inhabitants can sleep on summer nights, and to which they can ascend, out of the narrow, evil-smelling streets, to get a whiff of sweet odor from the orange gardens which surround the town. The ordinary pictures of Jaffa do it ample justice. The chief feature in the view is the hundreds of clumsy feluccas tossing about in the aggravating waves, diving endwise and dipping sidewise, guided a little by the long sweeps of the sailors, but apparently the sport of the most uncertain billows. A swarm of them, four or five deep, surrounds our vessel; they are rising and falling in the most sickly motion, and dashing into each other in the frantic efforts of their rowers to get near the gangway ladder. One minute the boat nearest the stairs rises as if it would mount into the ship, and the next it sinks below the steps into a frightful gulf. The passengers watch the passing opportunity to jump on board, as people dive into the "lift" of a hotel. Freight is discharged into lighters that are equally frisky; and it is taken on and off splashed with salt water and liable to a thousand accidents in the violence of the transit.

Before the town stretches a line of rocks worn for ages, upon which the surf is breaking and sending white jets into the air. It is through a narrow opening in this that our boat is borne on the back of a great wave, and we come into a strip of calmer water and approach the single landing-stairs. These stairs are not so convenient as those of the vessel we have just left, and two persons can scarcely pass on them. But this is the only sea entrance to Jaffa; if the Jews attempt to return and enter their ancient kingdom this way, it will take them a long time to get in. A sea-wall fronts the town, fortified by a couple of rusty cannon at one end, and the passage is through the one gate at the head of these stairs.

It seems forever that we are kept waiting at the foot of this shaky stairway. Two opposing currents are struggling to get up and down it: excited travellers, porters with trunks and knapsacks, and dragomans who appear to be pushing their way through simply to show their familiarity with the country. It is a dangerous ascent for a delicate woman. Somehow, as we wait at this gate where so many men of note have waited, and look upon this sea-wall upon which have stood so many of the mighty from Solomon to Origen, from Tiglath-Pileser to Richard Cœur de Lion, the historical figure which most pervades Jaffa is that of the whimsical Jonah, whose connection with it was the slightest. There is no evidence that he ever returned here. Josephus, who takes liberties with the Hebrew Scriptures, says that a whale carried the fugitive into the Euxine Sea, and there discharged him much nearer to Nineveh than he would have been if he had kept with the conveyance in which he first took passage and landed at Tarsus. Probably no one in Jaffa noticed the little man as he slipped through this gate and took ship, and yet his simple embarkation from the town has given it more notoriety than any other event. Thanks to an enduring piece of literature, the unheroic Jonah and his whale are better known than St. Jerome and his lion; they are the earliest associates and Oriental acquaintances of all well-brought-up children in Christendom. For myself, I confess that the strictness of many a New England Sunday has been relieved by the perusal of his unique adventure. He in a manner anticipated the use of the monitors and other cigar-shaped submerged sea-vessels.

When we have struggled up the slippery stairs and come through the gate, we wind about for some time in a narrow passage on the side of the sea, and then cross through the city, still on foot. It is a rubbishy place: the streets are steep and crooked; we pass through archways, we ascend steps, we make unexpected turns; the shops are a little like bazaars, but rather Italian than Oriental; we pass a pillared mosque and a Moslem fountain; we come upon an ancient square, in the centre of which is a round fountain with pillars and a canopy of stone, and close about it are the bazaars of merchants. This old fountain is profusely sculptured with Arabic inscriptions; the stones are worn and have taken the rich tint of age, and the sunlight blends it into harmony with the gay stuffs of the shops and the dark skins of the idlers on the pavement. We come into the great market of fruit and vegetables, where vast heaps of oranges, like apples in a New England orchard, line the way and fill the atmosphere with a golden tinge.

The Jaffa oranges are famous in the Orient; they grow to the size of ostrich eggs, they have a skin as thick as the hide of a rhinoceros, and, in their season, the pulp is sweet, juicy, and tender. It is a little late now, and we open one golden globe after another before we find one that is not dry and tasteless as a piece of punk. But one cannot resist buying such magnificent fruit.

Outside the walls, through broad dusty highways, by lanes of cactus hedges and in sight again of the sea breaking on a rocky shore, we come to the Hotel of the Twelve Tribes, occupied now principally by Cook's tribes, most of whom appear to be lost. In the adjacent lot are pitched the tents of Syrian travellers, and one of Cook's expeditions is in all the bustle of speedy departure. The bony, nervous Syrian horses are assigned by lot to the pilgrims, who are excellent people from England and America, and most of them as unaccustomed to the back of a horse as to that of an ostrich. It is touching to see some of the pilgrims walk around the animals which have fallen to them, wondering how they are to get on, which side they are to mount, and how they are to stay on. Some have already mounted, and are walking the steeds carefully round the enclosure or timidly essaying a trot. Nearly every one concludes, after a trial, that he would like to change, — something not quite so much up and down, you know, an easier saddle, a horse that more unites gentleness with spirit. Some of the dragomans are equipped in a manner to impress travellers with the perils of the country. One, whom I remember on the Nile as a mild though showy person, has bloomed here into a Bedawee : he is fierce in aspect, an arsenal of weapons, and gallops furiously about upon a horse loaded down with accoutrements. This, however, is only the beginning of our real danger.

After breakfast we sallied out to see the sights : besides the house of Simon the tanner, they are not many. The house of Simon is, as it was in the time of St. Peter, by the seaside. We went upon the roof (and it is more roof than anything else) where the apostle lay down to sleep and saw the vision, and looked around upon the other roofs and upon the wide sweep of the tumbling sea. In the court is a well, the stone curb of which is deeply worn in several places by the rope, showing long use. The water is brackish ; Simon may have tanned with it. The house has not probably been destroyed and rebuilt more than four or five times since St. Peter dwelt here; the Romans once built the entire city. The chief room is now a mosque. We inquired for the house of Dorcas, but that is not shown, although I understood that we could see her grave outside the city. It is a great oversight not to show the house of Dorcas, and one that I cannot believe will long annoy pilgrims in these days of multiplied discoveries of sacred sites.

Whether this is the actual spot where the house of Simon stood, I do not know, nor does it much matter. Here, or hereabouts, the apostle saw that marvellous vision which proclaimed to a weary world the brotherhood of man. From this spot issued the gospel of democracy : "Of a truth, I perceive that God is no respecter of persons." From this insignificant dwelling went forth the edict that broke the power of tyrants, and loosed the bonds of slaves, and ennobled the lot of woman, and enfranchised the human mind. Of all places on earth I think there is only one more worthy of pilgrimage by all devout and liberty-loving souls.

We were greatly interested, also, in a visit to the well-known school of Miss Arnot, a mission school for girls in the upper chambers of a house in the most crowded part of Jaffa. With modest courage and tact and self-devotion this lady has sustained it here for twelve years, and the fruits of it already begin to appear. We found twenty or thirty pupils, nearly all quite young, and most of them daughters of Christians; they are taught in Arabic the common branches, and some English, and they learn to sing. They sang for us English tunes like any Sunday school; a strange sound in a Moslem town. There are one or two other schools of a similar character in the Orient, conducted as private enterprises by ladies of culture; and I think there is no work nobler, and none more worthy of liberal support or more likely to result in giving women a decent position in Eastern society.

On a little elevation a half-mile outside the walls is a cluster of wooden houses, which were manufactured in America. There we found the remnants of the Adams colony, only half a dozen families out of the original two hundred and fifty persons; two or three men and some widows and children. The colony built in the centre of their settlement an ugly little church out of Maine timber; it now stands empty and staring, with broken windows. It is not difficult to make this adventure appear romantic. Those who engaged in it were plain New England people, many of them ignorant, but devout to fanaticism. They had heard the prophets expounded, and the prophecies of the latter days unravelled, until they came to believe that the day of the Lord was nigh, and that they had laid upon them a mission in the fulfilment of the divine purposes. Most of them were from Maine and New Hampshire, accustomed to bitter winters and to wring their living from a niggardly soil. I do not wonder that they were fascinated by the pictures of a fair land of blue skies, a land of vines and olives and palms, where they were undoubtedly called by the Spirit to a life of greater sanctity and considerable ease and abundance. I think I see their dismay when they first pitched their tents amid this Moslem squalor, and attempted to "squat," Western fashion, upon the skirts of the Plain of Sharon, which has been for some ages pre-empted. They erected houses, however, and joined the other inhabitants of the region in a struggle for existence. But Adams, the preacher and president, had not faith enough to wait for the unfolding of prophecy; he took to strong drink, and with general bad man-

agement the whole enterprise came to grief, and the deluded people were rescued from starvation only by the liberality of our
government.

There was the germ of a good idea in the rash undertaking.
If Palestine is ever to be repeopled, its coming inhabitants must
have the means of subsistence; and if those now here are to be
redeemed to a better life, they must learn to work; before all else
there must come a revival of industry and a development of the
resources of the country. To send here Jews or Gentiles, and to
support them by charity, only adds to the existing misery.

It was eight years ago that the Adams community exploded.
Its heirs and successors are Germans, a colony from Würtemberg,
an Advent sect akin to the American, but more single-minded
and devout. They own the ground upon which they have settled, having acquired a title from the Turkish government; they
have erected substantial houses of stone and a large hotel, The
Jerusalem, and give many evidences of shrewdness and thrift as
well as piety. They have established a good school, in which,
with German thoroughness, Latin, English, and the higher
mathematics are taught, and an excellent education may be obtained. More land the colony is not permitted to own; but they
hire ground outside the walls which they farm to advantage.

I talked with one of the teachers, a thin young ascetic in spectacles, whose severity of countenance and demeanor was sufficient
to rebuke all the Oriental levity I had encountered during the
winter. There was in him and in the other leaders an air of sincere fanaticism, and a sobriety and integrity in the common laborers, which are the best omens for the success of the colony. The
leaders told us that they thought the Americans came here with
the expectation of making money uppermost in mind, and hardly
in the right spirit. As to themselves, they do not expect to
make money; they repelled the insinuation with some warmth;
they have had, in fact, a very hard struggle, and are thankful for
a fair measure of success. Their sole present purpose is evidently to redeem and reclaim the land, and make it fit for the
expected day of jubilee. The Jews from all parts of the world,
they say, are to return to Palestine, and there is to issue out of

the Holy Land a new divine impulse which is to be the regeneration and salvation of the world. I do not know that anybody
but the Jews themselves would oppose their migration to Palestine, though their withdrawal from the business of the world
suddenly would create wide disaster. With these doubts, however, we did not trouble the youthful knight of severity. We
only asked him upon what the community founded its creed and
its mission. Largely, he replied, upon the prophets, and especially upon Isaiah; and he referred us to Isaiah xxxii. 1; xlix.
12 et seq.; and lii. 1. It is not every industrial community
that would flourish on a charter so vague as this.

A lad of twelve or fourteen was our guide to the Advent settlement; he was an early polyglot, speaking, besides English,
French, and German, Arabic, and, I think, a little Greek; a boy
of uncommon gravity of deportment and of precocious shrewdness. He is destined to be a guide and dragoman. I could see
that the whole Biblical history was a little *fade* to him, but he
does not lose sight of the profit of a knowledge of it. I could
not but contrast him with a Sunday-school scholar of his own age
in America, whose imagination kindles at the Old Testament stories, and whose enthusiasm for the Holy Land is awakened by
the wall maps and the pictures of Solomon's temple. Actual
contact has destroyed the imagination of this boy; Jerusalem is
not so much a wonder to him as Boston; Samson lived just over
there beyond the Plain of Sharon, and is not so much a hero as
Old Put.

The boy's mother was a good New Hampshire woman, whose
downright Yankeeism of thought and speech was in odd contrast
to her Oriental surroundings. I sat in a rocking-chair in the
sitting-room of her little wood cottage, and could scarcely convince myself that I was not in a prim New Hampshire parlor.
To her mind there were no more Oriental illusions, and perhaps
she had never indulged any; certainly, in her presence Palestine
seemed to me as commonplace as New England.

" I s'pose you 've seen the meetin' house? "

" Yes."

" Wal' it 's goin' to rack and ruin like everything else here.

1 *

There is n't enough here to have any service now. Sometimes I
go to the German; I try to keep up a little feeling."

I have no doubt it is more difficult to keep up a religious feeling in the Holy Land than it is in New Hampshire, but we did
not discuss that point. I asked, " Do you have any society ? "

" Precious little. The Germans are dreffle unsocial. The natives are all a low set. The Arabs will all lie; I don't think
much of any of 'em. The Mohammedans are all shiftless; you
can't trust any of 'em."

" Why don't you go home ? "

" Wal, sometimes I think I 'd like to see the old place, but I
reckon I could n't stand the winters. This is a nice climate,
that 's all there is here; and we have grapes and oranges, and
loads of flowers, — you see my garden there; I set great store by
that, and me and my daughter take solid comfort in it, especially
when *he* is away, and he has to be off most of the time with
parties, guidin' 'em. No, I guess I sha'n't ever cross the ocean
again."

It appeared that the good woman had consoled herself with a
second husband, who bears a Jewish name; so that the original
object of her mission, to gather in the chosen people, is not altogether lost sight of.

There is a curious interest in these New England transplanta-
tions. Climate is a great transformer. The habits and customs
of thousands of years will insensibly conquer the most stubborn
prejudices. I wonder how long it will require to blend these
scions of our vigorous civilization with the motley growth that
makes up the present Syriac population, — people whose blood is
streaked with a dozen different strains, Egyptian, Ethiopian, Arabian, Assyrian, Phœnician, Greek, Roman, Canaanite, Jewish, Persian, Turkish, with all the races that have in turn ravaged or occupied the land. I do not, indeed, presume to say what the Syrians
are who have occupied Palestine for so many hundreds of years,
but I cannot see how it can be otherwise than that their blood is
as mixed as that of the modern Egyptians. Perhaps these New
England offshoots will maintain their distinction of race for a
long time, but I should be still more interested to know how

long the New England mind will keep its integrity in these surroundings, and whether those ruggednesses of virtue and those
homely simplicities of character which we recognize as belonging
to the hilly portions of New England will insensibly melt away
in this relaxing air that so much wants moral tone. These Oriental countries have been conquered many times, but they have
always conquered their conquerors. I am told that even our
American consuls are not always more successful in resisting the
undermining seductions of the East than were the Roman pro-
consuls.

These reflections, however, let it be confessed, did not come to
me as I sat in the rocking-chair of my countrywoman. I was
rather thinking how completely her presence and accent dispelled
all my Oriental allusions and cheapened the associations of Jaffa.
There is I know not what in a real living Yankee that puts all
appearances to the test and dissipates the colors of romance.
It was not until I came again into the highway and found in
front of The Jerusalem hotel a company of Arab acrobats and
pyramid-builders, their swarthy bodies shining in the white sunlight, and a lot of idlers squatting about in enjoyment of the
exertions of others, that I recovered in any degree my delusions.

With the return of these, it seemed not so impossible to believe even in the return of the Jews; especially when we learned
that preparations for them multiply. A second German colony
has been established outside of the city. There is another at
Haifa ; on the Jerusalem road the beginning of one has been
made by the Jews themselves. It amounts to something like a
" movement."

At three o'clock in the afternoon we set out for Ramleh, igno-
miniously, in a wagon. There is a carriage-road from Jaffa to
Jerusalem, and our dragoman had promised us a "private carriage." We decided to take it, thinking it would be more comfortable than horseback for some of our party. We made a
mistake which we have never ceased to regret. The road I can
confidently commend as the worst in the world. The carriage
into which we climbed belonged to the German colony, and was
a compromise between the ancient ark, a modern dray, and a

threshing-machine. It was one of those contrivances that a German would evolve out of his inner consciousness, and its appearance here gave me grave doubts as to the adaptability of these honest Germans to the Orient. It was, however, a great deal worse than it looked. If it were driven over smooth ground it would soon loosen all the teeth of the passengers, and shatter their spinal columns. But over the Jerusalem road the effect was indescribable. The noise of it was intolerable, the jolting incredible. The little solid Dutchman, who sat in front and drove, shook like the charioteer of an artillery wagon; but I suppose he had no feeling. We pounded along over the roughest stone pavement, with the sensation of victims drawn to execution in a cart, until we emerged into the open country; but there we found no improvement in the road.

Jaffa is surrounded by immense orange groves, which are protected along the highways by hedges of prickly-pear. We came out from a lane of these upon the level and blooming Plain of Sharon, and saw before us, on the left, the blue hills of Judæa. It makes little difference what kind of conveyance one has, it is impossible for him to advance upon this historic, if not sacred plain, and catch the first glimpse of those pale hills which stood to him for a celestial vision in his childhood, without a great quickening of the pulse; and it is a most lovely view after Egypt, or after anything. The elements of it are simple enough, — merely a wide sweep of prairie and a line of graceful mountains; but the forms are pleasing, and the color is incomparable. The soil is warm and red, the fields are a mass of wild-flowers of the most brilliant and variegated hues, and, alternately swept by the shadows of clouds and bathed in the sun, the scene takes on the animation of incessant change.

It was somewhere here, outside the walls, I do not know the spot, that the massacre of Jaffa occurred. I purposely go out of my way to repeat the well-known story of it, and I trust that it will always be recalled whenever any mention is made of the cruel little Corsican who so long imposed the vulgarity and savageness of his selfish nature upon Europe. It was in March, 1799, that Napoleon, toward the close of his humiliating and disastrous campaign in Egypt, carried Jaffa by storm. The town was given over to pillage. During its progress four thousand Albanians of the garrison, taking refuge in some old khans, offered to surrender on condition that their lives should be spared; otherwise they would fight to the bitter end. Their terms were accepted, and two of Napoleon's aids-de-camp pledged their honor for their safety. They were marched out to the general's headquarters and seated in front of the tents with their arms bound behind them. The displeased commander called a council of war and deliberated two days upon their fate, and then signed the order for the massacre of the entire body. The excuse was that the general could not be burdened with so many prisoners. Thus in one day were murdered in cold blood about as many people as Jaffa at present contains. Its inhabitants may be said to have been accustomed to being massacred; eight thousand of them were butchered in one Roman assault; but I suppose all antiquity may be searched in vain for an act of perfidy and cruelty combined equal to that of the Grand Emperor.

The road over which we rattle is a causeway of loose stones; the country is a plain of sand, but clothed with a luxuriant vegetation. In the fields the brown husbandmen are plowing, turning up the soft red earth with a rude plough drawn by cattle yoked wide apart. Red-legged storks, on their way, I suppose, from Egypt to their summer residence further north, dot the meadows, and are too busy picking up worms to notice our halloo. Abd-el-Atti, who has a passion for shooting, begs permission to "go for" these household birds with the gun; but we explain to him that we would no more shoot a stork than one of the green birds of Paradise. Quails are scudding about in the newly turned furrows, and song birds salute us from the tops of swinging cypresses. The Holy Land is rejoicing in its one season of beauty, its spring-time.

Trees are not wanting to the verdant meadows. We still encounter an occasional grove of oranges; olives also appear, and acacias, sycamores, cypresses, and tamarisks. The pods of the carob-tree are, I believe, the husks upon which the prodigal son did not thrive. Large patches of barley are passed. But the

fields not occupied with grain are literally carpeted with wild-
flowers of the most brilliant hues, such a display as I never saw
elsewhere: scarlet and dark flaming poppies, the scarlet anemone,
marigolds, white daisies, the lobelia, the lupin, the vetch, the
gorse with its delicate yellow blossom, the pea, something that
we agreed to call the white rose of Sharon, the mallow, the aspho-
del; the leaves of a lily not yet in bloom. About the rose of
Sharon we no doubt were mistaken. There is no reason to suppose it was white; but we have somehow associated the purity of
that color with the song beginning, "I am the rose of Sharon
and the lily of the valleys." It was probably not even a rose.
We finally decided to cherish the red mallow as the rose of
Sharon; it is very abundant, and the botanist of our company
seemed satisfied to accept it. For myself, the rose by the name
of mallow does not smell sweet.

We come in sight of Ramleh, which lies on the swelling mounds
of the green plain, encompassed by emerald meadows and by
groves of orange and olive, and conspicuous from a great distance
by its elegant square tower, the most beautiful in form that we
have seen in the East. As the sun is sinking, we defer our visit
to it and drive to the Latin convent, where we are to lodge, permission to that effect having been obtained from the sister convent at Jaffa; a mere form, since a part of the convent was built
expressly for the entertainment of travellers, and the few monks
who occupy it find keeping a hotel a very profitable kind of hospitality. The stranger is the guest of the superior, no charge is
made, and the little fiction of gratuitous hospitality so pleases the
pilgrim that he will not at his departure be outdone in liberality.
It would be much more agreeable if all our hotels were upon this
system.

While the dragoman is unpacking the luggage in the court-yard
and bustling about in a manner to impress the establishment with
the importance of its accession, I climb up to the roofs to get the
sunset. The house is all roofs, it would seem, at different levels.
Steps lead here and there, and one can wander about at will; you
could not desire a pleasanter lounging-place in a summer evening.
The protecting walls, which are breast-high, are built in with cyl-

inders of tile, like the mud houses in Egypt; the tiles make the walls lighter, and furnish at the same time peep-holes through which the monks can spy the world, themselves unseen. I noticed that the tiles about the entrance court were inclined downwards, so that a curious person could study any new arrival at the convent without being himself observed. The sun went down behind the square tower which is called Saracenic and is entirely Gothic in spirit, and the light lay soft and rosy on the wide compass of green vegetation; I heard on the distant fields the bells of mules returning to the gates, and the sound substituted Italy in my mind for Palestine.

From this prospect I was summoned in haste; the superior of the convent was waiting to receive me, and I had been sought in all directions. I had no idea why I should be received, but I soon found that the occasion was not a trivial one. In the reception-room were seated in some state the superior, attended by two or three brothers, and the remainder of my suite already assembled. The abbot, if he is an abbot, arose and cordially welcomed "the general" to his humble establishment, hoped that he was not fatigued by the journey from Jaffa, and gave him a seat beside himself. The remainder of the party were ranged according to their rank. I replied that the journey was on the contrary delightful, and that any journey could be considered fortunate which had the hospitable convent of Ramleh as its end. The courteous monk renewed his solicitous inquiries, and my astonishment was increased by the botanist, who gravely assured the worthy father that "the general" was accustomed to fatigue, and that such a journey as this was a recreation to him.

"What in the mischief is all this about?" I seized a moment to whisper to the person next me.

"You are a distinguished American general, travelling with his lady in pursuit of Heaven knows what, and accompanied by his suite; don't make a mess of.it."

"Oh," I said, "if I *am* a distinguished American general, travelling with my lady in pursuit of Heaven knows what, I am glad to know it."

Fortunately the peaceful father did not know anything more of war than I did, and I suppose my hastily assumed modesty of the soldier seemed to him the real thing. It was my first experience of anything like real war, the first time I had ever occupied any military position, and it did not seem to be so arduous as has been represented.

Great regret was expressed by the superior that they had not anticipated my arrival, in order to have entertained me in a more worthy manner; the convent was uncommonly full of pilgrims, and it would be difficult to lodge my suite as it deserved. Then there followed a long discussion between the father and one of the monks upon our disposition for the night.

"If we give the general and his lady the south room in the court, then the doctor" — etc., etc.

"Or," urged the monk, "suppose the general and his lady occupy the cell number four, then mademoiselle can take" — etc., etc.

The military commander and his lady were at last shown into a cell opening out of the court, a lofty but narrow vaulted room, with brick floor and thick walls, and one small window near the ceiling. Instead of candles we had antique Roman lamps, which made a feeble glimmer in the cavern; the oddest water-jugs served for pitchers. It may not have been damp, but it felt as if no sun had ever penetrated the chill interior.

"What is all this nonsense of the general?" I asked Abd-el-Atti, as soon as I could get hold of that managing factotum.

"Dunno, be sure; these monk always pay more attention to 'stinguish people."

"But what did you say at the convent in Jaffa when you applied for a permit to lodge here?"

"Oh, I tell him my gentleman general American, but 'stinguish; mebbe he done gone wrote 'em that you 'stinguish American general. Very nice man, the superior, speak Italian beautiful; when I give him the letter, he say he do all he can for the general and his suite; he sorry I not let him know 'forehand."

The dinner was served in the long refectory, and there were some twenty-five persons at table, mostly pilgrims to Jerusalem, and most of them of the poorer class. One bright Italian had travelled alone with her little boy all the way from Verona, only to see the Holy Sepulchre. The monks waited at table and served a very good dinner. Travellers are not permitted to enter the portion of the large convent which contains the cells of the monks, nor to visit any part of the old building except the chapel. I fancied that the jolly brothers who waited at table were rather glad to come into contact with the world, even in this capacity.

In the dining-room hangs a notable picture. It is the Virgin enthroned, with a crown and aureole, holding the holy child, who is also crowned; in the foreground is a choir of white boys or angels. The Virgin and child are both *black*; it is the Virgin of Ethiopia. I could not learn the origin of this picture; it was rude enough in execution to be the work of a Greek artist of the present day; but it was said to come from Ethiopia, where it is necessary to a proper respect for the Virgin that she should be represented black. She seems to bear something the relation to the Virgin of Judæa that Astarte did to the Grecian Venus. And we are again reminded that the East has no prejudice of color: " I am black but comely, O ye daughters of Jerusalem "; " Look not upon me because I am black, because the sun hath looked upon me."

The convent bells are ringing at early dawn, and though we are up at half past five, nearly all the pilgrims have hastily departed for Jerusalem. Upon the roof I find the morning fair. There are more minarets than spires in sight, but they stand together in this pretty little town without discord. The bells are ringing in melodious persuasion, but at the same time, in voices as musical, the muezzins are calling from their galleries; each summoning men to prayer in its own way. From these walls spectators once looked down upon the battles of cross and crescent raging in the lovely meadows, — battles of quite as much pride as piety. A common interest always softens animosity, and I fancy that monks and Moslems will not again resort to the foolish practice of breaking each other's heads so long as they enjoy the profitable stream of pilgrims to the Holy Land.

After breakfast and a gift to the treasury of the convent according to our rank — I think if I were to stay there again it would

B

be in the character of a common soldier — we embarked again in
the ark, and jolted along behind the square-shouldered driver,
who seemed to enjoy the rattling and rumbling of his clumsy
vehicle.   But no minor infelicity could destroy for us the freshness of the morning or the enjoyment of the lovely country.   Although, in the jolting, one could not utter a remark about the
beauty of the way without danger of biting his tongue in two,
we feasted our eyes and let our imaginations loose over the vast
ranges of the Old Testament story.

After passing through the fertile meadows of Ramleh, we came
into a more rolling country, destitute of houses, but clothed on
with a most brilliant bloom of wild-flowers, among which the
papilionaceous flowers were conspicuous for color and delicacy.
I found by the roadside a *black calla* (which I should no more
have believed in than in the black Virgin, if I had not seen it).
Its leaf is exactly that of our calla-lily; its flower is similar to,
but not so open and flaring, as the white calla, and the pistil is
large and very long, and of the color of the interior of the flower.
The corolla is green on the outside, but the inside is incomparably
rich, like velvet, black in some lights and dark maroon in others.
Nothing could be finer in color and texture than this superb
flower.   Besides the blooms of yesterday we noticed buttercups,
various sorts of the ranunculus, among them the scarlet and the
  ooting-star, a light purple flower with a dark purple centre,
 he Star of Bethlehem, and the purple wind-flower.   Scarlet poppies and the still more brilliant scarlet anemones, dandelions,
marguerites, filled all the fields with masses of color.

Shortly we come into the hills, through which the road winds
upward, and the scenery is very much like that of the Adirondacks, or would be if the rocky hills of the latter were denuded
of trees.   The way begins to be lively with passengers, and it
becomes us to be circumspect, for almost every foot of ground
has been consecrated or desecrated, or in some manner made memorable.   This heap of rubbish is the remains of a fortress which
the Saracens captured, built by the Crusaders to guard the entrance
of the pass, upon the site of an older fortification by the Macca-
bees, or founded upon Roman substructions, and mentioned in

Judges as the spot where some very ancient Jew stayed overnight. It is also, no doubt, one of the stations that help us to determine with the accuracy of a surveyor the boundary between the territory of Benjamin and Judah. I try to ascertain all these localities and to remember them all, but I sometimes get Richard Cœur de Lion mixed with Jonathan Maccabæus, and I have no doubt I mistook " Job's convent " for the *Castellum boni Latronis*, a place we were specially desirous to see as the birthplace of the " penitent thief." But whatever we confounded, we are certain of one thing : we looked over into the Valley of Ajalon. It was over this valley that Joshua commanded the moon to tarry while he smote the fugitive Amorites on the heights of Gibeon, there to the east.

The road is thronged with pilgrims to Jerusalem, and with travellers and their attendants, — gay cavalcades scattered all along the winding way over the rolling plain, as in the picture of the Pilgrims to Canterbury. All the transport of freight as well as passengers is by the backs of beasts of burden. There are long files of horses and mules staggering under enormous loads of trunks, tents, and bags. Dragomans, some of them got up in fierce style, with baggy yellow trousers, yellow kuflias bound about the head with a twisted fillet, armed with long Damascus swords, their belts stuck full of pistols, and a rifle slung on the back, gallop furiously along the line, the signs of danger but the assurances of protection. Camp boys and waiters dash along also, on the pack-horses, with a great clatter of kitchen furniture ; even a scullion has an air of adventure as he pounds his rack-a-bone steed into a vicious gallop. And there are the Cook's tourists, called by everybody " Cookies," men and women struggling on according to the pace of their horses, conspicuous in hats with white muslin drapery hanging over the neck. Villanous-looking fellows with or without long guns, coming and going on the highway, have the air of being neither pilgrims nor strangers. We meet women returning from Jerusalem clad in white, seated astride their horses, or upon beds which top their multifarious baggage.

We are leaving behind us on the right the country of Samson, in which he passed his playful and engaging boyhood, and we look wistfully towards it. Of Zorah, where he was born, nothing is left but a cistern, and there is only a wretched hamlet to mark the site of Timnath, where he got his Philistine wife. "Get her for me, for she pleaseth me well," was his only reply to the entreaty of his father that he would be content with a maid of his own people.

The country gets wilder and more rocky as we ascend. Down the ragged side paths come wretched women and girls, staggering under the loads of brushwood which they have cut in the high ravines; loads borne upon the head that would tax the strength of a strong man. I found it no easy task to lift one of the bundles. The poor creatures were scantily clad in a single garment of coarse brown cloth, but most of them wore a profusion of ornaments; strings of coins, Turkish and Arabic, on the head and breast, and uncouth rings and bracelets. Farther on a rabble of boys besets us, begging for backsheesh in piteous and whining tones, and throwing up their arms in theatrical gestures of despair.

All the hills bear marks of having once been terraced to the very tops, for vines and olives. The natural ledges seem to have been humored into terraces and occasionally built up and broadened by stone walls; but where the hill was smooth, traces of terraces are yet visible. The grape is still cultivated low down the steeps, and the olives straggle over some of the hills to the very top; but these feeble efforts of culture or of nature do little to relieve the deserted aspect of the scene.

We lunch in a pretty olive grove, upon a slope long ago terraced and now grass-grown and flower-sown; lovely vistas open into cool glades, and paths lead upward among the rocks to inviting retreats. From this high perch in the bosom of the hills we look off upon Ramleh, Jaffa, the broad Plain of Sharon, and the sea. A strip of sand between the sea and the plain produces the effect of a mirage, giving to the plain the appearance of the sea. It would be a charming spot for a country-seat for a resident of Jerusalem, although Jerusalem itself is rural enough at present; and David and Solomon may have had summer pavilions in these cool shades in sight of the Mediterranean. David himself, however, perhaps had enough of this region — when he dodged about in these fastnesses between Ramah and Gath, from the pursuit of Saul — to make him content with a city life. There is nothing to hinder our believing that he often enjoyed this prospect; and we do believe it, for it is already evident that the imagination must be called in to create an enjoyment of this deserted land. David no doubt loved this spot. For David was a poet, even at this early period when his occupation was that of a successful guerilla; and he had all the true poet's adaptability, as witness the exquisite ode he composed on the death of his enemy Saul. I have no doubt that he enjoyed this lovely prospect often, for he was a man who enjoyed heartily everything lovely. He was in this as in all he did a *thorough* man; when he made a raid on an Amorite city, he left neither man, woman, nor child alive to spread the news.

We have already mounted over two thousand feet. The rocks are silicious limestone, crumbling and gray with ages of exposure; they give the landscape an ashy appearance. But there is always a little verdure amid the rocks, and now and then an olive-tree, perhaps a very old one, decrepit and twisted into the most fantastic form, as if distorted by a vegetable rheumatism, casting abroad its withered arms as if the tree writhed in pain. On such ghostly trees I have no doubt the five kings were hanged. Another tree or rather shrub is abundant, the dwarf-oak; and the hawthorn, now in blossom, is frequently seen. The rock-rose — a delicate white single flower — blooms by the wayside and amid the ledges, and the scarlet anemone flames out more brilliantly than ever. Nothing indeed could be more beautiful than the contrast of the clusters of scarlet anemones and white roses with the gray rocks.

We soon descend into a valley and reach the site of Kirjath-Jearim, which has not much ancient interest for me, except that the name is pleasing; but on the other side of the stream and opposite a Moslem fountain are the gloomy stone habitations of the family of the terrible Abu Ghaush, whose robberies of travellers kept the whole country in a panic a quarter of a century ago. He held the key of this pass, and let no one go by without toll. For fifty years he and his companions defied the Turkish government, and even went to the extremity of murdering two pashas who attempted to pass this way. He was disposed of in 1846, but his descendants still live here, having the inclination but not the courage of the old chief. We did not encounter any of them, but I have never seen any buildings that have such a wicked physiognomy as their grim houses.

Near by is the ruin of a low, thick-walled chapel, of a pure Gothic style, a remnant of the Crusaders' occupation. The gloomy wady has another association; a monkish tradition would have us believe it was the birthplace of Jeremiah; if the prophet was born in such a hard country it might account for his lamentations. As we pass out of this wady, the German driver points to a forlorn village clinging to the rocky slope of a hill to the right, and says, —

"That is where John Baptist was born."

The information is sudden and seems improbable, especially as there are other places where he was born.

" How do you know ? " we ask.

" O, I know *ganz wohl;* I been five years in dis land, and I ught to know."

Descending into a deep ravine we cross a brook, which we are told is the one that flows into the Valley of Elah, the valley of the " terebinth " or button trees ; and if so, it is the brook out of which David took the stone that killed Goliath. It is a bright, dashing stream. I stood upon the bridge, watching it dancing down the ravine, and should have none but agreeable recollections of it, but that close to the bridge stood a vile grog-shop, and in the doorway sat the most villanous-looking man I ever saw in Judæa, rapacity and murder in his eyes. The present generation have much more to fear from him and his drugged liquors than the Israelite had from the giant of Gath.

While the wagon zigzags up the last long hill, I mount by a short path and come upon a rocky plateau, across which runs a broad way, on the bed rock, worn smooth by many centuries of travel : by the passing of caravans and armies to Jerusalem, of innumerable generations of peasants, of chariots, of horses, mules, and foot-soldiers; here went the messengers of the king's pleasure, and here came the heralds and legates of foreign nations; this great highway the kings and prophets themselves must have trodden when they journeyed towards the sea; for I cannot learn that the Jews ever had any decent roads, and perhaps they never attained the civilization necessary to build them. We have certainly seen no traces of anything like a practicable ancient highway on this route.

Indeed, the greatest wonder to me in the whole East is that there has not been a good road built from Jaffa to Jerusalem; that the city sacred to more than half the world, to all the most powerful nations, to Moslems, Jews, Greeks, Roman Catholics, Protestants, the desire of all lands, and the object of pilgrimage with the delicate and the feeble as well as the strong, should not have a highway to it over which one can ride without being jarred and stunned and pounded to a jelly; that the Jews should never have made a road to their seaport; that the Romans, the road-builders, do not seem to have constructed one over this important route. The Sultan began this one over which we have been dragged, for the Empress Eugénie. But he did not finish it; most of the way it is a mere rubble of stones. The track is well engineered, and the road bed is well enough; soft stone is at hand to form an excellent dressing, and it might be, in a short time, as good a highway as any in Switzerland, if the Sultan would set some of his lazy subjects to work out their taxes on it. Of course, it is now a great improvement over the old path for mules; but as a carriage road it is atrocious. Imagine thirty-six miles of cobble pavement, with every other stone gone and the remainder sharpened!

Perhaps, however, it is best not to have a decent road to the Holy City of the world. It would make going there easy, even for delicate ladies and invalid clergymen; it would reduce the cost of the trip from Jaffa by two thirds; it would take away employment from a lot of vagabonds who harry the traveller over the route; it would make the pilgrimage too much a luxury, in these days of pilgrimages by rail, and of little faith, or rather of a sort of lacquer of faith which is only credulity.

Upon this plateau we begin to discern signs of the neighborhood of the city, and we press forward with the utmost eagerness,
disappointed at every turn that a sight of it is not disclosed.
Scattered settlements extend for some distance out on the Jaffa
road. We pass a school which the Germans have established for
Arab boys; an institution which does not meet the approval of
our restoration driver; the boys, when they come out, he says,
don't know what they are; they are neither Moslems nor Christians. We go rapidly on over the swelling hill, but the city will
not reveal itself. We expect it any moment to rise up before us,
conspicuous on its ancient hills, its walls shining in the sun.
We pass a guard-house, some towers, and newly built private
residences. Our pulses are beating a hundred to the minute, but
the city refuses to "burst" upon us as it does upon other travellers. We have advanced far enough to see that there is no elevation before us higher than that we are on. The great sight of all
our lives is only a moment separated from us; in a few rods more
our hearts will be satisfied by that long-dreamed-of prospect.
How many millions of pilgrims have hurried along this road, lifting up their eyes in impatience for the vision! But it does not
come suddenly. We have already seen it, when the driver stops,
points with his whip, and cries, —

"JERUSALEM!"

"What, _that?_"

We are above it and nearly upon it. What we see is chiefly
this: the domes and long buildings of the Russian Hospice, on
higher ground than the city and concealing a good part of it; a
large number of new houses, built of limestone prettily streaked
with the red oxyde of iron; the roofs of a few of the city houses,
and a little portion of the wall that overlooks the Valley of Hinnom. The remainder of the city of David is visible to the imagination.

The suburb through which we pass cannot be called pleasing.
Everything outside the walls looks new and naked; the whitish
glare of the stone is relieved by little vegetation, and the effect is
that of barrenness. As we drive down along the wall of the Russian convent, we begin to meet pilgrims and strangers, with whom

the city overflows at this season; many Russian peasants, unkempt, unsavory fellows, with long hair and dirty apparel, but
most of them wearing a pelisse trimmed with fur and a huge fur
hat. There are coffee-houses and all sorts of cheap booths and
shanty shops along the highway. The crowd is motley and far
from pleasant; it is sordid, grimy, hard, very different from the
more homogeneous, easy, flowing, graceful, and picturesque assemblage of vagabonds at the gate of an Egyptian town. There are
Russians, Cossacks, Georgians, Jews, Armenians, Syrians. The
northern dirt and squalor and fanaticism do not come gracefully
into the Orient. Besides, the rabble is importunate and impudent.

We enter by the Jaffa and Hebron gate, a big square tower,
with the exterior entrance to the north and the interior to the
east, and the short turn is choked with camels and horses and
a clamorous crowd. Beside it stands the ruinous citadel of
Saladin and the Tower of David, a noble entrance to a mean
street. Through the rush of footmen and horsemen, beggars,
venders of olive-wood, Moslems, Jews, and Greeks, we make our
way to the Mediterranean Hotel, a rambling new hostelry. In
passing to our rooms we pause a moment upon an open balcony
to look down into the green Pool of Hezekiah, and off over the
roofs to the Mount of Olives. Having secured our rooms, I·
hasten along narrow and abominably cobbled streets, mere ditches
of stone, lined with mean shops, to the Centre of the Earth, the
Church of the Holy Sepulchre.

II.

JERUSALEM.

IT was in obedience to a natural but probably mistaken impulse, that I went straight to the Church of the Holy Sepulchre during my first hour in the city. Perhaps it was a mistake to go there at all; certainly I should have waited until I had become more accustomed to holy places. When a person enters this memorable church, as I did, expecting to see only two sacred sites, and is brought immediately face to face with *thirty-seven*, his mind is staggered, and his credulity becomes so enfeebled that it is practically useless to him thereafter in any part of the Holy City. And this is a pity, for it is so much easier and sweeter to believe than to doubt.

It would have been better, also, to have visited Jerusalem many years ago; then there were fewer sacred sites invented, and scholarly investigation had not so sharply questioned the authenticity of the few. But I thought of none of these things as I stumbled along the narrow and filthy streets, which are stony channels of mud and water, rather than foot-paths, and peeped into the dirty little shops that line the way. I thought only that I was in Jerusalem; and it was impossible, at first, for its near appearance to empty the name of its tremendous associations, or to drive out the image of that holy city, "conjubilant with song."

I had seen the dome of the church from the hotel balcony; the building itself is so hemmed in by houses that only its south side, in which is the sole entrance, can be seen from the street. In front of this entrance is a small square; the descent to this square is by a flight of steps down Palmer Street, a lane given up to the traffic in beads, olive-wood, ivory-carving, and the thousand trinkets, most of them cheap and inartistic, which absorb the industry of the Holy City. The little square itself, surrounded by ancient buildings on three sides and by the blackened walls of the church on the north, might be set down in a mediæval Italian town without incongruity. And at the hour I first saw it, you would have said that a market or fair was in progress there. This, however, I found was its normal condition. It is always occupied by a horde of more clamorous and impudent merchants than you will find in any other place in the Orient.

It is with some difficulty that the pilgrim can get through the throng and approach the portal. The pavement is covered with heaps of beads, shells, and every species of holy fancy-work, by which are seated the traders, men and women, in wait for customers. The moment I stopped to look at the church, and it was discovered that I was a new-comer, a rush was made at me from every part of the square, and I was at once the centre of the most eager and hungry crowd. Sharp-faced Greeks, impudent Jews, fair-faced women from Bethlehem, sleek Armenians, thrust strings of rude olive beads and crosses into my face, forced upon my notice trumpery carving in ivory, in nuts, in seeds, and screamed prices and entreaties in chorus, bidding against each other and holding fast to me, as if I were the last man, and this were the last opportunity they would ever have of getting rid of their rubbish. Handfuls of beads rapidly fell from five francs to half a franc, and the dealers insisted upon my buying, with a threatening air; I remember one hard-featured and rapacious wretch who danced about and clung to me, and looked into my eyes with an expression that said plainly, " If you don't buy these beads I'll murder you." My recollection is that I bought, for I never can resist a persuasion of this sort. Whenever I saw the fellow in the square afterwards, I always fancied that he regarded me with a sort of contempt, but he made no further attempt on my life.

This is the sort of preparation that one daily has in approaching the Church of the Holy Sepulchre. The greed and noise of traffic around it are as fatal to sentiment as they are to devotion. You may be amused one day, you may be indignant the next;

at last you will be weary of the importunate crowd; and the only
consolation you can get from these daily scenes of the desecration
of the temple of pilgrimage is the proof they afford that this is
indeed Jerusalem, and that these are the legitimate descendants
of the thieves whom Christ scourged from the precincts of the
temple. Alas that they should thrive under the new dispensation
as they did under the old !

A considerable part of the present Church of the Holy Sepulchre is not more than sixty years old; but the massive, carved,
and dark south portal, and the remains of the old towers and walls
on this side, may be eight hundred. There has been some sort
of a church here ever since the time of Constantine (that is, three
centuries after the crucifixion of our Lord), which has marked the
spot that was then determined to be the site of the Holy Sepulchre. Many a time the buildings have been swept away by fire
or by the fanaticism of enemies, but they have as often been renewed. There would seem at first to have been a cluster of buildings here, each of which arose to cover a newly discovered sacred
site. Happily, all the sacred places are now included within the
walls of this many-roofed, heterogeneous mass of chapels, shrines,
tombs, and altars of worship of many warring sects, called the
Church of the Holy Sepulchre.

Happily also the exhaustive discussion of the question of the
true site of the sepulchre, conducted by the most devout and accomplished biblical scholars and the keenest antiquarians of the
age, relieves the ordinary tourist from any obligation to enter upon
an investigation that would interest none but those who have been
upon the spot. No doubt the larger portion of the Christian
world accepts this site as the true one.

I make with diffidence a suggestion that struck me, although
it may not be new. The Pool of Hezekiah is not over four hundred feet, measured on the map, from the dome of the sepulchre.
Under the church itself are several large excavations in the rocks,
which were once cisterns. Ancient Jerusalem depended for its
water upon these cisterns, which took the drainage from the roofs,
and upon a few pools, like that of Hezekiah, which were fed from
other reservoirs, such as Solomon's Pool, at a considerable dis-

tance from the city. These cisterns under the church may not date back to the time of our Lord, but if they do, they were doubtless at that time within the walls. And of course the Pool of Hezekiah, so near to this alleged site, cannot be supposed to have been beyond the walls.

Within the door of the church, upon a raised divan at one side, as if this were a bazaar and he were the merchant, sat a fat Turk, in official dress, the sneering warden of this Christian edifice, and the perhaps necessary guardian of peace within. His presence there, however, is at first a disagreeable surprise to all those who rebel at owing an approach to the holy place to the toleration of a Moslem; but I was quite relieved of any sense of obligation when, upon coming out, the Turk asked me for backsheesh!

Whatever one may think as to the site of Calvary, no one can approach a spot which even claims to be it, and which has been for centuries the object of worship of millions, and is constantly thronged by believing pilgrims, without profound emotion. It was late in the afternoon when I entered the church, and already the shades of evening increased the artificial gloom of the interior. At the very entrance lies an object that arrests one. It is a long marble slab resting upon the pavement, about which candles are burning. Every devout pilgrim who comes in kneels and kisses it, and it is sometimes difficult to see it for the crowds who press about it. Underneath it is supposed to be the Stone of Unction upon which the Lord's body was laid, according to the Jewish fashion, for anointing, after he was taken from the cross.

I turned directly into the rotunda, under the dome of which is the stone building enclosing the Holy Sepulchre, a ruder structure than that which covers the hut and tomb of St. Francis in the church at Assisi. I met in the way a procession of Latin monks, bearing candles, and chanting as they walked. They were making the round of the holy places in the church, this being their hour for the tour. The sects have agreed upon certain hours for these little daily pilgrimages, so that there shall be no collision. A rabble of pilgrims followed the monks. They had just come from incensing and adoring the sepulchre, and the crowd of other pilgrims who had been waiting their turn were now pressing in

at the narrow door.　As many times as I have been there, I have
always seen pilgrims struggling to get in and struggling to get
out.　The proud and the humble crowd there together; the
greasy boor from beyond the Volga jostles my lady from Naples,
and the dainty pilgrim from America pushes her way through a
throng of stout Armenian peasants.　But I have never seen any
disorder there, nor any rudeness, except the thoughtless eagerness of zeal.

Taking my chance in the line, I passed into the first apartment, called the Chapel of the Angel, a narrow and gloomy ante-
chamber, which takes its name from the fragment of stone in the
centre, the stone upon which the angel sat after it had been rolled
away from the sepulchre.　A stream of light came through the
low and narrow door of the tomb.　Through the passage to
this vault only one person can enter at a time, and the tomb will
hold no more than three or four.　Stooping along the passage,
which is cased with marble like the tomb, and may cover natural
rock, I came into the sacred place, and into a blaze of silver
lamps, and candles.　The vault is not more than six feet by
seven, and is covered by a low dome.　The sepulchral stone occupies all the right side, and is the object of devotion.　It is of
marble, supposed to cover natural stone, and is cracked and worn
smooth on the edge by the kisses of millions of people.　The
attendant who stood at one end opened a little trap-door, in which
lamp-cloths were kept, and let me see the naked rock, which is
said to be that of the tomb.　While I stood there in that very
centre of the faith and longing of so many souls, which seemed
almost to palpitate with a consciousness of its awful position,
pilgrim after pilgrim, on bended knees, entered the narrow way,
kissed with fervor or with coldness the unresponsive marble, and
withdrew in the same attitude.　Some approached it with streaming eyes and kissed it with trembling rapture; some ladies threw
themselves upon the cold stone and sobbed aloud.　Indeed, I did
not of my own will intrude upon these acts of devotion, which
have the right of secrecy, but it was some time before I could
escape, so completely was the entrance blocked up.　When I had
struggled out, I heard chanting from the hill of Golgotha, and

saw the gleaming of a hundred lights from chapel and tomb and remote recesses, but I cared to see no more of the temple itself that day.

The next morning (it was the 7th of April) was very cold, and the day continued so. Without, the air was keen, and within it was nearly impossible to get warm or keep so, in the thick-walled houses, which had gathered the damp and chill of dungeons. You might suppose that the dirtiest and most beggarly city in the world could not be much deteriorated by the weather, but it is. In a cheerful, sunny day you find that the desolation of Jerusalem has a certain charm and attraction: even a tattered Jew leaning against a ruined wall, or a beggar on a dunghill, is picturesque in the sunshine; but if you put a day of chill rain and frosty wind into the city, none of the elements of complete misery are wanting. There is nothing to be done, day or night; indeed, there is nothing ever to be done in the evening, except to read your guide-book — that is, the Bible — and go to bed. You are obliged to act like a Christian here, whatever you are.

Speaking of the weather, a word about the time for visiting Syria may not be amiss. In the last part of March the snow was a foot deep in the streets; parties who had started on their tour northward were snowed in and forced to hide in their tents three days from the howling winter. There is pleasure for you! We found friends in the city who had been waiting two weeks after they had exhausted its sights, for settled weather that would permit them to travel northward. To be sure, the inhabitants say that this last storm ought to have been rain instead of snow, according to the habit of the seasons; and it no doubt would have been if this region were not twenty-five hundred feet above the sea. The hardships of the Syrian tour are enough in the best weather, and I am convinced that our dragoman is right in saying that most travellers begin it too early in the spring.

Jerusalem is not a formidable city to the explorer who is content to remain above ground, and is not too curious about its substructions and buried walls, and has no taste, as some have, for crawling through its drains. I suppose it would elucidate the history of the Jews if we could dig all this hill away and lay bare

all the old foundations, and ascertain exactly how the city was
watered. I, for one, am grateful to the excellent man and great
scholar who crawled on his hands and knees through a subterranean conduit, and established the fact of a connection between
the Fountain of the Virgin and the Pool of Siloam. But I would
rather contribute money to establish a school for girls in the Holy
City, than to aid in laying bare all the aqueducts from Ophel to
the Tower of David. But this is probably because I do not
enough appreciate the importance of such researches among Jewish remains to the progress of Christian truth and morality in the
world. The discoveries hitherto made have done much to clear
up the topography of ancient Jerusalem; I do not know that
they have yielded anything valuable to art or to philology, any
treasures illustrating the habits, the social life, the culture, or the
religion of the past, such as are revealed beneath the soil of
Rome or in the ashes of Pompeii; it is, however, true that almost every tourist in Jerusalem becomes speedily involved in all
these questions of ancient sites, — the identification of valleys
that once existed, of walls that are now sunk under the accumulated rubbish of two thousand years, from thirty feet to ninety
feet deep, and of foundations that are rough enough and massive
enough to have been laid by David and cemented by Solomon.
And the fascination of the pursuit would soon send one underground, with a pickaxe and a shovel. But of all the diggings I
saw in the Holy City, that which interested me most was the
excavation of the church and hospital of the chivalric Knights of
St. John : concerning which I shall say a word further on.

The present walls were built by Sultan Suleiman in the middle
of the sixteenth century, upon foundations much older, and here
and there, as you can see, upon big blocks of Jewish workmanship. The wall is high enough and very picturesque in its zigzag
course and re-entering angles, and, I suppose, strong enough to
hitch a horse to ; but cannon-balls would make short work of it.

Having said thus much of the topography, gratuitously and
probably unnecessarily, for every one is supposed to know Jerusalem as well as he knows his native town, we are free to look at
anything that may chance to interest us. I do not expect, how-

ever, that any words of mine can convey to the reader a just conception of the sterile and blasted character of this promontory and the country round about it, or of the squalor, shabbiness, and unpicturesqueness of the city, always excepting a few of its buildings and some fragments of antiquity built into modern structures here and there. And it is difficult to feel that this spot was ever the splendid capital of a powerful state, that this arid and stricken country could ever have supplied the necessities of such a capital, and, above all, that so many Jews could ever have been crowded within this cramped space as Josephus says perished in the siege by Titus, when ninety-seven thousand were carried into captivity and eleven hundred thousand died by famine and the sword. Almost the entire Jewish nation must have been packed within this small area.

Our first walk through the city was in the Via Dolorosa, as gloomy a thoroughfare as its name implies. Its historical portion is that steep and often angled part between the Holy Sepulchre and the house of Pilate, but we traversed the whole length of it to make our exit from St. Stephen's Gate toward the Mount of Olives. It is only about four hundred years ago that this street obtained the name of the Via Dolorosa, and that the sacred "stations" on it were marked out for the benefit of the pilgrim. It is a narrow lane, steep in places, having frequent sharp angles, running under arches, and passing between gloomy buildings, enlivened by few shops. Along this way Christ passed from the Judgment Hall of Pilate to Calvary. I do not know how many times the houses along it have been destroyed and rebuilt since their conflagration by Titus, but this destruction is no obstacle to the existence intact of all that are necessary to illustrate the Passion-pilgrimage of our Lord. In this street I saw the house of Simon the Cyrenian, who bore the cross after Jesus; I saw the house of St. Veronica, from which that woman stepped forth and gave Jesus a handkerchief to wipe his brow, — the handkerchief, with the Lord's features imprinted on it, which we have all seen exhibited at St. Peter's in Rome; and I looked for the house of the Wandering Jew, or at least for the spot where he stood when he received that awful mandate of fleshly immortality. In

2*   c

this street are recognized the several " stations " that Christ made
in bearing the cross; we were shown the places where he fell, a
stone having the impress of his hand, a pillar broken by his fall,
and also the stone upon which Mary sat when he passed by.
Nothing is wanting that the narrative requires. We saw also in
this street the house of Dives, and the stone on which Lazarus
sat while the dogs ministered unto him. It seemed to me that I
must be in a dream, in thus beholding the houses and places of
resort of the characters in a *parable;* and I carried my dilemma
to a Catholic friend. But a learned father assured him that there
was no doubt that this is the house of Dives, for Christ often
took his parables from real life. After that I went again to look
at the stone, in a corner of a building amid a heap of refuse, upon
which the beggar sat, and to admire the pretty stone tracery of
the windows in the house of Dives.

At the end of the street, in a new Latin nunnery, are the
remains of the house of Pilate, which are supposed to be authentic.
The present establishment is called the convent of St. Anne, and
the community is very fortunate, at this late day, in obtaining
such a historic site for itself. We had the privilege of seeing
here some of the original rock that formed part of the foundations
of Pilate's house; and there are three stones built into the altar
that were taken from the pavement of Gabbatha, upon which
Christ walked. These are recent discoveries; it appears probable
that the real pavement of Gabbatha has been found, since Pilate's
house is so satisfactorily identified. Spanning the street in front
of this convent is the Ecce Homo arch, upon which Pilate showed
Christ to the populace. The ground of the new building was
until recently in possession of the Moslems, who would not sell
it for a less price than seventy thousand francs; the arch they
would not sell at all; and there now dwells, in a small chamber
on top of it, a Moslem saint and hermit. The world of pilgrims
flows under his feet; he looks from his window upon a daily
procession of Christians, who traverse the Via Dolorosa, having
first signified their submission to the Moslem yoke in the Holy
City by passing under this arch of humiliation. The hermit,
however, has the grace not to show himself, and few know that

he sits there, in the holy occupation of letting his hair and his nails grow.

From the house of the Roman procurator we went to the citadel of Sultan Suleiman. This stands close by the Jaffa Gate, and is the most picturesque object in all the circuit of the walls, and, although the citadel is of modern origin, its most characteristic portion lays claim to great antiquity. The massive structure which impresses all strangers who enter by the Jaffa Gate is called the Tower of Hippicus, and also the Tower of David. It is identified as the tower which Herod built and Josephus describes, and there is as little doubt that its foundations are the same that David laid and Solomon strengthened. There are no such stones in any other part of the walls as these enormous bevelled blocks; they surpass those in the Harem wall, at what is called the Jews' Wailing Place. The tower stands upon the northwest corner of the old wall of Zion, and being the point most open to attack it was most strongly built.

It seems also to have been connected with the palace on Zion which David built, for it is the tradition that it was from this tower that the king first saw Bathsheba, the wife of Uriah, when "it came to pass in an eventide that David arose from off his bed, and walked upon the roof of the king's house: and from the roof he saw a woman washing herself; and the woman was very beautiful to look upon." On the other side of the city gate we now look down upon the Pool of Bathsheba, in which there is no water, and we are informed that it was by that pool that the lovely woman, who was destined to be the mother of Solomon, sat when the king took his evening walk. Others say that she sat by the Pool of Gihon. It does not matter. The subject was a very fruitful one for the artists of the Renaissance, who delighted in a glowing reproduction of the biblical stories, and found in such incidents as this and the confusion of Susanna themes in which the morality of the age could express itself without any conflict with the religion of the age. It is a comment not so much upon the character of David as upon the morality of the time in which he lived, that although he repented, and no doubt sincerely, of his sin when reproved for it, his repentance

did not take the direction of self-denial; he did not send away
Bathsheba.

This square old tower is interiorly so much in ruins that it is
not easy to climb to its parapet, and yet it still has a guard-
house attached to it, and is kept like a fortification; a few rusty
old cannon, under the charge of the soldiers, would injure only
those who attempted to fire them; the entire premises have a
tumble-down, Turkish aspect. The view from the top is |the
best in the city of the city itself; we saw also from it the hills of
Moab and a bit of the Dead Sea. ·

Close by is the Armenian quarter, covering a large part of
what was once the hill of Zion. I wish it were the Christian
quarter, for it is the only part of the town that makes any pre-
tension to cleanliness, and it has more than any other the aspect
of an abode of peace and charity. This is owing to its being
under the government of one corporation, for the Armenian convent covers nearly the entire space of this extensive quarter. The
convent is a singular, irregular mass of houses, courts, and streets,
the latter apparently running over and under and through the
houses; you come unexpectedly upon stairways, you traverse
roofs, you enter rooms and houses on the roofs of other houses,
and it is difficult to say at any time whether you are on the earth
or in the air. The convent, at this season, is filled with pilgrims,
over three thousand of whom, I was told, were lodged here. We
came upon families of them in the little rooms in the courts and
corridors, or upon the roofs, pursuing their domestic avocations
as if they were at home, cooking, mending, sleeping, a boorish
but simple-minded lot of peasants.

The church is a large and very interesting specimen of religious architecture and splendid, barbaric decoration. In the vestibule hang the "bells." These are long planks of a sonorous
wood, which give forth a ringing sound when struck with a club.
As they are of different sizes, you get some variation of tone, and
they can be heard far enough to call the inmates of the convent
to worship. The interior walls are lined with ancient blue tiles
to a considerable height, and above them are rude and inartistic
sacred pictures. There is in the church much curious inlaid

work of mother-of-pearl and olive-wood, especially about the doors of the chapels, and one side shines with the pearl as if it were encrusted with silver. Ostrich eggs are strung about in profusion, with hooks attached for hanging lamps.

The first day of our visit to this church, in one of the doorways of what seemed to be a side chapel, and which was thickly encrusted with mother-of-pearl, stood the venerable bishop, in a light rose-colored robe and a pointed hood, with a cross in his hand, preaching to the pilgrims, who knelt on the pavement before him, talking in a familiar manner, and, our guide said, with great plainness of speech. The Armenian clergy are celebrated for the splendor of their vestments, and I could not but think that this rose-colored bishop, in his shining framework, must seem like a being of another sphere to the boors before him. He almost imposed upon us.

These pilgrims appeared to be of the poorest agricultural class of laborers, and their costume is uncouth beyond description. In a side chapel, where we saw tiles on the walls that excited our envy, — the quaintest figures and illustrations of sacred subjects, — the clerks were taking the names of pilgrims just arrived, who knelt before them and paid a Napoleon each for their lodging in the convent, as long as they should choose to stay. In this chapel were the shoes of the pilgrims who had gone into the church, a motley collection of foot-gear, covering half the floor: leather and straw, square shoes as broad as long, round shoes, pointed shoes, old shoes, patched shoes, shoes with the toes gone, a pathetic gathering that told of poverty and weary travel — and big feet. These shoes were things to muse on, for each pair, made maybe in a different century, seemed to have a character of its own, as it stood there awaiting the owner. People often make reflections upon a pair of shoes; literature is full of them. Poets have celebrated many a pretty shoe, — a queen's slipper, it may be, or the hobnail brogan of a peasant, or, oftener, the tiny shoes of a child; but it is seldom that one has an opportunity for such comprehensive moralizing as was here given. If we ever regretted the lack of a poet in our party, it was now.

We walked along the Armenian walls, past the lepers' quarter, and outside the walls, through the Gate of Zion, or the Gate of the Prophet David as it is also called, and came upon a continuation of the plateau of the hill of Zion, which is now covered with cemeteries, and is the site of the house of Caiaphas and of the tomb of David and those Kings of Jerusalem who were considered by the people worthy of sepulture here; for the Jews seem to have brought from Egypt the notion of refusing royal burial to their bad kings, and they had very few respectable ones.

The house of Caiaphas the high-priest had suffered a recent tumble-down, and was in such a state of ruin that we could with difficulty enter it or recognize any likeness of a house. On the premises is an Armenian chapel; in it we were shown the prison in which Christ was confined, also the stone door of the sepulchre, which the Latins say the Armenians stole. But the most remarkable object here is the little marble column (having carved on it a figure of Christ bound to a pillar) upon which the cock stood and crowed when Peter denied his Lord. There are some difficulties in the way of believing this now, but they will lessen as the column gets age.

Outside this gate lie the desolate fields strewn with the brown tombstones of the Greeks and Armenians, a melancholy spectacle. Each sect has its own cemetery, and the dead sleep peaceably enough, but the living who bury them frequently quarrel. I saw one day a funeral procession halted outside the walls; for some reason the Greek priest had refused the dead burial in the grave dug for him in the cemetery; the bier was dumped on the slope beside the road, and half overturned; the friends were sitting on the ground, wrangling. The man had been dead three days, and the coffin had been by the roadside in this place since the day before. This was in the morning; towards night I saw the same crowd there, but a Turkish official appeared and ordered the Greeks to bury their dead somewhere, and that without delay; to bury it for the sake of the public health, and quarrel about the grave afterwards if they must. A crowd collected, joining with fiery gesticulation and clamor in the dispute, the shrill voices of women being heard above all; but at last, four men roughly shouldered the box, handling it as if it contained merchandise, and trotted off with it.

As we walked over this pathless, barren necropolis, strewn, as it were, hap-hazard with shapeless, broken, and leaning head-stones, it was impossible to connect with it any sentiment of affection or piety. It spoke, like everything else about here, of mortality, and seemed only a part of that historical Jerusalem which is dead and buried, in which no living person can have anything more than an archæological interest. It was, then, with something like a shock that we heard Demetrius, our guide, say, pointing to a rude stone, —

"That is the grave of my mother!"

Demetrius was a handsome Greek boy, of a beautiful type which has almost disappeared from Greece itself, and as clever a lad as ever spoke all languages and accepted all religions, without yielding too much to any one. He had been well educated in the English school, and his education had failed to put any faith in place of the superstition it had destroyed. The boy seemed to be numerously if not well connected in the city; he was always exchanging a glance and a smile with some pretty, dark-eyed Greek girl whom we met in the way, and when I said, "Demetrius, who was that?" he always answered, "That is my cousin."

The boy was so intelligent, so vivacious, and full of the spirit of adventure, — begging me a dozen times a day to take him with me anywhere in the world, — and so modern, that he had not till this moment seemed to belong to Jerusalem, nor to have any part in its decay. This chance discovery of his intimate relation to this necropolis gave, if I may say so, a living interest to it, and to all the old burying-grounds about the city, some of which link the present with the remote past by an uninterrupted succession of interments for nearly three thousand years.

Just beyond this expanse, or rather in part of it, is a small plot of ground surrounded by high whitewashed walls, the entrance to which is secured by a heavy door. This is the American cemetery; and the stout door and thick wall are, I suppose, necessary to secure its graves from Moslem insult. It seems not to be visited often, for it was with difficulty that we could turn the huge key in the rusty lock. There are some half-dozen graves within; the graves are grass-grown and flower-sprinkled, and the

whole area is a tangle of unrestrained weeds and grass. The
high wall cuts off all view, but we did not for the time miss it,
rather liking for the moment to be secured from the sight of the
awful desolation, and to muse upon the strange fortune that had
drawn to be buried here upon Mount Zion, as a holy resting-
place for them, people alien in race, language, and customs to the
house of David, and removed from it by such spaces of time and
distance; people to whom the worship performed by David, if he
could renew it in person on Zion, would be as distasteful as is
that of the Jews in yonder synagogue.

Only a short distance from this we came to the mosque which
contains the tomb of David and probably of Solomon and other
Kings of Judah. No historical monument in or about Jerusalem
is better authenticated than this. Although now for many centuries the Moslems have had possession of it and forbidden access
to it, there is a tolerably connected tradition of its possession. It
was twice opened and relieved of the enormous treasure in gold
and silver which Solomon deposited in it; once by Hyrcanus
Maccabæus, who took what he needed, and again by Herod, who
found very little. There are all sorts of stories told about the
splendor of this tomb and the state with which the Moslems surround it. But they envelop it in so much mystery that no one
can know the truth. It is probable that the few who suppose
they have seen it have seen only a sort of cenotaph which is
above the real tomb in the rock below. The room which has
been seen is embellished with some display of richness in shawls
and hangings of gold embroidery, and contains a sarcophagus of
rough stone, and lights are always burning there. If the royal
tombs are in this place, they are doubtless in the cave below.

Over this spot was built a church by the early Christians; and
it is a tradition that in this building was the Cœnaculum. This
site may very likely be that of the building where the Last Supper was laid, and it may be that St. Stephen suffered martyrdom
here, and that the Virgin died here; the building may be as old
as the fourth century, but the chances of any building standing so
long in this repeatedly destroyed city are not good. There is a
little house north of this mosque in which the Virgin spent the

last years of her life; if she did, she must have lived to be over a thousand years old.

On the very brow of the hill, and overlooking the lower pool of Gihon, is the English school, with its pretty garden and its cemetery. We saw there some excavations, by which the bed-rock had been laid bare, disclosing some stone steps cut in it. Search is being made here for the Seat of Solomon, but it does not seem to me a vital matter, for I suppose he sat down all over this hill, which was covered with his palaces and harems and other buildings of pleasure, built of stones that " were of great value, such as are dug out of the earth for the ornaments of tem-ples and to make fine prospects in royal palaces, and which make the mines whence they are dug famous." Solomon's palace was constructed entirely of white stone, and cedar-wood, and gold and silver; in it " were very long cloisters, and those situate in an agreeable place in the palace, and among them a most glorious dining-room for feastings and compotations "; indeed, Josephus finds it difficult to reckon up the variety and the magnitude of the royal apartments, — " how many that were subterraneous and in-visible, the curiosity of those that enjoyed the fresh air, and the groves for the most delightful prospect, for avoiding the heat, and covering their bodies." If this most luxurious of monarchs in-troduced here all the styles of architecture which would repre-sent the nationality of his wives, as he built temples to suit their different religions, the hill of Zion must have resembled, on a small scale, the Munich of King Ludwig I.

Opposite the English school, across the Valley of Hinnom, is a long block of modern buildings which is one of the most conspic-uous objects outside the city. It was built by another rich Jew, Sir Moses Montefiore, of London, and contains tenements for poor Jews. Sir Moses is probably as rich as Solomon was in his own right, and he makes a most charitable use of his money; but I do not suppose that if he had at his command the public wealth that Solomon had, who made silver as plentiful as stones in the streets of Jerusalem, he could materially alleviate the lazy indi-gence of the Jewish exiles here. The aged philanthropist made a journey hither in the summer of 1875, to ascertain for himself the condition of the Jews. I believe he has a hope of establishing manufactories in which they can support themselves; but the minds of the Jews who are already restored are not set upon any sort of industry. It seems to me that they could be maintained much more cheaply if they were transported to a less barren land.

We made, one day, an exploration of the Jews' quarter, which enjoys the reputation of being more filthy than the Christian. The approach to it is down a gutter which has the sounding name of the Street of David; it was bad enough, but when we entered the Jews' part of the city we found ourselves in lanes and gutters of incomparable unpleasantness, and almost impassable, with nothing whatever in them interesting or picturesque, except the inhabitants. We had a curiosity to see if there were here any real Jews of the type that inhabited the city in the time of our Lord, and we saw many with fair skin and light hair, with straight nose and regular features. The persons whom we are accustomed to call Jews, and who were found dispersed about Europe at a very early period of modern history, have the Assyrian features, the hook nose, dark hair and eyes, and not at all the faces of the fair-haired race from which our Saviour is supposed to have sprung. The kingdom of Israel, which contained the ten tribes, was gobbled up by the Assyrians about the time Rome was founded, and from that date these tribes do not appear historically. They may have entirely amalgamated with their conquerors, and the modified race subsequently have passed into Europe; for the Jews claim to have been in Europe before the destruction of Jerusalem by Titus, in which nearly all the people of the kingdom of Judah perished.

Some scholars, who have investigated the problem offered by the two types above mentioned, think that the Jew as we know him in Europe and America is not the direct descendant of the Jews of Jerusalem of the time of Herod, and that the true offspring of the latter is the person of the light hair and straight nose who is occasionally to be found in Jerusalem to-day. Until this ethnological problem is settled, I shall most certainly withhold my feeble contributions for the " restoration " of the persons at present doing business under the name of Jews among the Western nations.

But we saw another type of Jew, or rather another variety, in this quarter. He called himself of the tribe of Benjamin, and is, I think, the most unpleasant human being I have ever encountered. Every man who supposes himself of this tribe wears a dark, corkscrew, stringy curl hanging down each side of his face, and the appearance of nasty effeminacy which this gives cannot be described. The tribe of Benjamin does not figure well in sacred history, — it was left-handed; it was pretty much exterminated by the other tribes once for an awful crime; it was held from going into the settled idolatry of the kingdom of Israel only by its contiguity to Judah, — but it was better than its descendants, if these are its descendants.

More than half of the eight thousand Jews in Jerusalem speak Spanish as their native tongue, and are the offspring of those expelled from Spain by Ferdinand. Now and then, I do not know whether it was Spanish or Arabic, we saw a good face, a noble countenance, a fine Oriental and venerable type, and occasionally, looking from a window, a Jewish beauty ; but the most whom we met were debased, mis-begotten, the remnants of sin, squalor, and bad living.

We went into two of the best synagogues, — one new, with a conspicuous green dome. They are not fine; on the contrary, they are slatternly places and very ill-kept. On the benches near the windows sat squalid men and boys reading, the latter, no doubt, students of the law ; all the passages, stairs, and by-rooms were dirty and disorderly, as if it were always Monday morning there, but never washing-day ; rags and heaps of ancient garments were strewn about ; and occasionally we nearly stumbled over a Jew, indistinguishable from a bundle of old clothes, and asleep on the floor. Even the sanctuary is full of unkempt people, and of the evidences of the squalor of the quarter. If this is a specimen of the restoration of the Jews, they had better not be restored any more.

The thing to do (if the worldliness of the expression will be pardoned) on Friday is to go and see the Jews wail, as in Con-

stantinople it is to see the Sultan go to prayer, and in Cairo to
hear the darwishes howl. The performance, being an open-air
one, is sometimes prevented by rain or snow, but otherwise it has
not failed for many centuries. This ancient practice is probably
not what it once was, having in our modern days, by becoming a
sort of fashion, lost its spontaneity; it will, however, doubtless
be long kept up, as everything of this sort endures in the East,
even if it should become necessary to hire people to wail.

The Friday morning of the day chosen for our visit to the wailing place was rainy, following a rainy night. The rough-paved
open alleys were gutters of mud, the streets under arches (for there
are shops in subterranean constructions and old vaulted passages)
were damper and darker than usual; the whole city, with its narrow lanes, and thick walls, and no sewers, was clammy and un-
comfortable. We loitered for a time in the dark and grave-like
gold bazaars, where there is but a poor display of attractions. Pilgrims from all lands were sopping about in the streets; conspicuous among them were Persians wearing high, conical frieze hats,
and short-legged, big-calfed Russian peasant women, — animated
meal-bags.

We walked across to the Zion Gate, and mounting the city wall
there — an uneven and somewhat broken, but sightly promenade
— followed it round to its junction with the Temple wall, and to
Robinson's Arch. Underneath the wall by Zion Gate dwell, in
low stone huts and burrows, a considerable number of lepers, who
form a horrid community by themselves. These poor creatures,
with toeless feet and fingerless hands, came out of their dens and
assailed us with piteous cries for charity. What could be done?
It was impossible to give to all. The little we threw them they
fought for, and the unsuccessful followed us with whetted eagerness. We could do nothing but flee, and we climbed the wall
and ran down it, leaving Demetrius behind as a rear-guard. I
should have had more pity for them if they had not exhibited so
much maliciousness. They knew their power, and brought all
their loathsomeness after us, thinking that we would be forced to
buy their retreat. Two hideous old women followed us a long
distance, and when they became convinced that further howling

and whining would be fruitless, they suddenly changed tone and cursed us with healthful vigor; having cursed us, they hobbled home to roost.

This part of the wall crosses what was once the Tyrophœan Valley, which is now pretty much filled up; it ran between Mount Moriah, on which the Temple stood, and Mount Zion. It was spanned in ancient times by a bridge some three hundred and fifty feet long, resting on stone arches whose piers must have been from one hundred to two hundred feet in height; this connected the Temple platform with the top of the steep side of Zion. It was on the Temple end of this bridge that Titus stood and held parley with the Jews who refused to surrender Zion after the loss of Moriah.

The exact locality of this interesting bridge was discovered by Dr. Robinson. Just north of the southwest corner of the Harem wall (that is, the Temple or Mount Moriah wall) he noticed three courses of huge projecting stones, which upon careful inspection proved to be the segment of an arch. The spring of the arch is so plainly to be seen now that it is a wonder it remained so long unknown.

The Wailing Place of the Jews is on the west side of the Temple enclosure, a little to the north of this arch; it is in a long, narrow court formed by the walls of modern houses and the huge blocks of stone of this part of the original wall. These stones are no doubt as old as Solomon's Temple, and the Jews can here touch the very walls of the platform of that sacred edifice.

Every Friday a remnant of the children of Israel comes here to weep and wail. They bring their Scriptures, and leaning against the honey-combed stone, facing it, read the Lamentations and the Psalms, in a wailing voice, and occasionally cry aloud in a chorus of lamentation, weeping, blowing their long noses with blue cotton handkerchiefs, and kissing the stones. We were told that the smoothness of the stones in spots was owing to centuries of osculation. The men stand together at one part of the wall and the women at another. There were not more than twenty Jews present as actors in the solemn ceremony the day we visited the spot, and they did not wail much, merely reading the Scriptures in a mumbling voice and swaying their bodies backward and forward. Still they formed picturesque and even pathetic groups : venerable old men with long white beards and hooked noses, clad in rags and shreds and patches in all degrees of decadence; lank creatures of the tribe of Benjamin with the corkscrew curls; and skinny old women shaking with weeping, real or assumed.

Very likely these wailers were as poor and wretched as they appeared to be, and their tears were the natural outcome of their grief over the ruin of the Temple nearly two thousand years ago. I should be the last one to doubt their enjoyment of this weekly bitter misery. But the demonstration had somewhat the appearance of a set and show performance; while it was going on, a shrewd Israelite went about with a box to collect mites from the spectators. There were many more travellers there to see the wailing than there were Jews to wail. This also lent an unfavorable aspect to the scene. I myself felt that if this were genuine, I had no business to be there with my undisguised curiosity, and if it were not genuine, it was the poorest spectacle that Jerusalem offers to the tourist. Cook's party was there in force, this being one of the things promised in the contract; and I soon found myself more interested in Cook's pilgrims than in the others.

The Scripture read and wailed this day was the fifty-first Psalm of David. If you turn to it (you may have already discovered that the covert purpose of these desultory notes is to compel you to read your Bible), you will see that it expresses David's penitence in the matter of Bathsheba.

III.

HOLY PLACÉS OF THE HOLY CITY.

THE sojourner in Jerusalem falls into the habit of dropping in at the Church of the Holy Sepulchre nearly every afternoon. It is the centre of attraction. There the pilgrims all resort; there one sees, in a day, many races, and the costumes of strange and distant peoples; there one sees the various worship of the many Christian sects. There are always processions making the round of the holy places, sect following sect, with swinging censers, each fumigating away the effect of its predecessor.

The central body of the church, answering to the nave, as the rotunda, which contains the Holy Sepulchre, answers to choir and apse, is the Greek chapel, and the most magnificent in the building. The portion of the church set apart to the Latins, opening also out of the rotunda, is merely a small chapel. The Armenians have still more contracted accommodations, and the poor Copts enjoy a mere closet, but it is in a sacred spot, being attached to the west end of the sepulchre itself.

On the western side of the rotunda we passed through the bare and apparently uncared-for chapel of the Syrians, and entered, through a low door, into a small grotto hewn in the rock. Lighted candles revealed to us some tombs, little pits cut in the rock, two in the side-wall and two in the floor. We had a guide who knew every sacred spot in the city, a man who never failed to satisfy the curiosity of the most credulous tourist.

" Whose tombs are these ? " we asked.

" That is the tomb of Joseph of Arimathea, and that beside it is the tomb of Nicodemus."

" How do you know ? "

" How do I know? You ask me how I know. Have n't I always lived in Jerusalem ?   I was born here."

" Then perhaps you can tell us, if this tomb belonged to Joseph of Arimathea and this to Nicodemus, whose is this third one ? "

" O yes, that other," replied the guide, with only a moment's paralysis of his invention, " that is the tomb of Arimathea himself."

One afternoon at four, service was going on in the Greek chapel, which shone with silver and blazed with tapers, and was crowded with pilgrims, principally Russians of both sexes, many of whom had made a painful pilgrimage of more than two thousand miles on foot merely to prostrate themselves in this revered place.   A Russian bishop and a priest, in the resplendent robes of their office, were intoning the service responsively.   In the very centre of this chapel is a round hole covered with a grating, and tapers are generally burning about it.   All the pilgrims kneeled there, and kissed the grating and adored the hole.   I had the curiosity to push my way through the throng in order to see the object of devotion, but I could discover nothing.   It is, however, an important spot : it is *the centre of the earth ;* though why Christians should worship the centre of the earth I do not know. The Armenians have in their chapel also a spot that they say is the real centre ; that makes three that we know of, for everybody understands that there is one in the Kaaba at Mecca.

We sat down upon a stone bench near the entrance of the chapel, where we could observe the passing streams of people, and were greatly diverted by a blithe and comical beggar who had stationed himself on the pavement there to intercept the Greek charity of the worshippers when they passed into the rotunda.   He was a diminutive man with distorted limbs ; he wore a peaked red cap, and dragged himself over the pavement, or rather skipped and flopped about on it like a devil-fish on land.   Never was seen in a beggar such vivacity and imperturbable good-humor, with so much deviltry in his dancing eyes.

As we appeared to him to occupy a neutral position as to him and his victims, he soon took us into his confidence and let us see his mode of operations. He said (to our guide) that he was a Greek from Damascus, — O yes, a Christian, a pilgrim, who always came down here at this season, which was his harvest-time. He hoped (with a wicked wink) that his devotion would be rewarded.

It was very entertaining to see him watch the people coming out, and select his victims, whom he would indicate to us by a motion of his head as he flopped towards them. He appeared to rely more upon the poor and simple than upon the rich, and he was more successful with the former. But he rarely, such was his insight, made a mistake. Whoever gave him anything he thanked with the utmost *empressement* of manner; then he crossed himself, and turned around and winked at us, his confederates. When an elegantly dressed lady dropped the smallest of copper coins into his cap, he let us know his opinion of her by a significant gesture and a shrug of his shoulders. But no matter from whom he received it, whenever he added a penny to his store the rascal chirped and laughed and caressed himself. He was in the way of being trodden under foot by the crowd; but his agility was extraordinary, and I should not have been surprised at any moment if he had vaulted over the heads of the throng and disappeared. If he failed to attract the attention of an eligible pilgrim, he did not hesitate to give the skirt of his elect a jerk, for which rudeness he would at once apologize with an indescribable grimace and a joke.

When the crowd had passed, he slid himself into a corner, by a motion such as that with which a fish suddenly darts to one side, and set himself to empty his pocket into his cap and count his plunder, tossing the pieces into the air and catching them with a chuckle, crossing himself and hugging himself by turns. He had four francs and a half. When he had finished counting his money he put it in a bag, and for a moment his face assumed a grave and business-like expression. We thought he would depart without demanding anything of us. But we were mistaken; he had something in view that he no doubt felt would insure him a liberal backsheesh. Wriggling near to us, he set his face into an expression of demure humility, held out his cap, and said, in English,

3   D

each word falling from his lips as distinctly and unnaturally as
if he had been a wooden articulating machine, —

"Come unto me all ye that labor and are heavy laden, and *I*
will give you rest."

The rascal's impiety lessened the charity which our intimacy
with him had intended, but he appeared entirely content, chirped,
saluted with gravity, and, with a flop, was gone from our sight.

At the moment, a procession of Franciscan monks swept by,
chanting in rich bass voices, and followed, as usual, by Latin pilgrims, making the daily round of the holy places; after they had
disappeared we could still hear their voices and catch now and
again the glimmer of their tapers in the vast dark spaces.

Opposite the place where we were sitting is the Chapel of the
Apparition, a room not much more than twenty feet square; it is
the Latin chapel, and besides its contiguity to the sepulchre has
some specialties of its own. The chapel is probably eight hundred years old. In the centre of the pavement is the spot upon
which our Lord stood when he appeared to the Virgin after the
resurrection; near it a slab marks the place where the three
crosses were laid after they were dug up by Helena, and where
the one on which our Lord was crucified was identified by the
miracle that it worked in healing a sick man. South of the altar
is a niche in the wall, now covered over, but a round hole is left
in the covering. I saw pilgrims thrust a long stick into this hole,
withdraw it, and kiss the end. The stick had touched a fragment of the porphyry column to which the Saviour was bound
when he was scourged.

In the semicircle at the east end of the nave are several interesting places : the prison where Christ was confined before his
execution, a chapel dedicated to the centurion who pierced the
side of our Lord, and the spot on which the vestments were
divided. From thence we descend, by a long flight of steps
partly hewn in the rock, to a rude, crypt-like chapel, in the heavy
early Byzantine style, a damp, cheerless place, called the Chapel
of Helena. At the east end of it another flight of steps leads
down into what was formerly a cistern, but is now called the
Chapel of the Invention of the Cross. Here the cross was found,

and at one side of the steps stands the marble chair in which the
mother of Constantine sat while she superintended the digging.
Nothing is wanting that the most credulous pilgrim could wish
to see ; that is, nothing is wanting in *spots* where things were.
This chapel belongs to the Latins ; that of Helena to the Greeks ;
the Abyssinian convent is above both of them.

On the south side of the church, near the entrance, is a dark
room called the Chapel of Adam, in which there is never more
light than a feeble taper can give. I groped my way into it
often, in the hope of finding something ; perhaps it is purposely
involved in an obscurity typical of the origin of mankind. There
is a tradition that Adam was buried on Golgotha, but the only
tomb in this chapel is that of Melchizedek ! The chapel formerly
contained that of Godfrey de Bouillon, elected the first king of
Jerusalem in 1099, and of Baldwin, his brother. We were shown
the two-handed sword of Godfrey, with which he clove a Saracen
lengthwise into two equal parts, a genuine relic of a heroic and
barbarous age. At the end of this chapel a glimmering light lets
us see through a grating a crack in the rock made by the earthquake at the crucifixion.

The gloom of this mysterious chapel, which is haunted by the
spectre of that dim shadow of unreality, Melchizedek, prepared
us to ascend to Golgotha, above it. The chapels of Golgotha
are supported partly upon a rock which rises fifteen feet above
the pavement of the church. The first is that of the Elevation
of the Cross, and belongs to the Greeks. Under the altar at the
east end is a hole in the marble which is over the hole in the rock
in which the cross stood ; on either side of it are the holes of the
crosses of the two thieves. The altar is rich with silver and gold
and jewels. The chamber, when we entered it, was blazing with
light, and Latin monks were performing their adorations, with
chanting and swinging of incense, before the altar. A Greek
priest stood at one side, watching them, and there was plain contempt in his face. The Greek priests are not wanting in fanaticism, but they never seem to me to possess the faith of the Latin
branch of the Catholic church. When the Latins had gone, the
Greek took us behind the altar, and showed us another earth-
quake-rent in the rock.

Adjoining this chapel is the Latin Chapel of the Crucifixion, marking the spot where Christ was nailed to the cross; from that we looked through a window into an exterior room dedicated to the Sorrowing Virgin, where she stood and beheld the crucifixion. Both these latter rooms do not rest upon the rock, but upon artificial vaults, and of course can mark the spots commemorated by them only *in space*.

Perhaps this sensation of being in the air, and of having no standing-place even for tradition, added something to the strange feeling that took possession of me; a mingled feeling that was no more terror than is the apprehension that one experiences at a theatre from the manufactured thunder behind the scenes. I suppose it arose from cross currents meeting in the mind, the thought of the awful significance of the events here represented and the sight of this theatrical representation. The dreadful name, Golgotha, the gloom of this part of the building, — a sort of mount of darkness, with its rent rock and preternatural shadow, — the blazing contrast of the chapel where the cross stood with the dark passages about it, the chanting and flashing lights of pilgrims ever coming and going, the neighborhood of the sepulchre itself, were well calculated to awaken an imagination the least sensitive. And, so susceptible is the mind to the influence of that mental electricity — if there is no better name for it — which proceeds from a mass of minds having one thought (and is sometimes called public opinion), be it true or false, that whatever one may believe about the real location of the Holy Sepulchre, he cannot witness, unmoved, the vast throng of pilgrims to these shrines, representing as they do every section of the civilized and of the uncivilized world into which a belief in the cross has penetrated. The undoubted sincerity of the majority of the pilgrims who worship here makes us for the time forget the hundred inventions which so often allure and as often misdirect that worship.

The Church of the Holy Sepulchre offers at all times a great spectacle, and one always novel, in the striking ceremonies and the people who assist at them. One of the most extraordinary, that of the Holy Fire, at the Greek Easter, which is three weeks later than the Roman, and which has been so often described, we did not see. I am not sure that we saw even all the thirty-seven holy places and objects in the church. It may not be unprofitable to set down those I can recall. They are, —

The Stone of Unction.

The spot where the Virgin Mary stood when the body of our Lord was anointed.

The Holy Sepulchre.

The stone on which the angel sat.

The tombs of Joseph of Arimathea and Nicodemus.

The well of Helena.

The stone marking the spot where Christ in the form of a gardener appeared to Mary Magdalene.

The spot where Mary Magdalene stood.

The spot where our Lord appeared to the Virgin after his resurrection.

The place where the true cross, discovered by Helena, was laid, and identified by a miracle.

The fragment of the Column of Flagellation.

The prison of our Lord.

The " Bonds of Christ," a stone with two holes in it.

The place where the *title* on the cross was preserved.

The place of the division of the vestments.

The centre of the earth (Greek).

The centre of the earth (Armenian).

The altar of the centurion who pierced the body of Christ.

The altar of the penitent thief.

The Chapel of Helena.

The chair in which Helena sat when the cross was found.

The spot where the cross was found.

The Chapel of the Mocking, with a fragment of the column upon which Jesus sat when they crowned him with thorns.

The Chapel of the Elevation of the Cross.

The spot where the cross stood.

The spots where the crosses of the thieves stood.

The rent rock near the cross.

The spot where Christ was nailed to the cross.

The spot where the Virgin stood during the crucifixion.

The Chapel of Adam.

The tomb of Melchizedek.

The rent rock in the Chapel of Adam.

The spots where the tombs of Godfrey and Baldwin stood.

No, we did not see them all. Besides, there used to be a piece of the cross in the Latin chapel; but the Armenians are accused of purloining it. All travellers, I suppose, have seen the celebrated Iron Crown of Lombardy, which is kept in the church at Monza, near Milan. It is all of gold except the inner band, which is made of a nail of the cross brought from Jerusalem by Helena. The Church of the Holy Sepulchre has not all the relics it might have, but it is as rich in them as any church of its age.

A place in Jerusalem almost as interesting to Christians as the Holy Sepulchre, and more interesting to antiquarians, is the Harem, or Temple area, with its ancient substructions and its resplendent Saracenic architecture. It is largely an open place, green with grass; it is clean and wholesome, and the sun lies lovingly on it. There is no part of the city where the traveller would so like to wander at will, to sit and muse, to dream away the day on the walls overhanging the valley of the Kidron, to recall at leisure all the wonderful story of its splendor and its disaster. But admission to the area is had only by special permit. Therefore the ordinary tourist goes not so much as he desires to the site of the Temple that Solomon built, and of the porch where Jesus walked and talked with his disciples. When he does go, he feels that he treads upon firm historical ground.

We walked down the gutter (called street) of David; we did not enter the Harem area by the Bâb es-Silsileh (Gate of the Chain), but turned northward and went in by the Bâb el-Katanîn (Gate of the Cotton-Merchants), which is identified with the Beautiful Gate of the Temple. Both these gates have twisted columns and are graceful examples of Saracenic architecture. As soon as we entered the gate the splendor of the area burst upon us; we passed instantly out of the sordid city into a green plain, out of which — it could have been by a magic wand only — had sprung the most charming creations in stone: minarets, domes, colonnades, cloisters, pavilions, columns of all orders, horseshoe arches and pointed arches, every joyous architectural thought expressed in shining marble and brilliant color.

Our dragoman, Abd-el-Atti, did the honors of the place with the air of proprietorship. For the first time in the Holy City he felt quite at home, and appeared to be on the same terms with the Temple area that he is with the tombs of the Pharaohs. The Christian antiquities are too much for him, but his elastic mind expands readily to all the marvels of the Moslem situation. The Moslems, indeed, consider that they have a much better right to the Temple than the Christians, and Abd-el-Atti acted as our cicerone in the precincts with all the delight of a boy and with the enthusiasm of faith. It was not unpleasant to him, either, to have us see that he was treated with consideration by the mosque attendants and ulemas, and that he was well known and could pass readily into the most reserved places. He had said his prayers that morning, at twelve, in this mosque, a privilege only second to that of praying in the mosque at Mecca, and was in high spirits, as one who had (if the expression is allowable) got a little ahead in the matter of devotion.

Let me give in a few words, without any qualifications of doubt, what seem to be the well-ascertained facts about this area. It is at present a level piece of ground (in the nature of a platform, since it is sustained on all sides by walls), a quadrilateral with its sides not quite parallel, about fifteen hundred feet long by one thousand feet broad. The northern third of it was covered by the Fortress of Antonia, an ancient palace and fortress, rebuilt with great splendor by Herod. The small remains of it in the northeast corner are now barracks.

This level piece of ground is nearly all artificial, either filled in or built up on arches. The original ground (Mount Moriah) was a rocky hill, the summit of which was the rock about which there has been so much controversy. Near the centre of this ground, and upon a broad raised platform, paved with marble, stands the celebrated mosque Kubbet es-Sukhrah, "The Dome of the Rock." It is built over the Sacred Rock.

This rock marks the site of the threshing-floor of Ornan, the

Jebusite, which David bought, purchasing at the same time the
whole of Mount Moriah.   Solomon built the Temple over this
rock, and it was probably the "stone of sacrifice."   At the time
Solomon built the Temple, the level place on Moriah was scarcely
large enough for the *naos* of that building, and Solomon extended
the ground to the east and south by erecting arches and filling in
on top of them, and constructing a heavy retaining-wall outside.
On the east side also he built a porch, or magnificent colonnade,
which must have produced a fine effect of Oriental grandeur when
seen from the deep valley below or from the Mount of Olives
opposite.

To this rock the Jews used to come, in the fourth century, and
anoint it with oil, and wail over it, as the site of the Temple.   On
it once stood a statue of Hadrian.   When the Moslems captured
Jerusalem, it became, what it has ever since been, one of their
most venerated places.   The Khalif Omar cleared away the rubbish from it, and built over it a mosque.   The Khalif Abd-el-
Melek began to rebuild it in A. D. 686.   During the Crusades it
was used as a Christian church.   Allowing for decay and repairs,
the present mosque is probably substantially that built by Abd-
el-Melek.

At the extreme south of the area is the vast Mosque of Aksa,
a splendid basilica with seven aisles, which may or may not be
the Church of St. Mary built by Justinian in the sixth century;
architects differ about it.   This question it seems to me very
difficult to decide from the architecture of the building, because
of the habit that Christians and Moslems both had of appropriat-
ing columns and capitals of ancient structures in their buildings;
and because the Moslems at that time used both the round and
the pointed arch.

This platform is beyond all comparison the most beautiful
place in Jerusalem, and its fairy-like buildings, when seen from
the hill opposite, give to the city its chief claim to Oriental picturesqueness.

The dome of the mosque Kubbet-es-Sukhrah is perhaps the
most beautiful in the world; it seems to float in the air like a
blown bubble; this effect is produced by a slight drawing in of

the base. This contraction of the dome is not sufficient to give the spectator any feeling of insecurity, or to belittle this architectural marvel to the likeness of a big toy; the builder hit the exact mean between massiveness and expanding lightness. The mosque is octagonal in form, and although its just proportions make it appear small, it is a hundred and fifty feet in diameter; outside and in, it is a blaze of color in brilliant marbles, fine mosaics, stained glass, and beautiful Saracenic tiles. The lower part of the exterior wall is covered with colored marbles in intricate patterns; above are pointed windows with stained glass; and the spaces between the windows are covered by glazed tiles, with arabesque designs and very rich in color. In the interior, which has all the soft warmth and richness of Persian needlework, are two corridors, with rows of columns and pillars; within the inner row is the Sacred Rock.

This rock, which is the most remarkable stone in the world, if half we hear of it be true, and which by a singular fortune is sacred to three religions, is an irregular bowlder, standing some five feet above the pavement, and is something like sixty feet long. In places it has been chiselled, steps are cut on one side, and various niches are hewn in it; a round hole pierces it from top to bottom. The rock is limestone, a little colored with iron, and beautiful in spots where it has been polished. One would think that by this time it ought to be worn smooth all over.

If we may believe the Moslems and doubt our own senses, this rock is suspended in the air, having no support on any side. It was to this rock that Mohammed made his midnight journey on El Burâk; it was from here that he ascended into Paradise, an excursion that occupied him altogether only forty minutes. It is, I am inclined to think, the miraculous suspension of this stone that is the basis of the Christian fable of the suspension of Mohammed's coffin,—a miracle unknown to all Moslems of whom I have inquired concerning it.

"Abd-el-Atti," I said, "does this rock rest on nothing?"

"So I have hunderstood; thim say so."

"But do you believe it?"

"When I read him, I believe; when I come and see him, I can't help what I see."

At the south end of the rock we descended a flight of steps and stood under the rock in what is called the Noble Cave, a small room about six feet high, plastered and whitewashed. This is supposed to be the sink into which the blood of the Jewish sacrifices drained. The plaster and whitewash hide the original rock, and give the Moslems the opportunity to assert that there is no rock foundation under the big stone.

"But," we said to Abd-el-Atti, "if this rock hangs in the air, why cannot we see all around it? Why these plaster walls that seem to support it?"

"So him used to be. This done so, I hear, on account of de women. Thim come here, see this rock, thim berry much frightened. Der little shild, what you call it, get born in de world before him wanted. So thim make this wall under it."

There are four altars in this cave, one of them dedicated to David; here the Moslem prophets, Abraham, David, Solomon, and Jesus, used to pray. In the rock is a round indentation made by Mohammed's head when he first attempted to rise to heaven; near it is the hole through which he rose. On the upper southeast corner of the rock is the print of the prophet's foot, and close to it the print of the hand of the angel Michael, who held the rock down from following Mohammed into the skies.

In the mosque above, Abd-el-Atti led us, with much solemnity, to a small stone set in the pavement near the north entrance. It was perforated with holes, in some of which were brass nails.

"How many holes you make 'em there?"

"Thirteen."

"How many got nails?"

"Four."

"Not so many. Only three and a half nails. Used to be thirteen nails. Now only three and a half. When these gone, then the world come to an end. I t'ink it not berry long."

"I should think the Moslems would watch this stone very carefully."

"What difference? You not t'ink it come when de time come?"

We noticed some pieces of money on the stone, and asked why that was.

"Whoever he lay backsheesh on this stone, he certain to go into Paradise, and be took by our prophet in his bosom."

We wandered for some time about the green esplanade, dotted with cypress-trees, and admired the little domes : the Dome of the Spirits, the dome that marks the spot where David sat in judgment, etc. ; some of them cover cisterns and reservoirs in the rock, as old as the foundations of the Temple.

In the corridor of the Mosque of Aksa are two columns standing close together, and like those at the Mosque of Omar, in Cairo, they are a test of character ; it is said that whoever can squeeze between them is certain of Paradise, and must, of course, be a good Moslem. I suppose that when this test was established the Moslems were all lean. A black stone is set in the wall of the porch ; whoever can walk, with closed eyes, across the porch pavement and put his finger on this stone may be sure of entering Paradise. According to this criterion, the writer of this is one of the elect of the Mohammedan Paradise and his dragoman is shut out. We were shown in this mosque the print of Christ's foot in a stone ; and it is said that with faith one can feel in it, as he can in that of Mohammed's in the rock, the real flesh. Opening from this mosque is the small Mosque of Omar, on the spot where that zealous khalif prayed.

The massive pillared substructions under Aksa are supposed by Moslems to be of Solomon's time. That wise monarch had dealings with the invisible, and no doubt controlled the genii, who went and came and built and delved at his bidding. Abd-el-Atti, with haste and an air of mystery, drew me along under the arches to the window in the south end, and showed me the opening of a passage under the wall, now half choked up with stones. This is the beginning of a subterranean passage made by the prophet Solomon, that extends all the way to Hebron, and has an issue in the mosque over the tomb of Abraham. This fact is known only to Moslems, and to very few of them, and is considered one of the great secrets. Before I was admitted to share it, I am glad that I passed between the two columns, and touched, with my eyes shut, the black stone.

In the southeast corner of the Harem is a little building called the Mosque of Jesus. We passed through it, and descended the stairway into what is called Solomon's Stables, being shown on our way a stone trough which is said to be the cradle of the infant Jesus. These so-called stables are subterranean vaults, built, no doubt, to sustain the south end of the Temple platform. We saw fifteen rows of massive square pillars of unequal sizes and at unequal distances apart (as if intended for supports that would not be seen), and some forty feet high, connected by round arches. We were glad to reascend from this wet and unpleasant cavern to the sunshine and the greensward.

I forgot to mention the Well of the Leaf, near the entrance, in the Mosque of Aksa, and the pretty Moslem legend that gave it a name, which Abd-el-Atti relates, though not in the words of the hand-book : —

" This well berry old ; call him Well of the Leaf; water same as Pool of Solomon, healthy water ; I like him very much. Not so deep as Bir el-Arwâh ; that small well, you see it under the rock ; they say it goes down into Gehenna."

" Why is this called the Well of the Leaf? "

" Once, time of Sulciman [it was Omar], a friend of our prophet come here to pray, and when he draw water to wash he drop the bucket in the bottom of the well. No way to get it up, but he must go down. When he was on the bottom, there he much surprised by a door open in the ground, and him berry cur'ous to see what it is. Nobody there, so he look in, and then walk through berry fast, and look over him shoulder to the bucket left in the well. The place where he was come was the most beautiful garden ever was, and he walk long time and find no end, always more garden, so cool, and water run in little streams, and sweet smell of roses and jasmine, and little birds that sing, and big trees and dates and oranges and palms, more kind, I t'ink, than you see in the garden of his vice-royal. When the man have been long time in the garden he begin to have fright, and pick a green leaf off a tree. and run back and come up to his friends. He show 'em the green leaf, but nobody have believe what he say. Then they tell him story to the kadi, and the kadi send men to see the garden in the bottom of the well. They not find any, not find any door. Then the kadi he make him a letter to the Sultau — berry wise man — and he say (so I read it in our history), ' Our prophet say, One of my friends shall walk in Paradise while he is alive. If this is come true, you shall see the leaf, if it still keep green.' Then the kadi make examine of the leaf, and find him green. So it is believe the man has been in Paradise.''

" And do you believe it ? "

" I cannot say edzacly where him been. Where you t'ink he done got that leaf ? "

Along the east wall of the Harem there are no remains of the long colonnade called Solomon's Porch, not a column of that resplendent marble pavilion which caught the first rays of the sun over the mountains of Moab, and which, with the shining temple towering behind it, must have presented a more magnificent appearance than Babylon, and have rivalled the architectural glories of Baalbek. The only thing in this wall worthy of note now is the Golden Gate, an entrance no longer used. We descended into its archways, and found some fine columns with composite capitals, and other florid stone-work of a rather tasteless and debased Roman style.

We climbed the wall by means of the steps, a series of which are placed at intervals, and sat a long time looking upon a landscape, every foot of which is historical. Merely to look upon it is to recall a great portion of the Jewish history and the momentous events in the brief life of the Saviour, which, brief as it was, sufficed to newly create the earth. There is the Mount of Olives, with its commemorative chapels, heaps of stone, and scattered trees ; there is the ancient foot-path up which David fled as a fugitive by night from the conspiracy of Absalom, what time Shimei, the relative of Saul, stoned him and cursed him ; and down that Way of Triumph, the old road sweeping round its base, came the procession of the Son of David, in whose path the multitude cast their garments and branches of trees, and cried, " Hosanna in the highest." There on those hills, Mount Scopus and Olivet, were once encamped the Assyrians, and again the Persians ; there shone the eagles of Rome, borne by her conquering legions ;

and there, in turn, Crusaders and Saracens pitched their tents.
How many times has the air been darkened with missiles hurled
thence upon this shining prize, and how many armies have closed
in about this spot and swarmed to its destruction! There the
Valley of Jehoshaphat curves down until it is merged in the Valley of the Brook Kidron.   There, at the junction of the roads that
run over and around Olivet, is a clump of trees surrounded by
a white wall; that is the Garden of Gethsemane. Near it is the
tomb of Mary. Farther down you see the tomb of Absalom, the
tomb of St. James, the monolith pyramid-tipped tomb of Zacharias
(none of them apparently as old as they claim to be), and the remains of a little temple, the model of which came from the banks
of the Nile, that Solomon built for his Egyptian wife, the daughter
of Pharaoh, wherein they worshipped the gods of her country. It
is tradition also that near here were some of the temples he built
for others of his strange wives : a temple to Chemosh, the Moabite god, and the image of Moloch, the devourer of children.   Solomon was wiser than all men, wiser than Heman, and Chalcol,
and Darda, the sons of Mahol; his friend Hiram of Tyre used to
send riddles to him which no one in the world but Solomon could
guess; but his wisdom failed him with the other sex, and there
probably never was another Oriental court so completely ruled
and ruined by women as his.

This valley below us is perhaps the most melancholy on earth:
nowhere else is death so visibly master of the scene; nature is
worn out, man tired out; a gray despair has settled down upon
the landscape. Down there is the village of Siloam, a village of
huts and holes in the rocks, opposite the cave of that name. If it
were the abode of wolves it would have a better character than it
has now. There is the grim cast of sin and exhaustion upon the
scene. I do not know exactly how much of this is owing to the
Jewish burying-ground, which occupies so much of the opposite
hill. The slope is thickly shingled with gray stones, that lie in a
sort of regularity which suggests their purpose. You fall to com-
puting how many Jews there may be in that hill, layer upon layer;
for the most part they are dissolved away into the earth, but you
think that if they were to put on their mortal bodies and come

forth, the valley itself would be filled with them almost to the height of the wall. Out of these gates, giving upon this valley of death, six hundred thousand bodies of those who had starved were thrown during the siege, and long before Titus stormed the city. I do not wonder that the Moslems think of this frightful vale as Gehenna itself.

From an orifice in the battlemented wall where we sat projects a round column, mounted there like a cannon, and perhaps intended to deceive an enemy into the belief that the wall is fortified. It is astride this column, overhanging this dreadful valley, that Mohammed will sit at the last, the judgment day. A line finer than a hair and sharper than a razor will reach from it to the tower on the Mount of Olives, stretching over the valley of the dead. This is the line Es-Serat. Mohammed will superintend the passage over it. For in that day all who ever lived, risen to judgment, must walk this razor-line; the good will cross in safety; the bad will fall into hell, that is, into Gehenna, this blasted gulf and side-hill below, thickly sown with departed Jews. It is in view of this perilous passage that the Moslem every day, during the ablution of his feet, prays: "O, make my feet not to slip on Es-Serat, on that day when feet shall slip."

IV.

NEIGHBORHOODS OF JERUSALEM.

WHEREVER we come upon traces of the Knights of St. John, there a door opens for us into romance; the very name suggests valor and courtesy and charity. Every town in the East that is so fortunate as to have any memorials of them, whatever its other historic associations, obtains an additional and special fame from its connection with this heroic order. The city of Acre recalls the memory of their useless prowess in the last struggle of the Christians to retain a foothold in Palestine; the name of the Knights of Rhodes brings before every traveller, who has seen it, the picturesque city in which the armorial insignia of this order have for him a more living interest than any antiquities of the Grecian Rose; the island fortress at the gate of the Levant owes all the interest we feel in it to the Knights of Malta; and even the city of David and of the Messiah has an added lustre as the birthplace of the Knights of St. John of Jerusalem.

From the eleventh century to the fifteenth, they are the chief figures who in that whirlwind of war contested the possession of the Levant with the Saracens and the Turks. In the forefront of every battle was seen their burnished mail, in the gloomy rear of every retreat were heard their voices of constancy and of courage; wherever there were crowns to be cracked, or wounds to be bound up, or broken hearts to be ministered to, there were the Knights of St. John, soldiers, priests, servants, laying aside the gown for the coat of mail if need be, or exchanging the cuirass for the white cross on the breast. Originally a charitable order, dwelling in the Hospital of St. John to minister to the pilgrims to Jerusalem, and composed of young soldiers of Godfrey, who took the vows of poverty, chastity, and obedience, they resumed their arms upon the pressure of infidel hostility, and subsequently divided the order into three classes : soldiers, priests, and servants. They speedily acquired great power and wealth ; their palaces, their fortifications, their churches, are even in their ruins the admiration and wonder of our age. The purity of the order was in time somewhat sullied by luxury, but their valor never suffered the slightest eclipse; whether the field they contested was lost or won, their bravery always got new honor from it.

Nearly opposite the court of the Church of the Holy Sepulchre is the green field of Muristan, the site of the palace, church, and hospital of the Knights of St. John. The field was, on an average, twenty-five feet above the surrounding streets, and a portion of it was known to rest upon vaults. This plot of ground was given to the Prussian government, and its agents have been making excavations there ; these were going on at the time of our visit. The disclosures are of great architectural and historical interest. The entrance through a peculiar Gothic gateway leads into a court. Here the first excavations were made several years ago, and disclosed some splendid remains : the apse of the costly church, cloisters, fine windows and arches of the best Gothic style. Beyond, the diggings have brought to light some of the features of the palace and hospital ; an excavation of twenty-five feet reaches down to the arches of the substructure, which rest upon pillars from forty to fifty feet high. This gives us some notion of the magnificent group of buildings that once occupied this square, and also of the industry of nature as an entomber, since some four centuries have sufficed her to bury these ruins so far beneath the soil, that peasants ploughed over the palaces of the knights without a suspicion of what lay beneath.

In one corner of this field stands a slender minaret, marking the spot where the great Omar once said his prayers : four centuries after this, Saladin is said to have made his military headquarters in the then deserted palace of the Knights of St. John. There is no spot in Jerusalem where one touches more springs of romance than in this field of Muristan.

E

Perhaps the most interesting and doleful walk one can take near Jerusalem is that into the Valley of Kidron and through Aceldama, round to the Jaffa Gate, traversing "the whole valley of the dead bodies, and of the ashes," in the cheerful words of Jeremiah.

We picked our way through the filthy streets and on the slippery cobble-stones, — over which it seems dangerous to ride and is nearly impossible to walk, — out through St. Stephen's Gate. Near the gate, inside, we turned into an alley and climbed a heap of rubbish to see a pool, which the guide insisted upon calling Bethesda, although it is Birket Israil. Having seen many of these pools, I did not expect much, but I was still disappointed. We saw merely a hole in the ground, which is void of all appearance of ever having been even damp. The fact is, we have come to Jerusalem too late; we ought to have been here about two thousand years ago.

The slope of the hill outside the gate is covered with the turbaned tombs of Moslems; we passed under the walls and through this cemetery into the deep valley below, crossing the bed of the brook near the tombs of Absalom, Jehoshaphat, St. James, and Zacharias. These all seem to be of Roman construction; but that called Absalom's is so firmly believed to be his that for centuries every Jew who has passed it has cast a stone at it, and these pebbles of hate partially cover it. We also added to the heap, but I do not know why, for it is nearly impossible to hate any one who has been dead so long.

The most interesting phenomenon in the valley is the Fountain of the Virgin, or the Fountain of Accused Women, as it used to be called. The Moslem tradition is that it was a test of the unfaithfulness of women; those who drank of it and were guilty, died; those who were innocent received no harm. The Virgin Mary herself, being accused, accepted this test, drank of the water, and proved her chastity. Since then the fountain has borne her name. The fountain, or well, is in the side-hill, under the rocks of Ophel, and the water springs up in an artificial cave. We descended some sixteen steps to a long chamber, arched with ancient masonry; we passed through that and descended fourteen steps more into a grotto, where we saw the water flowing in and escaping by a subterranean passage. About this fountain were lounging groups of Moslem idlers, mostly women and children. Not far off a Moslem was saying his prayers, prostrating himself before a prayer-niche. We had difficulty in making our way down the steps, so encumbered were they with women. Several of them sat upon the lowest steps in the damp cavern, gossiping, filling their water-skins, or paddling about with naked feet.

The well, like many others in Syria, is intermittent and irregular in its rising and falling; sometimes it is dry, and then suddenly it bubbles up and is full again. Some scholars think this is the Pool Bethesda of the New Testament, others think that Bethesda was Siloam, which is below this well and fed by it, and would exhibit the same irregular rising and falling. This intermittent character St. John attributed to an angel who came down and troubled the water; the Moslems, with the same superstition, say that it is caused by a dragon, who sleeps therein and checks the stream when he wakes.

On our way to the Pool of Siloam, we passed the village of Siloam, which is inhabited by about a thousand Moslems, — a nest of stone huts and caves clinging to the side-hill, and exactly the gray color of its stones. The occupation of the inhabitants appears to be begging, and hunting for old copper coins, mites, and other pieces of Jewish money. These relics they pressed upon us with the utmost urgency. It was easier to satisfy the beggars than the traders, who sallied out upon us like hungry wolves from their caves. There is a great choice of disagreeable places in the East, but I cannot now think of any that I should not prefer as a residence to Siloam.

The Pool of Siloam, magnified in my infant mind as "Siloam's shady rill," is an unattractive sink-hole of dirty water, surrounded by modern masonry. The valley here is very stony. Just below we came to Solomon's Garden, an arid spot, with patches of stone-walls, struggling to be a vegetable-garden, and somewhat green with lettuce and Jerusalem artichokes. I have no doubt it was quite another thing when Solomon and some of his wives used to walk here in the cool of the day, and even when Shallum, the son of Col-hozeh, set up "the wall of the Pool of Siloah by the king's garden."

We continued on, down to Joab's Well, passing on the way Isaiah's Tree, a decrepit sycamore propped up by a stone pillar, where that prophet was sawn asunder. There is no end to the cheerful associations of the valley. The Well of Joab, a hundred and twenty-five feet deep, and walled and arched with fine masonry, has a great appearance of antiquity. We plucked maidenhair from its crevices, and read the Old Testament references. Near it is a square pool fed by its water. Some little distance below this, the waters of all these wells, pools, drains, sinks, or whatever they are, reappear bursting up through a basin of sand and pebbles, as clear as crystal, and run brawling off down the valley under a grove of large olive-trees, — a scene rural and inviting.

I suppose it would be possible to trace the whole system of underground water ways and cisterns, from Solomon's Pool, which sends its water into town by an aqueduct near the Jaffa Gate, to Hezekiah's Pool, to the cisterns under the Harem, and so out to the Virgin's Well, the Pool of Siloam, and the final gush of sweet water below. This valley drains, probably artificially as well as naturally, the whole city, for no sewers exist in the latter.

We turned back from this sparkling brook, which speedily sinks into the ground again, absorbed by the thirsty part of the valley called Tophet, and went up the Valley of Hinnom, passing under the dark and frowning ledges of Aceldama, honey-combed with tombs. In this "field of blood" a grim stone structure forms the front of a natural cave, which is the charnel-house where the dead were cast pell-mell, in the belief that the salts in the earth would speedily consume them. The path we travel is rugged, steep, and incredibly stony. The whole of this region is inexpressibly desolate, worn-out, pale, uncanny. The height above this rocky terrace, stuffed with the dead, is the Hill of Evil Counsel, where the Jews took counsel against Jesus; and to add the last touch of an harmonious picture, just above this Potter's Field stands the accursed tree upon which Judas hanged himself, raising its gaunt branches against the twilight sky, a very gallows-tree to the imagination. It has borne no fruit since Iscariot. Towards dusk, sometimes, as you stand on the wall by Zion Gate, you almost fancy you can see *him* dangling there. It is of no use to tell me that the seed that raised this tree could not have sprouted till a thousand years after Judas was crumbled into dust; one must have faith in something.

This savage gorge, for the Valley of Hinnom is little more than that in its narrowest part, has few associations that are not horrible. Here Solomon set up the images ("the groves," or the graven images), and the temples for the lascivious rites of Ashtaroth or the human sacrifices to Moloch. Here the Jews, the kings and successors of Solomon, with a few exceptions, and save an occasional spasmodic sacrifice to Jehovah when calamity made them fear him, practised all the abominations of idolatry in use in that age. The Jews had always been more or less addicted to the worship of the god of Ammon, but Solomon first formally established it in Hinnom. Jeremiah writes of it historically, "They have built the high places of Tophet, which is in the valley of the son of Hinnom, to burn their sons and their daughters in the fire." This Moloch was as ingenious a piece of cruelty as ever tried the faith of heretics in later times, and, since it was purely a means of human sacrifice, and not a means of grace (as Inquisitorial tortures were supposed to be), its use is conclusive proof of the savage barbarity of the people who delighted in it. Moloch was the monstrous brass image of a man with the head of an ox. It was hollow, and the interior contained a furnace by which the statue was made red-hot. Children — the offerings to the god — were then placed in its glowing arms, and drums were beaten to drown their cries. It is painful to recall these things, but the traveller should always endeavor to obtain the historical flavor of the place he visits.

Continuing our walks among the antiquities of Jerusalem, we went out of the Damascus Gate, a noble battlemented structure, through which runs the great northern highway to Samaria and Damascus. The road, however, is a mere path over ledges and through loose stones, fit only for donkeys. If Rehoboam went this way in his chariot to visit Jeroboam in Samaria, there must

have existed then a better road, or else the king endured hard
pounding for the sake of the dignity of his conveyance. As soon
as we left the gate we encountered hills of stones and paths of
the roughest description. There are several rock tombs on this
side of the city, but we entered only one, that called by some the
Tombs of the Kings, and by others, with more reason, the Tomb
of Helena, a heathen convert to Judaism, who built this sepulchre
for herself early in the first century. The tomb, excavated entirely in the solid rock, is a spacious affair, having a large court
and ornamented vestibule and many chambers, extending far into
the rock, and a singular network of narrow passages and recesses
for the deposit of the dead. It had one device that is worthy
of the ancient Egyptians. The entrance was closed by a heavy
square stone, so hung that it would yield to pressure from without, but would swing to its place by its own weight, and fitted so
closely that it could not be moved from the inside. If any thief
entered the tomb and left this slab unsecured, he would be instantly caught in the trap and become a permanent occupant.
Large as the tomb is, its execution is mean compared with the
rock tombs of Egypt; but the exterior stone of the court, from
its exposure in this damp and variable climate, appears older than
Egyptian work which has been uncovered three times as long.

At the tomb we encountered a dozen students from the Latin
convent, fine-looking fellows in long blue-black gowns, red caps,
and red sashes. They sat upon the grass, on the brink of the
excavation, stringing rosaries and singing student songs, with
evident enjoyment of the hour's freedom from the school; they
not only made a picturesque appearance, but they impressed us
also as a Jerusalem group which was neither sinful nor dirty.
Beyond this tomb we noticed a handsome modern dwelling-house;
you see others on various eminences outside the city, and we
noted them as the most encouraging sign of prosperity about
Jerusalem.

We returned over the hill and by the city wall, passing the
Cave of Jeremiah and the door in the wall that opens into the
stone quarries of Solomon. These quarries underlie a considerable portion of the city, and furnished the stone for its ancient

buildings. I will not impose upon you a description of them; for it would be unfair to send you into disagreeable places that I did not explore myself.

The so-called Grotto of Jeremiah is a natural cavern in the rocky hill, vast in extent, I think thirty feet high and a hundred feet long by seventy broad, — as big as a church. The tradition is that Jeremiah lived and lamented here. In front of the cave are cut stones and pieces of polished columns built into walls and seats; these fragments seem to indicate the former existence here of a Roman temple. The cave is occupied by an old dervish, who has a house in a rock near by, and uses the cavern as a cool retreat and a stable for his donkey. His rocky home is shared by his wife and family. He said that it was better to live alone, apart from the world and its snares. He, however, finds the reputation of Jeremiah profitable, selling admission to the cave at a franc a head, and, judging by the women and children about him, he seemed to have family enough not to be lonely.

The sojourner in Jerusalem who does not care for antiquities can always entertain himself by a study of the pilgrims who throng the city at this season. We hear more of the pilgrimage to Mecca than of that to Jerusalem; but I think the latter is the more remarkable phenomenon of our modern life; I believe it equals the former, which is usually overrated, in numbers, and it certainly equals it in zeal and surpasses it in the variety of nationalities represented. The pilgrims of the cross increase yearly; to supply their wants, to minister to their credulity, to traffic on their faith, is the great business of the Holy City. Few, I imagine, who are not in Palestine in the spring, have any idea of the extent of this vast yearly movement of Christian people upon the Holy Land, or of the simple zeal which characterizes it. If it were in any way obstructed or hindered, we should have a repetition of the Crusades, on a vaster scale and gathered from a broader area than the wildest pilgrimage of the holy war. The driblets of travel from America and from Western Europe are as nothing in the crowds thronging to Jerusalem from Ethiopia to Siberia, from the Baltic to the Ural Mountains. Already for a year before the Easter season have they been on foot, slowly

pushing their way across great steppes, through snows and over
rivers, crossing deserts and traversing unfriendly countries; the
old, the infirm, women as well as men, their faces set towards
Jerusalem.   No common curiosity moves this mass, from Ethiopia, from Egypt, from Russia, from European Turkey, from Asia
Minor, from the banks of the Tagus and the Araxes; it is a true
pilgrimage of faith, the one event in a life of dull monotony and
sordid cares, the one ecstasy of poetry in an existence of poverty
and ignorance.

We spent a morning in the Russian Hospice, which occupies
the hill to the northwest of the city.   It is a fine pile of buildings, the most conspicuous of which, on account of its dome, is
the church, a large edifice with a showy exterior, but of no great
merit or interest.   We were shown some holy pictures which are
set in frames incrusted with diamonds, emeralds, rubies, and
other precious gems, the offerings of rich devotees, and displaying their wealth rather than their taste.

The establishment has one building for the accommodation of
rich pilgrims, and a larger one set apart for peasants.   The hospice lodges, free of charge, all the Russian pilgrims.   The exterior court was full of them.   They were sunning themselves,
but not inclined to lay aside their hot furs and heavy woollens.
We passed into the interior, entering room after room occupied
by the pilgrims, who regarded our intrusion with good-natured
indifference, or frankly returned our curiosity.   Some of the
rooms were large, furnished with broad divans about the sides,
which served for beds and lounging-places, and were occupied
by both sexes.   The women, rosy-cheeked, light-haired, broad,
honest-looking creatures, were mending their clothes; the men
were snoozing on the divans, flat on their backs, presenting to
the spectator the bottoms of their monstrous shoes, which had
soles eight inches broad ; a side of leather would be needed for a
pair.   In these not very savory rooms they cook, eat, and sleep.
Here stood their stoves; here hung their pilgrim knapsacks; here
were their kits of shoemaker's tools, for mending their foot-gear,
which they had tugged thousands of miles; here were household
effects that made their march appear more like an emigration

than a pilgrimage; here were the staring pictures of St. George and the Dragon, and of other saints, the beads and the other relics, which they had bought in Jerusalem.

Although all these pilgrims owed allegiance to the Czar, they represented a considerable variety of races. They came from Archangel, from Tobolsk, from the banks of the Ural, from Kurland; they had found their way along the Danube, the Dnieper, the Don. I spoke with a group of men and women who had walked over two thousand miles before they reached Odessa and took ship for Jaffa. There were among them Cossacks, wild and untidy, light-haired barbarians from the Caucasus, dark-skinned men and women from Moscow, representatives from the remotest provinces of great Russia; for the most part simple, rude, clumsy, honest boors. In an interior court we found men and women seated on the sunny flagging, busily occupied in arranging and packing the souvenirs of their visit. There was rosemary spread out to dry; there were little round cakes of blessed bread stamped with the image of the Saviour; there were branches of palm, crowns of thorns, and stalks of cane cut at the Jordan; there were tin cases of Jordan water; there were long strips of cotton cloth stamped in black with various insignia of death, to serve at home for coffin-covers; there were skull-caps in red, yellow, and white, also stamped with holy images, to be put on the heads of the dead. I could not but in mind follow these people to their distant homes, and think of the pride with which they would show these trophies of their pilgrimage; how the rude neighbors would handle with awe a stick cut on the banks of the Jordan, or eat with faith a bit of the holy bread. How sacred, in those homes of frost and snow, will not these mementos of a land of sun, of a land so sacred, become! I can see the wooden chest in the cabin where the rosemary will be treasured, keeping sweet, against the day of need, the caps and the shrouds.

These people will need to make a good many more pilgrimages, and perhaps to quit their morose land altogether, before they can fairly rank among the civilized of the earth. They were thickset, padded-legged, short-bodied, unintelligent. The faces of many of them were worn, as if storm-beaten, and some kept

4

their eyes half closed, as if they were long used to face the sleet and blasts of winter; and I noticed that it gave their faces a very different expression from that produced by the habit the Egyptians have of drawing the eyelids close together on account of the glare of the sun.

We took donkeys one lovely morning, and rode from the Jaffa Gate around the walls on our way to the Mount of Olives. The Jerusalem donkey is a good enough donkey, but he won't go. He is ridden with a halter, and never so elegantly caparisoned as his more genteel brother in Cairo. In order to get him along at all, it needs one man to pull the halter and another to follow behind with a stick; the donkey then moves by inches, — if he is in the humor. The animal that I rode stopped at once, when he perceived that his driver was absent. No persuasions of mine, such as kicks and whacks of a heavy stick, could move him on; he would turn out of the road, put his head against the wall, and pretend to go to sleep. You would not suppose it possible for a beast to exhibit so much contempt for a man.

On the high ground outside the wall were pitched the tents of travellers, making a very pretty effect amid the olive-trees and the gray rocks. Now and then an Arab horseman came charging down the road, or a Turkish official cantered by; women, veiled, clad in white balloon robes that covered them from head to foot, flitted along in the sunshine, mere white appearances of women, to whom it was impossible to attribute any such errand as going to market; they seemed always to be going to or returning from the cemetery.

Our way lay down the rough path and the winding road to the bottom of the Valley of Jehoshaphat. Leaving the Garden of Gethsemane on our right, we climbed up the rugged, stony, steep path to the summit of the hill. There are a few olive-trees on the way, enough to hinder the view where the stone-walls would permit us to see anything; importunate begging Moslems beset us; all along the route we encountered shabbiness and squalor. The *rural* sweetness and peace that we associate with this dear mount appear to have been worn away centuries ago. We did not expect too much, but we were not prepared for such a shabby show-place. If we could sweep away all the filthy habitations and hideous buildings on the hill, and leave it to nature, or, indeed, convert the surface into a well-ordered garden, the spot would be one of the most attractive in the world.

We hoped that when we reached the summit we should come into an open, green, and shady place, free from the disagreeable presence of human greed and all the artificiality that interposed itself between us and the sentiment of the place. But the traveller need not expect *that* in Palestine. Everything is staked out and made a show of. Arrived at the summit, we could see little or nothing ; it is crowned with the dilapidated Chapel of the Ascension. We entered a dirty court, where the custodian and his family and his animals live, and from thence were admitted to the church. In the pavement is shown the footprint of our ascending Lord, although the Ascension was made at Bethany. We paid the custodian for permission to see this manufactured scene of the Ascension. The best point of view to be had here is the old tower of the deserted convent, or the narrow passage to it on the wall, or the top of the minaret near the church. There is no place on wall or tower where one can sit ; there is no place anywhere here to sit down, and in peace and quiet enjoy the magnificent prospect, and meditate on the most momentous event in human history. We snatched the view in the midst of annoyances. The most minute features of it are known to every one who reads. The portion of it I did not seem to have been long familiar with is that to the east, comprising the Jordan valley, the mountains of Moab, and the Dead Sea.

Although this mount is consecrated by the frequent presence of Christ, who so often crossed it in going to and from Bethany, and retired here to meditate and to commune with his loved followers, everything that the traveller at present encounters on its summit is out of sympathy with his memory. We escaped from the beggars and the showmen, climbed some stone-walls, and in a rough field near the brow of the hill, in a position neither comfortable nor private, but the best that we found, read the chief events in the life of Christ connected with this mount, the triumphal entry, and the last scenes transacted on yonder hill. And we endeavored to make the divine man live again, who so often and so sorrowfully regarded the then shining city of Zion from this height.

To the south of the church and a little down the hill is the so-called site of the giving of the Lord's Prayer. I do not know on what authority it is thus named. A chapel is built to mark the spot, and a considerable space is enclosed before it, in which are other objects of interest, and these were shown to us by a pleasant-spoken lady, who is connected with the convent, and has faith equal to the demands of her position. We first entered a subterranean vaulted room, with twelve rough half-pillars on each side, called the room where the Apostles composed the creed. We then passed into the chapel. Upon the four walls of its arcade is written, in great characters, the Lord's Prayer in *thirty-two* languages ; among them the " Canadian."

In a little side chapel is the tomb of Aurelia de Bossa, Princesse de la Tour d'Auvergne, Duchesse de Bouillon, the lady whose munificence established this chapel and executed the prayer in so many tongues. Upon the side of the tomb this fact of her benevolence is announced, and the expectation is also expressed, in French, that " God will overwhelm her with blessing for ever and ever for her good deed." Stretched upon the sarcophagus is a beautiful marble effigy of the princess ; the figure is lovely, the face is sweet and seraphic, and it is a perfect likeness of her ladyship.

I do not speak at random. I happen to know that it is a perfect likeness, for a few minutes after I saw it, I met her in the corridor, in a semi-nunlike costume, with a heavy cross hanging by a long gold chain at her side. About her forehead was bound a barbarous frontlet composed of some two hundred gold coins, and ornaments not unlike those worn by the ladies of the ancient Egyptians. This incongruity of costume made me hesitate whether to recognize in this dazzling vision of womanhood a priestess of Astarte or of Christ. At the farther door, Aurelia de Bossa, Princesse de la Tour d'Auvergne, Duchesse de Bouillon, stopped and blew shrilly a silver whistle which hung at her girdle, to call her straying poodle, or to summon a servant. In the rear of the chapel this lady lives in a very pretty house, and

near it she was building a convent for Carmelite nuns. I cannot
but regard her as the most fortunate of her sex. She enjoys not
only this life, but, at the same time, all the posthumous reputation that a lovely tomb and a record of her munificence engraved
thereon can give. We sometimes hear of, but we seldom see, a
person, in these degenerate days, living in this world as if already
in the other.

We went on over the hill to Bethany ; we had climbed up by
the path on which David fled from Absalom, and we were to return
by the road of the Triumphal Entry. All along the ridge we
enjoyed a magnificent panorama : a blue piece of the Dead Sea,
the Jordan plain extending far up towards Hermon with the
green ribbon of the river winding through it, and the long, even
range of the Moab hills, blue in the distance. The prospect was
almost Swiss in its character, but it is a mass of bare hills, with
scarcely a tree except in the immediate foreground, and so naked
and desolate as to make the heart ache ; it would be entirely desolate but for the deep blue of the sky and an atmosphere that
bathes all the great sweep of peaks and plains in color.

Bethany is a squalid hamlet clinging to the rocky hillside,
with only one redeeming feature about it, — the prospect. A few
wretched one-story huts of stone, and a miserable handful of
Moslems, occupy this favorite home and resting-place of our
Lord. Close at hand, by the roadside, cut in the rock and
reached by a steep descent of twenty-six steps, is the damp and
doubtful tomb of Lazarus, down into which any one may go for
half a franc paid to the Moslem guardian. The house of Mary
and Martha is exhibited among the big rocks and fragments of
walls ; upon older foundations loose walls are laid, rudely and
recently patched up with cut stones in fragments, and pieces of
Roman columns. The house of Simon the leper, overlooking
the whole, is a mere heap of ruins. It does not matter, however,
that all these dwellings are modern ; this is Bethany, and when
we get away from its present wretchedness we remember only that
we have seen the very place that Christ loved.

We returned along the highway of the Entry slowly, pausing to
identify the points of that memorable progress, up to the crest

where Jerusalem broke upon the sight of the Lord, and whence
the procession, coming round the curve of the hill, would have
the full view of the city. He who rides that way to-day has a
grand prospect. One finds Jerusalem most poetic when seen from
Olivet, and Olivet most lovely when seen from the distance of the
city walls.

At the foot of the descent we turned and entered the enclosure
of the Garden of Gethsemane. Three stone-wall enclosures here
claim to be the real garden; one is owned by the Greeks, another
by the Armenians, the third by the Latins. We chose the last,
as it is the largest and pleasantest; perhaps the garden, which
was certainly in this vicinity, once included them all. After some
delay we were admitted by a small door in the wall, and taken
charge of by a Latin monk, whose young and sweet face was not
out of sympathy with the place. The garden contains a few aged
olive-trees, and some small plots of earth, fenced about and secured by locked gates, in which flowers grow. The guardian
gave us some falling roses, and did what he could to relieve the
scene of its artificial appearance; around the wall, inside, are the
twelve stations of the Passion, in the usual tawdry style.

But the birds sang sweetly in the garden, the flowers of spring
were blooming, and, hemmed in by the high wall, we had some
moments of solemn peace, broken only by the sound of a Moslem
darabooka drum throbbing near at hand. Desecrated as this spot
is, and made cheap by the petty creations of superstition, one cannot but feel the awful significance of the place, and the weight of
history crowding upon him, where battles raged for a thousand
years, and where the greatest victory of all was won when Christ
commanded Peter to put up his sword. Near here Titus formed
his columns which stormed the walls and captured the heroic city
after its houses, and all this valley itself, were filled with Jewish
dead; but all this is as nothing to the event of that awful night
when the servants of the high-priest led away the unresisting
Lord.

It is this event, and not any other, that puts an immeasurable
gulf between this and all other cities, and perhaps this difference
is more felt the farther one is from Jerusalem. The visitor

expects too much; he is unreasonably impatient of the contrast between the mean appearance of the theatre and the great events that have been enacted on it; perhaps he is not prepared for the ignorance, the cupidity, the credulity, the audacious impostures under Christian names, on the spot where Christianity was born.

When one has exhausted the stock sights of Jerusalem, it is probably the dullest, least entertaining city of the Orient; I mean, in itself, for its pilgrims and its religious fêtes, in the spring of the year, offer always some novelties to the sight-seer; and, besides, there is a certain melancholy pleasure to be derived from roaming about outside the walls, enveloped in a historic illusion that colors and clothes the nakedness of the landscape.

The chief business of the city and the region seems to be the manufacture of religious playthings for the large children who come here. If there is any factory of relics here I did not see it. Nor do I know whether the true cross has still the power of growing, which it had in the fourth century, to renew itself under the constant demand for pieces of it. I did not go to see the place where the tree grew of which it was made; the exact spot is shown in a Greek convent about a mile and a half west of the city. The tree is said to have been planted by Abraham and Noah. This is evidently an error; it may have been planted by Adam and watered by Noah.

There is not much trade in antiquities in the city; the shops offer little to tempt the curiosity-hunter. Copper coins of the Roman period abound, and are constantly turned up in the fields outside the city, most of them battered and defaced beyond recognition. Jewish mites are plenty enough, but the silver shekel would be rare if the ingenious Jews did not keep counterfeits on hand. The tourist is waited on at his hotel by a few patient and sleek sharks with cases of cheap jewelry and doubtful antiques, and if he seeks the shops of the gold and silver bazaars he will find little more. I will not say that he will not now and then pick up a piece of old pottery that has made the journey from Central Asia, or chance upon a singular stone with a talismanic inscription. The hope that he may do so carries the traveller through a great many Eastern slums. The chief shops, however, are those of trinkets manufactured for the pilgrims, of olive-wood, ivory, bone, camels' teeth, and all manner of nuts and seeds. There are more than fifty sorts of beads, strung for profane use or arranged for rosaries, and some of them have pathetic names, like "Job's tears." Jerusalem is entitled to be called the City of Beads.

There is considerable activity in Jewish objects that are old and rather unclean; and I think I discovered something like an attempt to make a "corner" in phylacteries, that is, in old ones, for the new are made in excess of the demand. If a person desires to carry home a phylactery to exhibit to his Sunday school, in illustration of the religion of the Jews, he wants one that has been a long time in use. I do not suppose it possible that the education of any other person is as deficient as mine was in the matter of these ornamental aids in worship. But if there is one, this description is for him: the phylactery, common size, is a leathern box about an inch and a half square, with two narrow straps of leather, about three feet long, sewed to the bottom corners. The box contains a parchment roll of sacred writing. When the worshipper performs his devotions in the synagogue, he binds one of the phylacteries about his left arm and the other about his head, so that the little box has something of the appearance of a leathern horn sprouting out of his forehead. Phylacteries are worn only in the synagogue, and in this respect differ from the greasy leathern talismans of the Nubians, which contain scraps from the Koran, and are never taken off. Whatever significance the phylactery once had to the Jew it seems now to have lost, since he is willing to make it an article of merchandise. Perhaps it is poverty that compels him also to sell his ancient scriptures; parchment rolls of favorite books, such as Esther, that are some centuries old, are occasionally to be bought, and new rolls, deceitfully doctored into an appearance of antiquity, are offered freely.

A few years ago the antiquarian world was put into a ferment by what was called the "Shœpira collection," a large quantity of clay pottery, — gods, votive offerings, images, jars, and other vessels, — with inscriptions in unknown characters, which was said to have been dug up in the land of Moab, beyond the Jordan, and was expected to throw great light upon certain passages of Jewish history, and especially upon the religion of the heathen who occupied Palestine at the time of the conquest. The collection was sent to Berlin; some eminent German *savans* pronounced it genuine; nearly all the English scholars branded it as an impudent imposture. Two collections of the articles have been sent to Berlin, where they are stored out of sight of the public generally, and Mr. Shœpira has made a third collection, which he still retains.

Mr. Shœpira is a Hebrew antiquarian and bookseller, of somewhat eccentric manners, but an enthusiast. He makes the impression of a man who believes in his discoveries, and it is generally thought in Jerusalem that if his collection is a forgery, he himself is imposed on. The account which he gives of the places where the images and utensils were found is anything but clear or definite. We are required to believe that they have been dug up in caves at night and by stealth, and at the peril of the lives of the discoverers, and that it is not safe to visit these caves in the daytime on account of the Bedaween. The fresh-baked appearance of some of the articles is admitted, and it is said that it was necessary to roast them to prevent their crumbling when exposed to the air. Our theory in regard to these singular objects is that a few of those first shown were actually discovered, and that all the remainder have been made in imitation of them. Of the characters (or alphabet) of the inscriptions, Mr. Shœpira says he has determined twenty-three; sixteen of these are Phœnician, and the others, his critics say, are meaningless. All the objects are exceedingly rude and devoid of the slightest art; the images are many of them indecent; the jars are clumsy in shape, but the inscriptions are put on with some skill. The figures are supposed to have been votive offerings, and the jars either memorial or sepulchral urns.

The hideous collection appeared to me *sui generis*, although some of the images resemble the rudest of those called Phœnician which General di Cesnola unearthed in Cyprus. Without merit, they seem to belong to a rude age rather than to be the inartistic product of this age. That is, supposing them to be forgeries, I

4 *   F

cannot see how these figures could be conceived by a modern
man, who was capable of inventing a fraud of this sort. He
would have devised something better, at least something less simple, something that would have somewhere betrayed a little
modern knowledge and feeling. All the objects have the same
barbarous tone, a kind of character that is distinct from their
rudeness, and the same images and designs are repeated over and
over again. This gives color to the theory that a few genuine
pieces of Moabite pottery were found, which gave the idea for a
large manufacture of them. And yet, there are people who see
these things, and visit all the holy places, and then go away and
lament that there are no manufactories in Jerusalem.

Jerusalem attracts while it repels; and both it and all Palestine
exercise a spell out of all proportion to the consideration they had
in the ancient world. The student of the mere facts of history,
especially if his studies were made in Jerusalem itself, would be
at a loss to account for the place that the Holy City occupies in
the thought of the modern world, and the importance attached to
the history of the handful of people who made themselves a home
in this rocky country. The Hebrew nation itself, during the little time it was a nation, did not play a part in Oriental affairs at
all commensurate with its posthumous reputation. It was not
one of the great kingdoms of antiquity, and in that theatre of
war and conquest which spread from Ethiopia to the Caspian Sea,
it was scarcely an appreciable force in the great drama.

The country the Hebrews occupied was small; they never conquered or occupied the whole of the Promised Land, which extended from the Mediterranean Sea to the Arabian plain, from
Hamath to Sinai. Their territory in actual possession reached
only from Dan to Beersheba. The coast they never subdued;
the Philistines, who came from Crete and grew to be a great
people in the plain, held the lower portion of Palestine on the sea,
and the Phœnicians the upper. Except during a brief period in
their history, the Jews were confined to the hill-country. Only
during the latter part of the reign of David and two thirds of that
of Solomon did the Jewish kingdom take on the proportions of a
great state. David extended the Israelitish power from the Gulf

of Akaba to the Euphrates; Damascus paid him tribute; he occupied the cities of his old enemies, the Philistines, but the kingdom of Tyre, still in the possession of Hiram, marked the limit
of Jewish sway in that direction.   This period of territorial consequence was indeed brief.   Before Solomon was in his grave,
the conquests bequeathed to him by his father began to slip from
his hand.   The life of the Israelites as a united nation, as anything but discordant and warring tribes, after the death of Joshua,
is all included in the reigns of David and Solomon, — perhaps
sixty or seventy years.

The Israelites were essentially highlanders.   Some one has
noticed their resemblance to the Scotch Highlanders in modes of
warfare.   In fighting they aimed to occupy the heights.   They
descended into the plain reluctantly; they made occasional forays
into the lowlands, but their hills were their strength, as the Psalm-
ist said; and they found security among their crags and secluded
glens from the agitations which shook the great empires of the
Eastern world.   Invasions, retreats, pursuits, the advance of de-
vouring hosts or the flight of panic-stricken masses, for a long
time passed by their ridge of country on either side, along the
Mediterranean or through the land of Moab.   They were out of
the track of Oriental commerce as well as of war.   So removed
were they from participation in the stirring affairs of their era that
they seem even to have escaped the omnivorous Egyptian conquerors.   For a long period conquest passed them by, and it was not
till their accumulation of wealth tempted the avarice of the great
Asiatic powers that they were involved in the conflicts which
finally destroyed them.   The small kingdom of Judah, long after
that of Israel had been utterly swept away, owed its continuance
of life to its very defensible position.   Solomon left Jerusalem a
strong city, well supplied with water, and capable of sustaining a
long siege, while the rugged country around it offered little comfort to a besieging army.

For a short time David made the name of Israel a power in the
world, and Solomon, inheriting his reputation, added the triumphs
of commerce to those of conquest.   By a judicious heathen alliance with Hiram of Tyre he was able to build vessels on the Red

Sea and man them with Phœnician sailors, for voyages to India and Ceylon; and he was admitted by Hiram to a partnership in his trading adventures to the Pillars of Hercules. But these are only episodes in the Jewish career; the nation's part in Oriental history is comparatively insignificant until the days of their great calamities. How much attention its heroism and suffering attracted at that time we do not know.

Though the Israelites during their occupation of the hill-country of Palestine were not concerned in the great dynastic struggles of the Orient, they were not, however, at peace. Either the tribes were fighting among themselves or they were involved in sanguinary fights with the petty heathen chiefs about them. We get a lively picture of the habits of the time in a sentence in the second book of Samuel: "And it came to pass, after the year was expired, at the time when kings go forth to battle, that David sent Joab and his servants with him, and all Israel; and they destroyed the children of Ammon, and besieged Rabbah." It was a pretty custom. In that season when birds pair and build their nests, when the sap mounts in the trees and travellers long to go into far countries, kings felt a noble impulse in their veins to go out and fight other kings. But this primitive simplicity was mingled with shocking barbarity; David once put his captives under the saw, and there is nothing to show that the Israelites were more moved by sentiments of pity and compassion than their heathen neighbors. There was occasionally, however, a grim humor in their cruelty. When Judah captured King Adonibezek, in Bezek, he cut off his great toes and his thumbs. Adonibezek, who could appreciate a good thing, accepted the mutilation in the spirit in which it was offered, and said that he had himself served seventy kings in that fashion; "threescore and ten kings, having their thumbs and great toes cut off, gathered their meat under my table."

From the death of Joshua to the fall of Samaria, the history of the Jews is largely a history of civil war. From about seven hundred years before Christ, Palestine was essentially a satrapy of the Assyrian kings, as it was later to become one of the small provinces of the Roman empire. At the time when Sennacherib was waiting before Jerusalem for Hezekiah to purchase his withdrawal by stripping the gold from the doors of the Temple, the foundations of a city were laid on the banks of the Tiber, which was to extend its sway over the known world, to whose dominion the utmost power of Jerusalem was only a petty sovereignty, and which was destined to rival Jerusalem itself as the spiritual capital of the earth.

If we do not find in the military power or territorial consequence of the Jews an explanation of their influence in the modern world, still less do we find it in any faithfulness to a spiritual religion, the knowledge of which was their chief distinction among the tribes about them. Their lapses from the worship of Jehovah were so frequent, and of such long duration, that their returns to the worship of the true God seem little more than breaks in their practice of idolatry. And these spasmodic returns were due to calamities, and fears of worse judgments. Solomon sanctioned by national authority gross idolatries which had been long practised. At his death, ten of the tribes seceded from the dominion of Judah and set up a kingdom in which idolatry was . made and remained the state religion, until the ten tribes vanished from the theatre of history. The kingdom of Israel, in order to emphasize its separation from that of Judah, set up the worship of Jehovah in the image of a golden calf. Against this state religion of image-worship the prophets seem to have thought it in vain to protest; they contented themselves with battling against the more gross and licentious idolatries of Baal and Ashtaroth; and Israel always continued the idol-worship established by Jeroboam. The worship of Jehovah was the state religion of the little kingdom of Judah, but during the period of its existence, before the Captivity, I think that only four of its kings were not idolaters. The people were constantly falling away into the heathenish practices of their neighbors.

If neither territorial consequence nor religious steadfastness gave the Jews rank among the great nations of antiquity, they would equally fail of the consideration they now enjoy but for one thing, and that is, after all, the chief and enduring product of any nationality; we mean, of course, its literature. It is by that, that the little kingdoms of Judah and Israel hold their sway over the world. It is that which invests ancient Jerusalem with its charm and dignity. Not what the Jews did, but the songs of their poets, the warnings and lamentations of their prophets, the touching tales of their story-tellers, draw us to Jerusalem by the most powerful influences that affect the human mind. And most of this unequalled literature is the product of seasons of turbulence, passion, and insecurity. Except the Proverbs and Song of Solomon, and such pieces as the poem of Job and the story of Ruth, which seem to be the outcome of literary leisure, the Hebrew writings were all the offspring of exciting periods. David composed his Psalms — the most marvellous interpreters of every human aspiration, exaltation, want, and passion — with his sword in his hand; and the prophets always appear to ride upon a whirlwind. The power of Jerusalem over the world is as truly a literary one as that of Athens is one of art. That literature was unknown to the ancients, or unappreciated : otherwise contemporary history would have considered its creators of more consequence than it did.

We speak, we have been speaking, of the Jerusalem before our era, and of the interest it has independent of the great event which is, after all, its chief claim to immortal estimation. It becomes sacred ground to us because there, in Bethlehem, Christ was born ; because here — not in these streets, but upon this soil — he walked and talked and taught and ministered ; because upon Olivet, yonder, he often sat with his disciples, and here, somewhere, — it matters not where, — he suffered death and conquered death.

This is the scene of these transcendent events. We say it to ourselves while we stand here. We can clearly conceive it when we are at a distance. But with the actual Jerusalem of to-day before our eyes, its naked desolation, its superstition, its squalor, its vivid contrast to what we conceive should be the City of our King, we find it easier to feel that Christ was born in New England than in Judæa.

V.

GOING DOWN TO JERICHO.

IT is on a lovely spring morning that we set out through the land of Benjamin to go down among the thieves of Jericho, and to the Jordan and the Dead Sea. For protection against the thieves we take some of them with us, since you cannot in these days rely upon finding any good Samaritans there.

For some days Abd-el-Atti has been in mysterious diplomatic relations with the robbers of the wilderness, who live in Jerusalem, and farm out their territory. "Thim is great rascals," says the dragoman; and it is solely on that account that we seek their friendship: the real Bedawee is never known to go back on his word to the traveller who trusts him, so long as it is more profitable to keep it than to break it. We are under the escort of the second sheykh, who shares with the first sheykh the rule of all the Bedaween who patrol the extensive territory from Hebron to the fords of the Jordan, including Jerusalem, Bethlehem, Mar Saba, and the shores of the Dead Sea; these rulers would have been called kings in the old time, and the second sheykh bears the same relation to the first that the Cæsar did to the Augustus in the Roman Empire.

Our train is assembled in the little market-place opposite the hotel, or rather it is assembling. for horses and donkeys are slow to arrive, saddles are wanting, the bridles are broken, and the unpunctuality and shiftlessness of the East manifest themselves. Abd-el-Atti is in fierce altercation with a Koorland nobleman about a horse, which you would not say would be likely to be a bone of contention with anybody. They are both endeavoring

to mount at once. Friends are backing each combatant, and the
air is thick with curses in guttural German and maledictions in
shrill Arabic. Unfortunately I am appealed to.

"What for this Dutchman, he take my horse?"

"Perhaps he hired it first?"

"P'aps not. I make bargain for him with the owner day before yesterday."

"I have become dis *pferd* for four days," cries the Baron.

There seems to be no reason to doubt the Baron's word; he
has ridden the horse to Bethlehem, and become accustomed to his
jolts, and no doubt has the prior lien on the animal. The owner
has let him to both parties, a thing that often happens when the
second comer offers a piastre more. Another horse is sent for,
and we mount and begin to disentangle ourselves from the
crowd. It is no easy matter, especially for the ladies. Our own
baggage-mules head in every direction. Donkeys laden with
mountains of brushwood push through the throng, scraping right
and left; camels shamble against us, their contemptuous noses in
the air, stretching their long necks over our heads; market-women
from Bethlehem scream at us; and greasy pilgrims block our
way and curse our horses' hoofs.

One by one we emerge and get into a straggling line, and begin to comprehend the size of our expedition. Our dragoman
has made as extensive preparations as if we were to be the first
to occupy Gilgal and Jericho, and that portion of the Promised
Land. We are equipped equally well for fighting and for famine. A party of Syrians, who desire to make the pilgrimage to
the Jordan, have asked permission to join us, in order to share
the protection of our sheykh, and they add both picturesqueness
and strength to the grand cavalcade which clatters out of Jaffa
Gate and sweeps round the city wall. Heaven keep us from un-
due pride in our noble appearance!

Perhaps our train would impress a spectator as somewhat
mixed, and he would be unable to determine the order of its
march. It is true that the horses and the donkeys and the
mules all have different rates of speed, and that the Syrian horse
has only two gaits, — a run and a slow walk. As soon as we

gain the freedom of the open country, these differences develop. The ambitious dragomen and the warlike sheykh put their horses into a run and scour over the hills, and then come charging back upon us, like Don Quixote upon the flock of sheep. The Syrians imitate this madness. The other horses begin to agitate their stiff legs; the donkeys stand still and protest by braying; the pack-mules get temporarily crazy, charge into us with the protruding luggage, and suddenly wheel into the ditch and stop. This playfulness is repeated in various ways, and adds to the excitement without improving the dignity of our march.

We are of many nationalities. There are four Americans, two of them ladies. The Doctor, who is accustomed to ride the mustangs of New Mexico and the wild horses of the Western deserts, endeavors to excite a spirit of emulation in his stiff-kneed animal, but with little success. Our dragoman is Egyptian, a decidedly heavy weight, and sits his steed like a pyramid.

The sheykh is a young man, with the treacherous eye of an eagle; a handsome fellow, who rides a lean white horse, anything but a beauty, and yet of the famous Nedjed breed from Mecca. This desert warrior wears red boots, white trousers and skirt, blue jacket, a yellow kufia, confined about the head by a black cord and falling upon his shoulders, has a long rifle slung at his back, an immense Damascus sword at his side, and huge pistols, with carved and inlaid stocks, in his belt. He is a riding arsenal and a visible fraud, this Bedawee sheykh. We should no doubt be quite as safe without him, and perhaps less liable to various extortions. But on the road, and from the moment we set out, we meet Bedaween, single and in squads, savage-looking vagabonds, every one armed with a gun, a long knife, and pistols with blunderbuss barrels, flaring in such a manner as to scatter shot over an acre of ground. These scarecrows are apparently paraded on the highway to make travellers think it is insecure. But I am persuaded that none of them would dare molest any pilgrim to the Jordan.

Our allies, the Syrians, please us better. There is a Frenchified Syrian, with his wife, from Mansura, in the Delta of Egypt. The wife is a very pretty woman (would that her

example were more generally followed in the East), with olive
complexion, black eyes, and a low forehead; a native of Sidon.
She wears a dark green dress, and a yellow kufia on her head,
and is mounted upon a mule, man-fashion, but upon a saddle as broad as a feather-bed. Her husband, in semi-Syrian
costume, with top-boots, carries a gun at his back and a frightful
knife in his belt. Her brother, who is from Sidon, bears also a
gun, and wears an enormous sword. Very pleasant people these,
who have armed themselves in the spirit of the hunter rather
than of the warrior, and are as completely equipped for the chase
as any Parisian who ventures in pursuit of game into any of the
dangerous thickets outside of Paris.

The Sidon wife is accompanied by two servants, slaves from
Soudan, a boy and a girl, each about ten years old, — two grin-
ning, comical monkeys, who could not by any possibility be of the
slightest service to anybody, unless it is a relief to their pretty
mistress to vent her ill-humor upon their irresponsible persons.
You could n't call them handsome, though their skins are of
dazzling black, and their noses so flat that you cannot see them
in profile. The girl wears a silk gown, which reaches to her feet
and gives her the quaint appearance of an old woman, and a
yellow vest; the boy is clad in motley European clothes, bought
second-hand with reference to his growing up to them, — upon
which event the trousers-legs and cuffs of his coat could be turned
down, — and a red fez contrasting finely with his black face.
They are both mounted on a decrepit old horse, whose legs are like
sled-stakes, and they sit astride on top of a pile of baggage, beds,
and furniture, with bottles and camp-kettles jingling about them
The girl sits behind the boy and clings fast to his waist with
one hand, while with the other she holds over their heads a rent
white parasol, to prevent any injury to their jet complexions.
When the old baggage-horse starts occasionally into a hard trot,
they both bob up and down, and strike first one side and then
the other, but never together; when one goes up the other goes
down, as if they were moved by different springs; but both show
their ivory and seem to enjoy themselves. Heaven knows why
they should make a pilgrimage to the Jordan.

Our Abyssinian servant, Abdallah, is mounted also on a pack-horse, and sits high in the air amid bags and bundles; he guides his brute only by a halter, and when the animal takes a fancy to break into a gallop, there is a rattling of dishes and kettles that sets the whole train into commotion; the boy's fez falls farther than ever back on his head, his teeth shine, and his eyes dance as he jolts into the midst of the mules and excites a panic, which starts everything into friskiness, waking up even the Soudan party, which begins to bob about and grin. There are half a dozen mules loaded with tents and bed furniture; the cook, and the cook's assistants, and the servants of the kitchen and the camp are mounted on something, and the train is attended besides by drivers and ostlers, of what nations it pleases Heaven. But this is not all. We carry with us two hunting dogs, the property of the Syrian. The dogs are not for use; they are a piece of ostentation, like the other portion of the hunting outfit, and contribute, as do the Soudan babies, to our appearance of Oriental luxury.

We straggle down through the Valley of Jehoshaphat, and around the Mount of Olives to Bethany; and from that sightly slope our route is spread before us as if we were looking upon a map. It lies through the "wilderness of Judæa." We are obliged to revise our Western notions of a wilderness as a region of gross vegetation. The Jews knew a wilderness when they saw it, and how to name it. You would be interested to know what a person who lived at Jerusalem, or anywhere along the backbone of Palestine, would call a wilderness. Nothing but the absolute nakedness of desolation could seem to him dreary. But this region must have satisfied even a person accustomed to deserts and pastures of rocks. It is a jumble of savage hills and jagged ravines, a land of limestone rocks and ledges, whitish gray in color, glaring in the sun, even the stones wasted by age, relieved nowhere by a tree, or rejoiced by a single blade of grass. Wild beasts would starve in it, the most industrious bird could n't collect in its length and breadth enough soft material to make a nest of; it is what a Jew of Hebron or Jerusalem or Ramah would call a "wilderness"! This exhausts the language of description. How vividly in this desolation stands out the figure of the prophet of God, clothed with camel's hair and with a girdle of skin about his loins, "the voice of one crying in the wilderness."

The road is thronged with Jordan pilgrims. We overtake them, they pass us, we meet them in an almost continuous train. Most of them are peasants from Armenia, from the borders of the Black Sea, from the Caucasus, from Abyssinia. The great mass are on foot, trudging wearily along with their bedding and provisions, the thick-legged women carrying the heaviest loads; occasionally you see a pilgrim asleep by the roadside, his pillow a stone. But the travellers are by no means all poor or unable to hire means of conveyance, — you would say that Judæa had been exhausted of its beasts of burden of all descriptions for this pilgrimage, and that even the skeletons had been exhumed to assist in it. The pilgrims are mounted on sorry donkeys, on wrecks of horses, on mules, sometimes an entire family on one animal. Now and then we encounter a " swell " outfit, a wealthy Russian well mounted on a richly-caparisoned horse and attended by his servants; some ride in palanquins, some in chairs. We overtake an English party, the central figure of which is an elderly lady, who rides in a sort of high cupboard slung on poles, and borne by a mule before and a mule behind; the awkward vehicle sways and tilts backwards and forwards, and the good woman looks out of the window of her coop as if she were sea-sick of the world. Some ladies, who are unaccustomed to horses, have arm-chairs strapped upon the horses' backs, in which they sit. Now and then two chairs are strapped upon one horse, and the riders sit back to back. Sometimes huge panniers slung on the sides of the horse are used instead of chairs, the passengers riding securely in them without any danger of falling out. It is rather a pretty sight when each basket happens to be full of children. There is, indeed, no end to the strange outfits and the odd costumes. Nearly all the women who are mounted at all are perched upon the top of all their household goods and furniture, astride of a bed on the summit. There approaches a horse which seems to have a sofa on its back, upon which four persons are seated in a row, as much at ease as if at home; it is not, however, a sofa; four baskets have been ingeniously fastened into a frame, so that four persons can ride in them abreast. This is an admirable contrivance for the riders, much better than riding in a row lengthwise on the horse, when the one in front hides the view from those behind.

Diverted by this changing spectacle, we descend from Bethany. At first there are wild-flowers by the wayside and in the fields, and there is a flush of verdure on the hills, all of which disappears later. The sky is deep blue and cloudless, the air is exhilarating; it is a day for enjoyment, and everything and everybody we encounter are in a joyous mood, and on good terms with the world. The only unamiable exception is the horse with which I have been favored. He is a stocky little stallion, of good shape, but ignoble breed, and the devil — which is, I suppose, in the horse what the old Adam is in man — has never been cast out of him. At first I am in love with his pleasant gait and mincing ways, but I soon find that he has eccentricities that require the closest attention on my part, and leave me not a moment for the scenery or for biblical reflections. The beast is neither content to go in front of the caravan nor in the rear; he wants society, but the instant he gets into the crowd he lets his heels fly right and left. After a few performances of this sort, and when he has nearly broken the leg of the Syrian, my company is not desired any more by any one. No one is willing to ride within speaking distance of me. This sort of horse may please the giddy and thoughtless, but he is not the animal for me. By the time we reach the fountain 'Ain el-Huad, I have quite enough of him, and exchange steeds with the dragoman, much against the latter's fancy; he keeps the brute the remainder of the day cantering over stones and waste places along the road, and confesses at night that his bridle-hand is so swollen as to be useless.

We descend a steep hill to this fountain, which flows from a broken Saracenic arch, and waters a valley that is altogether stony and unfertile except in some patches of green. It is a general halting-place for travellers, and presents a most animated appearance when we arrive. Horses, mules, and men are struggling together about the fountain to slake their thirst; but there is no

trough nor any pool, and the only mode to get the water is to
catch it in the mouth as it drizzles from the hole in the arch. It
is difficult for a horse to do this, and the poor things are beside
themselves with thirst. Near by are some stone ruins in which
a man and woman have set up a damp coffee-shop, sherbet-shop,
and smoking station. From them I borrow a shallow dish, and
succeed in getting water for my horse, an experiment which seems
to surprise all nations. The shop is an open stone shed with a
dirt floor, offering only stools to the customers; yet when the motley crowd are seated in and around it, sipping coffee and smoking
the narghilehs (water-pipes) with an air of leisure as if to-day
would last forever, you have a scene of Oriental luxury.

Our way lies down a winding ravine. The country is exceedingly rough, like the Wyoming hills, but without trees or verdure.
The bed of the stream is a mass of rock in shelving ledges; all
the rock in sight is a calcareous limestone. After an hour of this
sort of secluded travel we ascend again and reach the Red Khan,
and a scene still more desolate because more extensive. The
khan takes its name from the color of the rocks; perched upon
a high ledge are the ruins of this ancient caravansary, little more
now than naked walls. We take shelter for lunch in a natural
rock grotto opposite, exactly the shadow of a rock longed for in
a weary land. Here we spread our gay rugs, the servants un-
pack the provision hampers, and we sit and enjoy the wide view
of barrenness and the picturesque groups of pilgrims. The spot
is famous for its excellent well of water. It is, besides, the locality usually chosen for the scene of the adventure of the man who
went down to Jericho and fell among thieves, this being the khan
at which he was entertained for twopence. We take our siesta
here, reflecting upon the great advance in hotel prices, and endeavoring to re-create something of that past when this was the
highway between great Jerusalem and the teeming plain of the
Jordan. The Syro-Phœnician woman smoked a narghileh, and,
looking neither into the past nor the future, seemed to enjoy the
present.

From this elevation we see again the brown Jordan Valley and
the Dead Sea. Our road is downward more precipitously than it

has been before. The rocks are tossed about tumultuously, and the hills are rent, but there is no evidence of any volcanic action. Some of the rock strata are bent, as you see the granite in the White Mountains, but this peculiarity disappears as we approach nearer to the Jordan. The translator of M. François Lenormant's "Ancient History of the East" says that "the miracles which accompanied the entrance of the Israelites into Palestine seem such as might have been produced by volcanic agency." No doubt they might have been; but this whole region is absolutely without any appearance of volcanic disturbance.

As we go on, we have on our left the most remarkable ravine in Palestine; it is in fact a cañon in the rocks, some five hundred feet deep, the sides of which are nearly perpendicular. At the bottom of it flows the brook Cherith, finding its way out into the Jordan plain. We ride to the brink and look over into the abyss. It was about two thousand seven hundred and eighty-nine years ago, and probably about this time of the year (for the brook went dry shortly after), that Elijah, having incurred the hostility of Ahab, who held his luxurious court at Samaria, by prophesying against him, came over from Gilead and hid himself in this ravine.

"Down there," explains Abd-el-Atti, "the prophet Elijah fed him the ravens forty days. Not have that kind of ravens now."

Unattractive as this abyss is for any but a temporary summer residence, the example of Elijah recommended it to a great number of people in a succeeding age. In the wall of the precipice are cut grottos, some of them so high above the bed of the stream that they are apparently inaccessible, and not unlike the tombs in the high cliffs along the Nile. In the fourth and fifth centuries monks swarmed in all the desert places of Egypt and Syria like rabbits; these holes, near the scene of Elijah's miraculous support, were the abodes of Christian hermits, most of whom starved themselves down to mere skin and bones waiting for the advent of the crows. On the ledge above are the ruins of ancient chapels, which would seem to show that this was a place of some resort, and that the hermits had spectators of their self-denial. You might as well be a woodchuck and sit in a hole as a monk, unless somebody comes and looks at you.

As we advance, the Jordan valley opens more broadly upon our sight. At this point, which is the historical point, the scene of the passage of the Jordan and the first appearance of the Israel-itish clans in the Promised Land, the valley is ten miles broad. It is by no means a level plain : from the west range of mountains it slopes to the river, and the surface is broken by hillocks, ravines, and water-courses. The breadth is equal to that between the Connecticut River at Hartford and the Talcott range of hills. To the north we have in view the valley almost to the Sea of Galilee, and can see the white and round summit of Hermon beyond; on the east and on the west the barren mountains stretch in level lines; and on the south the blue waters of the Dead Sea continue the valley between ranges of purple and poetic rocky cliffs.

The view is magnificent in extent, and plain and hills glow with color in this afternoon light. Yonder, near the foot of the eastern hills, we trace the winding course of the Jordan by a green belt of trees and bushes. The river we cannot see, for the " bottom " of the river, to use a Western phrase, from six hundred to fifteen hundred feet in breadth, is sunk below the valley a hundred feet and more. This bottom is periodically overflowed. The general aspect of the plain is that of a brown desert, the wild vegetation of which is crisped by the scorching sun. There are, however, threads of verdure in it, where the brook Cherith and the waters from the fountain 'Ain es-Sultân wander through the neglected plain, and these strips of green widen into the thickets about the little village of Riha, the site of ancient Gilgal. This valley is naturally fertile; it may very likely have been a Paradise of fruit-trees and grass and sparkling water when the Jews looked down upon it from the mountains of Moab; it certainly bloomed in the Roman occupation ; and the ruins of sugar-mills still existing show that the crusading Christians made the cultivation of the sugar-cane successful here ; it needs now only the waters of the Jordan and the streams from the western foot-hills directed by irrigating ditches over its surface, moistening its ashy and nitrous soil, to become again a fair and smiling land.

Descending down the stony and precipitous road, we turn

north, still on the slope of the valley. The scant grass is already crisped by the heat, the bushes are dry skeletons. A ride of a few minutes brings us to some artificial mounds and ruins of buildings upon the bank of the brook Cherith. The brickwork is the fine reticulated masonry such as you see in the remains of Roman villas at Tusculum. This is the site of Herod's Jericho, the Jericho of the New Testament. But the Jericho which Joshua destroyed and the site of which he cursed, the Jericho which Hiel rebuilt in the days of the wicked Ahab, and where Elisha abode after the translation of Elijah, was a half-mile to the north of this modern town.

We have some difficulty in fording the brook Cherith, for the banks are precipitous and the stream is deep and swift; those who are mounted upon donkeys change them for horses, the Arab attendants wade in, guiding the stumbling animals which the ladies ride, the lumbering beast with the Soudan babies comes splashing in at the wrong moment, to the peril of those already in the torrent, and is nearly swept away; the sheykh and the servants who have crossed block the narrow landing; but with infinite noise and floundering about we all come safely over, and gallop along a sort of plateau, interspersed with thorny *nubk* and scraggy bushes. Going on for a quarter of an hour, and encountering cultivated spots, we find our tents already pitched on the bushy bank of a little stream that issues from the fountain of 'Ain es-Sultân a few rods above. Near the camp is a high mound of rubbish. This is the site of our favorite Jericho, a name of no majesty like that of Rome, and endeared to us by no associations like Jerusalem, but almost as widely known as either; probably even its wickedness would not have preserved its reputation, but for the singular incident that attended its first destruction. Jericho must have been a city of some consequence at the time of the arrival of the Israelites; we gain an idea of the civilization of its inhabitants from the nature of the plunder that Joshua secured; there were vessels of silver and of gold, and of brass and iron; and this was over fourteen hundred years before Christ.

Before we descend to our encampment, we pause for a survey of this historic region. There, towards Jordan, among the trees,

is the site of Gilgal (another name that shares the half-whimsical
reputation of Jericho), where the Jews made their first camp. The
king of Jericho, like his royal cousins roundabout, had "no more
spirit in him" when he saw the Israelitish host pass the Jordan.
He shut himself up in his insufficient walls, and seems to have
made no attempt at a defence. Over this upland the Jews swarmed,
and all the armed host with seven priests and seven ram's-horns
marched seven days round and round the doomed city, and on
the seventh day the people shouted the walls down. Every living
thing in the city was destroyed except Rahab and her family, the
town was burned, and for five hundred years thereafter no man
dared to build upon its accursed foundations. Why poor Jericho
was specially marked out for malediction we are not told.

When it was rebuilt in Ahab's time, the sons of the prophets
found it an agreeable place of residence; large numbers of them
were gathered here while Elijah lived, and they conversed with
that prophet when he was on his last journey through this valley,
which he had so often traversed, compelled by the Spirit of the
Lord. No incident in the biblical story so strongly appeals to the
imagination, nor is there anything in the poetical conception of
any age so sublime as the last passage of Elijah across this plain
and his departure into heaven beyond Jordan. When he came
from Bethel to Jericho, he begged Elisha, his attendant, to tarry
here; but the latter would not yield either to his entreaty or to
that of the sons of the prophets. We can see the way the two
prophets went hence to Jordan. Fifty men of the sons of the
prophets went and stood to view them afar off, and they saw the
two stand by Jordan. Already it was known that Elijah was to
disappear, and the two figures, lessening in the distance, were followed with a fearful curiosity. Did they pass on swiftly, and was
there some premonition, in the wind that blew their flowing man-
tles, of the heavenly gale? Elijah smites the waters with his
mantle, the two pass over dry-shod, and "as they still went on
and talked, behold there appeared a chariot of fire, and horses of
fire, and parted them both asunder; and Elijah went up by a
whirlwind into heaven. And Elisha saw it, and he cried, My
father, my father, the chariot of Israel and the horsemen thereof.
And he saw him no more."

Elisha returned to Jericho and abode there while the sons of the prophets sought for Elijah beyond Jordan three days, but did not find him. And the men of the city said to Elisha, "Behold, I pray thee, the situation of this city is pleasant, as my lord seeth, but the water is naught and the ground is barren." Then Elisha took salt and healed the spring of water; and ever since, to this day, the fountain, now called 'Ain es-Sultân, has sent forth sweet water.

Turning towards the northwest, we see the passage through the mountain, by the fountain 'Ain Dûk, to Bethel. It was out of some woods there, where the mountain is now bare, that Elisha called the two she-bears which administered that dreadful lesson to the children who derided his baldness. All the region, indeed, recalls the miracles of Elisha. It was probably here that Naaman the Syrian came to be healed; there at Gilgal Elisha took the death out of the great pot in which the sons of the prophets were seething their pottage; and it was there in the Jordan that he made the iron axe to swim.

Of all this celebrated and ill-fated Jericho, nothing now remains but a hillock and Elisha's spring. The wild beasts of the desert prowl about it, and the night-bird hoots over its fall, — a sort of echo of the shouts that brought down its walls. Our tents are pitched near the hillock, and the animals are picketed on the open ground before them by the stream. The Syrian tourist in these days travels luxuriously. Our own party has four tents, — the kitchen tent, the dining tent, and two for lodging. They are furnished with tables, chairs, all the conveniences of the toilet, and carpeted with bright rugs. The cook is an artist, and our table is one that would have astonished the sons of the prophets. The Syrian party have their own tents; a family from Kentucky has camped near by; and we give to Jericho a settled appearance. The elder sheykh accompanies the other party of Americans, so that we have now all the protection possible.

The dragoman of the Kentuckians we have already encountered in Egypt and on the journey, and been impressed by his respectable gravity. It would perhaps be difficult for him to tell his nationality or birthplace; he wears the European dress, and his gold spectacles and big stomach would pass him anywhere for a German professor. He seems out of place as a dragoman, but if any one desired a *savant* as a companion in the East, he would be the man. Indeed, his employers soon discover that his *forte* is information, and not work. While the other servants are busy about the camps Antonio comes over to our tent, and opens up the richness of his mind, and illustrates his capacity as a Syrian guide.

"You know that mountain, there, with the chapel on top?" he asks.

"No."

"Well, that is Mt. Nebo, and that one next to it is Pisgah, the mountain of the prophet Moses."

Both these mountains are of course on the other side of the Jordan in the Moab range, but they are not identified, — except by Antonio. The sharp mountain behind us is Quarantania, the Mount of Christ's Temptation. Its whole side to the summit is honey-combed with the cells of hermits who once dwelt there, and it is still the resort of many pilgrims.

The evening is charming, warm but not depressing; the atmosphere is even exhilarating, and this surprises us, since we are so far below the sea level. The Doctor says that it is exactly like Colorado on a July night. We have never been so low before, not even in a coal-mine. We are not only about thirty-seven hundred feet below Jerusalem, we are over twelve hundred below the level of the sea. Sitting outside the tent under the starlight, we enjoy the novelty and the mysteriousness of the scene. Tents, horses picketed among the bushes, the firelight, the groups of servants and drivers taking their supper, the figure of an Arab from Gilgal coming forward occasionally out of the darkness, the singing, the occasional violent outbreak of kicking and squealing among the ill-assorted horses and mules, the running of loose-robed attendants to the rescue of some poor beast, the strong impression of the locality upon us, and I know not what Old Testament flavor about it all, conspire to make the night memorable.

"This place very dangerous," says Antonio, who is standing round, bursting with information. "Him berry wise," is Abd-el-Atti's opinion of him. "Know a great deal; I tink him not live long."

"What is the danger?" we ask.

"Wild beasts, wild boars, hyenas, — all these bush full of them. It was three years now I was camped here with Baron Kronkheit. 'Bout twelve o'clock I heard a noise and came out. Right there, not twenty feet from here, stood a hyena as big as a donkey, his two eyes like fire. I did not shoot him for fear tó wake up the Baron."

"Did he kill any of your party?"

"Not any man. In the morning I find he has carried off our only mutton."

Notwithstanding these dangers, the night passes without alarm, except the barking of jackals about the kitchen tent. In the morning I ask Antonio if he heard the hyenas howling in the night. "Yes, indeed, plenty of them; they came very near my tent."

We are astir at sunrise, breakfast, and start for the Jordan. It is the opinion of the dragoman and the sheykh that we should go first to the Dead Sea. It is the custom. Every tourist goes to the Dead Sea first, bathes, and then washes off the salt in the Jordan. No one ever thought of going to the Jordan first. It is impossible. We must visit the Dead Sea, and then lunch at the Jordan. We wished, on the contrary, to lunch at the Dead Sea, at which we should otherwise only have a very brief time. We insisted upon our own programme, to the great disgust of all our camp attendants, who predicted disaster.

The Jordan is an hour and a half from Jericho; that is the distance to the bathing-place of the Greek pilgrims. We descend all the way. Wild vegetation is never wanting; wild-flowers abound; we pass through thickets of thorns, bearing the yellow "apples of the Dead Sea," which grow all over this plain. At Gilgal (now called Rîha) we find what is probably the nastiest village in the world, and its miserable inhabitants are credited with all the vices of Sodom. The wretched huts are surrounded by a thicket of *nubk* as a protection against the plundering Bed-aween. The houses are rudely built of stone, with a covering of

cane or brush, and each one is enclosed in a hedge of thorns.
These thorns, which grow rankly on the plain, are those of which
the " crown of thorns " was plaited, and all devout pilgrims carry
away some of them.   The habitations within these thorny
enclosures are filthy beyond description, and poverty-stricken.
And this is in a watered plain which would bloom with all manner
of fruits with the least care.   Indeed, there are a few tangled
gardens of the rankest vegetation; in them we see the orange,
the fig, the deceptive pomegranate with its pink blossoms, and the
olive.   As this is the time of pilgrimage, a company of Turkish
soldiers from Jerusalem is encamped at the village, and the broken
country about it is covered with tents, booths, shops, kitchens,
and presents the appearance of a fair and a camp-meeting combined.   There are hundreds, perhaps thousands, of pilgrims, who
go every morning, as long as they remain here, to dip in the Jordan.   Near the village rises the square tower of an old convent,
probably, which is dignified with the name of the " house of
Zacchæus."   This plain was once famed for its fertility; it was
covered with gardens and palm-groves; the precious balsam,
honey, and henna were produced here; the balsam gardens were
the royal gift of Antony to Cleopatra, who transferred the balsam-
trees to Heliopolis in Egypt.

As we ride away from Gilgal and come upon a more open and
desert plain, I encounter an eagle sitting on the top of a thorn-
tree, not the noblest of his species, but, for Palestine, a very fair
eagle.   Here is a chance for the Syrian hunter; he is armed with
gun and pistols; he has his dogs; now, if ever, is the time for
him to hunt, and I fall back and point out his opportunity.   He
does not embrace it.   It is an easy shot; perhaps he is looking
for wild boars; perhaps he is a tender-minded hunter.   At any
rate, he makes no effort to take the eagle, and when I ride forward
the bird gracefully rises in the air, sweeping upward in magnificent circles, now veering towards the Mount of Temptation, and
now towards Nebo, but always as serene as the air in which he
floats.

And now occurs one of those incidents which are not rare to
travellers in Syria, but which are rare and scarcely believed else-

where. As the eagle hangs for a second motionless in the em-
pyrean far before me, he drops a feather. I see the gray plume
glance in the sun and swirl slowly down in the lucid air. In
Judæa every object is as distinct as in a photograph. You can
see things at a distance you can make no one believe at home.
The eagle plume, detached from the noble bird, begins its leisurely
descent.

I see in a moment my opportunity. I might never have another. All travellers in Syria whose books I have ever read have
one or more startling adventures. Usually it is with a horse. I
do not remember any with a horse and an eagle. I determine at
once to have one. Glancing a moment at the company behind
me, and then fixing my eye on the falling feather, I speak a word
to my steed, and dart forward.

A word was enough. The noble animal seemed to comprehend
the situation. He was of the purest Arab breed; four legs, four
white ankles, small ears, slender pasterns, nostrils thin as tissue
paper, and dilating upon the fall of a leaf; an eye terrible in rage,
but melting in affection; a round barrel; gentle as a kitten, but
spirited as a game-cock. His mother was a Nedjed mare from
Medina, who had been exchanged by a Bedawee chief for nine
beautiful Circassians, but only as a compromise after a war by the
Pasha of Egypt for her possession. Her father was one of the
most respectable horses in Yemen. Neither father, mother, nor
colt had ever eaten anything but selected dates.

At the word, Abdallah springs forward, bounding over the sand,
skimming over the thorn bushes, scattering the Jordan pilgrims
right and left. He does not seem to be so much a horse as a creation of the imagination,—a Pegasus. At every leap we gain upon
the feather, but it is still far ahead of us, and swirling down,
down, as the air takes the plume or the weight of gravity acts
upon the quill. Abdallah does not yet know the object of our
fearful pace, but his docility is such that every time I speak to
him he seems to shoot out of himself in sudden bursts of enthusiasm. The terrible strain continues longer than I had supposed
it would, for I had undercalculated both the height at which the
feather was cast and my distance to the spot upon which it must

fall. None but a horse fed on dates could keep up the awful gait. We fly and the feather falls; and it falls with increasing momentum. It is going, going to the ground, and we are not there. At this instant, when I am in despair, the feather twirls, and Abdallah suddenly casts his eye up and catches the glint of it. The glance suffices to put him completely in possession of the situation. He gives a low neigh of joy; I plunge both spurs into his flanks about six or seven inches; he leaps into the air, and sails like a bird, — of course only for a moment; but it is enough; I stretch out my hand and catch the eagle's plume before it touches the ground. We light on the other side of a clump of thorns, and Abdallah walks on as quietly as if nothing had happened; he was not blown; not a hair of his glossy coat was turned. I have the feather to show.

Pilgrims are plenty, returning from the river in a continuous procession, in numbers rivalling the children of Israel when they first camped at Gilgal. We descend into the river-bottom, wind through the clumps of tangled bushes, and at length reach an open place where the river for a few rods is visible. The ground is trampled like a watering-spot for cattle; the bushes are not large enough to give shade; there are no trees of size except one or two at the water's edge; the banks are slimy, there seems to be no comfortable place to sit except on your horse — on Jordan's stormy banks I *stand* and cast a wistful eye; the wistful eye encounters nothing agreeable.

The Jordan here resembles the Arkansas above Little Rock, says the Doctor; I think it is about the size of the Concord where it flows through the classic town of that name in Massachusetts; but it is much swifter. Indeed, it is a rapid current, which would sweep away the strongest swimmer. The opposite bank is steep, and composed of sandy loam or marl. The hither bank is low, but slippery, and it is difficult to dip up water from it. Close to the shore the water is shallow, and a rope is stretched out for the protection of the bathers. This is the Greek bathing-place, but we are too late to see the pilgrims enter the stream; crowds of them are still here, cutting canes to carry away, and filling their tin cans with the holy water. We taste

the water, which is very muddy, and find it warm but not unpleasant. We are glad that we have decided to lunch at the
Dead Sea, for a more uninviting place than this could not be
found; above and below this spot are thickets and boggy ground.
It is beneath the historical and religious dignity of the occasion
to speak of lunch, but all tourists know what importance it
assumes on such an excursion, and that their high reflections
seldom come to them on the historical spot. Indeed, one must
be removed some distance from the vulgar Jordan before he can
glow at the thought of it. In swiftness and volume it exceeds
our expectations, but its beauty is entirely a creation of the
imagination.

We had the opportunity of seeing only a solitary pilgrim bathe.
This was a shock-headed Greek young man, who reluctantly ventured into the dirty water up to his knees and stood there shiver-
ing, and whimpering over the orders of the priest on the bank,
who insisted upon his dipping. Perhaps the boy lacked faith;
perhaps it was his first experiment with water; at any rate, he
stood there until his spiritual father waded in and ducked the
blubbering and sputtering neophyte under. This was not a
baptism, but a meritorious bath. Some seedy fellahs from
Gilgal sat on the bank fishing. When I asked them if they had
anything, they produced from the corners of their gowns some
Roman copper coins, picked up at Jericho, and which they swore
were dropped there by the Jews when they assaulted the city with
the rams'-horns. These idle fishermen caught now and then a
rather soft, light-colored perch, with large scales, — a sickly-look-
ing fish, which the Greeks, however, pronounced "tayeb."

We leave the river and ride for an hour and a half across a
nearly level plain, the earth of which shows salts here and there,
dotted with a low, fat-leaved plant, something like the American
sage-bush. Wild-flowers enliven the way, and although the
country is not exactly cheerful, it has no appearance of desolation
except such as comes from lack of water.

The Dead Sea is the least dead of any sheet of water I know.
When we first arrived the waters were a lovely blue, which
changed to green in the shifting light, but they were always

animated and sparkling. It has a sloping sandy beach, strewn with pebbles, up which the waves come with a pleasant murmur. The plain is hot; here we find a cool breeze. The lovely plain of water stretches away to the south between blue and purple ranges of mountains, which thrust occasionally bold promontories into it, and add a charm to the perspective.

The sea is not inimical either to vegetable or animal life on its borders. Before we reach it I hear bird-notes high in the air like the song of a lark; birds are flitting about the shore and singing, and gulls are wheeling over the water; a rabbit runs into his hole close by the beach. Growing close to the shore is a high woody stonewort, with abundance of fleshy leaves and thousands of blossoms, delicate protruding stamens hanging over the waters of the sea itself. The plant with the small yellow fruit, which we take to be that of the apples of Sodom, also grows here. It is the *Solanum spinosa*, closely allied to the potato, egg-plant, and tomato; it has a woody stem with sharp recurved thorns, sometimes grows ten feet high, and is now covered with round orange berries.

It is not the scene of desolation that we expected, although some branches and trunks of trees, gnarled and bleached, the drift-wood of the Jordan, strewn along the beach, impart a dead aspect to the shore. These dry branches are, however, useful; we build them up into a wigwam, over which we spread our blankets; under this we sit, sheltered from the sun, enjoying the delightful breeze and the cheering prospect of the sparkling sea. The improvident Arabs, now that it is impossible to get fresh water, begin to want it; they have exhausted their own jugs and ours, having neglected to bring anything like an adequate supply. To see water and not be able to drink it is too much for their philosophy.

The party separates along the shore, seeking for places where bushes grow out upon tongues of land and offer shelter from observation for the bather. The first impression we have of the water is its perfect clearness. It is the most innocent water in appearance, and you would not suspect its saltness and extreme bitterness. No fish live in it; the water is too salt for anything but codfish. Its buoyancy has not been exaggerated by travellers, but I did not expect to find bathing in it so agreeable as it is. The water is of a happy temperature, soft, not exactly oily, but exceedingly agreeable to the skin, and it left a delicious sensation after the bath ; but it is necessary to be careful not to get any of it into the eyes. For myself, I found swimming in it delightful, and I wish the Atlantic Ocean were like it ; nobody then would ever be drowned. Floating is no effort ; on the contrary, sinking is impossible. The only annoyance in swimming is the tendency of the feet to strike out of water, and of the swimmer to go over on his head. When I stood upright in the water it came about to my shoulders ; but it was difficult to stand, from the constant desire of the feet to go to the surface. I suppose that the different accounts of travellers in regard to the buoyancy of the water are due to the different specific gravity of the writers. We cannot all be doctors of divinity. I found that the best way to float was to make a bow of the body and rest with feet and head out of water, which was something like being in a cushioned chair. Even then it requires some care not to turn over. The bather seems to himself to be a cork, and has little control of his body.

About two hundred yards from the shore is an artificial island of stone, upon which are remains of regular masonry. Probably some crusader had a castle there. We notice upon looking down into the clear depths, some distance out, in the sunlight, that the lake seems, as it flows, to have translucent streaks, which are like a thick solution of sugar, showing how completely saturated it is with salts. It is, in fact, twelve hundred and ninety-two feet below the Mediterranean, nothing but a deep, half-dried-up sea ; the chloride of magnesia, which gives it its extraordinarily bitter taste, does not crystallize and precipitate itself so readily as the chloride of sodium.

We look in vain for any evidence of volcanic disturbance or action of fire. Whatever there may be at the other end of the lake, there is none here. We find no bitumen or any fire-stones, although the black stones along the beach may have been supposed to be bituminous. All the pebbles and all the stones of

the beach are of chalk flint, and tell no story of fire or volcanic
fury.

Indeed, the lake has no apparent hostility to life. An enterprising company could draw off the Jordan thirty miles above
here and make all this valley a garden, producing fruits and
sugar-cane and cotton, and this lake one of the most lovely water-
ing-places in the world. I have no doubt maladies could be discovered which its waters are exactly calculated to cure. I confidently expect to hear some day that great hotels are built upon
this shore, which are crowded with the pious, the fashionable, and
the diseased. I seem to see this blue and sunny lake covered
with a gay multitude of bathers, floating about the livelong day
on its surface; parties of them making a pleasure excursion to the
foot of Pisgah; groups of them chatting, singing, amusing themselves as they would under the shade of trees on land, having um-
brellas and floating awnings, and perhaps servants to bear their
parasols; couples floating here and there at will in the sweet
dream of a love that seems to be suspended between the heaven
and the earth. No one will be at any expense for boats, for every
one will be his own boat, and launch himself without sail or oars
whenever he pleases. How dainty will be the little feminine
barks that the tossing mariner will hail on that peaceful sea! No
more wailing of wives over husbands drowned in the waves, no
more rescuing of limp girls by courageous lovers. People may
be shipwrecked if there comes a squall from Moab, but they cannot be drowned. I confess that this picture is the most fascinating that I have been able to conjure up in Syria.

We take our lunch under the wigwam, fanned by a pleasant
breeze. The persons who partake it present a pleasing variety of
nations and colors, and the "spread" itself, though simple, was
gathered from many lands. Some one took the trouble to note
the variety: raisins from Damascus, bread, chicken, and mutton from Jerusalem, white wine from Bethlehem, figs from
Smyrna, cheese from America, dates from Nubia, walnuts from
Germany, water from Elisha's well, eggs from Hen.

We should like to linger till night in this enchanting place, but
for an hour the sheykh and dragoman have been urging our de-

parture; men and beasts are represented as suffering for water,—
all because we have reversed the usual order of travel. As soon
as we leave the lake we lose its breeze, the heat becomes severe;
the sandy plain is rolling and a little broken, but it has no shade,
no water, and is indeed a weary way. The horses feel the want
of water sadly. The Arabs, whom we had supposed patient in
deprivation, are almost crazy with thirst. After we have ridden
for over an hour the sheykh's horse suddenly wheels off and runs
over the plain; my nag follows him, apparently without reason,
and in spite of my efforts I am run away with. The horses dash
along, and soon the whole cavalcade is racing after us. The object is soon visible,—a fringe of trees, which denotes a brook;
the horses press on, dash down the steep bank, and plunge their
heads into the water up to the eyes. The Arabs follow suit. The
sheykh declares that in fifteen minutes more both men and horses
would have been dead. Never before did anybody lunch at the
Dead Sea.

When the train comes up, the patient donkey that Madame rides
is pushed through the brook and not permitted to wet his muzzle.
I am indignant at such cruelty, and spring off my horse, push the
two donkey-boys aside, and lead the eager donkey to the stream.
At once there is a cry of protest from dragomans, sheykh, and the
whole crowd, "No drink donkey, no drink donkey, no let donkey,
bad for donkey." There could not have been a greater outcry
among the Jews when the ark of the covenant was likely to touch
the water. I desist from my charitable efforts. Why the poor beast,
whose whole body craved water as much as that of the horse, was
denied it, I know not. It is said that if you give a donkey water
on the road he won't go thereafter. Certainly the donkey is never
permitted to drink when travelling. I think the patient and chas-
tened creature will get more in the next world than his cruel
masters.

Nearly all the way over the plain we have the long snowy range
of Mt. Hermon in sight, a noble object, closing the long northern
vista, and a refreshment to the eyes wearied by the parched vegetation of the valley and dazzled by the aerial shimmer. If we
turn from the north to the south, we have the entirely different

but equally poetical prospect of the blue sea enclosed in the re-
ceding hills, which fall away into the violet shade of the horizon.
The Jordan Valley is unique; by a geologic fault it is dropped
over a thousand feet below the sea-level; it is guarded by moun-
tain-ranges which are from a thousand to two thousand feet high;
at one end is a mountain ten thousand feet high, from which the
snow never disappears; at the other end is a lake forty miles long,
of the saltest and bitterest water in the world. All these contrasts
the eye embraces at one point.

We dismount at the camp of the Russian pilgrims by Riha, and
walk among the tents and booths. The sharpers of Syria attend
the strangers, tempt them with various holy wares, and entice
them into their dirty coffee-shops. It is a scene of mingled credulity and knavery, of devotion and traffic. There are great booths
for the sale of vegetables, nuts, and dried fruit. The whole may
be sufficiently described as a camp-meeting without any prayer-
tent.

At sunset I have a quiet hour by the fountain of Elisha. It is
a remarkable pool. Under the ledge of limestone rocks the water
gushes out with considerable force, and in such volume as to form
a large brook which flows out of the basin and murmurs over a
stony bed. You cannot recover your surprise to see a river in
this dry country burst suddenly out of the ground. A group of
native women have come to the pool with jars, and they stay to
gossip, sitting about the edge upon the stones with their feet in
the water. One of them wears a red gown, and her cheeks are as
red as her dress; indeed, I have met several women to-day who
had the complexion of a ripe Flemish Beauty pear. As it seems
to be the fashion, I also sit on the bank of the stream with my
feet in the warm swift water, and enjoy the sunset and the strange
concourse of pilgrims who are gathering about the well. They
are worthy Greeks, very decent people, men and women, who salute me pleasantly as they arrive, and seem to take my participation in the bath as an act of friendship.

Just below the large pool, by a smaller one, a Greek boy, having bathed, is about to dress, and I am interested to watch the
process. The first article to go on is a white shirt; over this he

puts on two blue woollen shirts ; he then draws on a pair of large, loose trousers ; into these the shirts are tucked, and the trousers are tied at the waist, — he is bothered with neither pins nor buttons. Then comes the turban, which is a soft gray and yellow material ; a red belt is next wound twice about the waist ; the vest is yellow and open in front ; and the costume is completed by a jaunty jacket of yellow, prettily embroidered. The heap of clothes on the bank did not promise much, but the result is a very handsome boy, dressed, I am sure, most comfortably for this climate. While I sit here the son of the sheykh rides his horse to the pool. He is not more than ten years old, is very smartly dressed in gay colors, and exceedingly handsome, although he has somewhat the supercilious manner of a lad born in the purple. The little prince speaks French, and ostentatiously displays in his belt a big revolver. I am glad of the opportunity of seeing one of the desert robbers in embryo.

When it is dusk we have an invasion from the neighboring Bedaween, an imposition to which all tourists are subjected, it being taken for granted that we desire to see a native dance. This is one of the ways these honest people have of levying tribute ; by the connivance of our protectors, the head sheykhs, the entertainment is forced upon us, and the performers will not depart without a liberal backsheesh. We are already somewhat familiar with the fascinating dances of the Orient, and have only a languid curiosity about those of the Jordan ; but before we are aware there is a crowd before our tents, and the evening is disturbed by doleful howling and drum-thumping. The scene in the flickering firelight is sufficiently fantastic.

The men dance first. Some twenty or thirty of them form in a half-circle, standing close together ; their gowns are in rags, their black hair is tossed in tangled disorder, and their eyes shine with animal wildness. The only dancing they perform consists in a violent swaying of the body from side to side in concert, faster and faster as the excitement rises, with an occasional stamping of the feet, and a continual howling like darwishes. Two vagabonds step into the focus of the half-circle and hop about in the most stiff-legged manner, swinging enormous swords

over their heads, and giving from time to time a war-whoop, — it
seems to be precisely the dance of the North American Indians.
We are told, however, that the howling is a song, and that the
song relates to meeting the enemy and demolishing him. The
longer the performance goes on the less we like it, for the un-
couthness is not varied by a single graceful motion, and the monotony becomes unendurable. We long for the women to begin.

When the women begin, we wish we had the men back again.
Creatures uglier and dirtier than these hags could not be found.
Their dance is much the same as that of the men, a semicircle,
with a couple of women to jump about and whirl swords. But
the women display more fierceness and more passion as they warm
to their work, and their shrill cries, dishevelled hair, loose robes,
and frantic gestures give us new ideas of the capacity of the gentle
sex ; you think that they would not only slay their enemies, but
drink their blood and dance upon their fragments. Indeed, one
of their songs is altogether belligerent ; it taunts the men with
cowardice, it scoffs them for not daring to fight, it declares that
the women like the sword and know how to use it, — and thus,
and thus, and thus, lunging their swords into the air, would they
pierce the imaginary enemy. But these sweet creatures do not
sing altogether of war ; they sing of love in the same strident
voices and fierce manner : " My lover will meet me by the
stream, he will take me over the water."

When the performance is over they all clamor for backsheesh ;
it is given in a lump to their sheykh, and they retire into the
bushes and wrangle over its distribution. The women return to
us and say, " Why you give our backsheesh to sheykh ? We no
get any. Men get all." It seems that women are animated nowadays by the same spirit the world over, and make the same just
complaints of the injustice of men.

When we turn in, there is a light gleaming from a cell high up
on Mt. Temptation, where some modern pilgrim is playing hermit
for the night.

We are up early in the morning, and prepare for the journey
to Jerusalem. Near our camp some Abyssinian pilgrims, Christians so called, have encamped in the bushes, a priest and three

or four laymen, the cleverest and most decent Abyssinians we have met with. They are from Gondar, and have been a year and a half on their pilgrimage from their country to the Jordan. The priest is severely ill with a fever, and his condition excites the compassion of Abd-el-Atti, who procures for him a donkey to ride back to the city. About the only luggage of the party consists of sacred books, written on parchment and preserved with great care, among them the Gospel of St. John, the Psalms, the Pentateuch, and volumes of prayers to the Virgin. They are willing to exchange some of these manuscripts for silver, and we make up besides a little purse for the sick man. These Abyssinian Christians when at home live under the old dispensation, rather than the new, holding rather to the law of Moses than of Christ, and practise generally all the vices of all ages; the colony of them at Jerusalem is a disreputable lot of lewd beggars; so that we are glad to find some of the race who have gentle manners and are outwardly respectable. To be sure, we had come a greater distance than they to the Jordan, but they had been much longer on the way.

The day is very hot; the intense sun beats upon the white limestone rocks and is reflected into the valleys. Our view in returning is better than it was in coming; the plain and the foot of the pass are covered with a bloom of lilac-colored flowers. We meet and pass more pilgrims than before. We overtake them resting or asleep by the roadside, in the shade of the rocks. They all carry bundles of sticks and canes cut on the banks of the Jordan, and most of them Jordan water in cans, bottles, and pitchers. There are motley loads of baggage, kitchen utensils, beds, children. We see again two, three, and four on one horse or mule, and now and then a row, as if on a bench, across the horse's back, taking up the whole road.

We overtake one old woman, a Russian, who cannot be less than seventy, with a round body, and legs as short as ducks' and as big as the "limbs" of a piano. Her big feet are encased in straw shoes, the shape of a long vegetable-dish. She wears a short calico gown, an old cotton handkerchief enwraps her gray head, she carries on her back a big bundle of clothing, an extra pair of

H

straw shoes, a coffee-pot, and a saucepan, and she staggers under
a great bundle of canes on her shoulder. Poor old pilgrim! I
should like to give the old mother my horse and ease her way to
the heavenly city; but I reflect that this would detract from the
merit of her pilgrimage. There are men also as old hobbling
along, but usually not so heavily laden. One ancient couple are
riding in the deep flaps of a pannier, hanging each side of a mule;
they can just see each other across the mule's back, but the swaying, sickening motion of the pannier evidently lessens their interest in life and in each other.

Our Syrian allies are as brave as usual. The Soudan babies
did not go to the Jordan or the Dead Sea, and are consequently
fresh and full of antics. The Syrian armament has not thus far
been used; eagles, rabbits, small game of all sorts, have been
disregarded; neither of the men has unslung his gun or drawn
his revolvers. The hunting dogs have not once been called on to
hunt anything, and now they are so exhausted by the heat that
their master is obliged to carry them all the way to Jerusalem;
one of the hounds he has in his arms and the other is slung in a
pannier under the saddle, his master's foot resting in the other
side to balance the dog. The poor creature looks out piteously
from his swinging cradle. It is the most inglorious hunting-
expedition I have ever been attached to.

Our sheykh becomes more and more friendly. He rides up to
me occasionally, and, nobly striking his breast, exclaims, "Me!
sheykh, Jordan, Jerusalem, Mar Saba, Hebron, all round; me,
big." Sometimes he ends the interview with a demand for
tobacco, and again with a hint of the backsheesh he expects in
Jerusalem. I want to tell him that he is exactly like our stately
red man at home, with his "Me! Big Injun. Chaw-tobac?"

We are very glad to get out of the heat at noon and take shelter
in the rock grotto at the Red Khan. We sit here as if in a box
at the theatre, and survey the passing show. The Syro-Phœnician
woman smokes her narghileh again, the dogs crouching at her
feet, and the Soudan babies are pretending to wait on her, and
tumbling over each other and spilling everything they attempt to
carry. The woman says they are great plagues to her, and cost

thirty napoleons each in Soudan. As we sit here after lunch, an endless procession passes before us, — donkeys, horses, camels in long strings tied together, and pilgrims of all grades; and as they come up the hill one after the other, showing their heads suddenly, it is just as if they appeared on the stage; and they all — Bedaween, Negroes, Russians, Copts, Circassians, Greeks, Soudan slaves, and Arab masters — seem struck with a "glad surprise" upon seeing us, and tarry long enough for us to examine them.

Suddenly presents himself a tall, gayly dressed, slim fellow from Soudan (the slave of the sheykh), showing his white teeth, and his face beaming with good-nature. He is so peculiarly black that we ask him to step forward for closer inspection. Abd-el-Atti, who expresses great admiration for him, gets a coal from the fire, and holds it up by his check; the skin has the advantage of the coal, not only in lustre but in depth of blackness. He says that he is a Galgam, a tribe whose virtues Abd-el-Atti endorses: "Thim very sincere, trusty, thim good breed."

When we have made the acquaintance of the Galgam in this thorough manner, he asks for backsheesh. The Doctor offers him a copper coin. This, without any offence in his manner, and with the utmost courtesy, he refuses, bows very low, says "Thanks," with a little irony, and turns away. In a few moments he comes back, opens his wallet, takes out two silver franc pieces, hands them to the Doctor, says with a proud politeness, "Backsheesh, Bedawee!" bows, runs across the hill, catches his horse, and rides gallantly away. It is beautifully done. Once or twice during the ride to Jerusalem we see him careering over the hills, and he approaches within hail at Bethany, but he does not lower his dignity by joining us again.

The heat is intense until we reach the well within a mile of Bethany, where we find a great concourse of exhausted pilgrims. On the way, wherever there is an open field that admits of it, we have some display of Bedawee horsemanship. The white Arab mare which the sheykh rides is of pure blood and cost him £ 200, although I should select her as a broken-down stage-horse. These people ride "all abroad," so to say, arms, legs, accoutrements flying; but they stick on, which is the principal thing;

and the horses over the rough ground, soft fields, and loose
stones, run, stop short, wheel in a flash, and exhibit wonderful
training and bottom.

The high opinion we had formed of the proud spirit and generosity of the Bedawee, by the incident at the Red Khan, was not
to be maintained after our return to Jerusalem. Another of our
Oriental illusions was to be destroyed forever. The cool acceptance by the Doctor of the two francs so loftily tendered, as a
specimen of Bedawee backsheesh, was probably unexpected, and
perhaps unprovided for by adequate financial arrangements on the
part of the Galgam. At any rate, that evening he was hovering
about the hotel, endeavoring to attract the attention of the Doctor, and evidently unwilling to believe that there could exist in
the heart of the howadji the mean intention of retaining those
francs. The next morning he sent a friend to the Doctor to ask
him for the money. The Doctor replied that he should never
think of returning a gift, especially one made with so much courtesy ; that, indeed, the amount of the money was naught, but that
he should keep it as a souvenir of the noble generosity of his Bedawee friend. This sort of sentiment seemed inexplicable to the
Oriental mind. The son of the desert was as much astonished
that the Frank should retain his gift, as the Spanish gentleman
who presents his horse to his guest would be if the guest should
take it. The offer of a present in the East is a flowery expression of a sentiment that does not exist, and its acceptance neces-
sarily implies a return of something of greater value. After
another day of anxiety the proud and handsome slave came in
person and begged for the francs until he received them. He
was no better than his master, the noble sheykh, who waylaid us
during the remainder of our stay for additional sixpences in backsheesh. O superb Bedawee, we did not begrudge the money,
but our lost ideal !

VI.

BETHLEHEM AND MAR SABA.

BETHLEHEM lies about seven miles south of Jerusalem. It is also a hill village, reposing upon a stony promontory that is thrust out eastward from the central mountain-range; the abrupt slopes below three sides of it are terraced; on the north is a valley which lies in a direct line between it and Jerusalem; on the east are the yawning ravines and the "wilderness" leading to the Dead Sea; on the south is the wild country towards Hebron, and the sharp summit of the Frank mountain in the distance. The village lies on the ridge; and on the point at the east end of it, overlooking a vast extent of seamed and rocky and jagged country, is the gloomy pile of convents, chapels, and churches that mark the spot of the Nativity.

From its earliest mention till now the home of shepherds and of hardy cultivators of its rocky hillsides, it has been noted for the free spirit and turbulence of its inhabitants. The primal character of a place seems to have the power of perpetuating itself in all changes. Bethlehem never seems to have been afflicted with servility. During the period of David's hiding in the Cave Adullam the warlike Philistines occupied it, but David was a fit representative of the pluck and steadfastness of its people. Since the Christian era it has been a Christian town, as it is to-day, and the few Moslems who have settled there, from time to time, have found it more prudent to withdraw than to brave its hostility. Its women incline to be handsome, and have rather European than Oriental features, and they enjoy the reputation of unusual virtue; the men are industrious, and seem to have more self-respect than the Syrians generally.

Bethlehem is to all the world one of the sweetest of words. A tender and romantic interest is thrown about it as the burial-place of Rachel, as the scene of Ruth's primitive story, and of David's boyhood and kingly consecration; so that no other place in Judæa, by its associations, was so fit to be the gate through which the Divine Child should come into the world. And the traveller to-day can visit it, with, perhaps, less shock to his feelings of reverence, certainly with a purer and simpler enjoyment, than any other place in Holy Land. He finds its ruggedness and desolateness picturesque, in the light of old song and story, and even the puerile inventions of monkish credulity do not affect him as elsewhere.

From Jerusalem we reach Bethlehem by following a curving ridge, — a lovely upland ride, on account of the extensive prospect and the breeze, and because it is always a relief to get out of the city. The country is, however, as stony as the worst portions of New England, — the mountain sheep-pastures; thick, double stone-walls enclosing small fields do not begin to exhaust the stones. On both sides of the ridge are bare, unproductive hills, but the sides of the valleys are terraced, and covered with a good growth of olive-trees. These hollows were no doubt once very fruitful by assiduous cultivation, in spite of the stones. Bethlehem, as we saw it across a deep ravine, was like a castle on a hill; there is nowhere level ground enough for a table to stand, off the ridges, and we looked in vain for the "plains of Bethlehem" about which we had tried, trustfully, to sing in youth.

Within a mile of Bethlehem gate we came to the tomb of Rachel, standing close by the highway. "And Rachel died, and was buried in the way to Ephrath, which is Beth-lehem. And Jacob set a pillar upon her grave : that is the pillar of Rachel's grave unto this day." This is the testimony of the author of Genesis, who had not seen the pillar which remained to his day, but repeated the tradition of the sons of Jacob. What remained of this pillar, after the absence of the Israelites for some five centuries from Bethlehem, is uncertain; but it may be supposed that some spot near Bethlehem was identified as the tomb of Rachel upon their return, and that the present site is the one then selected. It is possible, of course, that the tradition of the pagan Canaanites may have preserved the recollection of the precise spot. At any rate, Christians seem to agree that this is one of the few ancient sites in Judæa which are authentic, and the Moslems pay it equal veneration. The square, unpretentious building erected over it is of modern construction, and the pilgrim has to content himself with looking at a sort of Moslem tomb inside, and reflecting, if he can, upon the pathetic story of the death of the mother of Joseph.

There is, alas! everywhere in Judæa something to drive away sentiment as well as pious feeling. The tomb of Rachel is now surrounded by a Moslem cemetery, and as we happened to be there on Thursday we found ourselves in the midst of a great gathering of women, who had come there, according to their weekly custom, to weep and to wail.

You would not see in farthest Nubia a more barbarous assemblage, and not so fierce an one. In the presence of these wild mourners the term " gentler sex " has a ludicrous sound. Yet we ought not to forget that we were intruders upon their periodic grief, attracted to their religious demonstration merely by curiosity, and fairly entitled to nothing but scowls and signs of aversion. I am sure that we should give bold Moslem intruders upon our hours of sorrow at home no better reception. The women were in the usual Syrian costume; their loose gowns gaped open at the bosom, and they were without veils, and made no pretence of drawing a shawl before their faces; all wore necklaces of coins, and many of them had circlets of coins on the head, with strips depending from them, also stiff with silver pieces. A woman's worth was thus easily to be reckoned, for her entire fortune was on her head. A pretty face was here and there to be seen, but most of them were flaringly ugly, and — to liken them to what they most resembled — physically and mentally the type of the North American squaws. They were accompanied by all their children, and the little brats were tumbling about the tombs, and learning the language of woe.

Among the hundreds of women present, the expression of grief took two forms, — one active, the other more resigned. A group seated itself about a tomb, and the members swayed their bodies to and fro, howled at the top of their voices, and pretended to weep. I had the infidel curiosity to go from group to group in search of a tear, but I did not see one. Occasionally some interruption, like the arrival of a new mourner, would cause the swaying and howling to cease for a moment, or it would now and then be temporarily left to the woman at the head of the grave, but presently all would fall to again and abandon themselves to the luxury of agony. It was perhaps unreasonable to expect tears from creatures so withered as most of these were; but they worked themselves into a frenzy of excitement, they rolled up their blue checked cotton handkerchiefs, drew them across their eyes, and then wrung them out with gestures of despair. It was the dryest grief I ever saw.

The more active mourners formed a ring in a clear spot. Some thirty women standing with their faces toward the centre, their hands on each other's shoulders, circled round with unrhythmic steps, crying and singing, and occasionally jumping up and down with all their energy, like the dancers of Horace, "striking the ground with equal feet," coming down upon the earth with a heavy thud, at the same time slapping their faces with their hands; then circling around again with faster steps, and shriller cries, and more prolonged ululations, and anon pausing to jump and beat the ground with a violence sufficient to shatter their frames. The loose flowing robes, the clinking of the silver ornaments, the wild gleam of their eyes, the Bacchantic madness of their saltations, the shrill shrieking and wailing, conspired to give their demonstration an indescribable barbarity. This scene has recurred every Thursday for, I suppose, hundreds of years, within a mile of the birthplace of Jesus.

Bethlehem at a little distance presents an appearance that its interior does not maintain; but it is so much better than most Syrian villages of its size (it has a population of about three thousand), and is so much cleaner than Jerusalem, that we are content with its ancient though commonplace aspect. But the atmosphere of the town is thoroughly commercial, or perhaps I should say industrial; you do not find in it that rural and reposeful air which you associate with the birthplace of our Lord. The people are sharp, to a woman, and have a keen eye for the purse of the stranger. Every other house is a shop for the manufacture or sale of some of the Bethlehem specialties, — carvings in olive-wood and ivory and mother-of-pearl, crosses and crucifixes, and models of the Holy Sepulchre, and every sort of sacred trinket, and beads in endless variety; a little is done also in silver-work, especially in rings. One may chance upon a Mecca ring there; but the ring peculiar to Bethlehem is a silver wedding-ring; it is a broad and ingular band of silver with pendants, and is worn upon the thumb. As soon as we come into the town, we are beset with sellers of various wares, and we never escape them except when we are in the convent.

The Latin convent opens its doors to tourists; it is a hospitable house, and the monks are very civil; they let us sit in a *salle-à-manger*, while waiting for dinner, that was as damp and chill as a dungeon, and they gave us a well-intended but uneatable meal, and the most peculiar wine, all at a good price. The wine, white and red, was made by the monks, they said with some pride; we tried both kinds, and I can recommend it to the American Temperance Union : if it can be introduced to the public, the public will embrace total abstinence with enthusiasm.

While we were waiting for the proper hour to visit the crypt of the Nativity, we went out upon the esplanade before the convent, and looked down into the terraced ravines which are endeared to us by so many associations. Somewhere down there is the patch of ground that the mighty man of wealth, Boaz, owned, in which sweet Ruth went gleaning in the barley-harvest. What a picture of a primitive time it is, — the noonday meal of Boaz and his handmaidens, Ruth invited to join them, and dip her morsel in the vinegar with the rest, and the hospitable Boaz handing her parched corn. We can understand why Ruth had good gleaning over this stony ground, after the rakes of the handmaidens. We know that her dress did not differ from that worn by Oriental women now; for her " veil," which Boaz filled with six measures of barley, was the head-shawl still almost universally worn, — though not by the Bethlehemite women. Their head-dress is

6

peculiar; there seems to be on top of the head a square frame, and over this is thrown and folded a piece of white cloth. The women are thus in a manner crowned, and the dress is as becoming as the somewhat similar head-covering of the Roman peasants. We learn also in the story of Ruth that the mother-in-law in her day was as wise in the ways of men as she is now. " Sit still, my daughter," she counselled her after she returned with the veil full of barley, " until thou know how the matter will fall, for the man will not be in rest until he have finished the thing this day."

Down there, somewhere in that wilderness of ravines, David, the great-grandson of Ruth, kept his father's sheep before he went to the combat with Goliath. It was there — the grotto is shown a little more than a mile from this convent — that the shepherds watched their flocks by night when the angel appeared and announced the birth of the Messiah, the Son of David. We have here within the grasp of the eye almost the beginning and the end of the old dispensation, from the burial of Rachel to the birth of our Lord, from the passing of the wandering sheykh, Jacob, with his family, to the end put to the exclusive pretensions of his descendants by the coming of a Saviour to all the world.

The cave called the Grotto of the Nativity has great antiquity. The hand-book says it had this repute as early as the second century. In the year 327 the mother of Constantine built a church over it, and this basilica still stands, and is the oldest specimen of Christian architecture in existence, except perhaps the lower church of St. Clement at Rome. It is the oldest basilica above ground retaining its perfect ancient form. The main part of the church consists of a nave and four aisles, separated by four rows of Corinthian marble columns, tradition says, taken from the temple of Solomon. The walls were once adorned with mosaics, but only fragments of them remain ; the roof is decayed and leaky, the pavement is broken. This part of the church is wholly neglected, because it belongs to the several sects in common, and is merely the arena for an occasional fight. The choir is separated from the nave by a wall, and is divided into two chapels, one of the Greeks, the other of the Armenians. The Grotto of the

Nativity is underneath these chapels, and each sect has a separate staircase of descent to it. The Latin chapel is on the north side of this choir, and it also has a stairway to the subterranean apartments.

Making an effort to believe that the stable of the inn in which Christ was born was a small subterranean cave cut in the solid rock, we descended a winding flight of stairs from the Latin chapel, with a monk for our guide, and entered a labyrinth from which we did not emerge until we reached the place of the nativity, and ascended into the Greek chapel above it. We walked between glistening walls of rock, illuminated by oil-lamps here and there, and in our exploration of the gloomy passages and chambers, encountered shrines, pictures, and tombs of the sainted. We saw, or were told that we saw, the spot to which St. Joseph retired at the moment of the nativity, and also the place where the twenty thousand children who were murdered by the order of Herod — a ghastly subject so well improved by the painters of the Renaissance — are buried. But there was one chamber, or rather vault, that we entered with genuine emotion. This was the cell of Jerome, hermit and scholar, whose writings have gained him the title of Father of the Church.

At the close of the fourth century Bethlehem was chiefly famous as the retreat of this holy student, and the fame of his learning and sanctity drew to it from distant lands many faithful women, who renounced the world and its pleasures, and were content to sit at his feet and learn the way of life. Among those who resigned, and, for his sake and the cross, despised, the allurements and honors of the Roman world, was the devout Paula, a Roman matron who traced her origin from Agamemnon, and numbered the Scipios and Gracchi among her ancestors, while her husband, Joxotius, deduced a no less royal lineage from Æneas. Her wealth was sufficient to support the dignity of such a descent; among her possessions, an item in her rent-roll, was the city of Nicopolis, which Augustus built as a monument of the victory of Actium. By the advice and in the company of Jerome, her spiritual guide, she abandoned Rome and all her vast estates, and even her infant son, and retired to the holy village of Bethlehem. The great Jerome, who wrote her biography, and transmitted the story of her virtues to the most distant ages, bestowed upon her the singular title of the Mother-in-law of God ! She was buried here, and we look upon her tomb with scarcely less interest than that of Jerome himself, who also rests in this thrice holy ground. At the beginning of the fifth century, when the Goths sacked Rome, a crowd of the noble and the rich, escaping with nothing saved from the wreck but life and honor, attracted also by the reputation of Jerome, appeared as beggars in the streets of this humble village. No doubt they thronged to the cell of the venerable father.

There is, I suppose, no doubt that this is the study in which he composed many of his more important treatises. It is a vaulted chamber, about twenty feet square by nine feet high. There is in Venice a picture of the study of Jerome, painted by Carpaccio, which represents a delightful apartment; the saint is seen in his study, in a rich *négligé* robe ; at the side of his desk are musical instruments, music-stands, and sheets of music, as if he were accustomed to give *soirées ;* on the chimney-piece are Greek vases and other objects of virtu, and in the middle of the room is a poodle-dog of the most worldly and useless of the canine breed. The artist should have seen the real study of the hermit, — a grim, unornamented vault, in which he passed his days in mortifications of the body, hearing always ringing in his ears, in his disordered mental and physical condition, the last trump of judgment.

We passed, groping our way along in this religious cellar, through a winding, narrow passage in the rock, some twenty-five feet long, and came into the place of places, the very Chapel of the Nativity. In this low vault, thirty-eight feet long and eleven feet wide, hewn in the rock, is an altar at one end. Before this altar — and we can see everything with distinctness, for sixteen silver lamps are burning about it — there is a marble slab in the pavement into which is let a silver star, with this sentence round it : *Hic de Virgine Maria Jesus Christus natus est.* The guardian of this sacred spot was a Turkish soldier, who stood there with his gun and fixed bayonet, an attitude which experience has taught him is necessary to keep the peace among the Christians who meet here. The altar is without furniture, and is draped by each sect which uses it in turn. Near by is the chapel of the "manger," but the manger in which Christ was laid is in the church of Santa Maria Maggiore in Rome.

There is in Bethlehem another ancient cave which is almost as famous as that of the Nativity; it is called the Milk Grotto, and during all ages of the Church a most marvellous virtue has attached to it; fragments of the stone have been, and still continue to be, broken off and sent into all Christian countries; women also make pilgrimages to it in faith. The grotto is on the edge of the town overlooking the eastern ravines, and is arranged as a show-place. In our walk thither a stately Bedawee, as by accident, fell into our company, and acted as our cicerone. He was desirous that we should know that he also was a man of the world and of travel, and rated at its proper value this little corner of the earth. He had served in the French army and taken part in many battles, and had been in Paris and seen the tomb of the great emperor, — ah, there was a man! As to this grotto, they say that the Virgin used to send to it for milk, — many think so. As for him, he was a soldier, and did not much give his mind to such things.

This grotto is an excavation in the chalky rock, and might be a very good place to store milk, but for the popular prejudice in cities against chalk and water. We entered it through the court of a private house, and the damsel who admitted us also assured us that the Virgin procured milk from it. The tradition is that the Virgin and Child were concealed here for a time before the flight into Egypt; and ever since then its stone has the miraculous power of increasing the flow of the maternal breast. The early fathers encouraged this and the like superstitions in the docile minds of their fair converts, and themselves testified to the efficacy of this remarkable stone. These superstitions belong rather to the Orient than to any form of religion. There is a famous spring at Assiout in Egypt which was for centuries much resorted to by ladies who desired offspring; and the Arabs on the Upper Nile to-day, who wish for an heir male, resort to a plant which grows in the remote desert, rare and difficult to find, the leaves of which are "good for boys." This grotto scarcely repays the visit, except for the view one obtains of the wild country below it. When we bade good by to the courtly Arab, we had too much delicacy to offer money to such a gentleman and a soldier of the empire; a delicacy not shared by him, however, for he let no false modesty hinder a request for a little backsheesh for tobacco.

On our return, and at some distance from the gate, we diverged into a lane, and sought, in a rocky field, the traditional well whose waters David longed for when he was in the Cave of Adullam, — "O that one would give me drink of the water of the well of Bethlehem, which is by the gate!" Howbeit, when the three mighty men had broken through the Philistine guards and procured him the water, David would not drink that which was brought at such a sacrifice. Two very comely Bethlehem girls hastened at our approach to draw water from the well and gave us to drink, with all the freedom of Oriental hospitality, in which there is always an expectation of backsheesh. The water is at any rate very good, and there is no reason why these pretty girls should not turn an honest penny upon the strength of David's thirst, whether this be the well whose water he desired or not. We were only too thankful that no miraculous property is attributed to its waters. As we returned, we had the evening light upon the gray walls and towers of the city, and were able to invest it with something of its historical dignity.

The next excursion that we made from Jerusalem was so different from the one to Bethlehem, that by way of contrast I put them together. It was to the convent of Mar Saba, which lies in the wilderness towards the Dead Sea, about two hours and a half from the city.

In those good old days, when piety was measured by frugality in the use of the bath, when the holy fathers praised most those hermits who washed least, when it might perhaps be the boast of more than one virgin, devoted to the ascetic life, that she had lived fifty-eight years during which water had touched neither her hands, her face, her feet, nor any part of her body, Palestine was, after Egypt, the favorite resort of the fanatical, the unfortunate, and the lazy, who, gathered into communities, or dwelling in solitary caves, offered to the barbarian world a spectacle of superstition and abasement under the name of Christianity. But of the swarm of hermits and monks who begged in the cities and burrowed in the caves of the Holy Land in the fifth century, no one may perhaps be spoken of with more respect than St. Sabas, who, besides a reputation for sanctity, has left that of manliness and a virile ability, which his self-mortifications did not extirpate. And of all the monasteries of that period, that of Mar Saba is the only one in Judæa which has preserved almost unbroken the type of that time. St. Sabas was a Cappadocian who came to Palestine in search of a permanent retreat, savage enough to satisfy his austere soul. He found it in a cave in one of the wildest gorges in this most desolate of lands, a ravine which opens into the mountains from the brook Kidron. The fame of his zeal and piety attracted thousands to his neighborhood, so that at one time there were almost as many hermits roosting about in the rocks near him as there are inhabitants in the city of Jerusalem now. He was once enabled to lead an army of monks to that city and chastise the Monophysite heretics. His cave in the steep side of a rocky precipice became the nucleus of his convent, which grew around it and attached itself to the face of the rock as best it could. For the convent of Mar Saba is not a building, nor a collection of buildings, so much as it is a group of nests attached to the side of a precipice.

It was a bright Saturday afternoon that a young divinity student and I, taking the volatile Demetrius with us for interpreter, rode out of St. Stephen's gate, into Jehoshaphat, past the gray field of Jewish graves, down through Tophet and the wild ravine of the Kidron.

It is unpleasant to interrupt the prosperous start of a pilgrimage by a trifling incident, but at our first descent and the slightest tension on the bridle-reins of my horse, they parted from the bit. This accident, which might be serious in other lands, is of the sort that is anticipated here, and I may say assured, by the forethought of the owners of saddle-horses. Upon dismounting with as much haste as dignity, I discovered that the reins had been fastened to the bit by a single rotten string of cotton. Luckily the horse I rode was not an animal to take advantage of the weakness of his toggery. He was a Syrian horse, a light sorrel, and had no one of the good points of a horse except the name and general shape. His walk was slow and reluctant, his trot a high and non-progressive jolt, his gallop a large up-and-down agitation. To his bridle of strings and shreds no martingale was attached; no horse in Syria is subject to that restraint. When I pull the bit he sticks up his nose; when I switch him he kicks. When I hold him in, he won't go; when I let him loose, he goes on his nose. I dismount and look at him with curiosity; I wonder all the journey what his *forte* is, but I never discover. I conclude that he is like the emperor Honorius, whom Gibbon stigmatizes as "without passions, and consequently without talents."

Yet he was not so bad as the roads, and perhaps no horse would do much better on these stony and broken foot-paths. This horse is not a model (for anything but a clothes-horse), but from my observation I think that great injustice has been done to Syrian horses by travellers, who have only themselves to blame for accidents which bring the horses into disrepute. Travellers are thrown from these steeds; it is a daily occurrence; we heard continually that somebody had a fall from his horse on his way to the Jordan, or to Mar Saba, or to Nablous, and was laid up, and it was always in consequence of a vicious brute. The fact is that excellent ministers of the gospel and doctors of divinity and students of the same, who have never in their lives been on the back of a horse in any other land, seem to think when they come here that the holy air of Palestine will transform them into accomplished horsemen; or perhaps they are emulous of Elisha, that they may go to heaven by means of a fiery steed.

For a while we had the company of the singing brook Kidron, flowing clear over the stones; then we left the ravine and wound over rocky steeps, which afforded us fine views of broken hills and interlacing ridges, and when we again reached the valley the brook had disappeared in the thirsty ground. The road is strewn, not paved, with stones, and in many places hardly practicable for horses. Occasionally we encountered flocks of goats and of long-wooled sheep feeding on the scant grass of the hills, and tended by boys in the coarse brown and striped garments of the country, which give a state-prison aspect to most of the inhabitants, — but there was no other life, and no trees offer relief to the hard landscape. But the way was now and then bright with flowers, thickly carpeted with scarlet anemones, the Star of Bethlehem, and tiny dandelions. Two hours from the city we passed several camps of Bedaween, their brown low camel's-hair tents pitched among the rocks and scarcely distinguishable in the sombre land-scape. About the tents were grouped camels and donkeys, and from them issued and pursued us begging boys and girls. A lazy Bedawee appeared here and there with a long gun, and we could imagine that this gloomy region might be unsafe after nightfall; but no danger ever seems possible in such bright sunshine and under a sky so blue and friendly.

When a half-hour from the convent, we turned to the right from the road to the Dead Sea, and ascending a steep hill found ourselves riding along the edge of a deep winding gorge; a brook flows at the bottom, and its sides are sheer precipices of rock, generally parallel, but occasionally widening into amphitheatres of the most fantastic rocky formation. It is on one side of this narrow ravine that the convent is built, partly excavated in the rock, partly resting on jutting ledges, and partly hung out in the form of balconies, — buildings clinging to the steep side like a comb of wild bees or wasps to a rock.

Our first note of approach to it was the sight of a square tower and of the roofs of buildings below us. Descending from the road by several short turns, and finally by two steep paved inclines, we came to a lofty wall in which is a small iron door. As we could go no farther without aid from within, Demetrius shouted, and soon we had a response from a slit in the wall fifty feet above us to the left. We could see no one, but the voice demanded who we were, and whether we had a pass. Above the slit from which the angelic voice proceeded a stone projected, and in this was an opening for letting down or drawing up articles. This habit of caution in regard to who or what shall come into the convent is of course a relic of the gone ages of tumult, but it is still neces-sary as a safeguard against the wandering Bedaween, who would

6 *   I

no doubt find means to plunder the convent of its great wealth of gold, silver, and jewels if they were not at all times rigorously excluded. The convent with its walls and towers is still a fortress strong enough to resist any irregular attempts of the wandering tribes. It is also necessary to strictly guard the convent against women, who in these days of speculation, if not scientific curiosity, often knock impatiently and angrily at its gates, and who, if admitted, would in one gay and chatty hour destroy the spell of holy seclusion which has been unbroken for one thousand three hundred and ninety-two years. I know that sometimes it seems an unjust ordination of Providence that a woman cannot *be* a man, but I cannot join those who upbraid the monks of Mar Saba for inhospitality because they refuse to admit women under any circumstances into the precincts of the convent; if I do not sympathize with the brothers, I can understand their adhesion to the last shred of man's independence, which is only to be maintained by absolute exclusion of the other sex. It is not necessary to revive the defamation of the early Christian ages, that the devil appeared oftener to the hermit in the form of a beautiful woman than in any other; but we may not regret that there is still one spot on the face of the earth, if it is no bigger than the sod upon which Noah's pioneer dove alighted, in which weak men may be safe from the temptation, the criticism, and the curiosity of the superior being. There is an airy tower on the rocks outside the walls which women may occupy if they cannot restrain their desire to lodge in this neighborhood, or if night overtakes them here on their way from the Dead Sea; there Madame Pfeiffer, Miss Martineau, and other famous travellers of their sex have found refuge, and I am sorry to say abused their proximity to this retreat of shuddering man by estimating the piety of its inmates according to their hospitality to women. So far as I can learn, this convent of Mar Saba is now the only retreat left on this broad earth for MAN; and it seems to me only reasonable that it should be respected by his generous and gentle, though inquisitive foe.

After further parley with Demetrius and a considerable interval, we heard a bell ring, and in a few moments the iron door opened, and we entered, stepping our horses carefully over the stone threshold, and showing our pass from the Jerusalem Patriarch to an attendant, and came into a sort of stable hewn in the rock. Here we abandoned our horses, and were taken in charge by a monk whom the bell had summoned from below. He conducted us down several long flights of zigzag stairs in the rock, amid hanging buildings and cells, until we came to what appears to be a broad ledge in the precipice, and found ourselves in the central part of this singular hive, that is, in a small court, with cells and rocks on one side and the convent church, which overhangs the precipice, on the other. Beside the church and also at another side of the court are buildings in which pilgrims are lodged, and in the centre of the court is the tomb of St. Sabas himself. Here our passports were examined, and we were assigned a cheerful and airy room looking upon the court and tomb.

One of the brothers soon brought us coffee, and the promptness of this hospitality augured well for the remainder of our fare; relying upon the reputation of the convent for good cheer, we had brought nothing with us, not so much as a biscuit. Judge of our disgust, then, at hearing the following dialogue between Demetrius and the Greek monk.

" What time can the gentlemen dine ? "

" Any time they like."

" What have you for dinner ? "

" Nothing."

" You can give us no dinner ? "

" To be sure not. It is fast."

" But we have n't a morsel, we shall starve."

" Perhaps I can find a little bread."

" Nothing else ? "

" We have very good raisins."

" Well," we interposed, " kill us a chicken, give us a few oysters, stewed or broiled, we are not particular." This levity, which was born of desperation, for the jolting ride from Jerusalem had indisposed us to keep a fast, especially a fast established by a church the orthodoxy of whose creed we had strong reasons to doubt, did not affect the monk. He replied, " Chicken ! it is impossible." We shrunk our requisition to eggs.

" If I can find an egg, I will see." And the brother departed, with *carte blanche* from us to squeeze his entire establishment.

Alas, fasting is not in Mar Saba what it is in New England, where an appointed fast-day is hailed as an opportunity to forego lunch in order to have an extraordinary appetite for a better dinner than usual !

The tomb of St. Sabas, the central worship of this hive, is a little plastered hut in the middle of the court; the interior is decorated with pictures in the Byzantine style, and a lamp is always burning there. As we stood at the tomb we heard voices chanting, and, turning towards the rock, we saw a door from which the sound came. Pushing it open, we were admitted into a large chapel, excavated in the rock. The service of vespers was in progress, and a band of Russian pilgrims were chanting in rich bass voices, producing more melody than I had ever heard in a Greek church. The excavation extends some distance into the hill; we were shown the cells of St. John of Damascus and other hermits, and at the end a charnel-house piled full of the bones of men. In the dim light their skulls grinned at us in a horrid familiarity; in that ghastly jocularity which a skull always puts on, with a kind of mocking commentary upon the strong chant of the pilgrims, which reverberated in all the recesses of the gloomy cave, — fresh, hearty voices, such as these skulls have heard (if they can hear) for many centuries. The pilgrims come, and chant, and depart, generation after generation; the bones and skulls of the fourteen thousand martyrs in this charnel-bin enjoy a sort of repulsive immortality. The monk, who was our guide, appeared to care no more for the remains of the martyrs than for the presence of the pilgrims. In visiting such storehouses one cannot but be struck by the light familiarity with the relics and insignia of death which the monks have acquired.

This St. John of Damascus, whose remains repose here, was a fiery character in his day, and favored by a special miracle before he became a saint. He so distinguished himself by his invectives against Leo and Constantine and other iconoclast emperors at Constantinople who, in the eighth century, attempted to extirpate image-worship from the Catholic church, that he was sentenced to lose his right hand. The story is that it was instantly restored by the Virgin Mary. It is worthy of note that the superstitious Orient more readily gave up idolatry or image-worship under the Moslems than under the Christians.

As the sun was setting we left the pilgrims chanting to the martyrs, and hastened to explore the premises a little, before the light should fade. We followed our guide up stairs and down stairs, sometimes cut in the stone, sometimes wooden stairways, along hanging galleries, through corridors hewn in the rock, amid cells and little chapels, — a most intricate labyrinth, in which the uninitiated would soon lose his way. Here and there we came suddenly upon a little garden spot as big as a bed-blanket, a ledge upon which soil had been deposited. We walked also under grape-trellises, we saw orange-trees, and the single palm-tree that the convent boasts, said to have been planted by St. Sabas himself. The plan of this establishment gradually developed itself to us. It differs from an ordinary convent chiefly in this, — the latter is spread out flat on the earth, Mar Saba is set up edgewise. Put Mar Saba on a plain, and these little garden spots and graperies would be courts and squares amid buildings, these galleries would be bridges, these cells or horizontal caves would be perpendicular tombs and reservoirs.

When we arrived, we supposed that we were almost the only guests. But we found that the place was full of Greek and Russian pilgrims; we encountered them on the terraces, on the flat roofs, in the caves, and in all out-of-the-way nooks. Yet these were not the most pleasing nor the most animated tenants of the place; wherever we went the old rookery was made cheerful by the twittering notes of black birds with yellow wings, a species of grakle, which the monks have domesticated, and which breed in great numbers. Steeled as these good brothers are against the other sex, we were glad to discover this streak of softness in their nature. High up on the precipice there is a bell-tower attached to a little chapel, and in it hang twenty small bells, which are rung to call the inmates to prayer. Even at this height, and indeed wherever we penetrated, we were followed by the monotonous chant which issued from the charnel-house.

We passed by a long row of cells occupied by the monks, but were not permitted to look into them; nor were we allowed to see the library, which is said to be rich in illuminated manuscripts. The convent belongs to the Greek church; its monks take the usual vows of poverty, chastity, and obedience, and fortify themselves in their holiness by opposing walls of adamant to all womankind. There are about fifty monks here at present, and uncommonly fine-looking fellows, — not at all the gross and greasy sort of monk that is sometimes met. Their outward dress is very neat, consisting of a simple black gown and a round, high, flat-topped black cap.

Our dinner, when it was brought into our apartment, answered very well one's idea of a dessert, but it was a very good Oriental dinner. The chief articles were a piece of hard black bread, and two boiled eggs, cold, and probably brought by some pilgrim from Jerusalem; but besides, there were raisins, cheese, figs, oranges, a bottle of golden wine, and tea. The wine was worthy to be celebrated in classic verse; none so good is, I am sure, made elsewhere in Syria; it was liquid sunshine; and as it was manufactured by the monks, it gave us a new respect for their fastidious taste.

The vaulted chamber which we occupied was furnished on three sides with a low divan, which answered the double purpose of chairs and couch. On one side, however, and elevated in the wall, was a long niche, exactly like the recessed tombs in cathedrals, upon which, toes turned up, lie the bronze or wooden figures of the occupants. This was the bed of honor. It was furnished with a mattress and a thick counterpane having one sheet sewed to it. With reluctance I accepted the distinction of climbing into it, and there I slept, laid out, for all the world, like my own effigy. From the ceiling hung a dim oil-lamp, which cast a gloom rather than a light upon our sepulchral place of repose. Our windows looked out towards the west, upon the court, upon the stairs, upon the terraces, roofs, holes, caves, grottos, wooden balconies, bird-cages, steps entering the rock and leading to cells; and, towards the south, along the jagged precipice. The convent occupies the precipice from the top nearly to the bottom of the ravine; the precipice opposite is nearly perpendicular, close at hand, and permits no view in that direction. Heaven is the only object in sight from this retreat.

Before the twilight fell the chanting was still going on in the cavern, monks and pilgrims were gliding about the court, and numbers of the latter were clustered in the vestibule of the church, in which they were settling down to lodge for the night; and high above us I saw three gaudily attired Bedaween, who had accompanied some travellers from the Dead Sea, leaning over the balustrade of the stairs, and regarding the scene with Moslem complacency. The hive settled slowly to rest.

But the place was by no means still at night. There was in the court an old pilgrim who had brought a cough from the heart of Russia, who seemed to be trying to cough himself inside out. There were other noises that could not be explained. There was a good deal of clattering about in wooden shoes. Every sound was multiplied and reduplicated from the echoing rocks. The strangeness of the situation did not conduce to sleep, not even to an effigy-like repose; but after looking from the window upon the march of the quiet stars, after watching the new moon disappear between the roofs, and after seeing that the door of St. Sabas's tomb was closed, although his light was still burning, I turned in; and after a time, during which I was conscious that not even vows of poverty, chastity, and obedience are respected by fleas, I fell into a light sleep.

From this I was aroused by a noise that seemed like the call to judgment, by the most clamorous jangle of discordant bells, — all the twenty were ringing at once, and each in a different key. It was not simply a din, it was an earthquake of sound. The peals were echoed from the opposite ledges, and reverberated among the rocks and caves and sharp angles of the convent, until the crash was intolerable. It was worse than the slam, bang, shriek, clang, clash, roar, dissonance, thunder, and hurricane with which all musicians think it absolutely necessary to close any overture, symphony, or musical composition whatever, however decent and quiet it may be. It was enough to rouse the deafest pilgrim, to wake the dead martyrs and set the fourteen thousand skulls hunting for their bones, to call even St. Sabas himself from his tomb. I arose. I saw in the starlight figures moving about the court, monks in their simple black gowns. It was, I comprehended then, the call to midnight prayer in the chapel, and, resolved not to be disturbed further by it, I climbed back into my tomb.

But the clamor continued; I heard such a clatter of hobnailed shoes on the pavement, besides, that I could bear it no longer, got up, slipped into some of my clothes, opened the door, and descended by our winding private stairway into the court.

The door of St. Sabas's tomb was wide open!

Were the graves opening, and the dead taking the air? Did this tomb open of its own accord? Out of its illuminated interior would the saint stalk forth and join this great procession, the *reveille* of the quick and the slow?

From above and from below, up stairs and down stairs, out of caves and grottos and all odd roosting-places, the monks and pilgrims were pouring and streaming into the court; and the bells incessantly called more and more importunately as the loiterers delayed.

The church was open, and lighted at the altar end. I glided in with the other ghostly, hastily clad, and yawning pilgrims. The screen at the apse before the holy place, a mass of silver and gilding, sparkled in the candlelight; the cross above it gleamed like a revelation out of the gloom; but half of the church was in heavy shadow. From the penetralia came the sound of priestly chanting; in the wooden stalls along each side of the church stood, facing the altar, the black and motionless figures of the brothers. The pilgrims were crowding and jostling in at the door. A brother gave me a stall near the door, and I stood in it, as statue-like as I could, and became a brother for the time being.

At the left of the door stood a monk with impassive face; before him on a table were piles of wax tapers and a solitary lighted candle. Every pilgrim who entered bought a taper and paid two coppers for it. If he had not the change the monk gave him change, and the pilgrim carefully counted what he received and objected to any piece he thought not current. You may wake these people up any time of night, and find their perceptions about money unobscured. The seller never looked at the buyer, nor at anything except the tapers and the money.

The pilgrims were of all ages and grades; very old men, stout, middle-aged men, and young athletic fellows; there were Russians from all the provinces; Greeks from the isles, with long black locks and dark eyes, in fancy embroidered jackets and leggins, swarthy bandits and midnight pirates in appearance. But it 'ends to make anybody look like a pirate to wake him up at . .elve o'clock at night, and haul him into the light with no time to comb his hair. I dare say that I may have appeared to these honest people like a Western land-pirate. And yet I should rather meet some of those Greeks in a lighted church than outside the walls at midnight.

Each pilgrim knelt and bowed himself, then lighted his taper and placed it on one of the tripods before the screen. In time the church was very fairly illuminated, and nearly filled with standing worshippers, bowing, crossing themselves, and responding to the reading and chanting in low murmurs. The chanting was a very nasal intoning, usually slow, but now and then breaking into a lively gallop. The assemblage, quiet and respectful, but clad in all the vagaries of Oriental colors and rags, contained some faces that appeared very wild in the half-light. When the service had gone on half an hour, a priest came out with a tinkling censer and incensed carefully every nook and corner and person (even the vestibule, where some of the pilgrims slept, which needed it), until the church was filled with smoke and perfume. The performance went on for an hour or more, but I crept back to bed long before it was over, and fell to sleep on the drone of the intoning.

We were up before sunrise on Sunday morning. The pilgrims were already leaving for Jerusalem. There was no trace of the last night's revelry; everything was commonplace in the bright daylight. We were served with coffee, and then finished our exploration of the premises.

That which we had postponed as the most interesting sight was the cell of St. Sabas. It is a natural grotto in the rock, somewhat enlarged either by the saint or by his successors. When St. Sabas first came to this spot, he found a lion in possession. It was not the worst kind of a lion, but a sort of Judæan lion, one of those meek beasts over whom the ancient hermits had so much control. St. Sabas looked at the cave and at the lion, but the cave suited him better than the lion. The lion looked at the saint, and evidently knew what was passing in his mind. For the lions in those days were nearly as intelligent as anybody else. And then St. Sabas told the lion to go away, that he wanted that lodging for himself. And the lion, without a growl, put his tail down, and immediately went away. There is a picture of this interview still preserved at the convent, and any one can see that it is probable that such a lion as the artist has represented would move on when requested to do so.

In the cave is a little recess, the entrance to which is a small hole, a recess just large enough to accommodate a person in a sitting posture. In this place St. Sabas sat for seven years, without once coming out. That was before the present walls were built in front of the grotto, and he had some light, — he sat seven years on that hard stone, as long as the present French Assembly intends to sit. It was with him also a provisional sitting, in fact, a Septennate.

In the court-yard, as we were departing, were displayed articles to sell to the pious pilgrims: canes from the Jordan; crosses painted, and inlaid with cedar or olive wood, or some sort of Jordan timber; rude paintings of the sign-board order done by the monks, St. George and the Dragon being the favorite subject; hyperbolical pictures of the convent and the saint, stamped in black upon cotton cloth; and holy olive-oil in tin cans.

Perhaps the most taking article of merchandise offered was dates from the palm-tree that St. Sabas planted. These dates have no seeds. There was something appropriate about this; childless monks, seedless dates. One could understand that. But these dates were bought by the pilgrims to carry to their wives who desire but have not sons. By what reasoning the monks have convinced them that fruitless dates will be a cause of fruitfulness, I do not know.

We paid our tribute, climbed up the stairways and out the grim gate into the highway, and had a glorious ride in the fresh morning air, the way enlivened by wild-flowers, blue sky, Bedaween, and troops of returning pilgrims, and finally ennobled by the sight of Jerusalem itself, conspicuous on its hill.

VII.

THE FAIR OF MOSES; THE ARMENIAN PATRIARCH.

THE Moslems believe that their religion superseded Judaism and Christianity, — Mohammed closing the culminating series of six great prophets, Adam, Noah, Abraham, Moses, Jesus, Mohammed, — and that they have a right to administer on the effects of both. They appropriate our sacred history and embellish it without the least scruple, assume exclusive right to our sacred places, and enroll in their own calendar all our notable heroes and saints.

On the 16th of April was inaugurated in Jerusalem the *fête* and fair of the Prophet Moses. The fair is held yearly at Neby Mûsa, a Moslem wely, in the wilderness of Judæa, some three or four hours from Jerusalem on a direct line to the Dead Sea. There Moses, according to the Moslem tradition, was buried, and thither the faithful resort in great crowds at this anniversary, and hold a four days' fair.

At midnight the air was humming with preparations; the whole city buzzed like a hive about to swarm. For many days pilgrims had been gathering for this festival, coming in on all the mountain roads, from Gath and Askalon, from Hebron, from Nablous and Jaffa, — pilgrims as zealous and as ragged as those that gather to the Holy Sepulchre and on the banks of the Jordan. In the early morning we heard the pounding of drums, the clash of cymbals, the squeaking of fifes, and an occasional gun, let off as it were by accident, — very much like the dawn of a Fourth of July at home. Processions were straggling about the streets, apparently lost, like ward-delegations in search of the beginning of St. Patrick's Day; a disorderly scramble of rags and color, a rabble hustling along without step or order, preceded usually by half a dozen enormous flags, green, red, yellow, and blue, embroidered with various devices and texts from the Koran, which hung lifeless on their staves, but grouped in mass made as lively a study of color as a bevy of sails of the Chioggia fishing-boats flocking into the port of Venice at sunrise. Before the banners walked the musicians, filling the narrow streets with a fearful uproar of rude drums and cymbals. These people seem to have inherited the musical talent of the ancient Jews, and to have the same passion for noise and discord.

As the procession would not move to the Tomb of Moses until afternoon, we devoted the morning to a visit to the Armenian Patriarch. Isaac, archbishop, and by the grace of God Patriarch of the Armenians of Jerusalem, occupant of the holy apostolic seat of St. James (the Armenian convent stands upon the traditional site of the martyrdom of St. James), claims to be the spiritual head of five millions of Armenians, in Turkey, Syria, Palestine, India, and Persia. By firman from the Sultan, the Copts and the Syrian and the Abyssinian Christians are in some sort under his jurisdiction, but the authority is merely nominal.

The reception-room of the convent is a handsome hall (for Jerusalem), extending over an archway of the street below and looking upon a garden. The walls are hung with engravings and lithographs, most of them portraits of contemporary sovereigns and princes of Europe, in whose august company the Patriarch seems to like to sun himself. We had not to wait long before he appeared and gave us a courteous and simple welcome. As soon as he learned that we were Americans, he said that he had something that he thought would interest us, and going to his table took out of the drawer an old number of an American periodical containing a portrait of an American publisher, which he set great store by. We congratulated him upon his possession of this treasure, and expressed our passionate fondness for this sort of thing, for we soon discovered the delight the Patriarch took in pictures and especially in portraits, and not least in photographs of himself in the full regalia of his sacred office. And with rea-

son, for he is probably the handsomest potentate in the world.
He is a tall, finely proportioned man of fifty years, and his
deportment exhibits that happy courtesy which is born of the love
of approbation and a kindly opinion of self.   He was clad in the
black cloak with the pointed hood of the convent, which made a
fine contrast to his long, full beard, turning white; his complexion is fair, white and red, and his eyes are remarkably pleasant and benignant.

The languages at the command of the Patriarch are two, the
Armenian and the Turkish, and we were obliged to communicate
with him through the medium of the latter, Abd-el-Atti acting as
interpreter.   How much Turkish our dragoman knew, and how
familiar his holiness is with it, we could not tell, but the conversation went on briskly, as it always does when Abd-el-Atti has
control of it.   When we had exhausted what the Patriarch knew
about America and what we knew about Armenia, which did not
take long (it was astonishing how few things in all this world of
things we knew in common), we directed the conversation upon
what we supposed would be congenial and common ground, the
dogma of the Trinity and the point of difference between the Armenian and the Latin church.   I cannot say that we acquired
much light on the subject, though probably we did better than
disputants usually do on this topic.   We had some signal advantages.   The questions and answers, strained through the Turkish
language, were robbed of all salient and noxious points, and
solved themselves without difficulty.   Thus, the "*Filioque* clause"
offered no subtle distinctions to the Moslem mind of Abd-el-Atti,
and he presented it to the Patriarch, I have no doubt, with perfect clarity.   At any rate, the reply was satisfactory : —

"His excellency, he much oblige, and him say he t'ink so."

The elucidation of this point was rendered the easier, probably,
by the fact that neither Abd-el-Atti nor the Patriarch nor ourselves knew much about it.   When I told his highness (if, through
Abd-el-Atti, I did tell him) that the great Armenian convent at
Venice, which holds with the Pope, accepts the Latin construction
of the clause, he seemed never to have heard of the great Armenian convent at Venice.   At this point of the conversation we

thought it wise to finish the subject by the trite remark that we believed a man's life was after all more important than his creed.

"So am I," responded the dragoman, and the Patriarch seemed to be of like mind.

A new turn was given to our interview by the arrival of refreshments, a succession of sweetmeats, cordials, candies, and coffee. The sweetmeats first served were a delicate preserve of plums. This was handed around in a jar, from which each guest dipped a spoonful, and swallowed it, drinking from a glass of water immediately,—exactly as we used to take medicine in childhood. The preserve was taken away when each person had tasted it, and shortly a delicious orange cordial was brought, and handed around with candy. Coffee followed. The Patriarch then led the way about his palace, and with some pride showed us the gold and silver insignia of his office and his rich vestments. On the wall of his study hung a curious map of the world, printed at Amsterdam in 1692, in Armenian characters. He was so kind also as to give us his photograph, enriched with his unreadable autograph, and a book printed at the convent, entitled *Deux Ans de Séjour en Abyssinie;* and we had the pleasure of seeing also the heroes and the author of the book,—two Armenian monks, who undertook, on an English suggestion, a mission to King Theodore, to intercede for the release of the English prisoners held by the tyrant of that land. They were detained by its treacherous and barbarous chiefs, robbed by people and priests alike, never reached the headquarters of the king, and were released only after two years of miserable captivity and suffering. This book is a faithful record of their journey, and contains a complete description of the religion and customs of the Abyssinians, set down with the candor and verbal nakedness of Herodotus. Whatever Christianity the Abyssinians may once have had, their religion now is an odd mixture of Judaism, fetichism, and Christian dogmas, and their morals a perfect reproduction of those in vogue just before the flood; there is no vice or disease of barbarism or of civilization that is not with them of universal acceptance. And the priest Timotheus, the writer of this narrative, gave the Abyssinians abiding in Jerusalem a character no better than that of their countrymen at home.

The Patriarch, with many expressions of civility, gave us into
the charge of a monk, who showed us all the parts of the convent
we had not seen on a previous visit. The convent is not only a
wealthy and clean, but also an enlightened establishment. Within
its precincts are nuns as well as monks, and good schools are maintained for children of both sexes. The school-house, with its
commodious apartments, was not unlike one of our buildings for
graded schools; in the rooms we saw many cases of antiquities
and curiosities from various countries, and specimens of minerals.
A map which hung on the wall, and was only one hundred years
old, showed the Red Sea flowing into the Dead Sea, and the river
Jordan emptying into the Mediterranean. Perhaps the scholars
learn ancient geography only.

At twelve the Moslems said prayers in the Mosque of Omar,
and at one o'clock the procession was ready to move out of St.
Stephen's Gate. We rode around to that entrance. The spectacle spread before us was marvellous. All the gray and ragged
slopes and ravines were gay with color and lively with movement.
The city walls on the side overlooking the Valley of Jehoshaphat
were covered with masses of people, clinging to them like bees;
so the defences may have appeared to Titus when he ordered the
assault from the opposite hill. The sunken road leading from St.
Stephen's Gate, down which the procession was to pass, was lined
with spectators, seated in ranks on ranks on the stony slopes.
These were mostly women, — this being one of the few days upon
which the Moslem women may freely come abroad, — clad in pure
white, and with white veils drawn about their heads. These
clouds of white robes were relieved here and there by flaming
spots of color, for the children and slaves accompanied the women,
and their dress added blue and red and yellow to the picture.
Men also mingled in the throng, displaying turbans of blue and
black and green and white. One could not say that any color or
nationality was wanting in the spectacle. Sprinkled in groups all
over the hillside, in the Moslem cemetery and beneath it, were
like groups of color, and streaks of it marked the descent of every
winding path. The Prince of Oldenburg, the only foreign digni-
tary present, had his tents pitched upon a knoll outside the gate,
and other tents dotted the roadside and the hill.

Crowds of people thronged both sides of the road to the Mount of Olives and to Gethsemane, spreading themselves in the valley and extending away up the road of the Triumphal Entry; everywhere were the most brilliant effects of white, red, yellow, gray, green, black, and striped raiment: no matter what these Orientals put on, it becomes picturesque, — old coffee-bags, old rags and carpets, anything. There could not be a finer place for a display' than these two opposing hillsides, the narrow valley, and the winding roads, which increased the apparent length of the procession and set it off to the best advantage. We were glad of the opportunity to see this ancient valley of bones revived in a manner to recall the pageants and shows of centuries ago, and as we rode down the sunken road in advance of the procession, we imagined how we might have felt if we had been mounted on horses or elephants instead of donkeys, and if we had been conquerors leading a triumph, and these people on either hand had been cheering us instead of jeering us. Turkish soldiers, stationed every thirty paces, kept the road clear for the expected cavalcade. In order to see it and the spectators to the best advantage, we took position on the opposite side of the valley and below the road around the Mount of Olives.

The procession was a good illustration of the shallow splendor of the Orient; it had no order, no uniformity, no organization; it dragged itself along at the whim of its separate squads. First came a guard of soldiers, then a little huddle of men of all sorts of colors and apparel, bearing several flags, among them the green Flag of Moses; after an interval another squad, bearing large and gorgeous flags, preceded by musicians beating drums and cymbals. In front of the drums danced, or rather hitched forward with stately steps, two shabby fellows, throwing their bodies from side to side and casting their arms about, clashing cymbals and smirking with infinite conceit. At long intervals came other like bands with flags and music, in such disorder as scarcely to be told from the spectators, except that they bore guns and pistols, which they continually fired into the air and close over the heads of the crowd, with a reckless profusion of powder and the most murderous appearance. To these followed mounted soldiers in

7   J

white, with a Turkish band of music, — worse than any military band in Italy; and after this the pasha, the governor of the city, a number of civil and military dignitaries and one or two high ulemas, and a green-clad representative of the Prophet, — a beggar on horseback, — on fiery horses which curveted about in the crowd, excited by the guns, the music, and the discharge of a cannon now and then, which was stationed at the gate of St. Stephen. Among the insignia displayed were two tall instruments of brass, which twirled and glittered in the sun, not like the golden candlestick of the Jews, nor the " host " of the Catholics, nor the sistrum of the ancient Egyptians, but, perhaps, as Moslemism is a reminiscence of all religions, a caricature of all three.

The crush in the narrow road round the hill and the grouping of all the gorgeous banners there produced a momentary fine effect ; but generally, save for the spectators, the display was cheap and childish. Only once did we see either soldiers or civilians marching in order ; there were five fellows in line carrying Nubian spears, and also five sappers and miners in line, wearing leathern aprons and bearing theatrical battle-axes. As to the arms, we could discover no two guns of the same pattern in all the multitude of guns ; like most things in the East, the demonstration was one of show, color, and noise, not to be examined too closely, but to be taken with faith, as we eat dates. A company of Sheridan's cavalry would have scattered the entire army.

The procession, having halted on the brow of the hill, countermarched and returned ; but the Flag of Moses and its guard went on to the camp, at his tomb, there to await the arrival of the pilgrims on the Monday following. And the most gorgeous Moslem demonstration of the year was over.

VIII.

DEPARTURE FROM JERUSALEM.

THE day came to leave Jerusalem. Circumstances rendered it impossible for us to make the overland trip to Damascus or even to Haifa. Our regret that we should not see Bethel, Shechem, Samaria, Nazareth, and the Sea of Galilee was somewhat lessened by the thought that we knew the general character of the country and the villages, by what we had already seen, and that experience had taught us the inevitable disenchantment of seeing the historical and the sacred places of Judæa. It is not that one visits a desert and a heap of ruins, — that would be endurable and even stimulating to the imagination; but every locality which is dear to the reader by some divine visitation, or wonderful by some achievement of hero or prophet, is degraded by the presence of sordid habitations, and a mixed, vicious, and unsavory population, or incrusted with the most puerile superstitions, so that the traveller is fain to content himself with a general view of the unchanged features of the country. It must be with a certain feeling of humiliation that at Nazareth, for instance, the object of his pilgrimage is belittled to the inspection of such inventions as the spot upon which the Virgin stood when she received the annunciation, and the carpenter-shop in which Joseph worked.

At any rate, we let such thoughts predominate, when we were obliged to relinquish the overland journey. And whatever we missed, I flatter myself that the readers of these desultory sketches will lose nothing. I should have indulged a certain curiosity in riding over a country as rich in memories as it is poor in aspect, but I should have been able to add nothing to the minute descrip-

tions and vivid pictures with which the Christian world is familiar; and, if the reader will excuse an additional personal remark,
I have not had the presumption to attempt a description of Palestine and Syria (which the volumes of Robinson and Thompson
and Porter have abundantly given), but only to make a record of
limited travel and observation.   What I most regretted was that
we could not see the green and fertile plain of Esdraelon, the
flower-spangled meadow of Jezreel, and the forests of Tabor and
Carmel, — seats of beauty and of verdure, and which, with the Plain
of Sharon, might serve to mitigate the picture of grim desolation
which the tourist carries away from the Holy Land.

Finally, it was with a feeling akin to regret that we looked our
last upon gray and melancholy Jerusalem.   We had grown a
little familiar with its few objects of past or present grandeur,
the Saracenic walls and towers, the Temple platform and its resplendent mosque, the agglomeration called the Church of the
Holy Sepulchre, the ruins of the palace and hospice of the Knights
of St. John, the massive convents and hospices of various nations
and sects that rise amid the indistinguishable huddle of wretched
habitations, threaded by filthy streets and noisome gutters.   And
yet we confessed to the inevitable fascination which is always ex-
ercised upon the mind by antiquity; the mysterious attraction of
association; the undefinable influence in decay and desolation
which holds while it repels; the empire, one might say the tyranny,
over the imagination and the will which an ancient city asserts, as
if by force of an immortal personality, compelling first curiosity,
then endurance, then sympathy, and finally love.   Jerusalem has
neither the art, the climate, the antiquities, nor the society which
draw the world and hold it captive in Rome, but its associations
enable it to exercise, in a degree, the same attraction.   Its attraction is in its historic spell and name, and in spite of the modern
city.

Jerusalem, in fact, is incrusted with layer upon layer of inventions, the product of credulity, cunning, and superstition, a monstrous growth always enlarging, so that already the simple facts
of history are buried almost beyond recognition beneath this mass
of rubbish.   Perhaps it would have been better for the growth of

Christianity in the world if Jerusalem had been abandoned, had become like Carthage and Memphis and Tadmor in the wilderness, and the modern pilgrim were free to choose his seat upon a fallen wall or mossy rock, and reconstruct for himself the pageant of the past, and recall that Living Presence, undisturbed by the impertinences which belittle the name of religion. It has always been held well that the place of the burial of Moses was unknown. It would perhaps have conduced to the purity of the Christian faith if no attempt had ever been made to break through the obscurity which rests upon the place of the sepulchre of Christ. Invention has grown upon invention, and we have the Jerusalem of to-day as a result of the exaggerated importance attached to the localization of the Divine manifestation. Whatever interest Jerusalem has for the antiquarian, or for the devout mind, it is undeniable that one must seek in other lands and among other peoples for the robust virtue, the hatred of shams and useless forms, the sweet charity, the invigorating principles, the high thinking, and the simple worship inculcated by the Founder of Christianity.

The horses were ready. Jerusalem had just begun to stir; an itinerant vender of coffee had set up his tray on the street, and was lustily calling to catch the attention of the early workmen, or the vagrants who pick themselves up from the doorsteps at dawn, and begin to reconnoitre for the necessary and cheap taste of coffee, with which the Oriental day opens; the sky was overcast, and a drop or two of rain fell as we were getting into the saddle, but " It is nothing," said the stirrup-holder, " it goes to be a beautiful time " ; and so it proved.

Scarcely were we outside the city when it cleared superbly, and we set forward on our long ride of thirty-six miles, to the sea-coast, in high spirits. We turned to catch the first sunlight upon the gray Tower of David, and then went gayly on over the cool free hills, inhaling the sparkling air and the perfume of wild-flowers, and exchanging greetings with the pilgrims, Moslem and Christian, who must have broken up their camps in the hills at the earliest light. There are all varieties of nationality and costume, and many of the peaceful pilgrims are armed as if going to a military rendezvous; perhaps our cavalcade, which is also an as-

sorted one of horses, donkeys, and mules, is as amusing as any
we meet.   I am certain that the horse that one of the ladies rides
is unique, a mere framework of bones which rattle as he agitates
himself; a rear view of the animal, and his twisting and interlacing legs, when he moves briskly, suggest a Chinese puzzle.

We halted at the outlet of Wady 'Aly, where there is an inn,
which has the appearance of a Den of Thieves, and took our
lunch upon some giant rocks under a fig-tree, the fruit of which
was already half grown.   Here I discovered another black calla,
and borrowed a pick of the landlord to endeavor to dig up its
bulb.   But it was impossible to extract it from the rocks, and
when I returned the tool, the owner demanded pay for the use of
it; I told him that if he would come to America, I would lend
him a pick, and let him dig all day in the garden, — a liberality
which he was unable to comprehend.

By four o'clock we were at Ramleh, and turned aside to inspect
the so-called Saracen tower; it stands upon one side of a large
enclosure of walls and arches, an extensive ruin; under ground
are vaulted constructions apparently extending as far as the ruins
above, reminding one of the remains of the Hospice of St. John
at Jerusalem.   In its form and treatment and feeling this noble
tower is Gothic, and, taking it in connection with the remains
about it, I should have said it was of Christian construction, in
spite of the Arabic inscription over one of the doorways, which
might have been added when the Saracens took possession of it;
but I believe that antiquarians have decided that the tower was
erected by Moslems.   These are the most "rural" ruins we had
seen in the East; they are time-stained and weather-colored, like
the remains of an English abbey, and stand in the midst of a
green and most lovely country; no sand, no nakedness, no beggars.   Grass fills all the enclosure, and grain-fields press close
about it.   No view could be more enchanting than that of the
tower and the rolling plain at that hour: the bloom on the wheat-
fields, flecked with flaming poppies; the silver of the olive
groves; the beds of scarlet anemones and yellow buttercups,
blotching the meadows with brilliant colors like a picture of
Turner; the soft gray hills of Judæa; the steeples and minarets

of the city. All Ramleh is built on and amid ruins, half-covered arches and vaults.

Twilight came upon us while we were yet in the interminable plain, but Jaffa announced itself by its orange-blossoms long before we entered its straggling suburbs; indeed, when we were three miles away, the odor of its gardens, weighted by the night-air, was too heavy to be agreeable. At a distance this odor was more perceptible than in the town itself; but next day, in the full heat of the sun, we found it so overpowering as to give a tendency to headache.

IX.

ALONG THE SYRIAN COAST.

OUR only business in Jaffa being to get away from it, we impatiently expected the arrival of the Austrian Lloyd steamer for Beyrout, the *Venus*, a fickle and unsteady craft, as its name implies. In the afternoon we got on board, taking note as we left the land of the great stones that jut out into the sea, " where the chains with which Andromeda was bound have left their footsteps, which attest [says Josephus] the antiquity of that fable." The *Venus*, which should have departed at three o'clock, lay rolling about amid the tossing and bobbing and crushing crowd of boats and barges till late in the evening, taking in boxes of oranges and bags of barley, by the slow process of hoisting up one or two at a time. The ship was lightly loaded with freight, but overrun with third-class passengers, returning pilgrims from Mecca and from Jerusalem (whom the waters of the Jordan seemed not to have benefited), who invaded every part of deck, cabin, and hold, and spreading their beds under the windows of the cabins of the first-class passengers, reduced the whole company to a common disgust. The light load caused the vessel to roll a little, and there was nothing agreeable in the situation.

The next morning we were in the harbor of Haifa, under the shadow of Mt. Carmel, and rose early to read about Elijah, and to bring as near to us as we could with an opera-glass the convent and the scene of Elijah's victory over the priests of Baal. The noble convent we saw, and the brow of Carmel, which the prophet ascended to pray for rain ; but the place of the miraculous sacrifice is on the other side, in view of the plain of Esdraelon, and

so is the plain by the river Kishon where Elijah slew the four
hundred and fifty prophets of Baal, whom he had already mocked
and defeated. The grotto of Elijah is shown in the hill, and the
monks who inhabit the convent regard themselves as the successors of an unbroken succession of holy occupants since the days
of the great prophet. Their sumptuous quarters would no doubt
excite the indignation of Elijah and Elisha, who would not properly discriminate between the modern reign of Mammon and the
ancient rule of Baal. Haifa itself is only a huddle of houses on
the beach. Ten miles across the curving bay we saw the battlements of Akka, on its triangle of land jutting into the sea, above
the mouth of Kishon, out of the fertile and world-renowned plain.
We see it more distinctly as we pass; and if we were to land we
should see little more, for few fragments remain to attest its many
masters and strange vicissitudes. A prosperous seat of the Phœnicians, it offered hospitality to the fat-loving tribe of Asher; it
was a Greek city of wealth and consequence; it was considered
the key of Palestine during the Crusades, and the headquarters
of the Templars and the Knights of St. John; and in more modern
times it had the credit of giving the checkmate to the feeble imitation of Alexander in the East attempted by Napoleon I.

The day was cloudy and a little cool, and not unpleasant; but
there existed all day a ground-swell which is full of all nastiness,
and a short sea which aggravated the ground-swell; and although
we sailed by the Lebanon mountains and along an historic coast,
bristling with suggestions, and with little but suggestions, of an
heroic past, by Akka and Tyre and Sidon, we were mostly indifferent to it all. The Mediterranean, on occasion, takes away one's
appetite even for ruins and ancient history.

We can distinguish, as we sail by it, the mean modern town
which wears still the royal purple name of Tyre, and the peninsula, formerly the island, upon which the old town stood and
which gave it its name. The Arabs still call it Tsur or Sur, "the
rock," and the ancients fancied that this island of rock had the
form of a ship and was typical of the maritime pursuits of its
people. Some have thought it more like the cradle of commerce
which Tyre is sometimes, though erroneously, said to be; for she

7 *

was only the daughter of Sidon, and did but inherit from her
mother the secret of the mastery of the seas. There were two
cities of Tyre, — the one on the island, and another on the shore.
Tyre is not an old city in the Eastern reckoning, the date of its
foundation as a great power only rising to about 1200 b. c.,
about the time of the Trojan war, and after the fall of Sidon,
although there was a city there a couple of centuries earlier, when
Joshua and his followers conquered the hill-countries of Palestine;
it could never in its days of greatness have been large, probably
containing not more than 30,000 to 40,000 inhabitants, but its
reputation was disproportionate to its magnitude; Joshua calls
it the "strong city Tyre," and it had the entire respect of Jerusalem in the most haughty days of the latter. Tyre seems to have
been included in the "inheritance" allotted to Asher, but that
luxurious son of Jacob yielded to the Phœnicians and not they to
him; indeed, the parcelling of territory to the Israelitish tribes,
on condition that they would conquer it, recalls the liberal dying
bequest made by a tender Virginian to his son, of one hundred
thousand dollars if he could make it. The sea-coast portion of
the Canaanites, or the Phœnicians, was never subdued by the Jews;
it preserved a fortunate independence, in order that, under the
Providence that protected the Phœnicians, after having given the
world "letters" and the first impulse of all the permanent civilization that written language implies, they could still bless it by
teaching it commerce, and that wide exchange of products which
is a practical brotherhood of man. The world was spared the calamity of the descent of the tribes of Israel upon the Phœnician
cities of the coast, and art was permitted to grow with industry;
unfortunately the tribes who formed the kingdom of Israel were
capable of imitating only the idolatrous worship and the sensuality of their more polished neighbors. Such an ascendency did
Tyre obtain in Jewish affairs through the princess Jezebel and
the reception of the priests of Baal, that for many years both Samaria and Jerusalem might almost be called dependencies of the
city of the god, "the lord Melkarth, Baal of Tyre."

The arts of the Phœnicians the Jews were not apt to learn; the
beautiful bronze-work of their temples was executed by Tyrians,

and their curious work in wood also; the secret of the famous purple dye of the royal stuffs which the Jews coveted was known only to the Tyrians, who extracted from a sea-mussel this dark red violet; when the Jews built, Tyrian workmen were necessary; when Solomon undertook his commercial ventures into the far Orient, it was Tyrians who built his ships at Ezion-geber, and it was Tyrian sailors who manned them; the Phœnicians carried the manufacture of glass to a perfection unknown to the ancient Egyptians, producing that beautiful ware the art of which was revived by the Venetians in the sixteenth century; the Jews did not learn from the Phœnicians, but the Greeks did, how to make that graceful pottery and to paint the vases which are the despair of modern imitators; the Tyrian mariners, following the Sidonian, supplied the Mediterranean countries, including Egypt, with tin for the manufacture of bronze, by adventurous voyages as far as Britain, and no people ever excelled them in the working of bronze, as none in their time equalled them in the carving of ivory, the engraving of precious metals, and the cutting and setting of jewels.

Unfortunately scarcely anything remains of the abundant literature of the Phœnicians, — for the Canaanites were a literary people before the invasion of Joshua; their language was Semitic, and almost identical with the Hebrew, although they were descendants of Ham; not only their light literature but their historical records have disappeared, and we have small knowledge of their kings or their great men. The one we are most familiar with is the shrewd and liberal Hiram (I cannot tell why he always reminds me of General Grant), who exchanged riddles with Solomon, and shared with the mountain king the profits of his maritime skill and experience. Hiram's tomb is still pointed out to the curious, at Tyre; and the mutations of religions and the freaks of fortune are illustrated by the chance that has grouped so closely together the graves of Hiram, of Frederick Barbarossa, and of Origen.

Late in the afternoon we came in sight of Sidon, that ancient city which the hand-book infers was famous at the time of the appearance of Joshua, since that skilful captain speaks of it as "Great Zidon." Famous it doubtless had been long before his arrival, but the epithet "great" merely distinguished the two cities; for Sidon was divided like Tyre, "Great Sidon" being on the shore and "Little Sidon" at some distance inland. Tradition says it was built by Sidon, the great-grandson of Noah; but however this may be, it is doubtless the oldest Phœnician city except Gebel, which is on the coast north of Beyrout. It is now for the antiquarian little more than a necropolis, and a heap of stones, on which fishermen dry their nets, although some nine to ten thousand people occupy its squalid houses. What we see of it is the ridge of rocks forming the shallow harbor, and the picturesque arched bridge (with which engravings have made us familiar) that connects a ruined fortress on a detached rock with the rocky peninsula.

Sidon carries us far back into antiquity. When the Canaanitish tribes migrated from their seat on the Persian Gulf, a part of them continued their march as far as Egypt. It seems to be settled that the Hittites (or Khitas) were the invaders who overran the land of the Pharaohs, sweeping away in their barbarous violence nearly all the monuments of the civilization of preceding eras, and placing upon the throne of that old empire the race of Shepherd kings. It was doubtless during the dynasty of the Shepherds that Abraham visited Egypt, and it was a Pharaoh of Hittite origin who made Joseph his minister. It was after the expulsion of the Shepherds and the establishment of a dynasty "which knew not Joseph" that the Israelites were oppressed.

But the Canaanites did not all pass beyond Syria and Palestine; some among them, who afterwards were distinctively known as Phœnicians, established a maritime kingdom, and founded among other cities that of Sidon. This maritime branch no doubt kept up an intercourse with the other portions of the Canaanite family in Southern Syria and in Egypt, before the one was driven out of Egypt by the revolution which restored the rule of the Egyptian Pharaohs, and the other expelled by the advent of the Philistines. And it seems altogether probable that the Phœnicians received from Egypt many arts which they afterwards improved and perfected. It is tolerably certain that they borrowed from Egypt the hieratic writing, or some of its characters, which taught them to represent the sounds of their language by the alphabet which they gave to the world.   The Sidonians were subjugated by Thotmes III., with all Phœnicia, and were for centuries the useful allies of the Egyptians; but their dominion was over the sea, and they spread their colonies first to the Grecian isles and then along the African coast; and in the other direction sent their venturesome barks as far as Colchis on the Black Sea. They seem to have thrived most under the Egyptian supremacy, for the Pharaohs had need of their sailors and their ships.   In the later days of the empire, in the reign of Necho, it was Phœnician sailors who, at his command, circumnavigated Africa, passing down the Red Sea and returning through the Pillars of Hercules.

The few remains of Sidon which we see to-day are only a few centuries old, — six or seven; there are no monuments to carry us back to the city famous in arts and arms, of which Homer sang; and if there were, the antiquity of this hoary coast would still elude us.   Herodotus says that the temple of Melkarth at Tyre (the "daughter of Sidon") was built about 2300 B. C.   Probably he errs by a couple of centuries; for it was only something like twenty-three centuries before Christ that the Canaanites came into Palestine, that is to say, late in the thirteenth Egyptian dynasty, — a dynasty which, according to the list of Manetho and Mariette Bey, is separated from the reign of the first Egyptian king by an interval of twenty-seven centuries.   When Abraham wandered from Mesopotamia into Palestine he found the Canaanites in possession.   But they were comparatively new comers; they had found the land already occupied by a numerous population who were so far advanced in civilization as to have built many cities. Among the peoples holding the land before them were the Rephaim, who had sixty strong towns in what is now the wilderness of Bashan; there were also the Emim, the Zamzummim, and the Anakim, — perhaps primitive races and perhaps conquerors of a people farther back in the twilight, remnants of whom still remained in Palestine when the Jews began, in their turn, to level its cities to the earth, and who lived in the Jewish traditions as "giants."

X.

BEYROUT. — OVER THE LEBANON.

ALL the afternoon we had the noble range of Mt. Lebanon in view, and towards five o'clock we saw the desert-like promontory upon which Beyrout stands. This bold headland, however, changed its appearance when we had rounded it and came into the harbor; instead of sloping sand we had a rocky coast, and rising from the bay a couple of hundred feet, Beyrout, first the shabby old city, and then the new portion higher up, with its villas embowered in trees. To the right, upon the cliffs overlooking the sea, is the American college, an institution whose conspicuous position is only a fair indication of its pre-eminent importance in the East; and it is to be regretted that it does not make a better architectural show. Behind Beyrout, in a vast circular sweep, rise the Lebanon mountains, clothed with trees and vineyards, terraced, and studded with villas and villages. The view is scarcely surpassed anywhere for luxuriance and variety. It seems to us that if we had an impulse to go on a mission anywhere it would be to the wicked of this fertile land.

At Beyrout also passengers must land in small boats. We were at once boarded by the most ruffianly gang of boatmen we had yet seen, who poured through the gangways and climbed over the sides of the vessel, like privileged pirates, treading down people in their way. It was only after a severe struggle that we reached our boats and landed at the custom-house, and fell into the hands of the legalized plunderers, who made an attack upon our baggage and demanded our passports, simply to obtain backsheesh for themselves.

"Not to show 'em passport," says Abd-el-Atti, who wastes no affection on the Turks; "tiefs, all of dem; you be six months, not so? in him dominion, come now from Jaffa; I tell him if the kin' of Constantinople want us, he find us at the hotel."

The hotel Bellevue, which looks upon the sea and hears always the waves dashing upon the worn and jagged rocks, was overflowed by one of those swarms, which are the nuisance of independent travellers, known as a "Cook's Party," excellent people individually no doubt, but monopolizing hotels and steamboats, and driving everybody else into obscurity by reason of their numbers and compact organization. We passed yesterday one of the places on the coast where Jonah is said to have left the whale; it is suspected — though without any contemporary authority — that he was in a Cook's Party of his day, and left it in disgust for this private conveyance.

Our first care in Beyrout was to secure our passage to Damascus. There is a carriage-road over the Lebanons, constructed, owned, and managed by a French company; it is the only road in Syria practicable for wheels, but it is one of the best in the world; I suppose we shall celebrate our second centennial before we have one to compare with it in the United States. The company has the monopoly of all the traffic over it, forwarding freight in its endless trains of wagons, and despatching a diligence each way daily, and a night mail. We went to the office to secure seats in the diligence.

"They are all taken," said the official.

"Then we would like seats for the day after to-morrow."

"They are taken, and for the day after that — for a week."

"Then we must go in a private carriage."

"At present we have none. The two belonging to the company are at Damascus."

"Then we will hire one in the city."

"That is not permitted; no private carriage is allowed to go over the road farther than five kilometres outside of Beyrout."

"So you will neither take us yourselves nor let any one else?"

"Pardon; when the carriage comes from Damascus, you shall have the first chance."

Fortunately one of the carriages arrived that night, and the next morning at nine o'clock we were *en route*. The diligence left at 4 A. M., and makes the trip in thirteen hours; we were to break the journey at Stoura and diverge to Ba'albek. The carriage was a short omnibus, with seats inside for four, a broad seat in front, and a deck for the baggage, painted a royal yellow; three horses were harnessed to it abreast,—one in the shafts and one on each side. As the horses were to be changed at short stages, we went forward at a swinging pace, rattling out of the city and commanding as much respect as if we had been the diligence itself with its six horses, three abreast, and all its haughty passengers.

We leave the promontory of Beyrout, dip into a long depression, and then begin to ascend the Lebanon. The road is hard, smooth, white; the soil on either side is red; the country is exceedingly rich; we pass villas, extensive plantations of figs, and great forests of the mulberry; for the silk culture is the chief industry, and small factories of the famous Syrian silks are scattered here and there. As the road winds upward, we find the hillsides are terraced and luxuriant with fig-trees and grapevines, — the latter flourishing, in fact, to the very top of the mountains, say 5,200 feet above the blue Mediterranean, which sparkles below us. Into these hills the people of Beyrout come to pass the heated months of summer, living in little villas which are embowered in foliage all along these lovely slopes. We encounter a new sort of house; it is one story high, built of limestone in square blocks and without mortar, having a flat roof covered with stones and soil, — a very primitive construction, but universal here. Sometimes the building is in two parts, like a double log-cabin, but the opening between the two is always arched : so much for art ; but otherwise the house, without windows, or with slits only, looks like a section of stone-wall.

As we rise, we begin to get glimpses of the snowy peaks which make a sharp contrast with the ravishing view behind us, — the terraced gorges, the profound ravines, the vineyards, gardens, and orchards, the blue sea, and the white road winding back through all like a ribbon. As we look down, the limestone walls of the terraces are concealed, and all the white cliffs are hidden by the ample verdure. Entering farther into the mountains, and ascending through the grim Wady Hammâna, we have the considerable village of that name below us on the left, lying at the bottom of a vast and ash-colored mountain basin, like a gray heap of cinders on the edge of a crater broken away at one side. We look at it with interest, for there Lamartine once lived for some months in as sentimental a seclusion as one could wish. A little higher up we come to snow, great drifts of it by the roadside, — a phenomenon entirely beyond the comprehension of Abdallah, who has never seen sand so cold as this, which, nevertheless, melts in his hands. After encountering the snow, we drive into a cold cloud, which seems much of the time to hang on the top of Lebanon, and have a touch of real winter, — a disagreeable experience which we had hoped to eliminate from this year; snow is only tolerable when seen at a great distance, as the background in a summer landscape; near at hand it congeals the human spirits.

When we were over the summit and had emerged from the thick cloud, suddenly a surprise greeted us. Opposite was the range of Anti-Lebanon; two thousand feet below us, the broad plain, which had not now the appearance of land, but of some painted scene, — a singularity which is partially explained by the red color of the soil. But, altogether, it presented the most bewildering mass of color; if the valley had been strewn with watered silks over a carpet of Persian rugs, the effect might have been the same. There were patches and strips of green and of brown, dashes of red, blotches of burnt-umber and sienna, alternations of ploughed field and young grain, and the whole, under the passing clouds, took the sheen of the opal. The hard, shining road lay down the mountain-side in long loops, in ox-bows, in curves ever graceful, like a long piece of white tape flung by chance from the summit to the valley. We dashed down it at a great speed, winding backwards and forwards on the mountain-side, and continually shifting our point of view of the glowing picture.

At the little post-station of Stoura we left the Damascus road and struck north for an hour towards Ba'albek, over a tolerable carriage-road. But the road ceased at Mu'allakah; beyond that,

K

a horseback journey of six or seven hours, there is a road-bed to Ba'albek, stoned a part of the way, and intended to be passable some day. Mu'allakah lies on the plain at the opening of the wild gorge of the Berdûny, a lively torrent which dances down to join the Litâny, through the verdure of fruit-trees and slender poplars. Over a mile up the glen, in the bosom of the mountains, is the town of Zahleh, the largest in the Lebanon; and there we purposed to pass the night, having been commended to the hospitality of the missionaries there by Dr. Jessup of Beyrout.

Our halted establishment drew a crowd of curious spectators about it, mostly women and children, who had probably never seen a carriage before; they examined us and commented upon us with perfect freedom, but that was the extent of their hospitality, not one of them was willing to earn a para by carrying our baggage to Zahleh; and we started up the hill, leaving the dragoman in an animated quarrel with the entire population, who, in turn, resented his comments upon their want of religion and good manners.

Climbing up a stony hill, threading gullies and ravines, and finally rough streets, we came into the amphitheatre in the hills which enclose Zahleh. The town is unique in its construction. Imagine innumerable small whitewashed wooden houses, rising in concentric circles, one above the other, on the slopes of the basin, like the chairs on the terraces of a Roman circus. The town is mostly new, for the Druses captured it and burned it in 1860, and reminds one of a New England factory village. Its situation is a stony, ragged basin, three thousand feet above the sea; the tops of the hills behind it were still covered with snow, and we could easily fancy that we were in Switzerland. The ten or twelve thousand inhabitants are nearly all Maronites, a sect of Christians whom we should call Greeks, but who are in communion with the Latin church; a people ignorant and superstitious, governed by their priests, occasionally turbulent, and always on the point of open rupture with the mysterious and subtle Druses. Having the name of Christians and few of the qualities, they are most unpromising subjects of missionary labor. Yet the mission here makes progress and converts, and we were glad to see that the American missionaries were universally respected.

Fortunately the American name and Christianity are exceedingly well represented in Northern Syria by gentlemen who unite a thorough and varied scholarship with Christian simplicity, energy, and enthusiasm. At first it seems hard that so much talent and culture should be hidden away in such a place as Zahleh, and we were inclined to lament a lot so far removed from the living sympathies of the world. It seems, indeed, almost hopeless to make any impression in this antique and conceited mass of superstition. But if Syria is to be regenerated, and to be ever the home of an industrious, clean, and moral people, in sympathy with the enlightened world, the change is to be made by exhibiting to the people a higher type of Christianity than they have known hitherto, — a Christianity that reforms manners, and betters the social condition, and adds a new interest to life by lifting it to a higher plane ; physical conditions must visibly improve under it. It is not enough in a village like this of Zahleh, for instance, to set up a new form of Christian worship, and let it drone on in a sleepy fashion, however devout and circumspect. It needs *men* of talent, scientific attainment, practical sagacity, who shall make the Christian name respected by superior qualities, as well as by devout lives. They must show a better style of living, more thrift and comfort, than that which prevails here. The people will by and by see a logical connection between a well-ordered house and garden, a farm scientifically cultivated, a prosperous factory, and the profitableness of honesty and industry, with the superior civilization of our Western Christianity. You can already see the influence in Syria of the accomplished scholars, skilful physicians and surgeons, men versed in the sciences, in botany and geology, who are able to understand the resources of the country, who are supported there, but not liberally enough supported, by the Christians of America.

XI.

BA'ALBEK.

WE were entertained at the house of the Rev. Mr. Wood, who accompanied us the next day to Ba'albek, his mission territory including that ancient seat of splendid paganism. Some sort of religious *fête* in the neighborhood had absorbed the best saddle-beasts, and we were indifferently mounted on the refuse of donkeys and horses, Abdallah, our most shining possession, riding, as usual, on the top of a pile of baggage. The inhabitants were very civil as we passed along; we did not know whether to attribute it to the influence of the missionaries or to the rarity of travellers, but the word " backsheesh " we heard not once in Zahleh.

After we had emerged from Mu'allakah upon the open plain, we passed on our left hand the Moslem village of Kerah Nun, which is distinguished as the burial-place of the prophet Noah; but we contented ourselves with a sight of the dome. The mariner lies there in a grave seventy feet long, or seventy yards, some scoffers say; but this, whatever it is, is not the measure of the patriarch. The grave proved too short, and Noah is buried with his knees bent, and his feet extending downward in the ground.

The plain of Bukâ'a is some ninety miles long, and in this portion of it about ten miles broad; it is well watered, and though the red soil is stuffed with small stones, it is very fertile, and would yield abundantly if cultivated; but it is mostly an abandoned waste of weeds. The ground rises gradually all the way to Ba'albek, starting from an elevation of three thousand feet;

the plain is rolling, and the streams which rush down from the near mountains are very swift. Nothing could be lovelier than the snowy ranges of mountains on either hand, in contrast with the browns and reds of the slopes, — like our own autumn foliage, — and the green and brown plain, now sprinkled with wild-flowers of many varieties.

The sky was covered with clouds, great masses floating about; the wind from the hills was cold, and at length drove us to our wraps; then a fine rain ensued, but it did not last long, for the rainy season was over. We crossed the plain diagonally, and lunched at a little khan, half house and half stable, raised above a stream, with a group of young poplars in front. We sat on a raised divan in the covered court, and looked out through the arched doorway over a lovely expanse of plain and hills. It was difficult to tell which part of the house was devoted to the stable and which to the family; from the door of the room which I selected as the neatest came the braying of a donkey. The landlord and his wife, a young woman and rather pretty, who had a baby in her arms, furnished pipes and tobacco, and the travellers or idlers — they are one — sat on the ground smoking narghilehs. A squad of ruffianly Metâwilch, a sect of Moslems who follow the Koran strictly, and reject the traditions, — perhaps like those who call themselves Bible Christians in distinction from theological Christians, — came from the field, deposited their ploughs, which they carried on their shoulders, on the platform outside, and, seating themselves in a row in the khan, looked at us stolidly. And we, having the opportunity of saying so, looked at them intelligently.

We went on obliquely across the plain, rising a little through a region rich, but only half cultivated, crossing streams and floundering in mud-holes for three hours, on a walk, the wind growing stronger from the snow mountains, and the cold becoming almost unendurable. It was in vain that Abd-el-Atti spun hour after hour an Arab romance; not even the warm colors of the Oriental imagination could soften the piteous blast. At length, when patience was nearly gone, in a depression in the plain, close to the foot-hills of Anti-Lebanon, behold the great

Ba'albek, that is to say, a Moslem village of three thousand to four thousand inhabitants, fairly clean and sightly, and the ruins just on the edge of it, the six well-known gigantic Corinthian pillars standing out against the gray sky. Never was sight more welcome.

Ba'albek, like Zahleh, has no inn, and we lodged in a private house near the ruins. The house was one story; it consisted of four large rooms in a row, looking upon the stone-wall enclosure, each with its door, and with no communication between them. The kitchen was in a separate building. These rooms had high ceilings of beams supporting the flat roof, windows with shutters but without glass, divans along one side, and in one corner a fire-place and chimney. Each room had a niche extending from the floor almost to the ceiling, in which the beds are piled in the day-time; at night they are made up on the divans or on the floor. This is the common pattern of a Syrian house, and when we got a fire blazing in the big chimney-place and began to thaw out our stiff limbs, and Abd-el-Atti brought in something from the kitchen that was hot and red in color and may have had spice on the top of it, we found this the most comfortable residence in the world.

It is the business of a dragoman to produce the improbable in impossible places. Abd-el-Atti rubbed his lamp and converted this establishment into a tolerable inn, with a prolific kitchen and an abundant table. While he was performing this revolution we went to see the ruins, the most noble portions of which have survived the religion and almost the memory of the builders.

The remains of the temples of Ba'albek, or Hieropolis, are only elevated as they stand upon an artificial platform; they are in the depression of the valley, and in fact a considerable stream flows all about the walls and penetrates the subterranean passages. This water comes from a fountain which bursts out of the Anti-Lebanon hills about half a mile above Ba'albek, in an immense volume, falls into a great basin, and flows away in a small river. These instantaneously born rivers are a peculiarity of Syria; and they often disappear as suddenly as they come. The water of this Ba'albek fountain is cold, pure, and sweet; it deserves to be called a "beverage," and is, so far as my experience goes, the most agreeable water in the world. The Moslems have a proverb which expresses its unique worth : " The water of Ba'albek never leaves its home." · It rushes past the village almost a river in size, and then disappears in the plain below as suddenly as it came to the light above.

We made our way across the stream and along aqueducts and over heaps of shattered walls and columns to the west end of the group of ruins. This end is defended by a battlemented wall some fifty feet high, which was built by the Saracens out of incongruous materials from older constructions. The northeast corner of this new wall rests upon the ancient Phœnician wall, which sustained the original platform of the sacred buildings ; and at this corner are found the three famous stones which at one time gave a name, " The Three-Stoned," to the great temple. As I do not intend to enter into the details of these often described ruins, I will say here, that this ancient Phœnician wall appears on the north side of the platform detached, showing that the most ancient temple occupied a larger area than the Greek and Roman buildings.

There are many stones in the old platform wall which are thirty feet long ; but the three large ones, which are elevated twenty feet above the ground, and are in a line, are respectively 64 feet long, 63 feet 8 inches, and 63 feet, and about 13 feet in height and in depth. When I measured the first stone, I made ʾit 128 feet long, which I knew was an error, but it was only by careful inspection that I discovered the joint of the two stones which I had taken for one. I thought this a practical test of the close fit of these blocks, which, laid without mortar, come together as if the ends had been polished. A stone larger than either of these lies in the neighboring quarry, hewn out but not detached.

These massive constructions, when first rediscovered, were the subject of a great deal of wonder and speculation, and were referred to a remote and misty if not fabulous period. I believe it is now agreed that they were the work of the Phœnicians, or Canaanites, and that they are to be referred to a period subsequent to the conquest of Egypt, or at least of the Delta of Egypt, by the Hittites, when the Egyptian influence was felt in Syria ; and that this Temple of the Sun was at least suggested, as well as the worship of the Sun god here, by the Temple of the Sun at Heliopolis on the Nile. There is, to be sure, no record of the great city of Ba'albek, but it may safely be referred to the period of the greatest prosperity of the Phœnician nation.

Much as we had read of the splendor of these ruins, and familiar as we were with photographs of them, we were struck with surprise when we climbed up into the great court, that is, to the platform of the temples. The platform extends over eight hundred feet from east to west, an elevated theatre for the display of some of the richest architecture in the world. The general view is broad, impressive, inspiring beyond anything else in Egypt or Syria; and when we look at details, the ruins charm us with their beauty. Round three sides of the great court runs a wall, the interior of which, recessed and niched, was once adorned with the most elaborate carving in designs more graceful than you would suppose stone could lend itself to, with a frieze of garlands of vines, flowers, and fruits. Of the so-called great Temple of Baal at the west end of the platform, only six splendid Corinthian columns remain. The so-called Temple of the Sun or Jupiter, to the south of the other and on a lower level, larger than the Parthenon, exists still in nearly its original form, although some of the exterior columns have fallen, and time and the art-hating Moslems have defaced some of its finest sculpture. The ceiling between the outer row of columns and the wall of this temple is, or was, one of the most exquisite pieces of stone-carving ever executed; the figures carved in the medallions seem to have anticipated the Gothic genius, and the exquisite patterns in stone to have suggested the subsequent Saracenic invention. The composite capitals of the columns offer an endless study; stone roses stand out upon their stems, fruit and flowers hang and bloom in the freedom of nature; the carving is all bold and spirited, and the invention endless. This is no doubt work of the Roman period after the Christian era, but it is pervaded by Greek feeling, and would seem to have been executed by Greek artists.

In the centre of the great court (there is a small six-sided court to the east of the larger one, which was once approached by a great flight of steps from below) are remains of a Christian basilica, referred to the reign of Theodosius. Underneath the platform are enormous vaults, which may have served the successive occupants for store-houses. The Saracens converted this position into a fortress, and this military impress the ruins still bear. We have therefore four ages in these ruins : the Phœnician, the Greek and Roman, the Christian, and the Saracenic. The remains of the first are most enduring. The old builders had no other method of perpetuating their memory except by these cyclopean constructions.

We saw the sunset on Ba'albek. The clouds broke away and lay in great rosy masses over Lebanon ; the white snow ridge for forty miles sparkled under them. The peak of Lebanon, over ten thousand feet above us, was revealed in all its purity. There was a red light on the columns and on the walls, and the hills of Anti-Lebanon, red as a dull garnet, were speckled with snow patches. The imagination could conceive nothing more beautiful than the rose-color of the ruins, the flaming sky, and the immaculate snow peaks, apparently so close to us.

On our return we stopped at the beautiful circular temple of Venus, which would be a wonder in any other neighborhood. Dinner awaited us, and was marked by only one novelty, — what we at first took to be brown napkins, fantastically folded and laid at each plate, a touch of elegance for which we were not prepared. But the napkins proved to be bread. It is made of coarse dark wheat, baked in circular cakes as thin as brown paper, and when folded its resemblance to a napkin is complete. We found it tolerably palatable, if one could get rid of the notion that he was eating a limp rag. The people had been advertised of our arrival, and men, women, and boys swarmed about us to sell copper coins ; most of them Roman, which they find in the ruins. Few are found of the Greeks ; the Romans literally sowed the ground with copper money wherever they went in the Orient. The inhabitants are Moslems, and rather decent in appearance, and the women incline to good looks, though not so modest in dress as Moslem women usually are ; they are all per-

8

sistent beggars, and bring babies in their arms, borrowing for
that purpose all the infants in the neighborhood, to incite us to
charity.

We yielded to the average sentiment of Christendom, and
sallied out in the cold night to see the ruins under the light of
a full moon; one of the party going simply that he might avoid
the reproach of other travellers, — "It is a pity you did not see
Ba'albek by moonlight." And it must be confessed that these
ruins stand the dim light of the moon better than most ruins;
they are so broad and distinct that they show themselves even in
this disadvantage, which those of Karnak do not. The six isolated columns seemed to float in the sky; between them snowy
Lebanon showed itself.

The next morning was clear and sparkling; the sky was almost
as blue as it is in Nubia. We were awakened by the drumming
of a Moslem procession. It was the great annual *fête* day, upon
which was to be performed the miracle of riding over the bodies
of the devout. The ceremony took place a couple of miles away
upon the hill, and we saw on all the paths leading thither files of
men and women in white garments. The sheykh, mounted on
horseback, rides over the prostrate bodies of all who throw themselves before him, and the number includes young men as well as
darwishes. As they lie packed close together and the horse treads
upon their spinal columns, their escape from death is called miraculous. The Christians tried the experiment here a year or two
ago, several young fellows submitting to let a horseman trample
over them, in order to show the Moslems that they also possessed
a religion which could stand horses' hoofs.

The ruins, under the intense blue sky, and in the splendid sunlight, were more impressive than in the dull gray of the day
before, or even in the rosy sunset; their imperial dignity is not
impaired by the excessive wealth of ornamentation. When upon
this platform there stood fifty-eight of these noble columns, instead of six, conspicuous from afar, and the sunlight poured into
this superb court, adorned by the genius of Athens and the wealth
of Rome, this must have been one of the most resplendent temples in existence, rivalling the group upon the Acropolis itself

Nothing more marks the contrast between the religions of the Greeks and Romans and of the Egyptians, or rather between the genius of the two civilizations, than their treatment of sacred edifices. And it is all the more to be noted, because the more modern nations accepted without reserve any god or object of veneration or mystery in the Egyptian pantheon. The Roman occupants of the temple of Philæ sacrificed without scruple upon the altars of Osiris, and the voluptuous Græco-Romans of Pompeii built a temple to Isis. Yet always and everywhere the Grecians and the Romans sought conspicuous situations for the temples of the gods; they felt, as did our Pilgrim Fathers, who planted their meeting-houses on the windiest hills of New England, that the deity was most honored when the house of his worship was most visible to men; but the Egyptians, on the contrary, buried the magnificence of their temples within wall around wall, and permitted not a hint of their splendor to the world outside. It is worth while to notice also that the Assyrians did not share the contemporary reticence of the Egyptians, but built their altars and temples high above the plain in pyramidal stages; and if we may judge by this platform at Ba'albek, the Phœnicians did not imitate the exclusive spirit of the Pharaonic worshippers.

We lingered, called again and again by the impatient dragoman, in this fascinating spot, amid the visible monuments of so many great races, bearing the marks of so many religious revolutions, and turned away with slow and reluctant steps, as those who abandon an illusion or have not yet thought out some suggestion of the imagination. We turned also with reluctance from a real illusion of the senses. In the clear atmosphere the ridge of Lebanon was startlingly near to us; the snow summit appeared to overhang Ba'albek as Vesuvius does Pompeii; and yet it is half a day's journey across the plain to the base of the mountain, and a whole day's journey from these ruins to the summit. But although this illusion of distance did not continue as we rode down the valley, we had on either hand the snow ranges all day, making by contrast with the brilliant colors of the plain a lovely picture.

XII.

ON THE ROAD TO DAMASCUS.

THE station at Stoura is a big stable and a dirty little inn,
which has the kitchen in one shanty, the dining-room in
another, and the beds in a third ; a swift mountain stream runs
behind it, and a grove of poplars on the banks moans and rustles
in the wind that draws down the Lebanon gorge. It was after
dark when we arrived, but whether our coming put the establishment into a fluster, I doubt; it seems to be in a chronic state of
excitement. The inn was kept by Italians, who have a genius for
this sort of hotel; the landlord was Andrea, but I suspect the
real authority resided in his plump, bright, vivacious wife. They
had an heir, however, a boy of eight, who proved to be the tyrant
of the house when he appeared upon the scene. The servants
were a tall slender Syrian girl, an active and irresponsible boy,
and a dark-eyed little maid, in the limp and dirty single garment
which orphans always wear on the stage, and who in fact was an
orphan, and appeared to take the full benefit of her neglected
and jolly life. The whole establishment was on a lark, and in a
perpetual giggle, and communicated its overflowing good-humor
even to tired travellers. The well-favored little wife, who exhibited the extremes of fortune in a diamond ring and a torn and
draggled calico gown, sputtered alternately French and Italian
like a magpie, laughed with a contagious merriment, and actually
made the cheerless accommodations she offered us appear desir-
able. The whole family waited on us, or rather kept us waiting
on them, at table, bringing us a dish now and then as if its pro-
duction were a joke, talking all the while among themselves in

Arabic, and apparently about us, and laughing at their own observations, until we, even, came to conceive ourselves as a party· in a most comical light; and so amusing did we grow that the slim girl and the sorry orphan were forced to rush into a corner every few minutes and laugh it out.

I spent a pleasant hour in the kitchen, — an isolated, smoke-dried room with an earth floor, — endeavoring to warm my feet at the little fires of charcoal kindled in holes on top of a bank of earth and stone, and watching the pranks of this merry and industrious family. The little heir amused himself by pounding the orphan, kicking the shins of the boy, and dashing water in the face of the slim girl, — treatment which the servants dared not resent, since the father laughed over it as an exhibition of bravery and vivacity. Fragrant steam came from a pot, in which quail were stewing for the passengers by the night mail, and each person who appeared in the kitchen, in turn, gave this pot a stir; the lively boy pounded coffee in a big mortar, put charcoal on the fire, had a tussle with the heir, threw a handspring, doing nothing a min-ute at a time; the orphan slid in with a bucket of water, slop-ping it in all directions; the heir set up a howl and kicked his father because he was not allowed to kick the orphan any more; the little wife came in like a breeze, whisking everybody one side, and sympathized with dear little Robby, whose cruel and ugly papa was holding the love from barking his father's shins. You do not often see a family that enjoys itself so much as this.

It was late next morning when we tore ourselves from this en-chanting household, and went at a good pace over the fertile plain, straight towards Anti-Lebanon, having a glimpse of the snow of Mount Hermon, — a long ridge peering over the hills to the southeast, and crossing in turn the Litâny and the deep Anjar, which bursts forth from a single fountain about a mile to the north. On our left we saw some remains of what was once a capital city, Chalcis, of unknown origin, but an old city before it was possessed by the Ptolemies, or by Mark Antony, and once the luxurious residence of the Herod family. At Medjel, a vil-lage scattered at the foot of small *tells* rising in the plain, we turned into the hills, leaving unvisited a conspicuous Roman tem-

ple on a peak above the town.   The road winds gradually up a
wady.   As we left the plain, and looked back across it to Lebanon, the colors of Bukâ'a and the mountain gave us a new surprise ; they were brilliant and yet soft, as gay and splendid as the
rocks of the Yellowstone, and yet exquisitely blended as in a Persian rug.

The hill-country was almost uninhabited ; except the stations
and an occasional Bedaween camp there was small sign of occupation ; the ground was uncultivated ; peasants in rags were grub-
bing up the roots of cedars for fuel.   We met Druses with trains
of mules, Moslems with camels and mules, and long processions of
white-topped wagons, — like the Western " prairie schooner " —
drawn each by three mules tandem.   Thirty and forty of these
freight vehicles travel in company, and we were continually meeting or passing them ; their number is an indication of the large trade
that Damascus has with Beyrout and the Mediterranean.   There
is plenty of color in the people and in their costume.   We were
told that we could distinguish the Druses by their furtive and bad
countenances ; but for this information I should not have seen that
they differed much from the Maronites ; but I endeavored to see the
treacherous villain in them.   I have noticed in Syria that the Catholic travellers have a good opinion of the Maronites and hate the
Druses, that the American residents think little of the Maronites,
and that the English have a lenient side for the Druses.   The
Moslems consistently despise all of them.   The Druse has been a
puzzle.   There are the same horrible stories current about him
that were believed of the early Christians ; the Moslem believes
that infants are slain and eaten in his midnight assemblies, and
that once a year the Druse community meets in a cavern at midnight, the lights are extinguished, and the sexes mingling by
chance in the license of darkness choose companions for the
year.   But the Druse creed, long a secret, is now known ; they
are the disciples of Hâkim, a Khalif of the Fatimite dynasty ;
they believe in the unity of God and his latest manifestation in
Hâkim ; they are as much a political as a religious society ; they
are accomplished hypocrites, cunning in plotting and bold in
action ; they profess to possess " the truth," and having this, they

are indifferent to externals, and are willing to be Moslems with the Moslems and Christians with the Christians, while inwardly feeling a contempt for both. They are the most supercilious of all the Eastern sects. What they are about to do is always the subject of anxiety in the Lebanon regions.

At the stations of the road we found usually a wretched family or two dwelling in a shanty, half stable and half *café*, always a woman with a baby in her arms, and the superabundant fountains for nourishing it displayed to all the world; generally some slatternly girls, and groups of rough muleteers and drivers smoking. At one, I remember a Jew who sold antique gems, rings, and coins, with a shocking face, which not only suggested the first fall of his race, but all the advantages he has since taken of his innocent fellows, by reason of his preoccupation of his position of knowledge and depravity.

We made always, except in the steep ascents, about ten miles an hour. The management of the route is the perfection of French system and bureaucracy. We travel with a way-bill of numbered details, as if we were a royal mail. At every station we change one horse, so that we always have a fresh animal. The way-bill is at every station signed by the agent, and the minute of arrival and departure exactly noted; each horse has its number, and the number of the one taken and the one left is entered. All is life and promptness at the stations; changes are quickly made. The way-bill would show the company the exact time between stations; but I noticed that our driver continually set his watch backwards and forwards, and I found that he and the dragoman had a private understanding to conceal our delays for lunch, for traffic with Jews, or for the enjoyment of scenery.

After we had crossed the summit of the first ridge we dashed down the gate of a magnificent cañon, the rocks heaved up in perpendicular strata, overhanging, craggy, crumbled, wild. We crossed then a dreary and nearly arid basin; climbed, by curves and zigzags, another ridge, and then went rapidly down until we struck the wild and narrow gorge of the sacred Abana. Immediately luxuriant vegetable life began. The air was sweet with the blossoms of the mish-mish (apricot), and splendid walnuts and poplars overshadowed us. The river, swollen and rushing amid the trees on its banks, was frightfully rapid. The valley winds sharply, and gives room only for the river and the road, and sometimes only for one of them. Sometimes the river is taken out of its bed and carried along one bank or the other; sometimes the road crosses it, and again pursues its way between its divided streams. We were excited by its rush and volume, and by the rich vegetation along its sides. We came to fantastic Saracenic country-seats, to arcaded and latticed houses set high up over the river, to evidences of wealth and of proximity to a great city.

Suddenly, for we seemed to have become a part of the rushing torrent and to share its rapidity, we burst out of the gorge, and saw the river, overpassing its narrow banks, flowing straight on before us, and beyond, on a level, the minarets and domes of Damascus! All along the river, on both banks of it, and along the high wall by the roadside, were crowds of men in Turkish costume, of women in pure white, of Arabs sitting quietly by the stream smoking the narghileh, squatting in rows along the wall and along the water, all pulling at the water-pipe. There were tents and booths erected by the river. In a further reach of it men and boys were bathing. Ranks and groups of veiled women and children crouched on the damp soil close to the flood, or sat immovable on some sandy point. It is a delicious holiday for two or three women to sit the livelong day by water, running or stagnant, to sit there with their veils drawn over their heads, as rooted as water-plants, and as inanimate as bags of flour. It was a striking Oriental picture, played on by the sun, enlivened by the swift current, which dashes full into the city.

As we spun on, the crowd thickened, — soldiers, grave Turks on caparisoned horses or white donkeys, Jews, blacks, Persians. We crossed a trembling bridge, and rattled into town over stony pavements, forced our way with difficulty into streets narrow and broken by sharp turns, the carriage-wheels scarcely missing men and children stretched on the ground, who refused, on the theory of their occupation of the soil prior to the invention of wheels, to draw in even a leg; and, in a confused whirl of novel sights and discordant yells, barks, and objurgations, we came to Dimitri's hotel. The carriage stopped in the narrow street; a small door in the wall, a couple of feet above the pavement, opened, and we stepped through into a little court occupied by a fountain and an orange-tree loaded with golden fruit. Thence we passed into a large court, the centre of the hotel, where the Abana pours a generous supply into a vast marble basin, and trees and shrubs offer shelter to singing birds. About us was a wilderness of balconies, staircases, and corridors, the sun flooding it all; and Dimitri himself, sleek, hospitable, stood bowing, in a red fez, silk gown, and long gold chain.

8 *   L

XIII.

THE OLDEST OF CITIES.

IT is a popular opinion that there is nothing of man's work older than Damascus; there is certainly nothing newer. The city preserves its personal identity as a man keeps his from youth to age, through the constant change of substance. The man has in his body not an atom of the boy; but if the boy incurred scars, they are perpetuated in the man. Damascus has some scars. We say of other ancient cities, " This part is old, that part is new." We say of Damascus, its life is that of a tree, decayed at heart, dropping branches, casting leaves, but always renewing itself.

How old is Damascus? Or, rather, how long has a city of that name existed here on the banks of the Abana? According to Jewish tradition, which we have no reason to doubt, it was founded by Uz, the son of Aram, the son of Shem. By the same tradition it was a great city when a remarkable man, of the tenth generation from the Deluge, — a person of great sagacity, not mistaken in his opinions, skilful in the celestial science, compelled to leave Chaldea when he was seventy-five years old, on account of his religious opinions, since he ventured to publish the notion that there was but one God, the Creator of the Universe, — came with an army of dependants and " reigned " in the city of Uz. After some time Abraham removed into Canaan, which was already occupied by the Canaanites, who had come from the Persian Gulf, established themselves in wall-towns in the hills, built Sidon on the coast, and carried their conquests into Egypt. It was doubtless during the reign of the Hittites, or

Shepherd Kings, that Abraham visited Egypt. Those usurpers occupied the throne of the Pharaohs for something like five hundred years, and it was during their occupancy that the Jews settled in the Delta.

Now, if we can at all fix the date of the reign of the Shepherd Kings, we can approximate to the date of the foundation of Damascus, for Uz was the third generation from Noah, and Abraham was the tenth. We do not know how to reckon a generation in those days, when a life-lease was such a valuable estate, but if we should assume it to be a century, we should have about seven hundred years between the foundation of Damascus and the visit of Abraham to Egypt, a very liberal margin. But by the chronology of Mariette Bey, the approximate date of the Shepherds' invasion is 2300 B. C. to 2200 B. C., and somewhat later than that time Abraham was in Damascus. If Damascus was then seven hundred years old, the date of its foundation would be about 3000 B. C. to 2900 B. C.

Assuming that Damascus has this positive old age, how old is it comparatively? When we regard it in this light, we are obliged to confess that it is a modern city. When Uz and his friends wandered out of the prolific East, and pitched their tents by the Abana, there was already on the banks of the Nile a civilized, polished race, which had nearly completed a cycle of national existence much longer than the duration of the Roman Empire. It was about the eleventh dynasty of the Egyptian kingdom, the Great Pyramid had been built more than a thousand years, and the already degenerate Egyptians of the " Old Empire " had forgotten the noble art which adorned and still renders illustrious the reigns of the pyramid-builders.

But if Damascus cannot claim the highest antiquity, it has outlived all its rivals on the earth, and has flourished in a freshness as perennial as the fountain to which it owes its life, through all the revolutions of the Orient. As a necessary commercial capital it has pursued a pretty uniform tenor under all its various masters. Tiglath-Pileser attempted to destroy it; it was a Babylonian and then a Persian satrapy for centuries; it was a Greek city; it was the capital of a Roman province for seven hundred years;

it was a Christian city and reared a great temple to John the Baptist; it was the capital of the Saracenic Empire, in which resided
the ruler who gave laws to all the lands from India to Spain; it
was ravaged by Tamerlane; it now suffers the blight of Turkish
imbecility. From of old it was a caravan station and a mart of
exchange, a camp by a stream; it is to-day a commercial hive,
swarming with an hundred and fifty thousand people, a city without monuments of its past or ambition for its future.

If one could see Damascus, perhaps he could invent a phrase
that would describe it; but when you have groped and stumbled
about in it for a couple of weeks, endeavoring in vain to get a
view of more than a few rods of it at a time, you are utterly at a
loss how to convey an impression of it to others.

If Egypt is the gift of the Nile, the river Abana is the life of
Damascus; its water is carried into the city on a dozen different
levels, making it literally one of fountains and running water.
Sometimes the town is flooded; the water had only just subsided
from the hotel when we arrived. This inundation makes the city
damp for a long time. Indeed, it is at all times rather soaked
with water, and is — with all respect to Uz and Abraham and the
dynasty of the Omeiyades — a sort of habitable frog-pond on a
grand scale. At night the noise of frogs, even at our hotel, is the
chief music, the gentle twilight song, broken, it is true, by the
incessant howling and yelping of savage dogs, packs of which
roam the city like wolves all night. They are mangy yellow curs,
without a single good quality, except that they sleep all the day-
time. In every quarter of the city you see ranks and rows of
them asleep in the sun, occupying half the street and nestling in
all the heaps of rubbish. But much as has been said of the dogs
here, I think the frogs are the feature of the town; they are as
numerous as in the marshes of Ravenna.

Still the water could not be spared. It gives sparkle, life, verdure. In walking you constantly get glimpses through heavy
doorways of fountains, marble tanks of running water, of a
blooming tree or a rose-trellis in a marble court, of a garden of
flowers. The crooked, twisted, narrow streets, mere lanes of mud-
walls, would be scarcely endurable but for these occasional

glimpses, and the sight now and then of the paved, pillared court of a gayly painted mosque.

One ought not to complain when the Arab barber who trims his hair gives him a narghileh to smoke during the operation; but Damascus is not so Oriental as Cairo, the predominant Turkish element is not so picturesque as the Egyptian. And this must be said in the face of the universal use of the narghileh, which more than any other one thing imparts an Oriental, luxurious tone to the city. The pipe of Egypt is the chibouk, a stem of cherry five feet long with a small clay bowl; however richly it may be ornamented, furnished with a costly amber mouthpiece, wound with wire of gold, and studded, as it often is, with diamonds and other stones of price, it is, at the best, a stiff affair; and even this pipe is more and more displaced by the cigar, just as in Germany the meerschaum has yielded to the cigar as the Germans have become accessible to foreign influences. But in Damascus the picturesque narghileh, encourager of idleness, is still the universal medium of smoke. The management of the narghileh requires that a person should give his undivided mind to it; in return for that, it gives him peace. The simplest narghileh is a cocoanut-shell, with a flexible stem attached, and an open metal bowl on top for the tobacco. The smoke is drawn through the water which the shell contains. Other narghilehs have a glass standard and water-bowl, and a flexible stem two or three yards in length. The smoker, seated cross-legged before this graceful object, appears to be worshipping his idol. The mild Persian tobacco is kept alight by a slowly burning piece of dried refuse which is kindly furnished by the camel for fuel; and the smoke is inhaled into the lungs, and slowly expelled from the nostrils and the mouth. Although the hastily rolled cigarette is the resort of the poor in Egypt, and is somewhat used here, it must be a very abandoned wretch who cannot afford a pull at a narghileh in Damascus. Its universality must excuse the long paragraph I have devoted to this pipe. You see men smoking it in all the cafés, in all the shops, by the roadside, seated in the streets, in every garden, and on the house-tops. The visible occupation of Damascus is sucking this pipe.

Our first walk in the city was on Sunday to the church of the Presbyterian mission; on our way we threaded a wilderness of bazaars, nearly all of them roofed over, most of them sombre and gloomy. Only in the glaring heat of summer could they be agreeable places of refuge. The roofing of these tortuous streets and lanes is not so much to exclude the sun, I imagine, as to keep out the snow, and the roofs are consequently substantial ; for Damascus has an experience of winter, being twenty-two hundred feet above the sea-level, nearly as high as Jerusalem. These bazaars, so much vaunted all through the Orient, disappointed us, not in extent, for they are interminable, but in wanting the picturesqueness, oddity, and richness of those of Cairo. And this, like the general appearance of the city, is a disappointment hard to be borne, for we have been taught to believe that Damascus is a Paradise on earth, and that here, if anywhere, we should come into that region of enchantment which the poets of the Arabian Nights' tales have imposed upon us as the actual Orient. Should we have recognized, in the low and partially flooded strip of grass-land through which we drove from the mouth of the Abana gorge to the western gate of the city, the green *Merj* of the Arabian poets, that gem of the earth? The fame of it has gone abroad throughout the world, as if it were a unique gift of Allah to his favorites. Why, every Occidental land has a million glades, watered, green-sodded, tree-embowered, more lovely than this, that no poet has thought it worth while to celebrate.

We found a little handful of worshippers at the mission church, and among them — Heaven forgive us for looking at her on Sunday ! — an eccentric and somewhat notorious English lady of title, who shares the bed and board of an Arab sheykh in his harem outside the walls. It makes me blush for the attractiveness of my own country, and the slighted fascination of the noble red man in his paint and shoddy blanket, when I see a lady, sated with the tame civilization of England, throw herself into the arms of one of these coarse bigamists of the desert. Has he no reputation in the Mother country, our noble, chivalrous Walk-Under-the-Ground ?

We saw something of the missionaries of Damascus, but as I

was not of the established religion at the court of Washington at
the time of my departure from home, and had no commission to
report to the government, either upon the condition of consulates
or of religion abroad, I am not prepared to remark much upon
the state of either in this city. I should say, however, that not
many direct converts were made either from Moslemism or from
other Christian beliefs, but that incalculable good is accomplished
by the schools which the missionaries conduct. The influence
of these, in encouraging a disposition to read, and to inquire into
the truth and into the conditions of a better civilization, is not
to be overestimated. What impressed me most, however, in the
fortune of these able, faithful servants of the propagandism of
Christian civilization, was their pathetic isolation. A gentleman
and his wife of this mission had been thirty years absent from
the United States. The friends who cheered or regretted their
departure, who cried over them, and prayed over them, and followed them with tender messages, had passed away, or become
so much absorbed in the ever-exciting life at home as to have
almost forgotten those who had gone away to the heathen a
generation ago. The Mission Board that personally knew them
and lovingly cared for them is now composed of strangers to
them. They were, in fact, expatriated, lost sight of. And yet
they had gained no country nor any sympathies to supply the
place of those lost. They must always be, to a great degree,
strangers in this fierce, barbarous city.

We wandered down through the Christian quarter of the town:
few shops are here; we were most of the time walking between
mud-walls, which have a door now and then. This quarter is
new; it was entirely burned by the Moslems and Druses in 1860,
when no less than twenty-five hundred adult male Christians,
heads of families, were slaughtered, and thousands more perished
of wounds and famine consequent upon the total destruction of
their property. That the Druses were incited to this persecution
by the Turkish rulers is generally believed. We went out of the
city by the eastern gate, called Bab Shurky, which name profanely
suggested the irrelevant colored image of Bob Sharkey, and found
ourselves in the presence of huge mounds of rubbish, the accumu-

lations of refuse carted out of the city during many centuries, which entirely concealed from view the country beyond. We skirted these for a while, with the crumbling city wall on the left hand, passed through the hard, gray, desolate Turkish cemetery, and came at length into what might be called country. Not that we could see any country, however; we were always between high mud-walls, and could see nothing beyond them, except the sky, unless we stepped through an open door into a garden.

Into one of these gardens, a public one, and one of the most celebrated in the rhapsodies of travellers and by the inventive poets, we finally turned. When you are walking for pleasure in your native land, and indulging a rural feeling, would you voluntarily go into a damp swale, and sit on a moist sod under a willow? This garden is low, considerably lower than the city, which has gradually elevated itself on its own decay, and is cut by little canals or sluiceways fed by the Abana, which run with a good current. The ground is well covered with coarse grass, of the vivid green that one finds usually in low ground, and is liberally sprinkled with a growth of willows and poplars. In this garden of the Hesperides, in which there are few if any flowers, and no promise of fruit, there is a rough wooden shed, rickety and decaying, having, if I remember rightly, a balcony, — it must have a balcony, — and there pipes, poor lemonade, and poorer ice-cream are served to customers. An Arab band of four persons, one of them of course blind of an eye, seated cross-legged on a sort of bedstead, was picking and thumping a monotonous, never-ending tune out of the usual instruments. You could not deny that the vivid greenery, and the gayly apparelled groups, sitting about under the trees and on the water's edge, made a lively scene. In another garden, farther on around the wall, the shanty of entertainment is a many-galleried shaky construction, or a series of platforms and terraces of wood, overhanging the swift Abana. In the daytime it is but a shabby sight; but at night, when a thousand colored globes light it without revealing its poverty, and the lights dance in the water, and hundreds of turbaned, gowned narghileh-smokers and coffee-drinkers lounge in the galleries, or gracefully take their ease by the sparkling current, and the faint thump of the darabouka is heard, and some gesticulating story-teller, mounted upon a bench, is reeling off to an attentive audience an interminable Arabian tale, you might fancy that the romance of the Orient is not all invented.

Of other and private gardens and enclosures we had glimpses, on our walk, through open gates, and occasionally over the walls ; we could imagine what a fragrance and color would greet the senses when the apricots are in bloom, and the oranges and lemons in flower, and how beautiful the view might be if the ugly walls did not conceal it. We returned by the saddlers' bazaar, and by a famous plane-tree, which may be as old as the Moslem religion ; its gnarled limbs are like the stems of ordinary trees, and its trunk is forty feet around.

The remark that Damascus is without monuments of its past needs qualification ; it was made with reference to its existence before the Christian era, and in comparison with other capitals of antiquity. Remains may, indeed, be met in its exterior walls, and in a broken column here and there built into a modern house, of Roman workmanship, and its Great Mosque is an historical monument of great interest, if not of the highest antiquity. In its structure it represents three religions and three periods of art ; like the mosque of St. Sophia at Constantinople, it was for centuries a Christian cathedral ; like the Dome of the Rock at Jerusalem, it is built upon a spot consecrated by the most ancient religious rites. Situated in the midst of the most densely peopled part of the city, and pressed on all sides by its most crowded bazaars, occupying a quadrangle nearly five hundred feet one way by over three hundred the other, the wanderer among the shops is constantly coming to one side or another of it, and getting glimpses through the spacious portals of the colonnaded court within. Hemmed in as it is, it is only by diving into many alleys and pushing one's way into the rear of dirty shops and climbing upon the roofs of houses, that one can get any idea of the exterior of the mosque. It is, indeed, only from an eminence that you can see its three beautiful minarets.

It does not appear that Chosroes, the Persian who encamped his army in the delicious gardens of Damascus, in the year 614,

when he was on his way to the destruction of Jerusalem and the
massacre of its Christian inhabitants, disturbed the church of
John the Baptist in this city. But twenty years later it fell into
the hands of the Saracens, who for a few years were content to
share it with the Christian worshippers. It is said that when
Khâled, the most redoubtable of the Friends of the Prophet,
whose deeds entitled him to the sobriquet of The Sword of God,
entered this old church, he asked to be conducted into the sacred
vault (which is now beneath the *kubbeh* of the mosque), and that
he was there shown the head of John the Baptist in a gold casket,
which had in Greek this inscription : "This casket contains the
head of John the Baptist, son of Zachariah."

The building had been then for over three centuries a Christian
church. And already, when Constantine dedicated it to Christian
use, it had for over three hundred years witnessed the worship of
pagan deities. The present edifice is much shorn of its original
splendor and proportions, but sufficient remains to show that it
was a worthy rival of the temples of Ba'albek, Palmyra, and Jerusalem. No part of the building is older than the Roman occupation, but the antiquarians are agreed to think that this was the
site of the old Syrian temple, in which Ahaz saw the beautiful
altar which he reproduced in the temple at Jerusalem.

Pieces of superb carving, recalling the temple of the Sun at
Ba'albek, may still be found in some of the gateways, and the
noble Corinthian columns of the interior are to be referred to
Roman or Greek workmen. Christian art is represented in the
building in some part of the walls and in the round-topped windows ; and the Moslems have superimposed upon all minarets, a
dome, and the gay decorations of colored marbles and flaring inscriptions.

The Moslems have either been too ignorant or too careless to
efface all the evidences of Christian occupation. The doors of the
eastern gate are embossed with brass, and among the emblems is
the Christian sacramental cup. Over an arch, which can only be
seen from the roof of the silversmiths' bazaar, is this inscription
in Greek : "Thy kingdom, O Christ, is an everlasting kingdom,
and thy dominion endureth throughout all generations."

It required a special permit to admit us to the mosque, but when we were within the sacred precincts and shod with slippers, lest our infidel shoes should touch the pavement, we were followed by a crowd of attendants who for the moment overcame their repugnance to our faith in expectation of our backsheesh. The interior view is impressive by reason of the elegant minarets and the fine colonnaded open court. Upon one of the minarets Jesus will descend when he comes to judge the world. The spacious mosque, occupying one side of the court, and open on that side to its roof, is divided in its length by two rows of Corinthian columns, and has a certain cheerfulness and hospitality. The tesselated marble pavement of the interior is much worn, and is nearly all covered with carpets of Persia and of Smyrna. The only tomb in the mosque is that of St. John the Baptist, which is draped in a richly embroidered cloth.

We were anew impressed by the home-like, democratic character of the great mosques. This, opening by its four gates into the busiest bazaars, as we said, is much frequented at all hours. At the seasons of prayer you may see great numbers prostrating themselves in devotion, and at all other times this cool retreat is a refuge for the poor and the weary. The fountains of running water in the court attract people, — those who desire only to sit there and rest, as well as those who wash and pray. About the fountains and in the mosque were seated groups of women, eating their noonday bread, or resting in that dumb attitude under which Eastern women disguise their discontent or their intrigues. This is, at any rate, a haven of rest for all, and it is a goodly sight to see all classes, rich and poor, flocking in here, leaving their shoes at the door or carrying them in their hands.

The view from the minaret which we ascended is peculiar. On the horizon we saw the tops of hills and mountains, snowy Hermon among them. Far over the plain we could not look, for the city is beset by a thicket of slender trees, which were just then in fresh leafage. Withdrawing our gaze from the environs, we looked down upon the wide-spread oval-shaped city. Most conspicuous were the minarets, then a few domes, and then thousands of dome-shaped roofs. You see the top of a covered city, but not the city. In fact, it scarcely looks like a city; you see no streets, and few roofs proper, for we have to look twice to convince ourselves that the flat spaces covered with earth and often green with vegetation (gardens in the air) are actually roofs of houses. The streets are either roofed over or are so narrow that we cannot see them from this height. Damascus is a sort of rabbit-burrow.

Not far from the Great Mosque is the tomb of Saladin. We looked from the street through a grated window, to the bars of which the faithful have tied innumerable rags and strings (pious offerings, which it is supposed will bring them good luck) into a painted enclosure, and saw a large catafalque, or sarcophagus, covered with a green mantle. The tomb is near a mosque, and beside a busy cotton-bazaar; it is in the midst of traffic and travel, among activities and the full rush of life, — just where a man would like to be buried in order to be kept in remembrance.

In going about the streets we notice the prevalence of color in portals, in the interior courts of houses, and in the baths; there is a fondness for decorating with broad gay stripes of red, yellow, and white. Even the white pet sheep which are led about by children have their wool stained with dabs of brilliant color, — perhaps in honor of the Greek Easter.

The baths of Damascus are many and very good, not so severe and violent as those of New York, nor so thorough as those of Cairo, but, the best of them, clean and agreeable. We push aside a gay curtain from the street and descend by steps into a square apartment. It has a dome like a mosque. Under the dome is a large marble basin into which water is running; the floor is tesselated with colored marbles. Each side is a recess with a half-dome, and in the recesses are elevated divans piled with cushions for reclining. The walls are painted in stripes of blue, yellow, and red, and the room is bright with various Oriental stuffs. There are turbaned and silken-attired attendants, whose gentle faces might make them mistaken for ministers of religion as well as of cleanliness, and upon the divans recline those who have come from the bath, enjoying *kief*, with pipes and coffee. There is an atmosphere of perfect contentment in the place, and I can imagine how an effeminate ruler might see, almost without a sigh, the empire of the world slip from his grasp while he surrendered himself to this delicious influence.

We undressed, were towelled, shod with wooden clogs, and led through marble paved passages and several rooms into an inner, long chamber, which has a domed roof pierced by bulls'-eyes of party-colored glass. The floor, of colored marbles, was slippery with water running from the overflowing fountains, or dashed about by the attendants. Out of this room open several smaller chambers, into which an unsocial person might retire. We sat down on the floor by a marble basin into which both hot and cold water poured. After a little time spent in contemplating the humidity of the world, and reflecting on the equality of all men before the law without clothes, an attendant approached, and began to deluge us with buckets of hot water, dashing them over us with a jocular enjoyment and as much indifference to our personality as if we had been statues. I should like to know how life looks to a man who passes his days in this dimly illumined chamber of steam, and is permitted to treat his fellow-men with every mark of disrespect. When we were sufficiently drenched, the agile Arab who had selected me as his mine of backsheesh, knelt down and began to scrub me with hair mittens, with a great show of energy, uttering jocose exclamations in his own language, and practising the half-dozen English words he had mastered, one of them being "dam," which he addressed to me both affirmatively and interrogatively, as if under the impression that it conveyed the same meaning as *tyeb* in his vocabulary. I suppose he had often heard wicked Englishmen, who were under his hands, use it, and he took it for an expression of profound satisfaction. He continued this operation for some time, putting me in a sitting position, turning me over, telling me to "sleep" when he desired me to lie down, encouraging me by various barbarous cries, and slapping his hand from time to time to make up by noise for his economical expenditure of muscular force.

After my hilarious bather had finished this process, he lathered me thoroughly, drenched me from head to heels in suds, and then let me put the crowning touch to my happiness by entering one of the little rooms, and sliding into a tank of water hot enough to take the skin off. It is easy enough to make all this process read like a martyrdom, but it is, on the contrary, so delightful that you do not wonder that the ancients spent so much time in the bath, and that next to the amphitheatre the emperors and tyrants lavished most money upon these establishments, of which the people were so extravagantly fond.

Fresh towels were wound round us, turbans were put on our heads, and we were led back to the room first entered, where we were re-enveloped in cloths and towels, and left to recline upon the cushioned divans; pipes and coffee were brought, and we enjoyed a delicious sense of repose and bodily lightness, looking dimly at the grave figures about us, and recognizing in them not men but dreamy images of a physical paradise. No rude voices or sharp movements broke the repose of the chamber. It was as in a dream that I watched a handsome boy, who, with a long pole, was handling the washed towels, and admired the unerring skill that tossed the strips of cloth high in the air and caused them to catch and hang squarely upon the cords stretched across the recesses. The mind was equal to the observation, but not to the comprehension, of this feat. When we were sufficiently cooled, we were assisted to dress, the various articles of Frank apparel affording great amusement to the Orientals. The charge for the whole entertainment was two francs each, probably about four times what a native would have paid.

XIV.

OTHER SIGHTS IN DAMASCUS.

DAY after day we continued, like the mourners, to go about the streets, in the tangle of the bazaars, under the dark roofs, endeavoring to see Damascus. When we emerged from the city gate, the view was not much less limited. I made the circuit of the wall on the north, in lanes, by running streams, canals, enclosed gardens, seeing everywhere hundreds of patient, summer-loving men and women squatting on the brink of every rivulet, by every damp spot, in idle and perfect repose.

We stumbled about also on the south side of the town, and saw the reputed place of St. Paul's escape, which has been lately changed. It is a ruined Saracenic tower in the wall, under which is Bab Kisan, a gate that has been walled up for seven hundred years. The window does not any more exist from which the apostle was let down in a basket, but it used to be pointed out with confidence, and I am told that the basket is still shown, but we did not see it. There are still some houses on this south wall, and a few of them have projecting windows from which a person might easily be lowered. It was in such a house that the harlot of Jericho lived, who contrived the escape of the spies of Joshua. And we see how thick and substantial the town walls of that city must have been to support human habitations. But they were blown down.

Turning southward into the country, we came to the tomb of the porter who assisted Paul's escape, and who now sleeps here under the weight of the sobriquet of St. George. A little farther out on the same road is located the spot of Saul's conversion.

Near it is the English cemetery, a small high-walled enclosure, containing a domed building surmounted by a cross; and in this historical spot, whose mutations of race, religion, and government would forbid the most superficial to construct for it any cast-iron scheme of growth or decay, amid these almost melancholy patches of vegetation which still hover in the Oriental imagination as the gardens of all delights, sleeps undisturbed by ambition or by criticism, having at last, let us hope, solved the theory of "averages," the brilliant Henry T. Buckle.

Not far off is the Christian cemetery. "Who is buried here?" I asked our thick-witted guide.

"O, anybody," he replied, cheerfully, "Greeks, French, Italians, anybody you like"; as if I could please myself by interring here any one I chose.

Among the graves was a group of women, hair dishevelled and garments loosened in the *abandon* of mourning, seated about a rough coffin open its entire length. In it lay the body of a young man who had been drowned, and recovered from the water after three days. The women lifted up his dead hands, let them drop heavily, and then wailed and howled, throwing themselves into attitudes of the most passionate grief. It was a piteous sight, there under the open sky, in the presence of an unsympathizing crowd of spectators.

Returning, we went round by the large Moslem cemetery, situated at the southwest corner of the city. It is, like all Moslem burying-grounds, a melancholy spectacle, — a mass of small whitewashed mounds of mud or brick, with an inscribed headstone, — but here rest some of the most famous men and women of Moslem history. Here is the grave of Ibn' Asâker, the historian of Damascus; here rests the fierce Moawyeh, the founder of the dynasty of the Omeiyades; and here are buried three of the wives of Mohammed, and Fâtimeh, his granddaughter, the child of Ali, whose place of sepulture no man knows. Upon nearly every tomb is a hollow for water, and in it is a sprig of myrtle, which is renewed every Friday by the women who come here to mourn and to gossip.

Much of the traveller's time, and perhaps the most enjoyable part of it, in Damascus, is spent in the bazaars, cheapening scarfs and rugs and the various silken products of Syrian and Persian looms, picking over dishes of antique coins, taking impressions of intaglios, hunting for curious amulets, and searching for the quaintest and most brilliant Saracenic tiles. The quest of the antique is always exciting, and the inexperienced is ever hopeful that he will find a gem of value in a heap of rubbish; this hope never abandons the most *blasé* tourist, though in time he comes to understand that the sharp-nosed Jew, or the oily Armenian, or the respectable Turk, who spreads his delusive wares before him, knows quite as well as the seeker the value of any bit of antiquity, not only in Damascus, but in Constantinople, Paris, and London, and is an adept in all the counterfeits and impositions of the Orient.

The bazaars of the antique, of old armor, ancient brasses, and of curiosities generally, and even of the silver and gold smiths, are disappointing after Cairo; they are generally full of rubbish from which the choice things seem to have been culled; indeed, the rage for antiquities is now so great that sharp buyers from Europe range all the Orient and leave little for the innocent and hopeful tourist, who is aghast at the prices demanded, and usually finds himself a victim of his own cleverness when he pays for any article only a fourth of the price at first asked.

The silk bazaars of Damascus still preserve, however, a sort of pre-eminence of opportunity, although they are largely supplied by the fabrics manufactured at Beyrout and in other Syrian towns. Certainly no place is more tempting than one of the silk khans, — gloomy old courts, in the galleries of which you find little apartments stuffed full of the seductions of Eastern looms. For myself, I confess to the fascination of those stuffs of brilliant dyes, shot with threads of gold and of silver. I know a tall, oily-tongued Armenian, who has a little chamber full of shelves, from which he takes down one rich scarf after another, unfolds it, shakes out its shining hues, and throws it on the heap, until the room is littered with gorgeous stuffs. He himself is clad in silk attire, he is tall, suave, insinuating, grave, and overwhelmingly condescending. I can see him now, when I question the value put upon a certain

9   M

article which I hold in my hand and no doubt betray my admiration of in my eyes, — I can see him now throw back his head, half
close his Eastern eyes, and exclaim, as if he had hot pudding in
his mouth, "Thot is ther larster price."

I can see Abd-el-Atti now, when we had made up a package
of scarfs, and offered a certain sum for the lot, which the sleek and
polite trader refused, with his eternal, "Thot is ther larster price,"
sling the articles about the room, and depart in rage. And I
can see the Armenian bow us into the corridor with the same
sweet courtesy, knowing very well that the trade is only just
begun; that it is, in fact, under good headway; that the Arab will
return, that he will yield a little from the "larster price," and
that we shall go away loaded with his wares, leaving him ruined
by the transaction, but proud to be our friend.

Our experience in purchasing old Saracenic and Persian tiles
is perhaps worth relating as an illustration of the character of the
traders of Damascus. Tiles were plenty enough, for several
ancient houses had recently been torn down, and the dealers continually acquire them from ruined mosques or those that are
undergoing repairs. The dragoman found several lots in private
houses, and made a bargain for a certain number at two francs
and a half each; and when the bargain was made, I spent half
a day in selecting the specimens we desired.

The next morning, before breakfast, we went to make sure that
the lots we had bought would be at once packed and shipped.
But a change had taken place in twelve hours. There was an
Englishman in town who was also buying tiles; this produced
a fever in the market; an impression went abroad that there was
a fortune to be made in tiles, and we found that our bargain was
entirely ignored. The owners supposed that the tiles we had
selected must have some special value; and they demanded for
the thirty-eight which we had chosen — agreeing to pay for them
two francs and a half apiece — thirty pounds. In the house where
we had laid aside seventy-three others at the same price, not a
tile was to be discovered; the old woman who showed us the
vacant chamber said she knew not what had become of them, but
she believed they had been sold to an Englishman.

We returned to the house first mentioned, resolved to devote the day if necessary to the extraction of the desired tiles from the grip of their owners. The contest began about eight o'clock in the morning; it was not finished till three in the afternoon, and it was maintained on our side with some disadvantage, the only nutriment that sustained us being a cup of tea which we drank very early in the morning. The scene of the bargain was the paved court of the house, in which there was a fountain and a lemon-tree, and some rose-trees trained on espaliers along the walls. The tempting enamelled tiles were piled up at one side of the court and spread out in rows in the *lewán*, — the open recess where guests are usually received. The owners were two Greeks, brothers-in-law, polite, cunning, sharp, the one inflexible, the other yielding, — a combination against which it is almost impossible to trade with safety, for the yielding one constantly allures you into the grip of the inflexible. The women of the establishment, comely Greeks, clattered about the court on their high wooden pattens for a time, and at length settled down, in an adjoining apartment, to their regular work of embroidering silken purses and tobacco-pouches, taking time, however, for an occasional cigarette or a pull at a narghileh, and, in a constant chatter, keeping a lively eye upon the trade going on in the court. The handsome children added not a little to the liveliness of the scene, and their pranks served to soften the asperities of the encounter; although I could not discover, after repeated experiments, that any affection lavished upon the children lowered the price of the tiles. The Greek does not let sentiment interfere with business, and he is much more difficult to deal with than an Arab, who occasionally has impulses.

Each tile was the subject of a separate bargain and conflict. The dicker went on in Arabic, Greek, broken English, and dislocated French, and was participated in not only by the parties most concerned, but by the young Greek guide and by the donkey-boys. Abd-el-Atti exhibited all the qualities of his generalship. He was humorous, engaging, astonished, indignant, serious, playful, threatening, indifferent. Beaten on one grouping of specimens, he made instantly a new combination; more than once the trans-

action was abruptly broken off in mutual rage, obstinacy, and
recriminations; and it was set going again by a timely jocularity
or a seeming concession. I can see now the soft Greek take up
a tile which had painted on it some quaint figure or some lovely
flower, dip it in the fountain to bring out its brilliant color, and
then put it in the sun for our admiration; and I can see the
dragoman shake his head in slow depreciation, and push it one
side, when that tile was the one we had resolved to possess of
all others, and was the undeclared centre of contest in all the
combinations for an hour thereafter.

When the day was two thirds spent we had purchased one hundred tiles, jealously watched the packing of each one, and seen
the boxes nailed and corded. We could not have been more
exhausted if we had undergone an examination for a doctorate of
law in a German university. Two boxes, weighing two hundred
pounds each, were hoisted upon the backs of mules and sent to
the French company's station; there does not appear to be a dray
or a burden-cart in Damascus; all freight is carried upon the back
of a mule or a horse, even long logs and whole trunks of trees.

When this transaction was finished, our Greek guide, who had
heard me ask the master of the house for brass trays, told me
that a fellow whom I had noticed hanging about there all the
morning had some trays to show me; in fact, he had at his house
" seventeen trays."   I thought this a rich find, for the beautiful
antique brasses of Persia are becoming rare even in Damascus;
and, tired as we were, we rode across the city for a mile to a secluded private house, and were shown into an upper chamber.
What was our surprise to find spread out there the same " seventy-
three " tiles that we had purchased the day before, and which had
been whisked away from us. By " seventeen tray," the guide
meant " seventy-three." We told the honest owner that he was
too late; we had already tiles enough to cover his tomb.

XV.

SOME PRIVATE HOUSES.

THE private houses of Damascus are a theme of wonder and admiration throughout the Orient. In a land in which a moist spot is called a garden, and a canal bordered by willows a Paradise, the fancy constructs a palace of the utmost splendor and luxury out of materials which in a less glowing country would scarcely satisfy moderate notions of comfort or of ostentation.

But the East is a region of contrasts as well as of luxury, and it is difficult to say how much of their reputation the celebrated mansions of Damascus owe to the wretchedness of the ordinary dwellings, and also to the raggedness of their surroundings. We spent a day in visiting several of the richest dwellings, and steeping ourselves in the dazzling luxury they offer.

The exterior of a private house gives no idea of its interior. Sometimes its plain mud-wall has a solid handsome street-door, and if it is very old, perhaps a rich Saracenic portal; but usually you slip from the gutter, lined with mud-walls, called a street, into an alley, crooked, probably dirty, pass through a stable-yard and enter a small court, which may be cheered by a tree and a basin of water. Thence you wind through a narrow passage into a large court, a parallelogram of tesselated marble, having a fountain in the centre and about it orange and lemon trees, and roses and vines. The house, two stories high, is built about this court, upon which all the rooms open without communicating with each other. Perhaps the building is of marble, and carved, or it may be highly ornamented with stucco, and painted in gay colors. If the establishment belongs to a Moslem, it will have beyond this court a second, larger and finer, with more fountains, trees, and flowers, and a house more highly decorated. This is the harem, and the way to it is a crooked alley, so that by no chance can the slaves or visitors of the master get a glimpse into the apartments of the women. The first house we visited was of this kind; all the portion the gentlemen of the party were admitted into was in a state of shabby decay; its court in disrepair, its rooms void of comfort, — a condition of things to which we had become well accustomed in everything Moslem. But the ladies found the court of the harem beautiful, and its apartments old and very rich in wood-carving and in arabesques, something like the best old Saracenic houses in Cairo.

The houses of the rich Jews which we saw are built like those of the Moslems, about a paved court with a fountain, but totally different in architecture and decoration.

In speaking of a fountain, in or about Damascus, I always mean a basin into which water is discharged from a spout. If there are any jets or upspringing fountains, I was not so fortunate as to see them.

In passing through the streets of the Jews' quarter we encountered at every step beautiful children, not always clean Sunday-school children, but ravishingly lovely, the handsomest, as to exquisite complexions, grace of features, and beauty of eyes, that I have ever seen. And looking out from the open windows of the balconies which hang over the street were lovely Jewish women, the mothers of the beautiful children, and the maidens to whom the humble Christian is grateful that they tire themselves and look out of windows now as they did in the days of the prophets.

At the first Jewish house we entered, we were received by the entire family, old and young, newly married, betrothed, cousins, uncles, and maiden aunts. ' They were evidently expecting company about these days, and not at all averse to exhibiting their gorgeous house and their rich apparel. Three dumpy, middle-aged women, who would pass for ugly anywhere, welcomed us at first in the raised recess, or lewân, at one end of the court; we were seated upon the divans, while the women squatted upon cushions. Then the rest of the family began to appear. There were the handsome owner of the house, his younger brother just married, and the wife of the latter, a tall and pretty woman of the strictly wax-doll order of beauty, with large, swimming eyes. She wore a short-waisted gown of blue silk, and diamonds, and, strange to say, a dark wig; it is the fashion at marriage to shave the head and put on a wig, a most disenchanting performance for a bride. The numerous children, very pretty and sweet-mannered, came forward and kissed our hands. The little girls were attired in white short-waisted dresses, and all, except the very smallest, wore diamonds. One was a bride of twelve years, whose marriage was to be concluded the next year. She wore an orange-wreath, her high corsage of white silk sparkled with diamonds, and she was sweet and engaging in manner, and spoke French prettily.

The girls evidently had on the family diamonds, and I could imagine that the bazaar of Moses in the city had been stripped to make a holiday for his daughters. Surely, we never saw such a display out of the Sultan's treasure-chamber. The head-dress of one of the cousins of the family, who was recently married, was a pretty hat, the coronal front of which was a mass of diamonds. We saw this same style of dress in other houses afterwards, and were permitted to admire other young women who were literally plastered with these precious stones, in wreaths on the head, in brooches and necklaces, — masses of dazzling diamonds, which after a time came to have no more value in our eyes than glass, so common and cheap did they seem. If a wicked person could persuade one of these dazzling creatures to elope with him, he would be in possession of treasure enough to found a college for the conversion of the Jews. I could not but be struck with the resemblance of one of the plump, glowing-cheeked young girls, who was set before us for worship, clad in white silk and inestimable jewels, to the images of the Madonna, decked with equal affection and lavish wealth, which one sees in the Italian churches.

All the women and children of the family walked about upon wooden pattens, ingeniously inlaid with ivory or pearl, the two supports of which raise them about three inches from the ground.

They are confined to the foot by a strap across the ball, but being otherwise loose, they clatter at every step; of course, graceful walking on these little stilts is impossible, and the women go about like hens whose toes have been frozen off. When they step up into the lewân, they leave their pattens on the marble floor, and sit in their stocking-feet. Our conversation with this hospitable collection of relations consisted chiefly in inquiries about their connection with each other, and an effort on their part to understand our relationship, and to know why we had not brought our entire families. They were also extremely curious to know about our houses in America, chiefly, it would seem, to enforce the contrast between our plainness and their luxury. When we had been served with coffee and cigarettes, they all rose and showed us about the apartments.

The first one, the *salon*, will give an idea of the others. It was a lofty, but not large room, with a highly painted ceiling, and consisted of two parts; the first, level with the court and paved with marble, had a marble basin in the centre supported on carved lions; the other two thirds of the apartment was raised about a foot, carpeted, and furnished with chairs of wood, inlaid with mother-of-pearl, stiffly set against the walls. The chairs were not comfortable to sit in, and they were the sole furniture. The wainscoting was of marble, in screen-work, and most elaborately carved. High up, near the ceiling, were windows, double windows in fact, with a space between like a gallery, so that the lace-like screen-work was exhibited to the utmost advantage. There was much gilding and color on the marble, and the whole was costly and gaudy. The sleeping-rooms, in the second story, were also handsome in this style, but they were literally all windows, on all sides; the space between the windows was never more than three or four inches. They are admirable for light and air, but to enter them is almost like stepping out of doors. They are all *en suite*, so that it would seem that the family must retire simultaneously, exchanging the comparative privacy of the isolated rooms below for the community of these glass apartments.

The *salons* that we saw in other houses were of the same general style of the first; some had marble niches in the walls, the arch of which was supported by slender marble columns, and these recesses, as well as the walls, were decorated with painting, usually landscapes and cities. The painting gives you a perfectly accurate idea of the condition of art in the Orient; it was not only pre-Raphaelite, it was pre-Adamite, worse than Byzantine, and not so good as Chinese. Money had been freely lavished in these dwellings, and whatever the Eastern chisel or brush could do to enrich and ornament them had been done. I was much pleased by the picture of a city, — it may have been Damascus, — freely done upon the wall. The artist had dotted the plaster with such houses as children are accustomed to make on a slate, arranging some of them in rows, and inserting here and there a minaret and a dome. There was not the slightest attempt at shading or perspective. Yet the owners contemplated the result with visible satisfaction, and took a simple and undisguised pleasure in our admiration of the work of art.

"Alas," I said to the delighted Jew connoisseur who had paid for this picture, "we have nothing like that in our houses in America, not even in the Capitol at Washington!"

"But your country is new," he replied with amiable consideration; "you will have of it one day."

In none of these veneered and stuccoed palaces did we find any comfort; everywhere a profuse expenditure of money in Italian marble, in carving, in gilding, and glaring color, but no taste, except in some of the wood-work, cut in Arabesque, and inlaid, — a reminiscence of the almost extinct Saracenic grace and invention. And the construction of all the buildings and the ornamentation were shabby and cheap in appearance, in spite of the rich materials; the marbles in the pavement or the walls were badly joined and raggedly cemented, and by the side of the most costly work was sure to be something mean and frail.

We supposed at first that we ought to feel a little delicacy about intruding our bare-faced curiosity into private houses, — perhaps an unpardonable feeling in a traveller who has been long enough in the Orient to lose the bloom of Occidental modesty. But we need not have feared. Our hosts were only too glad that we should see their state and luxury. There was something almost

9 *

comical in these Jewish women arraying themselves in their finest
gowns, and loading themselves with diamonds, so early in the
day (for they were ready to receive us at ten o'clock), and in their
naïve enjoyment of our admiration. Surely we ought not to have
thought that comical which was so kindly intended. I could not
but wonder, however, what resource for the rest of the day could
remain to a woman who had begun it by dressing in all her ornaments, by crowning herself with coronets and sprays of diamonds,
by hanging her neck and arms with glittering gems, as if she had
been a statue set up for idolatry. After this supreme effort of the
sex, the remainder of the day must be intolerably flat. For I
think one of the pleasures of life must be the gradual transforma-
tion, the blooming from the chrysalis of elegant morning *désha-
bille* into the perfect flower of the evening toilet.

These princesses of Turkish diamonds all wore dresses with
the classic short waist, which is the most womanly and becoming,
and perhaps their apparel imparted a graciousness to their manner.
We were everywhere cordially received, and usually offered coffee,
or sherbet and confections.

H. H. the Emir Abd-el-Kader lives in a house suitable to a
wealthy Moslem who has a harem. The old chieftain had expressed his willingness to receive us, and N. Meshaka, the American consular agent, sent his *kawass* to accompany us to his
residence at the appointed hour. The old gentleman met us at
the door of his reception-room, which is at one end of the foun-
tained court. He wore the plain Arab costume, with a white
turban. I had heard so much of the striking, venerable, and even
magnificent appearance of this formidable desert hero, that I
experienced a little disappointment in the reality, and learned
anew that the hero should be seen in action, or through the lenses
of imaginative description which can clothe the body with all the
attributes of the soul. The demigods so seldom come up to
their reputation! Abd-el-Kader may have appeared a gigantic
man when on horseback in the smoke and whirl of an Algerine
combat; but he is a man of medium size and scarcely medium
height; his head, if not large, is finely shaped and intellectual, and
his face is open and pleasing. He wore a beard, trimmed, which

I suspect ought to be white, but which was black, and I fear dyed. You would judge him to be, at least, seventy-five, and his age begins to show by a little pallor, by a visible want of bodily force, and by a lack of lustre in those once fiery and untamable eyes.

His manner was very gracious, and had a simple dignity, nor did our interview mainly consist in the usual strained compliments of such occasions. In reply to a question, he said that he had lived over twenty years in Damascus, but it was evident that his long exile had not dulled his interest in the progress of the world, and that he watched with intense feeling all movements of peoples in the direction of freedom. There is no such teacher of democracy as misfortune, but I fancy that Abd-el-Kader sincerely desires for others the liberty he covets for himself. He certainly has the courage of his opinions; while he is a very strict Moslem, he is neither bigoted nor intolerant, as he showed by his conduct during the massacre of the Christians here, in 1860. His face lighted up with pleasure when I told him that Americans remembered with much gratitude his interference in behalf of the Christians at that time.

The talk drifting to the state of France and Italy, he expressed his full sympathy with the liberal movement of the Italian government, but as to France he had no hope of a republic at present, he did not think the people capable of it.

"But America," he said with sudden enthusiasm, "that is the country, in all the world that is the *only* country, that is the land of real freedom. "I hope," he added, "that you will have no more trouble among yourselves."

We asked him what he thought of the probability of another outburst of the Druses, which was getting to be so loudly whispered. Nobody, he said, could tell what the Druses were thinking or doing; he had no doubt that in the former rising and massacre they were abetted by the Turkish government. This led him to speak of the condition of Syria; the people were fearfully ground down, and oppressed with taxation and exactions of all sorts; in comparison he did not think Egypt was any better off, but much the same.

In all our conversation we were greatly impressed by the calm and comprehensive views of the old hero, his philosophical temper, and his serenity; although it was easy to see that he chafed under the banishment which kept so eager a soul from participation in the great movements which he weighed so well and so longed to aid. When refreshments had been served, we took our leave; but the emir insisted upon accompanying us through the court and the dirty alleys, even to the public street where our donkeys awaited us, and bade us farewell with a profusion of Oriental salutations.

XVI.

SOME SPECIMEN TRAVELLERS.

IT is to be regretted that some one has not the leisure and the
genius — for it would require both — to study and to sketch
the more peculiar of the travellers who journey during a season
in the Orient, to photograph *their* impressions, and to unravel
the motives that have set them wandering. There was at our
hotel a countryman whose observations on the East pleased
me mightily. I inferred, correctly, from his slow and deliberate
manner of speech, that he was from the great West. A gentleman spare in figure and sallow in complexion, you might have
mistaken him for a "member" from Tennessee or Illinois. What
you specially admired in him was his entire sincerity, and his
imperviousness to all the glamour, historical or romantic, which
interested parties, like poets and historians, have sought to throw
over the Orient. A heap of refuse in the street or an improvident dependant on Allah, in rags, was just as offensive to him in
Damascus as it would be in Big Lickopolis. He carried his
scales with him; he put into one balance his county-seat and
into the other the entire Eastern civilization, and the Orient
kicked the beam, — and it was with a mighty, though secret joy
that you saw it.

It was not indeed for his own pleasure that he had left the familiar cronies of his own town and come into foreign and uncom-
fortable parts; you could see that he would much prefer to be
again among the "directors" and "stockholders" and operators,
exchanging the dry chips of gossip about stocks and rates; but,
being a man of "means," he had yielded to the imperious press-

ure of our modern society which insists on travel, and to the
natural desire of his family to see the world. Europe had not
pleased him, although it was interesting for an old country, and
there were a few places, the Grand Hotel in Paris for instance,
where one feels a little at home. Buildings, cathedrals? Yes,
some of them were very fine, but there was nothing in Europe to
equal or approach the Capitol in Washington. And galleries;
my wife likes them, and my daughter, — I suppose I have walked
through miles and miles of them. It may have been in the nature
of a confidential confession, that he was dragged into the East,
though he made no concealment of his repugnance to being here.
But when he had crossed the Mediterranean, Europe had attractions for him which he had never imagined while he was in it.
If he had been left to himself he would have fled back from Cairo
as if it were infested with plague; he had gone no farther up the
Nile; that miserable hole, Cairo, was sufficient for him.

"They talk," he was saying, speaking with that deliberate
pause and emphasis upon every word which characterizes the conversation of his section of the country, — "they talk about the climate of Egypt; it is all a humbug. Cairo is the most disagreeable city in the world, no sun, nothing but dust and wind. I
give you my word that we had only one pleasant day in a week;
cold, — you can't get warm in the hotel; the only decent day we
had in Egypt was at Suez. Fruit? What do you get? Some
pretend to like those dry dates. The oranges are so sour you
can't eat them, except the Jaffa, which are all peel. Yes, the pyr-
amids are big piles of stone, but when you come to architecture,
what is there in Cairo to compare to the Tuileries? The mosque
of Mohammed Ali *is* a fine building; it suits me better than the
mosque at Jerusalem. But what a city to live in!"

The farther our friend journeyed in the Orient, the deeper became his disgust. It was extreme in Jerusalem; but it had a
pathetic tone of resignation in Damascus; hope was dead within
him. The day after we had visited the private houses, some one
asked him at table if he was not pleased with Damascus.

"Damascus!" he repeated, "Damascus is the most God-for-
saken place I have ever been in. There is nothing to *eat*, and

nothing to *see*. I had heard about the bazaars of Damascus; my daughter must see the bazaars of Damascus. There is nothing in them; I have been from one end of them to the other, — it is a mess of rubbish. I suppose you were hauled through what they call the private houses? There is a good deal of marble and a good deal of show, but there is n't a house in Damascus that a respectable American would *live* in; there is n't one he could be comfortable in. The old mosque is an interesting place: I like the mosque, and I have been there a couple of times, and should n't mind going again; but I 've had enough of Damascus, I don't intend to go out doors again until my family are ready to leave."

All these intense dislikes of the Western observer were warmly combated by the ladies present, who found Damascus almost a paradise, and were glowing with enthusiasm over every place and incident of their journey. Having delivered his opinion, our friend let the conversation run on without interference, as it ranged all over Palestine. He sat in silence, as if he were patiently enduring anew the martyrdom of his pleasure-trip, until at length, obeying a seeming necessity of relieving his feelings, he leaned forward and addressed the lady next but one to him, measuring every word with judicial slowness, —

"Madame — I — hate — the — *name* — of Palestine — and Judæa — and — the Jordan — and — Damascus — and — Jeru-sa*lem*."

It is always refreshing in travel to meet a candid man who is not hindered by any weight of historic consciousness from expressing his opinions; and without exactly knowing why I felt under great obligations to this gentleman, — for gentleman he certainly was, even to an old-fashioned courtesy that shamed the best breeding of the Arabs. And after this wholesale sweep of the Oriental board, I experienced a new pleasure in going about and picking up the fragments of romance and sentiment that one might still admire.

There was another pilgrim at Damascus to whom Palestine was larger than all the world besides, and who magnified its relation to the rest of the earth as much as our more widely travelled friend

belittled it. In a waste but damp spot outside the Bab-el-Hadid
an incongruous Cook's Party had pitched its tents, — a camp
which swarmed during the day with itinerant merchants and beg-.
gars, and at night was the favorite resort of the most dissolute
dogs of Damascus. In knowing this party one had an opportunity to observe the various motives that bring people to the Holy
Land; there were a divinity student, a college professor, a well-
known publisher, some indomitable English ladies, some London
cockneys, and a group of young men who made a lark of the
pilgrimage, and saw no more significance in the tour than in a
jaunt to the Derby or a sail to Margate. I was told that the
guide-book most read and disputed over by this party was the
graphic itinerary of Mark Twain. The pilgrim to whom I refer,
however, scarcely needed any guide in the Holy Land. He was,
by his own representation, an illiterate shoemaker from the South
of England; of schooling he had never enjoyed a day, nor of
education, except such as sprung from his "conversion," which
happened in his twentieth year. At that age he joined the
" Primitive Methodists," and became, without abandoning his
bench, an occasional exhorter and field-preacher; his study, to
which he gave every moment not demanded by his trade, was the
Bible. To exhorting he added the labor on Sunday of teaching,
and for nearly forty years, without interruption, he had taken
charge of a Sunday-school class. He was very poor, and the
incessant labor of six days in the week hardly sufficed to the support of himself and his wife, and the family that began to fill his
humble lodging. Nevertheless, at the very time of his conversion he was seized with an intense longing to make a pilgrimage
to the Holy Land. This desire strengthened the more he read
the Bible and became interested in the scenes of its prophecies
and miracles. He resolved to go; yet to undertake so expensive
a journey at the time was impossible, nor could his family spare
his daily labor. But, early in his married life, he came to a notable resolution, and that was to lay by something every year, no
matter how insignificant the sum, as a fund for his pilgrimage.
And he trusted if his life were spared long enough he should be
able to see with his own eyes the Promised Land; if that might

be granted him, his object in life would be attained, and he should be willing to depart in peace.

Filled with this sole idea he labored at his trade without relaxation, and gave his Sundays and evenings to a most diligent study of the Bible ; and at length extended his reading to other books, commentaries and travels, which bore upon his favorite object. Years passed by ; his Palestine fund accumulated more slowly than his information about that land, but he was never discouraged ; he lost at one time a considerable sum by misplaced confidence in a comrade, but, nothing disheartened, he set to work to hammer out what would replace it. Of course such industry and singleness of purpose were not without result ; his business prospered and his fund increased ; but with his success new duties opened ; his children must be educated, for he was determined that they should have a better chance in England than their father had been given. The expenses of their education and his contributions to the maintenance of the worship of his society interfered sadly with his pilgrimage, and more than thirty years passed before he saw himself in possession of the sum that he could spare for the purchase of a Cook's ticket to the Holy Land. It was with pardonable pride that he told this story of his life, and added that his business of shoemaking was now prosperous, that he had now a shop of his own and men working under him, and that one of his sons, who would have as good an education as any nobleman in the kingdom, was a student at the college in London.

Of all the party with whom he travelled no one knew the Bible so well as this shoemaker ; he did not need to read it as they explored the historical places, he quoted chapter after chapter of it, without hesitation or consciousness of any great achievement, and he knew almost as well the books of travel that relate to the country. Familiarity with the English of the Bible had not, however, caused him to abandon his primitive speech, and he did not show his respect for the sacred book by adopting its grammatical forms. Such phrases as, " It does I good to see he eat," in respect to a convalescent comrade, exhibited this peculiarity. Indeed, he preserved his independence, and vindicated the

N

reputation of his craft the world over for a certain obstinacy of opinion, if not philosophic habit of mind, which pounding upon leather seems to promote. He surprised his comrades by a liberality of view and an absence of narrowness which were scarcely to be expected in a man of one idea. I was pained to think that the reality of the Holy Land might a little impair the celestial vision he had cherished of it for forty years; but perhaps it will be only a temporary obscuration; for the imagination is stronger than the memory, as we see so often illustrated in the writings of Oriental travellers; and I have no doubt that now he is again seated on his bench, the kingdoms he beholds are those of Israel and Judah, and not those that Mr. Cook showed him for an hundred pounds.

We should, perhaps, add, that our shoemaker cared for no part of the Orient except Palestine, and for no history except that in the Bible. He told me that he was forwarded from London to Rome, on his way to join Cook's Pilgrims at Cairo, in the company of a party of Select Baptists (so they were styled in the prospectus of their journey), and that, unexpectedly to himself (for he was a man who could surmount prejudices), he found them very good fellows; but that he was obliged to spend a whole day in Rome greatly against his will; it was an old and dilapidated city, and he did n't see why so much fuss was made over it. Egypt did not more appeal to his fancy; I think he rather loathed it, both its past and its present, as the seat of a vain heathenism. For ruins or antiquities not mentioned in the Bible he cared nothing, for profane architecture still less; Palestine was his goal, and I doubt if since the first crusade any pilgrim has trod the streets of Jerusalem with such fervor of enthusiasm as this illiterate, Bible-grounded, and spiritual-minded shoemaker.

We rode one afternoon up through the suburb of Salahiyeh to the sheykh's tomb on the naked hill north of the city, and down along the scarred side of it into the Abana gorge. This much-vaunted ride is most of the way between mud-walls so high that you have a sight of nothing but the sky and the tops of trees, and an occasional peep, through chinks in a rickety gate, into a damp and neglected garden, or a ragged field of grain under trees. But the view from the heights over the vast plain of Damascus, with the city embowered in its green, is superb, both for extent and color, and quite excuses the enthusiasm expended on this perennial city of waters. We had occasional glimpses of the Abana after it leaves the city, and we could trace afar off the course of the Pharpar by its winding ribbon of green. The view was best long before we reached the summit, at the cemetery and the ruined mosque, when the minarets showed against the green beyond. A city needs to be seen from some distance, and from not too high an elevation; looking directly down upon it is always uninteresting.

Somewhere in the side of the mountain, to the right of our course, one of the Moslem legends has located the cave of the Seven Sleepers. Knowing that the cave is really at Ephesus, we did not care to anticipate it.

The skeykh's tomb is simply a stucco dome on the ridge, and exposed to the draft of air from a valley behind it. The wind blew with such violence that we could scarcely stand there, and we made all our observations with great discomfort. What we saw was the city of Damascus, shaped like an oval dish with a long handle; the handle is the suburb on the street running from the Gate of God that sees the annual procession of pilgrims depart for Mecca. Many brown villages dot the emerald, — there are said to be forty in the whole plain. Towards the east we saw the desert and the gray sand fading into the gray sky of the horizon. That way lies Palmyra; by that route goes the dromedary post to Bagdad. I should like to send a letter by it.

The view of the Abana gorge from the height before we descended was unique. The narrow pass is filled with trees; but through them we could see the white French road, and the Abana divided into five streams, carried at different levels along the sides, in order to convey water widely over the plain. Along the meadow road, as we trotted towards the city, as, indeed, everywhere about the city at this season, we found the ground marshy and vivacious with frogs.

The street called Straight runs the length of the city from east to west, and is straight in its general intention, although it appears to have been laid out by a donkey, whose attention was con-

stantly diverted to one side or the other. It is a totally uninteresting lane. There is no reason, however, to suppose that St.
Paul intended to be facetious when he spoke of it. In his day it
was a magnificent straight avenue, one hundred feet wide; and
two rows of Corinthian colonnades extending a mile from gate to
gate divided it lengthwise. This was an architectural fashion of
that time; the colonnade at Palmyra, which is seen stalking in a
purposeless manner across the desert, was doubtless the ornament
of such a street.

The street life of Damascus is that panorama of the mean and
the picturesque, the sordid and the rich, of silk and rags, of many
costumes and all colors, which so astonishes the Oriental traveller
at first, but to which he speedily becomes so accustomed that it
passes almost unnoticed. The majority of the women are veiled,
but not so scrupulously as those of Cairo. Yet the more we see
of the women of the East the more convinced we are that they
are exceedingly good-hearted; it is out of consideration for the
feelings of the persons they meet in the street that they go veiled.
This theory is supported by the fact that the daughters of Bethlehem, who are all comely and many of them handsome, never
wear veils.

In lounging through the streets the whole life and traffic of
the town is exposed to you : donkeys loaded with panniers of
oranges, or with sickly watermelon cut up, stop the way (all
the melons of the East that I have tasted are flavorless); men
bearing trays of sliced boiled beets cry aloud their deliciousness
as if they were some fruit of paradise; boys and women seated
on the ground, having spread before them on a paper some sort
of uninviting candy; anybody planted by the roadside; dogs by
the dozen snoozing in all the paths,—the dogs that wake at night
and make Rome howl; the various tradesmen hammering in their
open shops; the silk-weavers plying the shuttle; the makers of
"sweets" stirring the sticky compounds in their shining copper
pots and pans; and what never ceases to excite your admiration
is the good-nature of the surging crowd, the indifference to being
jostled and run over by horses, donkeys, and camels.

Damascus may be — we have abundant testimony that it is — a

good city, if, as I said, one could see it. Arriving, you dive into a hole, and scarcely see daylight again ; you never can look many yards before you ; you move in a sort of twilight, which is deepened under the heavy timber roofs of the bazaars ; winding through endless mazes of lanes with no view except of a slender strip of sky, you occasionally may step through an opening in the wall into a court with a square of sunshine, a tank of water, and a tree or two. The city can be seen only from the hill or from a minaret, and then you look only upon roofs. After a few days the cooping up in this gorgeous Oriental paradise became oppressive.

We drove out of the city very early one morning. I was obliged to the muezzin of the nearest minaret for awakening me at four o'clock. From our window we can see his aerial balcony, — it almost overhangs us ; and day and night at his appointed hours we see the turbaned muezzin circling his high pinnacle, and hear him projecting his long call to prayer over the city roofs. When we came out at the west gate, the sun was high enough to color Hermon and the minarets of the west side of the city, and to gleam on the Abana. As we passed the diligence station, a tall Nubian, an employé of the company, stood there in the attitude of seneschal of the city ; ugliness had marked him for her own, giving him a large, damaged expanse of face, from which exuded, however, an inexpungible good-nature ; he sent us a cheerful *salâm aloykem*, — " the peace of God be with you " ; we crossed the shaky bridge, and got away up the swift stream at the rate of ten miles an hour.

Our last view, with the level sun coming over the roofs and spires, and the foreground of rapid water and verdure, gave us Damascus in its loveliest aspect.

XVII.

INTO DAYLIGHT AGAIN. — AN EPISODE OF TURKISH JUSTICE.

IT was an immense relief to emerge from Damascus into Beyrout, — into a city open, cheerful; it was to re-enter the
world. How brightly it lies upon its sunny promontory, climbing up the slopes and crowning every eminence with tree-embowered villas! What a varied prospect it commands of sparkling sea and curving shore; of country broken into the most pleasing diversity of hill and vale, woodlands and pastures; of precipices that are draped in foliage; of glens that retain their primitive
wildness, strips of dark pine forest, groups of cypresses and of
palms, spreading mulberry orchards, and terraces draped by vines;
of villages dotting the landscape; of convents clinging to the
heights, and the snowy peaks of Lebanon! Bounteous land of
silk and wine!

Beyrout is the brightest spot in Syria or Palestine, the only
pleasant city that we saw, and the centre of a moral and intellectual impulse the importance of which we cannot overestimate.
The mart of the great silk industry of the region, and the seaport
of Damascus and of all Upper Syria, the fitful and unintelligent
Turkish rule even cannot stifle its exuberant prosperity; but
above all the advantages which nature has given it, I should attribute its brightest prospects to the influence of the American
Mission, and to the establishment of Beyrout College. For almost
thirty years that Mission has sustained here a band of erudite
scholars, whose investigations have made the world more familiar
with the physical character of Palestine than the people of Con-

necticut are with the resources of their own State, and of wise managers whose prudence and foresight have laid deep and broad the foundations of a Syrian civilization.

I do not know how many converts have been made in thirty years, — the East has had ample illustration, from the Abyssinians to the Colchians, of "conversion" without knowledge or civilization, — nor do I believe that any "reports" of the workmen themselves to the "Board" can put in visible array adequately the results of the American Mission in Syria. But the transient visitor can see something of them, in the dawning of a better social life, in the beginning of an improvement in the condition of women, in an unmistakable spirit of inquiry, and a recognizable taste for intellectual pursuits. It is not too much to say that the birth of a desire for instruction, for the enjoyment of literature, and, to a certain extent, of science, is due to their schools; and that their admirably conducted press, which has sent out not only translations of the Scriptures, but periodicals of secular literature and information, and elementary geographies, histories, and scientific treatises, has satisfied the want which the schools created. And this new leaven is not confined to a sect, nor limited to a race; it is working, slowly it is true, in the whole of Syrian society.

The press establishment is near the pretty and substantial church of the Mission; it is a busy and well-ordered printing and publishing house; sending out, besides its religious works and school-books, a monthly and a weekly publication and a child's paper, which has a large and paying circulation, a great number of its subscribers being Moslems. These regenerating agencies — the schools and the press — are happily supplemented by the college, which offers to the young men of the Orient the chance of a high education, and attracts students even from the banks of the Nile. We were accompanied to the college by Dr. Jessup and Dr. Post, and spent an interesting morning in inspecting the buildings and in the enjoyment of the lovely prospect they command. As it is not my desire to enter into details regarding the Mission or the college any further than is necessary to emphasize the supreme importance of this enterprise to the civilization of the

Orient, I will only add that the college has already some interesting collections in natural history, a particularly valuable herbarium, and that the medical department is not second in promise to the literary.

It is sometimes observed that a city is like a man, in that it will preserve through all mutations and disasters certain fundamental traits; the character that it obtains at first is never wholly lost, but reappears again and again, asserting its individuality after, it may be, centuries of obscurity. Beyrout was early a seat of learning and a centre of literary influence; for nearly three hundred years before its desolation by an earthquake in the middle of the sixth century, and its subsequent devastation by the followers of the Arabian prophet, it was thronged with students from all the East, and its schools of philosophy and law enjoyed the highest renown. We believe that it is gradually resuming its ancient *prestige*.

While we were waiting day after day the arrival of the Austrian steamboat for Constantinople, we were drawn into a little drama which afforded us alternate vexation and amusement; an outline of it may not be out of place here as an illustration of the vicissitudes of travel in the East, or for other reasons which may appear. I should premise that the American consul who resided here with his family was not in good repute with many of the foreign residents; that he was charged with making personal contributions to himself the condition of the continuance in office of his sub-agents in Syria; that the character of his dragomans, or at least one of them named Ouardy, was exceedingly bad, and brought the consular office and the American name into contempt; and that these charges had been investigated by an agent sent from the ministerial bureau in Constantinople. The dragomans of the consulate, who act as interpreters, and are executors of the consul's authority, have no pay, but their position gives them a consideration in the community, and a protection which they turn to pecuniary account. It should be added that the salary of the consul at Beyrout is two thousand dollars, — a sum, in this expensive city, which is insufficient to support a consul, who has a family, in the style of a respectable citizen, and is wholly inadequate to the maintenance of any equality with the representatives of other nations; the government allows no outfit, nor does it provide for the return of its consul; the cost of transporting himself and family home would consume almost half a year's salary, and the tenure of the office is uncertain. To accept any of several of our Oriental consulships, a man must either have a private fortune or an unscrupulous knack of living by his wits. The English name is almost universally respected in the East, so far as my limited experience goes, in the character of its consuls; the same cannot be said of the American.

The morning after our arrival, descending the steps of the hotel, I found our dragoman in a violent altercation with another dragoman, a Jew, and a resident of Beyrout. There is always a latent enmity between the Egyptian and the Syrian dragomans, a national hostility, as old perhaps as the Shepherds' invasion, which it needs only an occasion to blow into a flame. The disputants were surrounded by a motley crowd, nearly all of them the adherents of the Syrian. I had seen Antoine Ouardy at Luxor, when he was the dragoman of an English traveller. He was now in Frank dress, wearing a shining hat, an enormous cluster shirt-pin, and a big seal ring; and with his aggressive nose and brazen face he had the appearance of a leading mock-auctioneer in the Bowery. On the Nile, where Abd-el-Atti enjoys the distinction of Sultan among his class, the fellow was his humble servant; but he had now caught the Egyptian away from home, and was disposed to make the most of his advantage. Chancing to meet Ouardy this morning, Abd-el-Atti had asked for the payment of two pounds lent at Luxor; the debt was promptly denied, and when his own due-bill for the money was produced, he declared that he had received the money from Abd-el-Atti in payment for some cigars which he had long ago purchased for him in Alexandria. Of course if this had been true, he would not have given a note for the money; and it happened that I had been present when the sum was borrowed.

The brazen denial exasperated our dragoman, and when I arrived the quarrel had come nearly to blows, all the injurious Arabic epithets having been exhausted. The lie direct had been

10

given back and forth, but the crowning insult was added, in English, when Abd-el-Atti cried, —

" You 're a humbug ! "

This was more than Ouardy could stand. Bursting with rage, he shook his fist in the Egyptian's face : —

" You call *me* humbug; you hum*bug*, yourself. You pay for this, I shall have satisfaction by the law."

We succeeded in separating and, I hoped, in reducing them to reason, but Antoine went off muttering vengeance, and Abd-el-Atti was determined to bring suit for his money. I represented the hopelessness of a suit in a Turkish court, the delay and the cost of lawyers, and the certainty that Ouardy would produce witnesses to anything he desired to prove.

" What I care for two pound ! " exclaimed the heated dragoman. " I go to spend a hundred pound, but I have justice."

Shortly after, as Abd-el-Atti was walking through the bazaars, with one of the ladies of our party, he was set upon by a gang of Ouardy's friends and knocked down ; the old man recovered himself and gave battle like a valiant friend of the Prophet ; Ouardy's brother sallied out from his shop to take a hand in the scrimmage, and happened to get a rough handling from Abd-el-Atti, who was entirely ignorant of his relationship to Antoine. The whole party were then carried off to the seraglio, where Abd-el-Atti, as the party attacked, was presumed to be in the wrong, and was put into custody. In the inscrutable administration of Turkish justice, the man who is knocked down in a quarrel is always arrested. When news was brought to us at the hotel of this mishap, I sent for the American consul, as our dragoman was in the service of an American citizen. The consul sent his son and his dragoman. And the dragoman sent to assist an American, embarrassed by the loss of his servant in a strange city, turned out to be the brother of Antoine Ouardy, and the very fellow that Abd-el-Atti had just beaten. Here was a complication. Dragoman Ouardy showed his wounds, and wanted compensation for his injuries. At the very moment we needed the protection of the American government, its representative appeared as our chief prosecutor.

However, we sent for Abd-el-Atti, and procured his release from the seraglio ; and after an hour of conference, in which we had the assistance of some of the most respectable foreign residents of the city, we flattered ourselves that a compromise was made. The injured Ouardy, who was a crafty rogue, was persuaded not to insist upon a suit for damages, which would greatly incommode an American citizen, and Abd-el-Atti seemed willing to drop his suit for the two pounds. Antoine, however, was still menacing.

"You heard him," he appealed to me, "you heard him call me humbug."

The injurious nature of this mysterious epithet could not be erased from his mind. It was in vain that I told him it had been freely applied to a well-known American, until it had become a badge of distinction. But at length a truce was patched up ; and, confident that there would be no more trouble, I went into the country for a long walk over the charming hills.

When I returned at six o'clock, the camp was in commotion. Abd-el-Atti was in jail ! There was a suit against him for 20,000 francs for horrible and unprovoked injuries to the dragoman of the American consul ! The consul, upon written application for assistance, made by the ladies at the hotel, had curtly declined to give any aid, and espoused the quarrel of his dragoman. It appeared that Abd-el-Atti, attempting again to accompany a lady in a shopping expedition through the bazaars, had been sent for by a messenger from the seraglio. As he could not leave the lady in the street, he carelessly answered that he would come by and by. A few minutes after he was arrested by a squad of soldiers, and taken before the military governor. Abd-el-Atti respectfully made his excuse that he could not leave the lady alone in the street, but the pasha said that he would teach him not to insult his authority. Both the Ouardy brothers were beside the pasha, whispering in his ear, and as the result of their deliberations Abd-el-Atti was put in prison. It was Saturday afternoon, and the conspirators expected to humiliate the old man by keeping him locked up till Monday. This was the state of the game when I came to dinner; the faithful Abdallah, who had

reluctantly withdrawn from watching the outside of the seraglio
where his master was confined, was divided in mind between
grief and alarm on the one side and his duty of habitual cheerfulness to us on the other, and consequently announced, "Abd-el-
Atti, seraglio," as a piece of good news; the affair had got wind
among the *cafés*, where there was a buzz of triumph over the
Egyptians; and at the hotel everybody was drawn into the excitement, discussing the assault and the arrest of the assaulted
party, the American consul and the character of his dragoman,
and the general inability of American consuls to help their countrymen in time of need.

The principal champion of Abd-el-Atti was Mohammed Achmed,
the dragoman of two American ladies who had been travelling in
Egypt and Palestine. Achmed was a character. He had the
pure Arab physiognomy, the vivacity of an Italian, the restless-
ness of an American, the courtesy of the most polished Oriental,
and a unique use of the English tongue. Copious in speech, at
times flighty in manner, gravely humorous, and more sharp-witted
than the "cutest" Yankee, he was an exceedingly experienced
and skilful dragoman, and perfectly honest to his employers.
Achmed was clad in baggy trousers, a silk scarf about his waist,
short open jacket, and wore his tarboosh on the back of his sloping head. He had a habit of throwing back his head and half
closing his wandering, restless black eyes in speaking, and his
gestures and attitudes might have been called theatrical but for a
certain simple sincerity; yet any extravagance of speech or action
was always saved from an appearance of absurdity by a humorous
twinkle in his eyes. Alexandria was his home, while Abd-el-Atti
lived in Cairo; the natural rivalry between the dragomans of the
two cities had been imbittered by some personal disagreement,
and they were only on terms of the most distant civility. But
Abd-el-Atti's misfortune not only roused his national pride, but
touched his quick generosity, and he surprised his employers by
the enthusiasm with which he espoused the cause and defended
the character of the man he had so lately regarded as anything
but a friend. He went to work with unselfish zeal to procure his
release; he would think of nothing else, talk of nothing else.

"How is it, Achmed," they said, "that you and Abd-el-Atti have suddenly become such good friends?"

"Ah, my lady," answers Achmed, taking an attitude, "you know not Abd-el-Atti, one of the firste-class men in all Egypt. Not a common dragoman like these in Beyrout, my lady; you shall ask in Cairo what a man of esteem. To tell it in Cairo that he is in jail! Abd-el-Atti is my friend. What has been sometime, that is nothing. It must not be that he is in jail. And he come out in half an hour, if your consul say so."

"That is not so certain; but what can we do?"

"Write to the consul American that he shall let Abd-el-Atti go. You, my lady," said Achmed, throwing himself on his knees before the person he was addressing, "make a letter, and say I want my dragoman immediate. If he will not, I go to the English consul, I know he will do it. Excuse me, but will you make the letter? When it was the English consul, he does something; when it was the American, I pick your pargin, my lady, he is not so much esteem here."

In compliance with Achmed's entreaty a note was written to the consul, but it produced no effect, except an uncivil reply that it was after office hours.

When I returned, Achmed was in a high fever of excitement. He believed that Abd-el-Atti would be released if I would go personally to the consul and insist upon it.

"The consul, I do not know what kind of man this is for consul; does he know what man is Abd-el-Atti? Take my advice," continued Achmed, half closing his eyes, throwing back his head and moving it alertly on the axis of his neck, and making at the same time a deprecatory gesture with the back of his hands turned out, — "take my advice, Mesr. Vahl, Abd-el-Atti is a man of respect; he is a man very rich, God forgive me! Firste-class man. There is no better family in Egypt than Abd-el-Atti Effendi. You have seen, he is the friend of governors and pashas. There is no man of more respect. In Cairo, to put Abd-el-Atti in jail, they would not believe it! When he is at home, no one could do it. The Khedive himself," he continued, warming with his theme, "would not touch Abd-el-Atti. He has houses in the

city and farms and plantations in the country, a man very well
known. Who in Cairo is to put him in jail? [This, with a smile
of derision.] I think he take out and put in prison almost anybody else he like, Mohammed Effendi Abd-el-Atti. See, when
this Ouardy comes in Egypt!"

We hastened to the consul's. I told the consul that I was deprived of the service of my dragoman, that he was unjustly imprisoned, simply for defending himself when he was assailed by a
lot of rowdies, and that as the complaint against him was supposed to issue from the consulate, I doubted not that the consul's
influence could release him. The consul replied, with suavity,
that he had nothing to do with the quarrel of his dragoman, and
was not very well informed about it, only he knew that Ouardy
had been outrageously assaulted and beaten by Abd-el-Atti; that
he could do nothing at any rate with the pasha, even if that func-
tionary had not gone to his harem outside the city, where nobody
would disturb him. I ventured to say that both the Ouardys had
a very bad reputation in the city,— it was, in fact, infamous,— and
that the consulate was brought into contempt by them. The consul
replied that the reputation of Antoine might be bad, but that his
dragoman was a respectable merchant; and then he complained
of the missionaries, who had persecuted him ever since he had
been in Beyrout. I said that I knew nothing of his grievances;
that my information about his dragoman came from general report, and from some of the bankers and most respectable citizens,
and that I knew that in this case my dragoman had been set upon
in the first instance, and that it was believed that the Ouardys
were now attempting to extort money from him, knowing him to
be rich, and having got him in their clutches away from his
friends. The consul still said that he could do nothing that
night; he was very sorry, very sorry for my embarrassment, and
he would send for Ouardy and advise him to relinquish his prosecution on my account. "Very well," I said, rising to go, "if
you cannot help me I must go elsewhere. Will you give me a
note of introduction to the pasha?" He would do that with pleasure, although he was certain that nothing would come of it.

Achmed, who had been impatiently waiting on the high piazza

(it is a charming situation overlooking the Mediterranean), saw
that I had not succeeded, and was for going at once to the English consul ; for all dragomans have entire confidence that English
consuls are all-powerful.

"No," I said, "we will try the pasha, to whom I have a letter,
though the consul says the pasha is a friend of Ouardy."

"I believe you. Ouardy has women in his house ; the pasha
goes often there ; so I hear. But we will go. I will speak to
the pasha also, and tell him what for a man is Abd-el-Atti. A
very pleasant man, the pasha, and speak all languages, very well
English."

It was encouraging to know this, and I began to feel that I
could make some impression on him. We took a carriage and
drove into the suburbs, to the house of the pasha. His Excellency
was in his harem, and dining, at that hour. I was shown by a
barefooted servant into a barren parlor furnished in the European
style, and informed that the pasha would see me presently. After
a while cigarettes and coffee — a poor substitute for dinner for a
person who had had none — were brought in ; but no pasha.
I waited there, I suppose, nearly an hour for the governor to
finish his dinner ; and meantime composed a complimentary ora-
tion to deliver upon his arrival. When his Excellency at last
appeared, I beheld a large, sleek Turk, whose face showed good-
nature and self-indulgence. I had hopes of him, and, advancing
to salute him, began an apology for disturbing his repose at this
unseasonable hour, but his Excellency looked perfectly blank. He
did not understand a word of English. I gave him the letter of
the consul, and mentioned the name "American Consul." The
pasha took the letter and opened it ; but as he was diligently examining it upside down, I saw that he did not read English. I
must introduce myself.

Opening the door, I called Achmed. In coming into the
presence of this high rank, all his buoyancy and bravado vanished ; he obsequiously waited. I told him to say to his Excellency how extremely sorry I was to disturb his repose at such an
unseasonable hour, but that my dragoman, whose services I
needed, had been unfortunately locked up ; that I was an Amer-

ican citizen, as he would perceive by the letter from the consul, and that I would detain him only a moment with my business. Achmed put this into choice Arabic. His Excellency looked more blank than before. He did not understand a word of Arabic. The interview was getting to be interesting.

The pasha then stepped to the door and called in his dragoman, a barefooted fellow in a tattered gown. The two interpreters stood in line before us, and the pasha nodded to me to begin. I opened, perhaps, a little too elaborately ; Achmed put my remarks into Arabic, and the second dragoman translated that again into Turkish. What the speech became by the time it reached the ear of the pasha I could not tell, but his face darkened at once, and he peremptorily shook his head. The word came back to me that the pasha would n't let him out ; Abd-el-Atti must stay in jail till his trial. I then began to argue the matter, — to say that there was no criminal suit against him, only an action for damages, and that I would be responsible for his appearance when required. The translations were made ; but I saw that I was every moment losing ground ; no one could tell what my solicitations became after being strained through Arabic and Turkish. My case was lost, because it could not be heard.

Suddenly it occurred to me that the pasha might know some European language. I turned to him, and asked him if he spoke German. O, yes ! The prospect brightened, and if I also had spoken that language, we should have had no further trouble. However, desperation beat up my misty recollection, and I gave the pasha a torrent of broken German that evidently astonished him. At any rate, he became gracious as soon as he understood me. He said that Abd-el-Atti was not confined on account of the suit, — he knew nothing and cared nothing for his difficulty with Ouardy, — but for his contempt of the police and soldiers. I explained that, and added that Abd-el-Atti was an old man, that I had been doctoring him for a fever ever since we were in Damascus, that I feared to have him stay in that damp jail over Sunday, and that I would be responsible for his appearance.

" Do you mean to say," he asked, "that you will be personally responsible that he appears at the seraglio Monday morning ? "

" Certainly," I said, "for his appearance at any time and place your Excellency may name."

" Then he may go." He gave the order to his dragoman to accompany us and procure his release, and we retired, with mutual protestations of the highest consideration. Achmed was nearly beside himself with joy. The horses seemed to him to crawl ; he could n't wait the moment to announce to Abd-el-Atti his deliverance. " Ah, they thought to keep Abd-el-Atti in jail all night, and sent word to Cairo, ' Abd-el-Atti is in jail.' Abd-el-Atti Effendi ! Take my advice, a man of respect."

The cobble-paved court of the old seraglio prison, to which the guards admitted us without question, was only dimly lighted by an oil-lamp or two, and we could distinguish a few figures flitting about, who looked like malefactors, but were probably keepers. We were shown into a side room, where sat upon the ground an official, perhaps a judge, and two assistants. Abd-el-Atti was sent for. The old man was brought in, swinging his string of beads in his hand, looking somewhat crest-fallen, but preserving a portentous gravity. I arose and shook hands with him, and told him we had come to take him out. When we were seated, a discussion of the case sprung up, the official talked, his two assistants talked, and Abd-el-Atti and Achmed talked, and there was evidently a disposition to go over the affair from the beginning. It was a pity to cut short so much eloquence, but I asked the pasha's dragoman to deliver his message, and told Achmed that we would postpone the discussion till Monday, and depart at once. The prisoner was released, and, declining coffee, we shook hands and got away with all haste. As we drove to the hotel, Abd-el-Atti was somewhat pensive, but declared that he would rather give a hundred pounds than not be let out that night ; and when we reached home, Achmed, whose spirits were exuberant, insisted on dragging him to the *café* opposite, to exhibit him in triumph.

When I came down in the morning, Achmed was in the hall.

" Well, Achmed, how are you ? "

" Firste-class," closing his eyes with a humorous twinkle. " I 'm in it now."

10 *

o

" In what ? "

" In the case with Mohammed Abd-el-Atti. That Ouardy says I pay him damage twenty thousand francs. Twenty thousand francs, I wish he may get it ! How much, I s'pose, for the consul ? Take my advice, the consul want money."

" Then the suit will keep you here with Abd-el-Atti ? "

" Keep, I don't know. I not pay him twenty thousand francs, not one thousand, not one franc. What my ladies do? Who go to Constantinople with my ladies? To-morrow morning come the steamer. To leave the old man alone with these thiefs, what would anybody say of Mohammed Achmed for that? What for consul is this? I want to go to Constantinople with my ladies, and then to see my family in Alexandria. For one day in five months have I see my wife and shild. O yes, I have very nice wife. Yes, one wife quite plenty for me. And I have a fine house, cost me twenty thousand dollars; I am not rich, but I have plenty, God forgive me. My shop is in the silk bazaar. I am merchant. My father-in-law say what for I go dragoman? I like to see nice peoples and go in the world. When I am dragoman, I am servant. When I am merchant, O, I am very well in Alexandria. I think I not go any more. Ah, here is Abd-el-Atti. Take my advice, he not need to be dragoman; he is pooty off. Good morning, my friend. Have they told you I am to be put in jail also? "

" So I hear; Ouardy sue you and Abdallah so you cannot be witness."

" O, they think they get money from us. Mebbe the pasha and the consul. I think so."

" So am I," responded Abd-el-Atti in his most serious manner. The " Eastern question," with these experienced dragomans, instantly resolves itself into a question of money, whoever is concerned and whatever is the tribunal. I said that I would see the consul in the morning, and that I hoped to have all proceedings stopped, so that we could get off in the steamer. Abd-el-Atti shook his head.

" The consul not to do anything. Ouardy have lent him money; so I hunderstood."

Beyrout had a Sunday appearance. The shops were nearly all closed, and the churches, especially the Catholic, were crowded. It might have been a peaceful day but for our imbroglio, which began to be serious; we could not afford the time to wait two weeks for the next Cyprus steamer, we did not like to abandon our dragomans, and we needed their services. The ladies who depended upon Achmed were in a quandary. Notes went to the consul, but produced no effect. The bankers were called into the council, and one of them undertook to get Achmed free. Travellers, citizens, and all began to get interested or entangled in the case. There was among respectable people but one opinion about the consul's dragoman. At night it was whispered about that the American consul had already been removed and that his successor was on his way to Beyrout. Achmed came to us in the highest spirits with the news.

All day Monday we expected the steamer. The day was frittered away in interviews with the consul and the pasha, and in endeavoring to learn something of the two cases, the suit for damages and for the debt, supposed to be going on somewhere in the seraglio. After my interview with the consul, who expressed considerable ignorance of the case and the strongest desire to stop it, I was surprised to find at the seraglio all the papers in the consul's name, and all the documents written on consular paper; so that when I appeared as an American citizen, to endeavor to get my dragoman released, it appeared to the Turkish officials that they would please the American government by detaining and punishing him.

The court-room was a little upper chamber, with no furniture except a long table and chairs; three Moslem judges sat at one end of the table, apparently waiting to see what would turn up. The scene was not unlike that in an office of a justice of the peace in America. The parties to the case, witnesses, attendants, spectators, came and went as it pleased them, talked or whispered to the judges or to each other. There seemed to be no rule for the reception or rejection of evidence. The judges smoked and gathered the facts as they drifted in, and would by and by make up their minds. It is truth to say, however, that they seemed to be endeavoring to get at the facts, and that they appeared to be above prejudice or interest. A new complication developed itself, however; Antoine Ouardy claimed to be a French citizen, and the French consul was drawn into the fray. This was a new device to delay proceedings.

When I had given my evidence to the judges, which I was required to put in writing, I went with Abd-el-Atti to the room of the pasha. This official was gracious enough, but gave us no hopes of release. He took me one side and advised me, as a traveller, to look out for another dragoman; there was no prospect that Abd-el-Atti could get away to accompany me on this steamer, — in fact, the process in court might detain him six months. However, the best thing to do would be to go to the American consul with Ouardy and settle it. He thought Ouardy would settle it for a reasonable amount. It was none of his business, but that was his advice. We were obliged to his Excellency for this glimpse behind the scenes of a Turkish court, and thanked him for his advice; but we did not follow it. Abd-el-Atti thought that if he abandoned the attempt to collect a debt in a Turkish city, he ought not, besides, to pay for the privilege of doing so.

Tuesday morning the steamer came into the harbor. Although we had registered our names at the office of the company for passage, nothing was reserved for us. Detained at the seraglio and the consul's, we could not go off to secure places, and the consequence was that we were subject to the black-mail of the steward when we did go. By noon there were signs of the failure of the prosecution; and we sent off our luggage. In an hour or two Abd-el-Atti appeared with a troop of friends, triumphant. Somewhere, I do not know how, he and Achmed had raked up fourteen witnesses in his favor; the judges would n't believe Ouardy nor any one he produced, and his case had utterly broken down. This mountain of a case, which had annoyed us so many days and absorbed our time, suddenly collapsed. We were not sorry to leave even beautiful Beyrout, and would have liked to see the last of Turkish rule as well. At sunset, on the steamer *Achille*, swarming above and below with pilgrims from Jerusalem and Mecca, we sailed for Cyprus.

XVIII.

CYPRUS.

.

IN the early morning we were off Cyprus, in the open harbor of Larnaka, — a row of white houses on the low shore. The town is not peculiar and not specially attractive, but the *Marina* lies prettily on the blue sea, and the palms, the cypresses, the minarets and church-towers, form an agreeable picture behind it, backed by the lovely outline of mountains, conspicuous among them Santa Croce. The highest, Olympus, cannot be seen from this point.

A night had sufficed to transport us into another world, a world in which all outlines are softened and colored, a world in which history appears like romance. We might have imagined that we had sailed into some tropical harbor, except that the island before us was bare of foliage; there was the calm of perfect repose in the sky, on the sea, and the land; Cyprus made no harsh contrast with the azure water in which it seemed to be anchored for the morning, as our ship was. You could believe that the calm of summer and of early morning always rested on the island, and that it slept exhausted in the memory of its glorious past.

Taking a cup of coffee, we rowed ashore. It was the festival of St. George, and the flags of various nations were hung out along the *riva*, or displayed from the staffs of the consular residences. It is one of the chief *fête* days of the year, and the foreign representatives, who have not too much excitement, celebrated it by formal visits to the Greek consul. Larnaka does not keep a hotel, and we wandered about for some time before we could discover its sole *locanda*, where we purposed to breakfast. This establishment would please an artist, but it had few attractions for a person wishing to break his fast, and our unusual demand threw it into confusion. The *locanda* was nothing but a kitchen in a tumble-down building, smoke-dried, with an earth floor and a rickety table or two. After long delay, the cheerful Greek proprietor and his lively wife — whose good-humored willingness both to furnish us next to nothing, but the best they had, from their scanty larder, and to cipher up a long reckoning for the same, excited our interest — produced some fried veal, sour bread, harsh wine, and tart oranges; and we breakfasted more sumptuously, I have no doubt, than any natives of the island that morning. The scant and hard fare of nearly all the common people in the East would be unendurable to any American; but I think that the hardy peasantry of the Levant would speedily fall into dyspeptic degeneracy upon the introduction of American rural cooking.

After we had killed our appetites at the *locanda*, we presented our letters to the American consul, General di Cesnola, in whose spacious residence we experienced a delightful mingling of Oriental and Western hospitality. The kawâss of the General was sent to show us the town. This kawâss was a gorgeous official, a kind of glorified being, in silk and gold-lace, who marched before us, huge in bulk, waving his truncheon of office, and gave us the appearance, in spite of our humility, of a triumphal procession. Larnaka has not many sights, although it was the residence of the Lusignan dynasty, — Richard Cœur de Lion having, toward the close of the twelfth century, made a gift of the island to Guy de Lusignan. It has, however, some mosques and Greek churches. The church of St. Lazarus, which contains the now vacant tomb of the Lazarus who was raised from the dead at Bethany and afterwards became bishop of Citium, is an interesting old Byzantine edifice, and has attached to it an English burial-ground, with tombs of the seventeenth century. The Greek priest who showed us the church does not lose sight of the gain of godliness in this life while pursuing in this remote station his heavenly journey. He sold my friend some exquisite old crucifixes, carved in wood, mounted in antique silver, which he took from the altar, and he let the church part with some of its quaint old pictures, commemorating the impossible exploits of St. Demetrius and St. George. But he was very careful that none of the Greeks who were lounging about the church should be witnesses of the transfer. He said that these ignorant people had a prejudice about these sacred objects, and might make trouble.

The excavations made at Larnaka have demonstrated that this was the site of ancient Citium, the birthplace of Zeno, the Stoic, and the Chittim so often alluded to by the Hebrew prophets ; it was a Phœnician colony, and when Ezekiel foretold the unrecoverable fall of Tyre, among the luxuries of wealth he enumerated were the " benches of ivory brought out of the isles of Chittim." Paul does not mention it, but he must have passed through it when he made his journey over the island from Salamis to Paphos, where he had his famous encounter with the sorcerer Bar-jesus. A few miles out of town on the road to Citti is a Turkish mosque, which shares the high veneration of Moslems with those of Mecca and Jerusalem.   In it is interred the wet-nurse of Mohammed.

We walked on out of the town to the most considerable church in the place, newly built by the Roman Catholics.   There is attached to it a Franciscan convent, a neat establishment with a garden ; and the hospitable monks, when they knew we were Americans, insisted upon entertaining us ; the contributions for their church had largely come from America, they said, and they seemed to regard us as among the number of their benefactors. This Christian charity expressed itself also in some bunches of roses, which the brothers plucked for our ladies.   One cannot but suspect and respect that timid sentiment the monk retains for the sex whose faces he flies from, which he expresses in the care of flowers ; the blushing rose seems to be the pure and only link between the monk and womankind ; he may cultivate it without sin, and offer it to the chance visitor without scandal.

The day was lovely, but the sun had intense power, and in default of donkeys we took a private carriage into the country to visit the church of St. George, at which the *fête* day of that saint was celebrated by a fair, and a concourse of peasants. Our carriage was a four-wheeled cart, a sort of hay-wagon, drawn by two steers, and driven by a Greek boy in an embroidered jacket. The Franciscans lent us chairs for the cart; the resplendent kawâss marched ahead; Abd-el-Atti hung his legs over the tail of the cart in an attitude of dejection; and we moved on, but so slowly that my English friend, Mr. Edward Rae, was able to sketch us, and the Cyprians could enjoy the spectacle.

The country lay bare and blinking under the sun; save here and there a palm or a bunch of cypresses, this part of the island has not a tree or a large shrub. The view of the town and the sea with its boats, as we went inland, was peculiar, not anything real, but a skeleton picture; the sky and sea were indigo blue. We found a crowd of peasants at the church of St. George, which has a dirty interior, like all the Greek churches. The Greeks, as well as the other Orientals, know how to mingle devotion with the profits of trade, and while there were rows of booths outside, and traffic went on briskly, the church was thronged with men and women who bought tapers for offerings, and kissed with fervor the holy relics which were exposed. The articles for sale at the booths and stands were chiefly eatables and the coarsest sort of merchandise. The only specialty of native manufacture was rude but pleasant-sounding little bells, which are sometimes strung upon the necks of donkeys. But so fond are these simple people of musical noise, that these bells are attached to the handles of sickles also. The barley was already dead-ripe in the fields, and many of the peasants at the fair brought their sickles with them. They were, both men and women, a good-humored, primitive sort of people, certainly not a handsome race, but picturesque in appearance; both sexes affect high colors, and the bright petticoats of the women matched the gay jackets of their husbands and lovers.

We do not know what was the ancient standard of beauty in Cyprus; it may have been no higher than it is now, and perhaps the swains at this *fête* of St. George would turn from any other type of female charms as uninviting. The Cyprian or Paphian Venus could not have been a beauty according to our notions.

The images of her which General di Cesnola found in her temple all have a long and sharp nose. These images are Phœnician, and were made six hundred to a thousand years before the Christian era, at the time that wonderful people occupied this fertile island. It is an interesting fact, and an extraordinary instance of the persistence of nature in perpetuating a type, that all the women of Cyprus to-day—who are, with scarcely any exception, ugly — have exactly the nose of the ancient Paphian Venus, that is to say, the nose of the Phœnician women whose husbands and lovers sailed the Mediterranean as long ago as the siege of Troy.

It was off the southern coast of this island, near Paphos, that Venus Aphrodite, born of the foam, is fabled to have risen from the sea. The anniversary of her birth is still perpetuated by an annual *fête* on the 11th of August, — a rite having its foundation in nature, that has proved to be stronger than religious instruction or prejudice. Originally, these *fêtes* were the scenes of a too literal worship of Venus, and even now the Cyprian maiden thinks that her chance of matrimony is increased by her attendance at this annual fair. Upon that day all the young people go upon the sea in small boats, and, until recently, it used to be the custom to dip a virgin into the water in remembrance of the mystic birth of Venus. That ceremony is still partially maintained ; instead of sousing the maiden in the sea, her companions spatter the representative of the goddess with salt water, — immersion has given way here also to sprinkling.

The lively curiosity of the world has been of late years turned to Cyprus as the theatre of some of the most important and extensive archæological discoveries of this century ; discoveries unique, and illustrative of the manners and religion of a race, once the most civilized in the Levant, of which only the slightest monuments had hitherto been discovered ; discoveries which supply the lost link between Egyptian and Grecian art. These splendid results, which by a stroke of good fortune confer some credit upon the American nation, are wholly due to the scholarship, patient industry, address, and enthusiasm of one man. To those who are familiar with the magnificent Cesnola Collection, which is the chief attraction of the Metropolitan Museum of New

York, I need make no apology for devoting a few paragraphs to the antiquities of Cyprus and their explorer.

Cyprus was the coveted prize of all the conquerors of the Orient in turn. The fair island, with an area not so large as the State of Connecticut, owns in its unequal surface the extremes of the temperate climate; snow lies during the greater part of the year upon its mountains, which attain an altitude of over seven thousand feet, and the palm spreads its fan-leaves along the southern coast and in the warm plains; irregular in shape, it has an extreme length of over one hundred and forty miles, and an average breadth of about forty miles, and its deeply indented coast gives an extraordinarily long shore-line and offers the facilities of harbors for the most active commerce.

The maritime Phœnicians early discovered its advantages, and in the seventeenth century B. C., or a little later, a colony from Sidon settled at Citium; and in time these Yankees of the Levant occupied all the southern portion of the island with their busy ports and royal cities. There is a tradition that Teucer, after the Trojan war, founded the city of Salamis on the east coast. But however this may be, and whatever may be the exact date of the advent of the Sidonians upon the island, it is tolerably certain that they were in possession about the year 1600 B. C., when the navy of Thotmes III., the greatest conqueror and states-man in the long line of Pharaohs, visited Cyprus and collected tribute. The Egyptians were never sailors, and the fleet of Thotmes III. was no doubt composed of Phœnician ships manned by Phœnician sailors. He was already in possession of the whole of Syria, the Phœnicians were his tributaries and allies, their ships alone sailed the Grecian seas and carried the products of Egypt and of Asia to the Pelasgic populations. The Phœnician supremacy, established by Sidon in Cyprus, was maintained by Tyre; and it was not seriously subverted until 708 B. C., when the Assyrian ravager of Syria, Sargon, sent a fleet and conquered Cyprus. He set up a *stele* in Citium, commemorating his exploit, which has been preserved and is now in the museum at Berlin. Two centuries later the island owned the Persians as masters, and was comprised in the fifth satrapy of Darius. It became a

part of the empire of the Macedonian Alexander after his conquest of Asia Minor, and was again an Egyptian province under
the Ptolemies, until the Roman eagles swooped down upon it.
Coins are not seldom found that tell the story of these occupa-
tions. Those bearing the head of Ptolemy Physcon, Euergetes
VII., found at Paphos and undoubtedly struck there, witness the
residence on the island of that licentious and literary tyrant,
whom a popular outburst had banished from Alexandria. Another
with the head of Vespasian, and on the obverse an outline of the
temple of Venus at Paphos, attests the Roman hospitality to the
gods and religious rites of all their conquered provinces.

Upon the breaking up of the Roman world, Cyprus fell to the
Greek Empire, and for centuries maintained under its ducal governors a sort of independent life, enjoying as much prosperity as
was possible under the almost uniform imbecility and corruption of
the Byzantine rule. We have already spoken of its transfer to the
Lusignans by Richard Cœur de Lion; and again a romantic chapter
was added to its history by the reign of Queen Catharine Cornaro,
who gave her kingdom to the Venetian republic. Since its final
conquest by the Turks in 1571, Cyprus has interested the world
only by its sufferings ; for Turkish history here, as elsewhere, is
little but a record of exactions, rapine, and massacre.

From time to time during the present century efforts have
been made by individuals and by learned societies to explore the
antiquities of Cyprus ; but although many interesting discoveries
were made, yet the field was comparatively virgin when General
di Cesnola was appointed American consul in 1866. Here and
there a *stele*, or some fragments of pottery, or the remains of a
temple, had been unearthed by chance or by superficial search,
but the few objects discovered served only to pique curiosity.
For one reason or another, the efforts made to establish the site
of ancient cities had been abandoned, the expeditions sent out
by France had been comparatively barren of results, and it seemed
as if the traces of the occupation of the Phœnicians, the Egyptians, the Assyrians, the Persians, and the Romans were irrecover-
ably concealed.

General L. P. di Cesnola, the explorer of Cyprus, is of a noble

Piedmontese family; he received a military and classical education at Turin; identified with the party of Italian unity, his sympathies were naturally excited by the contest in America; he offered his sword to our government, and served with distinction in the war for the Union. At its close he was appointed consul at Cyprus, a position of no pecuniary attraction, but I presume that the new consul had in view the explorations which have given his name such honorable celebrity in both hemispheres.

The difficulties of his undertaking were many. He had to encounter at every step the jealousy of the Turkish government, and the fanaticism and superstition of the occupants of the soil. Archæological researches are not easy in the East under the most favorable circumstances, and in places where the traces of ancient habitations are visible above ground, and ancient sites are known; but in Cyprus no ruins exist in sight to aid the explorer, and, with the exception of one or two localities, no names of ancient places are known to the present generation. But the consul was convinced that the great powers which had from age to age held Cyprus must have left some traces of their occupation, and that intelligent search would discover the ruins of the prosperous cities described by Strabo and mentioned by the geographer Ptolemy. Without other guides than the descriptions of these and other ancient writers, the consul began his search in 1867, and up to 1875 he had ascertained the exact sites of *eleven ancient cities* mentioned by Strabo and Ptolemy, most of which had ceased to exist before the Christian era, and none of which has left vestiges above the soil.

In the time of David and of Solomon the Phœnicians formed the largest portion of the population of the island; their royal cities of Paphos, Amathus, Carpassa, Citium, and Ammochosto, were in the most flourishing condition. Not a stone remained of them above ground; their sites were unknown in 1867.

When General di Cesnola had satisfied himself of the probable site of an ancient city or temple, it was difficult to obtain permission to dig, even with the authority of the Sultan's firman. He was obliged to wait for harvests to be gathered, in some cases, to take a lease of the ground; sometimes the religious fanaticism of the occupants could not be overcome, and his working parties were frequently beaten and driven away in his absence. But the consul exhibited tact, patience, energy, the qualities necessary, with knowledge, to a successful explorer. He evaded or cast down all obstacles.

In 1868 he discovered the necropoli of Ledra, Citium, and Idalium, and opened during three years in these localities over ten thousand tombs, bringing to light a mass of ancient objects of art which enable us to understand the customs, religion, and civilization of the earlier inhabitants. Idalium was famous of old as the place where Grecian pottery was first made, and fragments of it have been found from time to time on its site.

In 1869 and 1870 he surveyed Aphrodisium, in the northeastern part of the island, and ascertained, in the interior, the site of Golgos, a city known to have been in existence before the Trojan war. The disclosures at this place excited both the wonder and the incredulity of the civilized world, and it was not until the marvellous collection of the explorer was exhibited, partially in London, but fully in New York, that the vast importance of the labors of General di Cesnola began to be comprehended. In exploring the necropolis of Golgos, he came, a few feet below the soil, upon the remains of the temple of Venus, strewn with mutilated sculptures of the highest interest, supplying the missing link between Egyptian and Greek art, and indeed illustrating the artistic condition of most of the Mediterranean nations during the period from about 1200 to about 500 B. C. It would require too much space to tell how the British Museum missed and the Metropolitan of New York secured this first priceless " Cesnola Collection." Suffice it to say, that it was sold to a generous citizen of New York, Mr. John Taylor Johnson, for fifty thousand dollars, — a sum which would not compensate the explorer for his time and labor, and would little more than repay his pecuniary outlay, which reached the amount of over sixty thousand dollars in 1875. But it was enough that the treasure was secured by his adopted country ; the loss of it to the Old World, which was publicly called an " European misfortune," was a piece of good fortune to the United States, which time will magnify.

From 1870 to 1872 the General's attention was directed to the southwestern portion of the island, and he laid open the necropoli of Marium, Paphos, Alamas, and Soli, and three ancient cities whose names are yet unknown. In 1873 he explored and traced the cities of Throni, Leucolla, and Arsinöe, and the necropoli of several towns still unknown. In 1874 and 1875 he brought to light the royal cities of Amathus and Curium, and located the little town of Kury.

It would not be possible here to enumerate all the objects of art or worship, and of domestic use, which these excavations have yielded. The statuary and the thousands of pieces of glass, some of them rivalling the most perfect Grecian shapes in form, and excelling the Venetian colors in the iridescence of age, perhaps attract most attention in the Metropolitan Museum. From the tombs were taken thousands of vases of earthenware, some in alabaster and bronze, statuettes in terra-cotta, arms, coins, scarabæi, cylinders, intaglios, cameos, gold ornaments, and mortuary *steles*. In the temples were brought to light inscriptions, bas-reliefs, architectural fragments, and statues of the different nations who have conquered and occupied the island. The inscriptions are in the Egyptian, Assyrian, Phœnician, Greek, and the Cypriote languages; the last-mentioned being, in the opinion of the explorer, an ancient Greek dialect.

At Curium, nineteen feet below the surface of the ground, were found the remains of the Temple of Apollo Hylates; the sculptures contained in it belong to the Greek period from 700 to 100 B. C. At Amathus some royal tombs were opened, and two marble sarcophagi of large dimensions, one of them intact, were discovered, which are historically important, and positive additions to the remains of the best Greek art.

After Golgos, Paleo Paphos yielded the most interesting treasures. Here existed a temple to the Paphian Venus, whose birth-place was in sight of its portals, famous throughout the East; devotees and pilgrims constantly resorted to it, as they do now to the shrines of Mecca and Jerusalem. Not only the maritime adventurers and traders from Asia Minor and the Grecian mainland crowded to the temple of this pleasing and fortunate goddess, and quitted their vows or propitiated her favor by gifts, but the religious or the superstitious from Persia and Assyria and farthest Egypt deposited there their votive offerings. The collector of a museum of antiquity that should illustrate the manners and religion of the thousand years before the Christian era could ask nothing better than these deposits of many races during many centuries in one place.

The excavations at Paphos were attended with considerable danger; more than once the workmen were obliged to flee to save their lives from the fanatic Moslems. The town, although it has lost its physical form, and even its name (its site is now called Baffo), retains the character of superstition it had when St. Paul found it expedient to darken the vision of Elymas there, as if a city, like a man, possessed a soul that outlives the body.

We spent the afternoon in examining the new collection of General di Cesnola, not so large as that in the Metropolitan Museum, but perhaps richer in some respects, particularly in iridescent glass.

In the summer of 1875, however, the labors of the indefatigable explorer were crowned with a discovery the riches of which cast into the shade the real or pretended treasures of the "House of Priam," — a discovery not certainly of more value to art than those that preceded it, but well calculated to excite popular wonder. The finding of this subterranean hoard reads like an adventure of Aladdin.

In pursuing his researches at Curium, on the southwestern side of the island, General di Cesnola came upon the site of an ancient temple, and uncovered its broken mosaic pavement. Beneath this, and at the depth of twenty-five feet, he broke into a subterranean passage cut in the rock. This passage led to a door; no genie sat by it, but it was securely closed by a stone slab. When this was removed, a suite of four rooms was disclosed, but they were not immediately accessible; earth sifting through the roofs for ages had filled them, and it required the labor of a month to clean out the chambers. Imagine the feverish enthusiasm of the explorer as he slowly penetrated this treasure-house, where every stroke of the pick disclosed the gleam of buried treasure! In the first room were found only *gold* objects; in the second only *silver* and silver-gilt ornaments and utensils; in the third alabasters, terra-cottas, vases, and groups of figures; in the fourth *bronzes*, and nothing else. It is the opinion of the discoverer that these four rooms were the depositories where the crafty priests and priestesses of the old temple used to hide their treasures during times of war or sudden invasion. I cannot but think that the mysterious subterranean passages and chambers in the ancient temples of Egypt served a similar purpose. The treasure found scattered in these rooms did not appear to be the whole belonging to the temple, but only a part, left perhaps in the confusion of a hasty flight.

Among the articles found in the first room, dumped in a heap in the middle (as if they had been suddenly, in a panic, stripped from the altar in the temple and cast into a place of concealment), were a gold cup covered with Egyptian embossed work, and two bracelets of pure gold weighing over *three pounds*, inscribed with the name of "Etevander, King of Paphos." This king lived in 635 B. C., and in 620 B. C. paid tribute to the Assyrian monarch Assurbanapal (Sardanapalus), as is recorded on an Assyrian tablet now in the British Museum. There were also many gold necklaces, bracelets, ear-rings, finger-rings, brooches, seals, armlets, etc., in all four hundred and eighty gold articles.

In the silver-room, arranged on the benches at the sides, were vases, bottles, cups, bowls, bracelets, finger-rings, ear-rings, seals, etc. One of the most curious and valuable objects is a silver-gilt bowl, having upon it very fine embossed Egyptian work, and evidently of high antiquity.

In the third room of vases and terra-cottas were some most valuable and interesting specimens. The bronze-room yielded several high candelabra, lamp-holders, lamps, statuettes, bulls'-heads, bowls, vases, jugs, patera, fibula, rings, bracelets, mirrors, etc. Nearly all the objects in the four rooms seem to have been "votive offerings," and testify a pagan devotion to the gods not excelled by Christian generosity to the images and shrines of modern worship. The inscriptions betoken the votive character of these treasures; that upon the heavy gold amulets is in the genitive case, and would be literally translated "Etevandri Regis Paphi," the words "offering of" being understood to precede it.

I confess that the glitter of these treasures, and the glamour of these associations with the ingenious people of antiquity, transformed the naked island of Cyprus, as we lay off it in the golden sunset, into a region of all possibilities, and I longed to take my Strabo and my spade and wander off prospecting for its sacred placers. It seemed to me, when we weighed anchor at seven o'clock, that we were sailing away from subterranean passages stuffed with the curious treasures of antiquity, from concealed chambers in which one, if he could only remove the stone slab of the door, would pick up the cunning work of the Phœnician jewellers, the barbarous ornaments of the Assyrians, the conceits in gold and silver of the most ancient of peoples, the Egyptians.

XIX.

THROUGH SUMMER SEAS. — RHODES.

AT daylight next morning we could just discern Cyprus sinking behind us in the horizon. The day had all the charm
with which the poets have invested this region; the sea was of
the traditional indigo blue, — of which the Blue Grotto of Capri
is only a cheap imitation. No land was in sight, after we lost
Cyprus, but the spirit of the ancient romance lay upon the waters,
and we were soothed with the delights of an idle existence. As
good a world as can be made with a perfect sea and a perfect sky
and delicious atmosphere we had.

Through this summer calm voyages our great steamer, a world
in itself, an exhibition, a fair, a *fête*, a camp-meeting, cut loose
from the earth and set afloat. There are not less than eight hundred pilgrims on board, people known as first-class and second-
class stowed in every nook and corner. Forward of the first
cabin, the deck of the long vessel is packed with human beings,
two deep and sometimes crossed, a crowd which it is almost impossible to penetrate. We look down into the hold upon a mass
of bags and bundles and Russians heaped indiscriminately together, — and it is very difficult to distinguish a Russian woman
from a bundle of old clothes, when she is in repose. These people travel with their bedding, their babies, and their cooking
utensils, and make a home wherever they sit down.

The forward passengers have overflowed their limits and extend
back upon our portion of the deck, occupying all one side of it to
the stern, leaving the so-called privileged class only a narrow
promenade on the starboard side. These intruders are, however,

rather first-class second-class. Parties of them are camped down in small squares, which become at once miniature seraglios. One square is occupied by wealthy Moslems from Damascus, and in another is a stately person who is rumored to be the Prince of Damascus. These turbaned and silk-clad Orientals have spread their bright rugs and cushions, and lounge here all day and sleep here at night; some of them entertain themselves with chess, but the most of them only smoke and talk little. Why should they talk? has not enough already been said in the world? At intervals during the day, ascertaining, I do not know how, the direction of Mecca, these grave men arise, spread their prayer-carpets, and begin in unison their kneelings and prostrations, servants and masters together, but the servants behind their masters. Next to them, fenced off by benches, is a harem square, occupied by veiled women, perhaps the wives of these Moslems and perhaps " some others." All the deck is a study of brilliant costume.

A little later the Oriental prince turns out to be only a Turkish pasha, who has a state-room below for himself, and another for his harem; but in another compartment of our flower-bed of a deck is a merchant-prince of Damascus, whose gorgeousness would impose upon people more sophisticated than we.

" He no prince; merchant like me," explains Achmed, " and very rich, God be merciful."

" But why don't you travel about like that, Achmed, and make a fine display?"

" For why? Anybody say Mohammed Achmed any more respect? What for I show my rich? Take my advice. When I am dragoman, I am servant; and dress [here a comico-sarcastic glance at his plain but handsome dragoman apparel] not in monkey shine, like Selim — you remember him — at Jaffa, fierce like a Bedawee. I make business. When I am by my house, that is another thing."

The pasha has rooms below, and these contiguous squares on deck are occupied, the one by his suite and the other by *their* ladies and slaves, all veiled and presumably beautiful, lolling on the cushions in the *ennui* that appears to be their normal condition. One of them is puffing a cigarette under her white veil at the risk of a conflagration. One of the slaves, with an olive complexion and dark eyes, is very pretty, and rather likes to casually leave her face uncovered for the benefit of the infidels who are about; that her feet and legs are bare she cares still less. This harem is, however, encroached upon by Greek women, who sprawl about with more freedom, and regard the world without the hindrance of a veil. If they are not handsome, they are at least not self-conscious, as you would think women would be in baggy silk trousers and embroidered jackets.

In the afternoon we came in sight of the ancient coasts of Pamphylia and Lycia and a lovely range of what we took to be the Karamanian mountains, snow-covered and half hid in clouds, all remote and dim to our vision as the historical pageant of Assyrian, Persian, and Roman armies on these shores is to our memory. Eastward on that rugged coast we know is Cilicia and the Tarsus of Paul and Haroun al Raschid. The sunset on the Lycian mountains was glorious; the foot by the water was veiled in golden mist; the sea sank from indigo to purple, and when the light waves broke flecks of rose or blood flowed on the surface.

After dark, and before we were abreast of old Xanthus, we descried the famous natural light which is almost as mysterious to the moderns as it was to the ancients. The Handbook says of it: "About two miles from the coast, through a fertile plain, and then ascending a woody glen, the traveller arrives at the *Zanar*, or volcanic flame, which issues perpetually from the mountain." Pliny says: "*Mount Chimæra*, near Phaselis, emits an unceasing flame that burns day and night." Captain Beaufort observed it from the ship during the night as a small but steady light among the hills. We at first mistook it for a lighthouse. But it was too high above the water for that, and the flame was too large; it was rather a smoky radiance than a point of light, and yet it had a dull red centre and a duller luminous surrounding. We regarded with curiosity and some awe a flame that had been burning for over twenty centuries, and perhaps was alight before the signal-fires were kindled to announce the fall of Troy, — Nature's own Pharos to the ancient mariners who were without compass on these treacherous seas.

Otherwise, this classic coast is dark, extinguished is the fire on the altar of Apollo at Patera, silent is the winter oracle of this god, and desolate is the once luxurious metropolis of Lycia. Even Xanthus, the capital, a name disused by the present inhabitants, has little to show of Greek culture or Persian possession, and one must seek the fragments of its antique art in the British Museum.

Coming on deck the next morning at the fresh hour of sunrise, I found we were at Rhodes. We lay just off the semicircular harbor, which is clasped by walls — partly shaken down by earthquakes — which have noble round towers at each embracing end. Rhodes is, from the sea, one of the most picturesque cities in the Mediterranean, although it has little remains of that ancient splendor which caused Strabo to prefer it to Rome or Alexandria. The harbor wall, which is flanked on each side by stout and round stone windmills, extends up the hill, and, becoming double, surrounds the old town ; these massive fortifications of the Knights of St. John have withstood the onsets of enemies and the tremors of the earth, and, with the ancient moat, excite the curiosity of this so-called peaceful age of iron-clads and monster cannon. The city ascends the slope of the hill and passes beyond the wall. Outside and on the right towards the sea are a picturesque group of a couple of dozen stone windmills, and some minarets and a church-tower or two. Higher up the hill is sprinkled a little foliage, a few mulberry-trees, and an isolated palm or two ; and, beyond, the island is only a mass of broken, bold, rocky mountains. Of its forty-five miles of length, running southwesterly from the little point on which the city stands, we can see but little.

Whether or not Rhodes emerged from the sea at the command of Apollo, the Greeks expressed by this tradition of its origin their appreciation of its gracious climate, fertile soil, and exquisite scenery. From remote antiquity it had fame as a seat of arts and letters, and of a vigorous maritime power, and the romance of its early centuries was equalled if not surpassed when it became the residence of the Knights of St. John. I believe that the first impress of its civilization was given by the Phœnicians;

it was the home of the Dorian race before the time of the Trojan war, and its three cities were members of the Dorian Hexapolis ; it was in fact a flourishing maritime confederacy, strong enough to send colonies to the distant Italian coast, and Sybaris and Parthenope (modern Naples) perpetuated the luxurious refinement of their founders. The city of Rhodes itself was founded about four hundred years before Christ, and the splendor of its palaces, its statues and paintings, gave it a pre-eminence among the most magnificent cities of the ancient world. If the earth of this island could be made to yield its buried treasures as Cyprus has, we should doubtless have new proofs of the influence of Asiatic civilization upon the Greeks, and be able to trace in the early Doric arts and customs the superior civilization of the Phœnicians, and of the masters of the latter in science and art, the Egyptians.

Naturally, every traveller who enters the harbor of Rhodes hopes to see the site of one of the seven wonders of the world, the Colossus. He is free to place it on either mole at the entrance of the harbor, but he comprehends at once that a statue which was only one hundred and five feet high could never have extended its legs across the port. The fame of this colossal bronze statue of the sun is disproportioned to the period of its existence ; it stood only fifty-six years after its erection, being shaken down by an earthquake in the year 224 B. C., and encumbering the ground with its fragments till the advent of the Moslem conquerors.

When we landed, the town was not yet awake, except the boat-men and the coffee-houses by the landing-stairs. The Greek boatman, whom we accepted as our guide, made an unsuccessful excursion for bread, finding only a black uneatable mixture, sprinkled with aromatic seeds ; but we sat under the shelter of an old sycamore in a lovely place by the shore, and sipped our coffee, and saw the sun coming over Lycia, and shining on the old towers and walls of the Knights.

Passing from the quay through a highly ornamented Gothic gateway, we ascended the famous historic street, still called the Street of the Knights, the massive houses of which have withstood the shocks of earthquakes and the devastation of Saracenic and Turkish occupation. At this hour the street was as deserted as it was three centuries and a half ago, when the Knights sorrowfully sailed out of the harbor in search of a new home. Their four months' defence of the city, against the overwhelming force of Suleiman the Magnificent, added a new lustre to their valor, and extorted the admiration of the victor and the most honorable terms of surrender. With them departed the prosperity of Rhodes. This street, of whose palaces we have heard so much, is not imposing; it is not wide, its solid stone houses are only two stories high, and their fronts are now disfigured by cheap Arab balconies, but the façades are gray with age. All along are remains of carved windows. Gothic sculptured doorways, and shields and coats of arms, crosses and armorial legends, are set in the walls, partially defaced by time and accident; for the Moslems, apparently inheriting the respect of Suleiman for the Knights, have spared the mementos of their faith and prowess. I saw no inscriptions that are intact, but made out upon one shield the words *voluntas mei est.* The carving is all beautiful.

We went through the silent streets, waking only echoes of the past, out to the ruins of the once elegant church of St. John, which was shaken down by a powder-explosion some thirty years ago, and utterly flattened by an earthquake some years afterwards. Outside the ramparts we met, and saluted with the freedom of travellers, a gorgeous Turk who was taking the morning air, and whom our guide in bated breath said was the governor. In this part of the town is the Mosque of Suleiman; in the portal are two lovely marble columns, rich with age; the lintels are exquisitely carved with flowers, arms, casques, musical instruments, the crossed sword and the torch, and the mandolin, perhaps the emblem of some troubadour knight. Wherever we went we found bits of old carving, remains of columns, sections of battlemented roofs. The town is saturated with the old Knights. Near the mosque is a foundation of charity, a public kitchen, at which the poor were fed or were free to come and cook their food; it is in decay now, and the rooks were sailing about its old round-topped chimneys.

There are no Hellenic remains in the city, and the only remembrance of that past which we searched for was the antique
coin, which has upon one side the head of Medusa and upon the
other the rose (*rhoda*) which gave the town its name. The town
was quiet; but in pursuit of this coin in the Jews' quarter we
started up swarms of traders, were sent from Isaac to Jacob, and
invaded dark shops and private houses where Jewish women and
children were just beginning to complain of the morning light.
Our guide was a jolly Greek, who was willing to awaken the
whole town in search of a silver coin. The traders, when we had
routed them out, had little to show in the way of antiquities.
Perhaps the best representative of the modern manufactures of
Rhodes is the wooden shoe, which is in form like the Damascus
clog, but is inlaid with more taste. The people whom we encountered in our morning walk were Greeks or Jews.

The morning atmosphere was delicious, and we could well
believe that the climate of Rhodes is the finest in the Mediterranean, and also that it is the least exciting of cities.

"Is it always so peaceful here?" we asked the guide.

"Nothing, if you please," said he, "has happened here since
the powder-explosion, nothing in the least."

"And is the town as healthy as they say?"

"Nobody dies."

The town is certainly clean, if it is in decay. In one street we
found a row of mulberry-trees down the centre, but they were
half decayed, like the street. I shall always think of Rhodes as
a silent city, — except in the Jews' quarter, where the hope of
selling an old coin set the whole hive humming, — and I suspect
that is its normal condition.

XX.

AMONG THE ÆGEAN ISLANDS.

OUR sail all day among the Ægean islands was surpassingly
lovely; our course was constantly changing to wind among
them; their beautiful outlines and the soft atmosphere that en-
wrapped them disposed us to regard them in the light of Homeric
history, and we did not struggle against the illusion. They are
all treeless, and for the most part have scant traces of vegetation,
except a thin green grass which seems rather a color than a substance. Here are the little islands of Chalce and Syme, once
seats of Grecian culture, now the abode of a few thousand sponge-
fishers. We pass Telos, and Nisyros, which was once ruled by
Queen Artemisia, and had its share in the fortunes of the wars of
Athens and Sparta. It is a small round mass of rock, but it
rises twenty-two hundred feet out of the sea, and its volcanic soil
is favorable to the grape. Opposite is the site of the ruins of
Cnidus, a Dorian city of great renown, and famous for its shrine
of Venus, and her statue by Praxiteles. We get an idea of the
indentation of this coast of Asia Minor (and its consequent acces-
sibility to early settlement and civilization) from the fact that
Cnidus is situated on a very narrow peninsula ninety miles long.

Kos is celebrated not only for its size, loveliness, and fertility,
but as the birthplace of Apelles and of Hippocrates; the inhabitants still venerate an enormous plane-tree under which the
good physician is said to have dispensed his knowledge of healing. The city of Kos is on a fine plain, which gradually slopes
from the mountain to the sea and is well covered with trees.
The attractive town lies prettily along the shore, and is dis-

11*

tinguished by a massive square mediæval fortress, and by round stone windmills with specially long arms.

As we came around the corner of Kos, we had a view, distant but interesting, of the site of Halicarnassus, the modern town of Boudroum, with its splendid fortress, which the Turks wrested from the Knights of St. John. We sail by it with regret, for the student and traveller in the East comes to have a tender feeling for the simple nature of the father of history, and would forego some other pleasant experiences to make a pilgrimage to the birthplace of Herodotus. Here, also, was born the historian Dionysius. And here, a few years ago, were identified the exact site and rescued the remains of another of the Seven Wonders, the Tomb of Mausolus, built in honor of her husband by the Carian Artemisia, who sustained to him the double relation of sister and queen. This monument, which exhibited the perfection of Greek art, was four hundred and eleven feet in circumference and one hundred and forty feet high. It consisted of a round building, surrounded by thirty-six columns surmounted by a pyramid, and upon the latter stood a colossal group of a chariot and four horses. Some of the beautiful sculpture of this mausoleum can be seen in the British Museum.

We were all the afternoon endeavoring to get sight of Patmos, which the intervening islands hid from view. Every half-hour some one was discovering it, and announcing the fact. No doubt half the passengers will go to their graves comforted by the belief that they saw it. Some of them actually did have a glimpse of it towards night, between the islands of Lipso and Arki. It is a larger island than we expected to see; and as we had understood that the Revelations were written on a small rocky island, in fact a mere piece of rock, the feat seemed less difficult on a good-sized island. Its height is now crowned by the celebrated monastery of St. John, but the island is as barren and uninviting as it was when the Romans used it as a place of banishment.

We passed Astypalæa, Kalyminos, Leros, and a sprinkling of islets (as if a giant had sown this sea with rocks), each of which has a history, or is graced by a legend ; but their glory is of the past. The chief support of their poor inhabitants is now the sponge-fishery. At sunset we had before us Icaria and Samos, and on the mainland the site of Miletus, now a fever-smitten place, whose vast theatre is almost the sole remains of the metropolis of the Ionic confederacy. Perhaps the centre of Ionic art and culture was, however, the island of Samos, but I doubt not the fame of its Samian wine has carried its name further than the exploits of its warriors, the works of its artists, or the thoughts of its philosophers. It was the birthplace of Pythagoras; it was once governed by Polycrates; there for a time Antony and Cleopatra established their court of love and luxury. In the evening we sailed close under its high cliffs, and saw dimly opposite Icaria, whose only merit or interest lies in its association with the ill-judged aerial voyage of Icarus, the son of Dædalus.

Although the voyager amid these islands and along this historic coast profoundly feels the influence of the past, and, as he reads and looks and reflects, becomes saturated with its half-mysterious and delicious romance, he is nevertheless scarcely able to believe that these denuded shores and purple, rocky islets were the homes of heroes, the theatres of world-renowned exploits, the seats of wealth and luxury and power; that the marble of splendid temples gleamed from every summit and headland; that rich cities clustered on every island and studded the mainland; and that this region, bounteous in the fruits of the liberal earth, was not less prolific in vigorous men and beautiful women, who planted adventurous and remote colonies, and sowed around the Mediterranean the seeds of our modern civilization. In the present desolation and soft decay it is difficult to recall the wealth, the diversified industry, the martial spirit, the refinement of the races whose art and literature are still our emulation and despair. Here, indeed, were the beginnings of our era, of our modern life, — separated by a great gulf from the ancient civilization of the Nile, — the life of the people, the attempts at self-government, the individual adventure, the new development of human relations consequent upon commerce, and the freer exchange of products and ideas.

What these islands and this variegated and genial coast of Asia Minor might become under a government that did not paralyze effort and rob industry, it is impossible to say; but the impression is made upon the traveller that Nature herself is exhausted in these regions, and that it will need the rest or change of a geologic era to restore her pristine vigor. The prodigality and avarice of thousands of years have left the land — now that the flame of civilization has burned out — like the crater of an extinct volcano. But probably it is society and not nature that is dead. The island of Rhodes, for an example, might in a few years of culture again produce the forests that once supplied her hardy sons with fleets of vessels, and her genial soil, under any intelligent agriculture, would yield abundant harvests. The land is now divided into petty holdings, and each poor proprietor scratches it just enough to make it yield a scanty return.

During the night the steamer had come to Chios (Scio), and I rose at dawn to see — for we had no opportunity to land — the spot almost equally famous as the birthplace of Homer and the land of the Chian wine. The town lies along the water for a mile or more around a shallow bay opening to the east, a city of small white houses, relieved by a minaret or two; close to the water's edge are some three-story edifices, and in front is an ancient square fort, which has a mole extending into the water, terminated by a mediæval bastion, behind which small vessels find shelter. Low by the shore, on the north, are some of the sturdy windmills peculiar to these islands, and I can distinguish with a glass a few fragments of Byzantine and mediæval architecture among the common buildings. Staring at us from the middle of the town were two big signs, with the word "Hotel."

To the south of the town, amid a grove of trees, are the white stones of the cemetery; the city of the dead is nearly as large as that of the living. Behind the city are orange orchards and many a bright spot of verdure, but the space for it is not broad. Sharp, bare, serrated, perpendicular ridges of mountain rise behind the town, encircling it like an amphitheatre. In the morning light these mountains are tawny and rich in color, tinged with purple and red. Chios is a pretty picture in the shelter of these hills, which gather for it the rays of the rising sun.

It is now half a century since the name of Scio rang through

the civilized world as the theatre of a deed which Turkish history
itself can scarcely parallel, and the island is vigorously regaining
its prosperity. It only needs to recall the outlines of the story.
The fertile island, which is four times the extent of the Isle of
Wight, was the home of one hundred and ten thousand inhabitants, of whom only six thousand were Turks. The Greeks of
Scio were said to differ physically and morally from all their kin-
dred; their merchants were princes at home and abroad, art and
literature flourished, with grace and refinement of manner, and
there probably nowhere existed a society more industrious, gay,
contented, and intelligent. Tempted by some adventurers from
Samos to rebel, they drew down upon themselves the vengeance
of the Turks, who retaliated the bloody massacre of Turkish
men, women, and children by the insurrectionists, with a universal
destruction. The city of Scio, with its thirty thousand inhabitants, and seventy villages, were reduced to ashes; twenty-five
thousand of all ages and both sexes were slain, forty-five thousand were carried away as slaves, among them women and children
who had been reared in luxury, and most of the remainder escaped,
in a destitute state, into other parts of Greece. At the end of
the summer's harvest of death, only two thousand Sciotes were
left on the island. An apologist for the Turks could only urge
that the Greeks would have been as unmerciful under like circumstances.

None of the first-class passengers were up to see Chios, — not
one for poor Homer's sake; but the second-class were stirring for
their own, crawling out of their comfortables, giving the babies a
turn, and the vigilant flea a taste of the morning air. When the
Russian peasant, who sleeps in the high truncated frieze cap, and
in the coat which he wore in Jerusalem, — a garment short in the
waist, gathered in pleats underneath the shoulders, and falling in
stiff expanding folds below, — when he first gets up and rubs his
eyes, he is an astonished being. His short-legged wife is already
astir, and beginning to collect the materials of breakfast. Some
of the Greeks are making coffee; there is a smell of coffee, and
there are various other unanalyzed odors. But for pilgrims, and
pilgrims so closely packed that no one can stir without moving

the entire mass, these are much cleaner than they might be
expected to be, and cleaner, indeed, than they can continue to be,
and keep up their reputation. And yet, half an hour among
them, looking out from the bow for a comprehensive view of
Chios, is quite enough. I wished, then, that these people would
change either their religion or their clothes.

Last night we had singing on deck by an extemporized quar-
tette of young Americans, with harmonious and well-blended
voices, and it was a most delightful contrast to the caterwauling,
accompanied by the darabouka, which we constantly hear on the
forward deck, and which the Arabs call singing. Even the fat,
good-humored little Moslem from Damascus, who lives in the
pen with the merchant-prince of that city, listened with delight
and declared that it was *tyeb kateer*. Who knows but these people, who are always singing, have some appreciation of music
after all?

XXI.

SMYRNA AND EPHESUS.

WHEN we left Chios we sailed at first east, right into the sun, gradually turned north and rounded the promontory of the mainland, and then, east by south, came into the beautiful land-locked bay of Smyrna, in which the blue water changes into a muddy green. At length we passed on the right a Turkish for-tress, which appeared as formidable as a bathing establishment, and Smyrna lay at the bottom of the gulf, circling the shore, — white houses, fruit-trees, and hills beyond.

The wind was north, as it always is here in the morning, and the landing was difficult. We had the usual excitement of swarm-ing boats and clamorous boatmen and lively waves. One passen-ger went into the water instead of the boat, but was easily fished out by his baggy trousers, and, as he was a Greek pilgrim, it was thought that a little water would n't injure him. Coming to the shore we climbed with difficulty out of the bobbing boat upon the sea-wall; the shiftless Turkish government will do nothing to im-prove the landing at this great port, — if the Sultan can borrow any money he builds a new palace on the Bosphorus, or an iron-clad to anchor in front of it.

Smyrna may be said to have a character of its own in not having any character of its own. One of the most ancient cities on the globe, it has no appearance of antiquity; containing all nationalities, it has no nationality; the second commercial city of the East, it has no chamber of commerce, no *Bourse*, no commer-cial unity; its citizens are of no country and have no impulse of patriotism; it is an Asiatic city with a European face; it produces nothing, it exchanges everything,—the fabrics of Europe, the luxuries of the Orient; the children of the East are sent to its schools, but it has no literary character nor any influence of culture; it is hospitable to all religions, and conspicuous for none; it is the paradise of the Turks, the home of luxury and of beautiful women, but it is also a favorite of the mosquito, and, until recently, it has been the yearly camp of the plague; it is not the most healthful city in the world, and yet it is the metropolis of the drug-trade.

Smyrna can be compared to Damascus in its age and in its perpetuity under all discouragements and changes, — the shocks of earthquakes, the constant visitations of pestilence, and the rule of a hundred masters. It was a great city before the migration of the Ionians into Asia Minor, it saw the rise and fall of Sardis, it was restored from a paralysis of four centuries by Alexander. Under all vicissitudes it seems to have retained its character of a great mart of exchange, a necessity for the trade of Asia; and perhaps the indifference of its conglomerate inhabitants to freedom and to creeds contributed to its safety. Certainly it thrived as well under the Christians, when it was the seat of one of the seven churches, as it did under the Romans, when it was a seat of a great school of sophists and rhetoricians, and it is equally prosperous under the sway of the successor of Mohammed. During the thousand years of the always decaying Byzantine Empire it had its share of misfortunes, and its walls alternately, at a later day, displayed the star and crescent, and the equal arms of the cross of St. John. Yet, in all its history, I seem to see the trading, gay, free, but not disorderly Smyrna passing on its even way of traffic and of pleasure.

Of its two hundred thousand and more inhabitants, about ninety thousand are Rayah Greeks, and about eighty thousand are Turks. There is a changing population of perhaps a thousand Europeans, there are large bodies of Jews and Armenians, and it was recently estimated to have as many as fifteen thousand Levantines. These latter are the descendants of the marriage of Europeans with Greek and Jewish women; and whatever moral reputation the Levantines enjoy in the Levant, the women of this mixture are famous for their beauty. But the race is said to be not self-sustaining, and is yielding to the original types. The languages spoken in Smyrna are Turkish, a Greek dialect (the Romaic), Spanish, Italian, French, English, and Arabic, probably prevailing in the order named. Our own steamer was much more Oriental than the city of Smyrna. As soon as we stepped ashore we seemed to have come into a European city; the people almost all wear the Frank dress, the shops offer little that is peculiar. One who was unfamiliar with bazaars might wonder at the tangle of various lanes, but we saw nothing calling for comment. A walk through the Jewish quarter, here as everywhere else the dirtiest and most picturesque in the city, will reward the philosophic traveller with the sight of lovely women lolling at every window. It is not the fashion for Smyrniote ladies to promenade the streets, but they mercifully array themselves in full toilet and stand in their doorways.

The programme of the voyage of the *Achille* promised us a day and a half in Smyrna, which would give us time to visit Ephesus. We were due Friday noon; we did not arrive till Saturday noon. This vexatious delay had caused much agitation on board; to be cheated out of Ephesus was an outrage which the tourists could not submit to; they had come this way on purpose to see Ephesus. They would rather give up anything else in the East. The captain said he had no discretion, he must sail at 4 P. M. The passengers then prepared a handsome petition to the agent, begging him to detain the steamer till eight o'clock, in order to permit them to visit Ephesus by a special train. There is a proclivity in all those who can write to sign any and every thing except a subscription paper, and this petition received fifty-six eager and first-class signatures. The agent at Smyrna plumply refused our request, with unnecessary surliness; but upon the arrival of the captain, and a consultation which no doubt had more reference to freight than to the petition, the official agreed, as a special favor, to detain the steamer till eight o'clock, but not a moment longer.

We hastened to the station of the Aidin Railway, which runs eighty miles to Aidin, the ancient Tralles, a rich Lydian metropo-

lis of immemorial foundation. The modern town has perhaps
fifty thousand inhabitants, and is a depot for cotton and figs; that
sweetmeat of Paradise, the *halva*, is manufactured there, and its
great tanneries produce fine yellow Morocco leather. The town
lies only three miles from the famous tortuous Mæander, and all
the region about it is a garden of vines and fruit-trees. The railway company is under English management, which signifies
promptness, and the special train was ready in ten minutes;
when lo! of the fifty-six devotees of Ephesus only eleven appeared. We were off at once; good engine, solid track, clean,
elegant, comfortable carriages. As we moved out of the city the
air was full of the odor of orange-blossoms; we crossed the
Meles, and sped down a valley, very fertile, smiling with grain-
fields, green meadows, groves of mulberry, oranges, figs, with
blue hills, — an ancient Mount Olympus, beyond which lay green
Sardis, in the distance, a country as lovely and home-like as an
English or American farm-land. We had seen nothing so luxuriant and thriving in the East before. The hills, indeed, were
stripped of trees, but clad on the tops with verdure, the result of
plentiful rains.

We went "express." The usual time of trains is three hours;
we ran over the fifty miles in an hour and a quarter. We could
hardly believe our senses, that we were in a luxurious carriage,
flying along at this rate in Asia, and going to Ephesus! While
we were confessing that the lazy swing of the carriage was more
agreeable than that of the donkey or the dromedary, the train
pulled up at station Ayasolook, once the residence of the Sultans
of Ayasolook, and the camp of Tamerlane, now a cluster of coffee-
houses and railway-offices, with a few fever-stricken inhabitants,
who prey upon travellers, not with Oriental courtesy, but with
European insolence.

On our right was a round hill surmounted by a Roman castle;
from the hills on the left, striding across the railway towards
Ephesus, were the tall stone pillars of a Roman aqueduct, the
brick arches and conductor nearly all fallen away. On the summit of nearly every pillar a white, red-legged stork had built,
from sticks and grass, a high round nest, which covered the top;

and the bird stood in it motionless, a beautiful object at that height against the sky.

The station people had not obeyed our telegram to furnish enough horses, and those of us who were obliged to walk congratulated ourselves on the mistake, since the way was as rough as the steeds. The path led over a ground full of stone *débris*. This was the site of Ayasolook, which had been built out of the ruins of the old city; most picturesque objects were the small mosque-tombs and minarets, which revived here the most graceful forms and fancies of Saracenic art. One, I noticed, which had the ideal Persian arch and slender columns, Nature herself had taken into loving care and draped with clinging green and hanging vines. There were towers of brick, to which age has given a rich tone, flaring at the top in a curve that fascinated the eye. On each tomb, tower, and minaret the storks had nested, and upon each stood the mother looking down upon her brood. About the crumbling sides of a tower, thus draped and crowned, innumerable swallows had built their nests, so that it was alive with birds, whose cheerful occupation gave a kind of pathos to the human desertion and decay.

Behind the Roman castle stands the great but ruinous mosque of Sultan Selim, which was formerly the Church of St. John. We did not turn aside for its empty glory, but to the theologian or the student of the formation of Christian dogmas, and of the gladiatorial spectacles of an ancient convocation, there are few arenas in the East more interesting than this; for in this church it is supposed were held the two councils of A. D. 431 and 449. St. John, after his release from Patmos, passed the remainder of his life here; the Virgin Mary followed him to the city, so favored by the presence of the first apostles, and here she died and was buried. From her entombment, Ephesus for a long time enjoyed the reputation of the City of the Virgin, until that honor was transferred to Jerusalem, where, however, her empty tomb soon necessitated her resurrection and assumption, — the subject which inspired so many artists after the revival of learning in Europe. In the hill near this church Mary Magdalene was buried; in Ephesus also reposed the body of St. Timothy, its first bishop.

This church of St. John was at some distance from the heart of the city, which lay in the plain to the south and near the sea, but in the fifth century Ephesus was a city of churches. The reader needs to remember that in that century the Christian controversy had passed from the nature of the Trinity to the incarnation, and that the first council of Ephesus was called by the emperor Theodosius in the hope of establishing the opinion of the Syrian Nestorius, the primate of Constantinople, who refused to give to the mother of Christ the title, then come into use, of the Mother of God, and discriminated nicely the two natures of the Saviour. His views were anathematized by Cyril, the patriarch of Alexandria, and the dispute involved the entire East in a fierce contest. In the council convened of Greek bishops, Nestorius had no doubt but he would be sustained by the weight of authority; but the prompt Cyril, whose qualities would have found a conspicuous and useful theatre at the head of a Roman army against the Scythians, was first on the ground, with an abundance of spiritual and temporal arms. In reading of this council, one recalls without effort the once famous and now historical conventions of the Democratic party of the State of New York, in the days when political salvation, offered in the creeds of the "Hard Shells" and of the "Soft Shells," was enforced by the attendance of gangs of "Short boys" and "Tammany boys," who understood the use of slung-shot against heretical opinions. It is true that Nestorius had in reserve behind his prelates the stout slaves of the bath of Zeuxippus, but Cyril had secured the alliance of the bishop of Ephesus, and the support of the rabble of peasants and slaves who were easily excited to jealousy for the honor of the Virgin of their city; and he landed from Egypt, with his great retinue of bishops, a band of merciless monks of the Nile, of fanatics, mariners, and slaves, who took a ready interest in the theological discussions of those days. The council met in this church, surrounded by the fierce if not martial array of Cyril: deliberations were begun before the arrival of the most weighty supporters of Nestorius, — for Cyril anticipated the slow approach of John of Antioch and his bishops, — and in one day the primate of Constantinople was hastily deposed and cursed, together with his heresy. Upon the arrival of John, he also formed a council, which deposed and cursed the opposite party and heresy, and for three months Ephesus was a scene of clamor and bloodshed. The cathedral was garrisoned, the churches were shut against the Nestorians; the imperial troops assaulted them and were repelled; the whole city was thrown into a turmoil by the encounters of the rival factions, each council hurled its anathemas at the other, and peace was only restored by the dissolution of the council by command of the emperor. The second session, in the year 449, was shorter and more decisive; it made quick work of the heresy of Nestorius. Africa added to its delegation of bullies and fanatics a band of archers; the heresy of the two natures was condemned and anathematized, — " May those who divide Christ be divided with the sword, may they be hewn in pieces, may they be burned alive," — and the scene in the cathedral ended in a mob of monks and soldiers, who trampled upon Flavian, the then primate of Constantinople, so that in three days thereafter he died of his wounds.

It is as difficult to make real now upon this spot those fierce theologic wars of Ephesus, as it is the fabled exploits of Bacchus and Hercules and the Amazons in this valley; to believe that here were born Apollo and Diana, and that hither fled Latona, and that great Pan lurked in its groves.

We presently came upon the site of the great Temple of Diana, recently identified by Mr. Wood. We encountered on our way a cluster of stone huts, wretched habitations of the only representatives of the renowned capital. Before us was a plain broken by small hillocks and mounds, and strewn with cut and fractured stone. The site of the temple can be briefly and accurately described as a rectangular excavation, perhaps one hundred and fifty feet wide by three hundred long and twelve feet deep, with two feet of water in it, out of which rises a stump of a column of granite and another of marble, and two bases of marble. Round this hole are heaps of fractured stone and marble. In this excavation Mr. Wood found the statue of Diana, which we may hope is the ancient sacred image, guarded by the priests as the most precious treasure of the temple, and imposed upon the credu-

lity of men as heaven-descended. This is all that remains of one
of the Seven Wonders of the world, — a temple whose fame is second to none in antiquity ; a temple seven times burned and eight
times built, and always with increased magnificence; a temple
whose origin, referable doubtless to the Cyclopean builders of
this coast, cannot be less than fifteen hundred years before our
era ; a temple which still had its votaries and its rites in the fourth
century. We picked up a bit of marble from its ruins, as a help
both to memory and imagination, but we went our way utterly
unable to conceive that there ever existed any such person as
great Diana of the Ephesians.

We directed our steps over the bramble-grown plain to the hill
Pion. I suppose Pion may have been the acropolis of Ephesus, the spot of the earliest settlement, and on it and around it
clustered many of the temples and public buildings. The reader
will recall Argos, and Athens, and Corinth, and a dozen other
cities of antiquity, for which nature furnished in the midst of a
plain such a convenient and easily defended hill-fortress. On our
way thither we walked amid mounds that form a street of tombs ;
many of the sarcophagi are still in place, and little injured; but
we explore the weed-hid ground with caution, for it is full of pit-
falls.

North of the hill Pion is a low green valley, encircled with
hills, and in the face of one of its ledges, accessible only by a
ladder, we were pointed out the cave of the Seven Sleepers. This
favorite myth, which our patriotism has transferred to the high-
lands of the Hudson in a modified shape, took its most popular
form in the legend of the Seven Sleepers, and this grotto at
Ephesus was for many centuries the object of Christian and Moslem pilgrimage. The Christian legend, that in the time of the
persecution of Diocletian seven young men escaped to this cave
and slept there two centuries, and awoke to find Christianity the
religion of the empire, was adopted and embellished by Mohammed. In his version, the wise dog Ketmehr, or Al Rakim as the
Koran names him, becomes an important character.

" When the young men," says Abd-el-Atti, " go along the side
of the hill to the cave, the dog go to follow them. They take up

stones to make him go back, for they 'fraid of him bark, and let the people know where they hide. But the dog not to go back, he sit down on him hind, and him look berry wise. By and by he speak, he say the name of God.

"'How did you know that?' ask him the young men.

"'I know it,' the dog say, 'before you born!'

"Then they see the dog he wise by Allah, and know great deal, and let him to go with 'em. This dog, Ketmehr, he is gone, so our Prophet say, to be in Paradise; no other dog be there. So I hope."

The names of the Seven Sleepers and Ketmehr are in great talismanic repute throughout the East; they are engraved upon swords and upon gold and precious stones, and in Smyrna you may buy these charms against evil.

Keeping round the hill Pion, we reached the ruins of the gymnasium, heaps of stone amid brick arches, the remains of an enormous building; near it is the north gate of the city, a fine marble structure, now almost buried. Still circling Pion we found ourselves in a narrow valley, on the other side of which was the long ridge of Conessus, which runs southward towards the sea. Conessus seems to have been the burial-place of the old town. This narrow valley is stuffed with remains of splendid buildings, of which nothing is now to be seen but heaps of fine marble, walls, capitals, columns, in prodigal waste. We stopped to admire a bit of carving, or to notice a Greek inscription, and passed on to the Stadium, to the Little Theatre, to the tomb of St. Luke. On one of the lintels of the entrance of this tomb, in white marble, as fresh as if carved yesterday, is a cross, and under it the figure of an *Egyptian* ox, the emblem of that saint.

We emerged from this gorge to a wide view of the plain, and a glimpse of an arm of the sea. On this plain are the scattered ruins of the old city, brick, stone, and marble, — absolute desolation. On the left, near the sea, is a conical hill, crowned by one of the towers of the ancient wall, and dignified with the name of the "prison of St. Paul." In this plain is neither life nor cultivation, but vegetation riots over the crumbling remains of Ephesus, and fever waits there its chance human prey. We stood on the side of the hill Pion, amid the fallen columns and heaped walls of its Great Theatre. It was to this theatre that the multitude rushed when excited against Paul by Demetrius, the silversmith, who carried his religion into his business; and here the companions of Paul endeavored to be heard and could not, for "all with one voice about the space of two hours cried out, Great is Diana of the Ephesians." This amphitheatre for fifty thousand spectators is scooped out of the side of the hill, and its tiers of seats are still indicated. What a magnificent view they must have enjoyed of the city and the sea beyond; for the water then came much nearer; and the spectator who may have wearied of the strutting of the buskined heroes on the stage, or of the monotonous chant of the chorus, could rest his eye upon the purple slopes of Conessus, upon the colonnades and domes of the opulent city, upon the blue waves that bore the merchants' ships of Rome and Alexandria and Berytus.

The theatre is a mine of the most exquisite marbles, and we left its treasures with reluctance; we saw other ruins, bases of columns, the remains of the vast city magazines for the storage of corn, and solid walls of huge stones once washed by the sea; we might have wandered for days amid the fragments, but to what purpose?

At Ephesus we encountered no living thing. Man has deserted it, silence reigns over the plain, nature slowly effaces the evidence of his occupation, and the sea even slinks away from it. No great city that I have seen is left to such absolute desolation; not Pæstum in its marsh, not Thebes in its sand, not Ba'albek, not even Memphis, swept clean as it is of monuments, for its site is vocal with labor and bounteous in harvests. Time was, doubtless, when gold pieces piled two deep on this ground could not have purchased it; and the buyers or sellers never imagined that the city lots of Ephesus could become worth so little as they are to-day.

If one were disposed to muse upon the vagaries of human progress, this would be the spot. No civilization, no religion, has been wanting to it. Its vast Cyclopean foundations were laid by simple pagans; it was in the polytheistic belief of the Greeks that it

attained the rank of one of the most polished and wealthy cities
of antiquity, famed for its arts, its schools of poetry, of painting
and sculpture, of logic and magic, attracting to its opportunities
the devout, the seekers of pleasure and of wisdom, the poets, the
men of the world, the conquerors and the defeated ; here Artemisia sheltered the children of Xerxes after the disaster of Salamis ;
here Alexander sat for his portrait to Apelles (who was born in
the city) when he was returning from the capture of Sardis ;
Spartans and Athenians alike, Lysander and Alcibiades, sought
Ephesus, for it had something for all ; Hannibal here conferred
with Antiochus ; Cicero was entertained with games by the people
when he was on his way to his province of Cilicia ; and Antony
in the character of inebriate Bacchus, accompanied by Cleopatra,
crowned with flowers and attended by bands of effeminate musicians, made here one of the pageants of his folly.   In fact, scarcely
any famous name of antiquity is wanting to the adornment of this
hospitable city.   Under the religion of Christ it has had the good
fortune to acquire equal celebrity, thanks to the residence of
Paul, the tent-maker, and to its conspicuous position at the head
of the seven churches of Asia.   From Ephesus went forth the
news of the gospel, as formerly had spread the rites of Diana, and
Christian churches and schools of philosophy succeeded the temples and gymnasia of the polytheists.   And, in turn, the cross
was supplanted by the crescent ; but it was in the day when
Islamism was no longer a vital faith, and except a few beautiful
ruins the Moslem occupation has contributed nothing to the glory
of Ephesus.   And now paganism, Christianity, and Moslemism
seem alike to have forsaken the weary theatre of so much brilliant
history.   As we went out to the station, by the row of booths
and coffee-shops, a modern Greek, of I do not know what religion, offered to sell me an image of I do not know what faith.
There is great curiosity at present about the relics and idols of
dead religions, and a brisk manufacture of them has sprung up ;
it is in the hands of sceptics who indifferently propagate the
images of the Virgin Mary or of the chaste huntress Diana.

    The swift Asiatic train took us back to Smyrna in a golden
sunset.   We had been warned by the agent not to tarry a moment
12

beyond eight o'clock, and we hurried breathless to the boat. Fortunately the steamer had not sailed; we were in time, and should have been if we had remained on shore till eight the next morning. All night long we were loading freight, with an intolerable rattling of chains, puffing of the donkey-engine, and swearing of boatmen; after the novelty of swearing in an Oriental tongue has worn off, it is no more enjoyable than any other kind of profanity.

XXII.

THE ADVENTURERS.

WE sailed away from Smyrna Sunday morning, with the *Achille* more crowded than when we entered that port. The second-class passengers still further encroached upon the first-class. The Emir of Damascus, with all his rugs and beds, had been pushed farther towards the stern, and more harems occupied temporary pens on our deck, and drew away our attention from the natural scenery.

The venerable, white-bearded, Greek bishop of Smyrna was a passenger, also the tall noble-looking pasha of that city, just relieved and ordered to Constantinople, as pashas are continually, at the whim of the Sultan. We had three pashas on board,—one recalled from Haifa, who had been only twenty days at his post. The pasha of Smyrna was accompanied by his family, described on the register as his wife and "four others," an indefinite expression to define an indefinite condition. The wife had a room below ; the "four others" were penned up in a cushioned area on the saloon deck, and there they squatted all day, veiled and robed in white, poor things, without the least occupation for hand or mind. Near them, other harems of Greeks and Turks, women, babies, slaves, all in an Oriental mess, ate curds and green lettuce.

We coasted along the indented, picturesque shore of Asia, having in view the mountains about ancient Pergamus, the seat of one of the seven churches ; and before noon came to Mitylene, the ancient Lesbos, a large island which bears another Mount Olympus, and cast anchor in the bay upon which the city stands.

By the bend of the bay and the opposite coast, the town is charmingly land-locked. The site of Mitylene, like so many of these island cities, is an amphitheatre, and the mountain-slopes, green and blooming with fruit-trees, are dotted with white houses and villages. The scene is Italian rather than Oriental, and gives one the general impression of Castellamare or Sorrento ; but the city is prettier to look at than to explore, as its broad and clean streets, its ordinary houses and European-dressed inhabitants, take us out of our ideal voyaging, and into the regions of the commonplace. The shops were closed, and the country people, who in all countries appear to derive an unexplained pleasure in wandering about the streets of a city hand in hand, were seeking this mild recreation. A youthful Jew, to whom the Sunday was naught, under pretence of showing us something antique, led us into the den of a Greek, to whom it was also naught, and whose treasures were bags of defaced copper coins of the Roman period.

Upon the point above the city is a fine mediæval fortress, now a Turkish fort, where we encountered, in the sentinel at the gate, the only official in the Orient who ever refused backsheesh ; I do not know what his idea is. From the walls we looked upon the blue strait, the circling, purple hills of Asia, upon islands, pretty villages, and distant mountains, soft, hazy, serrated, in short, upon a scene of poetry and peace, into which the ancient stone bastion by the harbor, which told of days of peril, and a ruined aqueduct struggling down the hill back of the town, — the remnant of more vigorous days, — brought no disturbance.

In Lesbos we are at the source of lyric poetry, the Æolian spring of Greece ; here Alcæus was born. Here we come upon the footsteps of Sappho. We must go back to a period when this and all the islands of these heavenly seas were blooming masses of vegetation, the hills hung with forests, the slopes purple with the vine, the valleys laughing with flowers and fruit, and everywhere the primitive, joyful Greek life. No doubt, manners were somewhat rude, and passions, love, and hate, and revenge, were frankly exhibited ; but in all the homely life ran a certain culture, which seems to us beautiful even in the refinement of this shamefaced age. The hardy youth of the islands sailed into far seas, and in exchange for the bounty of their soil brought back foreign fabrics of luxury. We know that Lesbos was no stranger to the Athenian influence, its scholars had heard Plato and Aristotle, and the warriors of Athens respected it both as a foe and an ally. Charakos, a brother of Sappho, went to Egypt with a ship full of wine, and returned with the beautiful slave Doricha, as part at least of the reward of his venture.

After the return of Sappho and her husband from their flight into Sicily, the poet lived for many years at Mitylene; but she is supposed to have been born in Eresso, on the southwestern point of the island, where the ruins of the acropolis and remains of a sea-wall still mark the site of the famous town. At any rate, she lived there, with her husband Kerkylas, a landed proprietor and a person of consequence, like a dame of noble birth and gentle breeding as she was; and in her verse we have a glimpse of her walking upon the sandy shore, with her little daughter, the beautiful child whom she would not give up for the kingdom of Lydia, nor for heavenly Lesbos itself. That Sappho was beautiful as her image on the ancient coins represents her, and that she was consumed by passion for a handsome youth, the world likes to believe. But Maximus of Tyre says that she was small and dark; — graces are not so plenty, even in heaven, that genius and beauty can be lavished upon one person. We are prone to insist that the poet who revels in imagination and sounds the depth of passion is revealing his own heart, and that the tale that seems so real must be a personal experience. The little glimpse we have of Sappho's life does not warrant us to find in it the passionate tempest of her burning lyrics, nor is it consistent with her social position that she should expose upon the market-place her passion for the handsome Phaon, like a troubadour of the Middle Ages or a Zingara of Bohemia. If that consuming fire was only quenched in the sea at the foot of " Leucadia's far-projecting rock of woe," at least our emotion may be tempered by the soothing knowledge that the leap must have been taken when the enamored singer had passed her sixtieth year.

We did not see them at Mitylene, but travellers into the interior speak of the beautiful women, the descendants of kings' daughters, the rewards of Grecian heroes; near old Eresso the women preserve the type of that indestructible beauty, and in the large brown eyes, voluptuous busts, and elastic gait one may deem that he sees the originals of the antique statues.

Another famous woman flits for a moment before us at Lesbos. It is the celebrated Empress Irene, whose cruelty was hardly needed to preserve a name that her talent could have perpetuated. An Athenian virgin and an orphan, at seventeen she became the wife of Leo IV. (A. D. 780), and at length the ruler of the Eastern Empire. Left the guardian of the empire and her son Constantine VI., she managed both, until the lad in his maturity sent his mother into retirement. The restless woman conspired against him; he fled, was captured and brought to the palace and lodged in the porphyry chamber where he first had seen the light, and where he last saw it; for his eyes were put out by the order of Irene. His very existence was forgotten in the depths of the palace, and for several years the ambitious mother reigned with brilliancy and the respect of distant potentates, until a conspiracy of eunuchs overturned her power, and she was banished to Lesbos. Here history, which delights in these strokes of poetic justice, represents the empress earning her bread by the use of her distaff.

As we came from Mitylene into the open sea, the view was surpassingly lovely, islands green and poetic, a coast ever retreating and advancing, as if in coquetry with the blue waves, purple robing the hills, — a voyage for poets and lotus-eaters. We were coming at night to Tenedos, to which the crafty Greeks withdrew their fleet when they pretended to abandon the siege, and to old Troy, opposite; we should be able to feel their presence in the darkness.

Our steamer, as we have intimated, was a study of nationalities and languages, as well as of manners. We were English, American, Greek, Italian, Turkish, Arab, Russian, French, Armenian, Egyptian, Jew, Georgian, Abyssinian, Nubian, German, Koorland, Persian, Kurd; one might talk with a person just from Mecca or Medina, from Bagdad, from Calcutta, from every Greek or Turkish island, and from most of the capitals of Europe. A

couple of Capuchins, tonsured, in brown serge with hanging
crosses, walked up and down amid the throng of Christians, Moslems, and pagans, withdrawn from the world while in it, like beings of a new sex. There was a couple opposite us at table whom
we could not make out, — either recently married or recently
eloped, the man apparently a Turkish officer, and his companion
a tall, showy woman, you might say a Frenchman's idea of physical beauty, a little like a wax Madonna, but with nothing holy
about her; said by some to be a Circassian, by others to be a
French grisette on an Eastern tour; but she spoke Italian, and
might be one of the Continental countesses.

The square occupied by the emir and his suite — a sort of
bazaar of rugs and narghilehs — had music all day long ; a solo-
ist, on three notes, singing, in the Arab drawl, an unending impro-
vised ballad, and accompanying himself on the mandolin. When
we go to look at and listen to him, the musician betrays neither self-consciousness nor pride, unless you detect the latter in
a superior smile that plays about his lips, as he throws back
his head and lets his voice break into a falsetto. It probably
does not even occur to his Oriental conceit that he does well, —
that his race have taken for granted a thousand years, — and he
could not be instructed by the orchestra of Von Bulow, nor be
astonished by the Lohengrin of Wagner.

Among the adventurers on board — we all had more or less the
appearance of experiments in that odd assembly — I particularly
liked the French *prestidigitateur* Caseneau, for his bold eye, utter
self-possession, and that indefinable varnish upon him, which belonged as much to his dress as to his manner, and suggested the
gentleman without concealing the adventurer. He had a taste for
antiquities, and wore some antique gems, which had I know not
what mysterious about them, as if he had inherited them from an
Ephesian magician or a Saracenic doctor of the black art. At the
table after dinner, surrounded by French and Italians, the con-
jurer exhibited some tricks at cards. I dare say they were not
extraordinary, yet they pleased me just as well as the manifesta-
tions of the spiritists. One of them I noted. The trickster was
blindfolded. A gentleman counted out a pack of cards, and while

doing so mentally fixed upon one of them by number. Caseneau took the pack, still blinded, and threw out the card the gentleman had thought of. The experiment was repeated by sceptics, who suspected a confederate, but the result was always the same.

The Circassian beauty turned out to be a Jewess from Smyrna. I believe the Jewesses of that luxurious city imitate all the kinds of beauty in the world.

In the evening the Italians were grouped around the tables in the saloon, upon which cards were cast about, matched, sorted, and redistributed, and there were little piles of silver at the corners, the occasional chinking of which appeared to add to the interest of the amusement. On deck the English and Americans were singing the hymns of the Protestant faith; and in the lull of the strains of "O mother dear, Jerusalem," you might hear the twang of strings and the whine of some Arab improvisatore on the forward deck, and the chink of changing silver below. We were making our way through a superb night, — a thousand people packed so closely that you could not move without stepping into a harem or a mass of Greek pilgrims, — singing hymns, gambling, listening to a recital of the deeds of Antar, over silver waves, under a flooding moon, and along the dim shores of Asia. That mysterious continent lay in the obscurity of the past; here and there solitary lights, from some shepherd's hut in the hills or fortress casemate by the shore, were the rents in the veil through which we saw antiquity.

XXIII.

THROUGH THE DARDANELLES.

THE *Achille*, which has a nose for freight, but none for poetry, did not stop at Tenedos, puffed steadily past the plain of Troy, turned into the broad opening of the Dardanelles, and by daylight was anchored midway between the Two Castles. On such a night, if ever, one might see the evolution of shadowy armies upon the windy plain, — if, indeed, this conspicuous site was anything more than the theatre of Homer's creations, — the spectators on the walls of Ilium, the Greeks hastily embarking on their ships for Tenedos, the joyful procession that drew the fatal gift into the impregnable walls.

There is a strong current southward through the Dardanelles, which swung the vessel round as we came to anchor. The forts which, with their heavy modern guns, completely command this strait, are something less than a mile and a half apart, and near each is a large and handsome town, — Khilid-bahri on the European shore and Chanak-Kalesi on the Asiatic. The latter name signifies the pottery-castle, and is derived from the chief manufactory of the place; the town of a couple of thousand houses, gayly painted and decorated in lively colors, lies upon a sandy flat and presents a very cheerful appearance. It is a great Asiatic *entrepôt* for European products, and consular flags attest its commercial importance.

When I came upon deck its enterprising traders had already boarded the steamer, and encumbered it with their pottery, which found a ready market with the pilgrims, for it is both cheap and ugly. Perhaps we should rather say fantastic than ugly. You

12 *   R

see specimens of it all over the East, and in the bazaars of Cairo, Jerusalem, and Damascus it may be offered you as something rare. Whatever the vessel is,—a pitcher, cup, vase, jar, or cream-pot,— its form is either that of some impossible animal, some griffin, or dragon, or dog of the underworld, or its spout is the neck and head of some fantastic monster. The ware is painted in the most startling reds, greens, yellows, and blacks, and sometimes gilt, and then glazed. It is altogether hideous, and fascinating enough to drive the majolica out of favor.

Above these two towns the strait expands into a sort of bay, formed on the north by a promontory jutting out from the Asiatic shore, and upon this promontory it is now agreed stood old Abydos; it is occupied by a fort which grimly regards a corresponding one on the opposite shore, not a mile distant. Here Leander swam to Hero, Byron to aquatic fame, and here Xerxes laid his bridge. All this is plain to be seen; this is the narrowest part of the passage; exactly opposite this sloping site of Abydos is a depression between two high cliffs, the only point where the Persian could have rested the European extremity of his bridge; and it surely requires no stretch of the imagination to see Hero standing upon this projecting point holding the torch for her lover.

The shore is very pretty each side, not bold, but quiet river scenery; and yet there is a contrast : on the Asiatic horizon are mountains, rising behind each other, while the narrow peninsula, the Thracian Chersonesus of the ancients, which forms the western bank of the Dardanelles, offers only a range of moderate hills. What a beautiful stream, indeed, is this, and how fond history has been of enacting its spectacles upon it ! How the civilizations of the East and West, in a continual flow and reflow, push each other across it ! With a sort of periodic regularity it is the scene of a great movement, and from age to age the destinies of the race have seemed to hang upon its possession; and from time to time the attention of the world is concentrated upon this water-street between two continents. Under whatever name, the Oriental civilization has been a misfortune, and the Western a blessing to the border-land ; and how narrowly has Europe, more than once, from Xerxes to Chosroes, from Omar to the Osmanlis, seemed to escape the torrent of Eastern slavery. Once the culture of Greece passed these limits, and annexed all Asia Minor and the territory as far as the Euphrates to the empire of intelligence. Who shall say that the day is not at hand when the ancient movement of free thought, if not of Grecian art and arms, is about to be renewed, and Europe is not again to impose its laws and manners upon Little Asia? The conquest, which one sees going on under his eyes, is not indeed with the pomp of armies, but by the more powerful and enduring might of commerce, intercourse, and the weight of a world's opinion diffused by travel and literature. The Osmanli sits supinely and watches the change; the Greeks, the rajahs of all religions, establish schools, and the new generation is getting ready for the revolution; the Turk does not care for schools. That it may be his fate to abandon European Turkey and even Constantinople, he admits. But it is plain that if he goes thus far he must go farther; and that he must surrender a good part of the Roman Eastern Empire. For any one can see that the Hellespont could not be occupied by two powers, and that it is no more possible to divide the control of the Bosphorus than it is that of the Hudson or the Thames.

The morning was cold, and the temperature as well as the sky admonished us that we were passing out of the warm latitude. Twenty-five miles from the Chang and Eng forts we passed near but did not call at Gallipoli, an ancient city with few antiquities, but of great strategic importance. Whoever holds it has the key to Constantinople and the Black Sea; it was seized by the Moslems in the thirteenth century before they imposed the religion of the Koran upon the city of Constantine, and it was early occupied by the English and French, in 1854, in the war that secured that city to the successor of the Prophet.

Entering upon the Sea of Marmora, the "vexed Propontis," we had fortunately smooth water but a cold north-wind. The Propontis has enjoyed a nauseous reputation with all mariners, ancient and modern. I don't know that its form has anything to do with it, but if the reader will take the trouble to consult a map, he will see how nearly this bag of water, with its two ducts, the Bosphorus and the Hellespont, resembles a human stomach. There is nothing to be seen in the voyage from Gallipoli to Constantinople, except the island of Marmora, famous for the quarries which furnish marbles for the palaces of the Bosphorus and for Eyoub and Scutari, the two great cities of the dead. We passed near enough to distinguish clearly its fine perpendicular cliffs.

It was dark before we saw the lights of Stamboul rise out of the water; it is impossible, at night, to enter the Golden Horn through the mazes of shipping, and we cast anchor outside. The mile or two of gas-lights along the promontory of the old city and the gleams upon the coast of ancient Chalcedon were impressive and exciting to the imagination, but, owing to the lateness of our arrival, we lost all the emotions which have struck other travellers anything but dumb upon coming in sight of the capital of the Moslem Empire.

XXIV.

CONSTANTINOPLE.

THE capital which we know as Constantinople, lying in two continents, presents itself as three cities. The long, horn-shaped promontory, between the Sea of Marmora and the Golden Horn, is the site of ancient Byzantium, which Constantine baptized with his own name, and which the Turks call Stamboul. The ancient city was on the eastern extremity, now known as Seraglio Point; its important position was always recognized, and it was sharply contended for by the Spartans, the Athenians, the Macedonians, and the Persians. Like the city of Romulus, it occupies seven hills, and its noble heights are conspicuous from afar by sea or land. In the fourth century it was surrounded by a wall, which followed the water on three sides, and ran across the base of the promontory, over four miles from the Seven Towers on the Propontis to the Cemetery of Eyoub on the Golden Horn. The land-wall, which so many times saved the effeminate city from the barbarians of the north and the Saracens of Arabia, stands yet with its battered towers and score of crumbling gates.

The second city, on a blunt promontory between the Golden Horn and the Bosphorus, overlooks the ancient Byzantium, and is composed of three districts, — Galata and Tophanna, on the water and climbing up the hill; and Pera, which crowns the summit. Galata was a commercial settlement of the thirteenth century; Pera is altogether modern.

The third city is Scutari, exactly opposite the mouth of the Golden Horn, and a little north of ancient Chalcedon, which was for over a thousand years the camp of successive besieging armies, Georgians, Persians, Saracens, and Turks.

The city of the Crescent, like a veiled beauty of the harem, did not at once disclose to us its charms. It was at six o'clock in the morning on the eleventh day of blooming May, that we landed on the dirty quay of Tophanna. The morning was cloudy, cold, misty, getting its weather from the Black Sea, and during the day rain fell in a very Occidental dreariness. Through the mist loomed the heights of Seraglio Point; and a hundred minaret peaks and domes appeared to float in the air above the veiled city. Along the floating lower bridge, across the Golden Horn, poured an unceasing procession of spectres; caïques were shooting about in every direction, steamers for the Bosphorus, for Scutari, for the Islands, were momently arriving and departing from their stations below the bridge, and the huge bulk of the Turkish iron-clads could be discerned at their anchorage before the palace of Beshiktash. The scene was animated, but there was not visible as much shipping as I had expected to see in this great port.

The customs' official on the quay was of a very inquisitive turn of mind, but we could excuse him on the ground of his age and ignorance, for he was evidently endeavoring to repair the neg-lected opportunities of his youth. Our large luggage had gone to the custom-house in charge of Abd-el-Atti, who has a genius for free-trade, and only our small parcels and hand-bags were at the mercy of the inspector on the quay. But he insisted upon opening every bag and investigating every article of the toilet and garment of the night; he even ripped open a feather pillow which one of the ladies carried with her, and neither the rain on the open dock nor our respectable appearance saved our effects from his most searching attentions. The discoveries of General di Ces-nola and the interest that Europeans take in antiquities have recently convinced the Turks that these relics must have some value, and an order had been issued to seize and confiscate all curiosities of this sort. I trembled, therefore, when the inspector got his hands upon a baby's nursing-bottle, which I had brought from Cyprus, where it had been used by some Phœnician baby probably three thousand years ago. The fellow turned it round and regarded it with serious ignorance and doubt.

"What is that?" he asked Achmed.

"O, that's nothing but a piece of pottery, something for a shild without his mother, I think, — it is nothing, not worth two paras."

The confiscator of antiquities evidently had not the slightest knowledge of his business; he hesitated, but Achmed's perfect indifference of manner determined him, and he slowly put the precious relic back into the box. The inspector parted from us with regret, but we left him to the enjoyment of a virtue unassailed by the least bribe, — an unusual, and, I imagine, an unwelcome possession in this region.

Donkeys were not to be had, nor carriages, and we climbed on foot the very steep hill to the hotel in Pera; ascending roughly paved, crooked streets, lined with rickety houses, and occasionally mounting stairs for a mile through a quarter that has the shabbiness but not the picturesqueness of the Orient. A squad of porters seized our luggage and bore it before us. The porters are the beasts of burden, and most of them wear heavy saddles, upon which boxes and trunks can be strapped. No drays were visible. Heavy burdens, hogsheads, barrels, and cases of goods were borne between two long stout poles carried by four athletic men; as they move along the street, staggering under the heavy load, everybody is obliged, precipitately, to make way for them, for their impetus is such that they cannot check their career. We see these gigantic fellows at every street-corner, with their long poles, waiting for a job. Sedan-chairs, which were formerly in much request, are gradually disappearing, though there is nothing at present to exactly take the place of these lumbering conveyances. Carriages increase every year, but they are expensive, and they can only ascend the height of Pera by a long circuit. The place of the sedan and the carriage is, however, to some extent supplied by a railway in Galata, the cars of which are drawn up by a stationary engine. And on each side of the Golden Horn is a horse-railway, running wherever the ground is practicable.

To one coming from the West, I suppose that Constantinople would present a very mixed and bizarre appearance, and that he would be impressed by the silence of the busiest streets, in which the noise of wheels and the hum of a Western capital is wanting. But to one coming from the East, Galata and Pera seem a rather vulgarized European town. The Frank dress predominates, although it is relieved by the red fez, which the Turks generally and many Europeans wear. Variety enough there is in costumes, but the Grecian, the Bulgarian, the Albanian, etc., have taken the place of the purely Oriental ; and the traveller in the Turkish capital to-day beholds not only the conflux of Asia and Europe, but the transition, in buildings, in apparel, in manners, to modern fashions. Few veiled women are seen, and they wear a white strip of gauze which conceals nothing. The street hawkers, the sellers of sweets, of sponges, and of cakes, are not more peculiar in their cries than those of London and Paris.

When we had climbed the hill, we came into the long main street of Pera, the street of the chief shops, the hotels and foreign embassies, a quarter of the city which has been burned over as often as San Francisco, and is now built up substantially with stone and brick, and contains very little to interest the seeker of novelty. After we had secured rooms, and breakfasted, at the hotel Byzance, we descended the hill again to the water, and crossed the long, floating bridge to Stamboul. This bridge is a very good symbol of the Sultan's Empire ; its wooden upper works are decayed, its whole structure is rickety, the floats that support it are unevenly sunken, so that the bridge is a succession of swells and hollows ; it is crowded by opposing streams of the most incongruous people, foot and horse jumbled together ; it is encumbered by venders of eatables and auctioneers of cheap wares, and one has to pay toll to cross it. But it is a microcosm of the world. In an hour one may see pass there every nationality, adventurers from every clime, traders, priests, sailors, soldiers, fortune-hunters of Europe, rude peasants of the provinces, sleek merchants of the Orient, darwishes, furtive-eyed Jews ; here is a Circassian beauty seeking a lover through the carriage window ; here a Turkish grandee on a prancing, richly caparisoned horse ; here moves a squad of black soldiers, and now the bridge shakes under the weight of a train of flying artillery.

The water is alive with the ticklish caïques. The caïque is a long narrow boat, on the model of the Indian birch-bark canoe, and as thin and light on the water; the passenger, if he accomplishes the feat of getting into one without overturning it, sits upon the bottom, careful not to wink and upset it; the oars have a heavy swell near the handle, to counterbalance the weight of the long blade, and the craft skims the water with swiftness and a most agreeable motion. The caïques are as numerous on the water as the yellow, mangy dogs on shore, and the two are the most characteristic things in Constantinople.

We spent a good part of the day in wandering about the bazaars of Stamboul, and we need not repeat what has been heretofore said of these peculiar shops. During our stay in the city we very thoroughly explored them, and visited most of the great khans, where are to be found the silks of Broussa, of Beyrout and Damascus, the rugs of Persia, the carpets of Asia Minor, the arms and the cunning work in gold, silver, and jewels gathered from every region between Ispahan and Darfour. We found the bazaars extensive, well filled and dear, at least the asking price was enormous, and we wanted the time and patience which are needed for the slow siege of reducing the merchants to decent terms. The bazaars are solidly roofed arcades, at once more cleanly and less picturesque than those of Cairo, and not so Oriental or attractive. Book-stalls, which are infrequent in Cairo, abound here; and the long arcades lined with cases of glittering gems, enormous pearls, sparkling diamonds, emeralds fit for the Pope's finger, and every gold and silver temptation, exceed anything else in the East in magnificence. And yet they have a certain modern air, and you do not expect to find in them those quaint and fascinating antique patterns of goldsmiths' work, the inherited skill of the smiths of the Pharaohs, which draw you into the dingy recesses of the Copt artificers in the city of the Nile.

From the Valideh Khan we ascended to the public square, where stands the Seraskier's Fire-tower; a paved, open place, surrounded by government buildings of considerable architectural pretensions, and dedicated, I should say, to drumming, to the shifting about of squads of soldiers, and the cantering hither and thither of Turkish beys. Near it is the old mosque of Sultan. Beyezid II., which, with its magnificent arabesque gates, makes a fine external impression. The outer court is surrounded by a cloister with columns of verd-antique and porphyry, enclosing a fountain and three stately, venerable trees. The trees and the arcades are alive with doves, and, as we entered, more than a thousand flew towards us in a cloud, with a great rustling and cooing. They are protected as an almost sacred appendage of the mosque, and are said to be bred from a single pair which the Sultan bought of a poor woman and presented to the house he had built, three centuries and a half ago. This mosque has also another claim to the gratitude of animals; for all the dogs of Stamboul, none of whom have any home but the street, nor any other owner than the Prophet, resort here every Friday, as regularly, if not as piously, as the Sultan goes to pray, and receive their weekly bread.

Near this mosque are lines of booths and open-air shops, which had a fascination for me as long as I remained in the city. They extend from the trees in the place of the mosque down through lanes to the bazaars. The keepers of them were typical Orientals, honest Jews, honest Moslems, withered and one-eyed waiters on Providence and a good bargain, suave, gracious, patient, gowned and turbaned, sitting cross-legged behind their trays and show-cases. These are the dealers in stones, both precious and common, in old and new ornaments, and the thousand cheap adornments in glass and metal which the humbler classes love. Here are heaps of blood-stones, of carnelians, of agates, of jasper, of onyx, dishes of turquoise, strings of doubtful pearls, barbarous rings and brooches, charms and amulets, — a feast of color for the eye, and a sight to kindle the imagination. For these bawbles came out of the recesses of the Orient, were gathered by wild tribes in remote deserts, and transported by caravan to this common mart. These dealers buy of the Persian merchants, and of adventurous Jew travellers who range all the deserts from Teheran to Upper Nubia in search of these shining stones. Some of the turquoises are rudely set in silver rings, but most of them are merely glued to the end of little sticks; these generally are the refuse of the trade, for the finer stones go to the great jewellers in the bazaar, or to the Western markets. A large and perfect turquoise of good color is very rare, and commands a large price; but the cunning workmen of Persia have a method of at once concealing the defects of a good-sized turquoise which has the true color, and at the same time enhancing its value, by engraving upon it some sentence from the Koran, or some word which is a charm against the evil eye; the skill of the engraver is shown in fitting his letters and flourishes to the flaws in the surface of the stone. To further hide any appearance of imperfection, the engraved lines are often gilded. With a venerable Moslem, who sat day after day under a sycamore-tree, I had great content, and we both enjoyed the pleasure of endless bargaining without cheating each other, for except in some trifles we never came to an exact agreement. He was always promising me the most wonderful things for the next day, which he would procure from a mysterious Jew friend who carried on a clandestine commerce with some Bedawee in Arabia. When I was seated, he would pull from his bosom a knotted silk handkerchief, and, carefully untying it, produce a talisman, presenting it between his thumb and finger, with a lift of the eyebrows and a cluck of the tongue that expressed the rapture I would feel at the sight of it. To be sure, I found it a turquoise set in rude silver, faded to a sickly green, and not worth sixpence; but I handed it back with a sigh that such a jewel was beyond my means, and intimated that something less costly, and of a blue color, would suit me as well. We were neither of us deceived, while we maintained the courtesies of commercial intercourse. Sometimes he would produce from his bosom an emerald of real value or an opal of lovely hues, and occasionally a stone in some peculiar setting which I had admired the day before in the jewelry bazaar; for these trinkets, upon which the eye of the traveller has been seen longingly to rest, are shifted about among this mysterious fraternity to meet him again. I suppose it was known all over Stamboul that a Frank had been looking for a Persian amulet. As long as I sat with my friend, I never saw him actually sell anything, but he seemed to be the centre of mysterious transactions; furtive traders continually came to him to borrow or return a jewel, or to exchange a handful of trumpery. Delusive old man! I had no confidence in you, but I would go far to pass another day in your tranquil society. How much more agreeable you were than the young Nubian at an opposite stand, who repelled purchasers by his supreme indifference, and met all my feeble advances with the toss of the head and the cluck in the left cheek, which is the peremptory " no " in Nubia.

In this quarter are workers in shell and ivory, the makers of spoons of tortoise-shell with handles of ivory and coral, the fabricators of combs, dealers in books, and a long street of little shops devoted to the engraving of seals. To wander about among these craftsmen is one of the chief pleasures of the traveller. Vast as Stamboul is, if you remove from it the mosques and nests of bazaars, it would not be worth a visit.

XXV.

THE SERAGLIO AND ST. SOPHIA, HIPPODROME, ETC.

HAVING procured a firman, we devoted a day to the old
Seraglio and some of the principal mosques of Stamboul.
After an occupation of fifteen centuries as a royal residence, the
Seraglio has been disused for nearly forty years, and fire, neglect,
and decay have done their work on it, so that it is but a melancholy reminiscence of its former splendor. It occupies the ancient
site of Byzantium, upon the Point, and is enclosed by a crumbling wall three miles in circuit. No royal seat in the world has
a more lovely situation. Upon the summit of the promontory,
half concealed in cypresses, is the cluster of buildings, of all ages
and degrees of cheapness, in which are the imperial apartments
and offices; on the slopes towards the sea are gardens, terraces,
kiosks, and fountains.

We climbed up the hill on the side towards Pera, through a
shabby field, that had almost the appearance of a city dumping-
ground, and through a neglected grove of cypresses, where some
deer were feeding, and came round to the main entrance, a big,
ugly pavilion with eight openings over the arched *porte*, — the
gate which is known the world over as the Sublime Porte.
Through this we passed into a large court, and thence to the
small one into which the Sultan only is permitted to ride on
horseback. In the centre of this is a fountain where formerly
pashas foreordained to lose their heads lost them. On the right,
a low range of buildings covered with domes but no chimneys, are
the royal kitchens; there are nine of them, — one for the Sultan,
one for the chief sultanas, and so on down to the one devoted

to the cooking of the food for the servants. Hundreds of beasts,
hecatombs, were slaughtered daily and cooked here to feed the
vast household. From this court open the doors into the halls
and divans and various apartments; one of them, leading into
the interior, is called the Gate of Felicity; in the old times that
could only be called a gate of felicity which let a person out of this
spider's parlor. In none of these rooms is there anything specially attractive; cheap magnificence in decay is only melancholy.

We were better pleased in the gardens, where we looked upon
Galata and Pera, upon the Golden Horn and the long bridges
streaming with their picturesque processions, upon the Bosphorus
and its palaces, and thousands of sails, steamers, and caïques, and
the shining heights of Scutari. Overhanging the slope is the
kiosk or summer palace of Sultan Moorad, a Saracenic octagonal
structure, the interior walls lined with Persian tiles, the ceilings
painted in red arabesques and gilded in mosaics, the gates of
bronze inlaid with mother-of-pearl; a most charming building,
said to be in imitation of a kiosk of Bagdad. In it we saw the
Sultan's private library, a hundred or two volumes in a glass case,
that had no appearance of having been read either by the Sultan
or his wife.

The apartment in the Seraglio which is the object of curiosity
and desire is the treasure-room. I suppose it is the richest in
the world in gems; it is certainly a most wearisome place, and
gave me a contempt for earthly treasure. In the centre stands a
Persian throne, — a chair upon a board platform, and both incrusted with rubies, pearls, emeralds, diamonds; there are toilet-
tables covered to the feet with diamonds, pipe-stems glistening
with huge diamonds, old armor thickly set with precious stones,
saddle-cloths and stirrups stiff with diamonds and emeralds, robes
embroidered with pearls. Nothing is so cheap as wealth lavished
in this manner; at first we were dazzled by the flashing display,
but after a time these heaps of gems seemed as common in our
eyes as pebbles in the street. I did not even covet an emerald
as large as my fist, nor a sword-hilt in which were fifteen diamonds, each as large as the end of my thumb, nor a carpet sown
with pearls, some of which were of the size of pigeon's eggs, nor

aigrettes which were blazing with internal fires, nor chairs of state, clocks and vases, the whole surfaces of which were on fire with jewels. I have seen an old oaken table, carved in the fifteenth century, which gave me more pleasure than one of lapis lazuli, which is exhibited as the most costly article in this collection; though it is inlaid with precious stones, and the pillars that support the mirror are set with diamonds, and the legs and claws are a mass of diamonds, rubies, carbuncles, emeralds, topazes, etc., and huge diamond pendants ornament it, and the deep fringe in front is altogether of diamonds. This is but a barbarous, ostentatious, and tasteless use of the beautiful, and I suppose gives one an idea of the inartistic magnificence of the Oriental courts in centuries gone by.

This treasure-house has, I presume, nothing that belonged to the Byzantine emperors before the Moslem conquest, some of whom exceeded in their magnificence any of the Osmanli sultans. Arcadius, the first Eastern emperor after the division of the Roman world, rivalled, in the appointments of his palace (which stood upon this spot) and in his dress, the magnificence of the Persian monarchs; and perhaps the luxurious califs of Bagdad at a later day did not equal his splendor. His robes were of purple, a color reserved exclusively for his sacred person, and of silk, embroidered with gold dragons; his diadem was of gold set with gems of inestimable worth; his throne was massy gold, and when he went abroad he rode in a chariot of solid, pure gold, drawn by two milk-white mules shining in harness and trappings of gold.

No spot on earth has been the scene of such luxury, cruelty, treachery, murder, infidelity of women, and rapacity of men, as this site of the old palace; and the long record of the Christian emperors — the occasionally interrupted anarchy and usurpation of a thousand years — loses nothing in these respects in comparison with the Turkish occupation, although the world shudders at the unrevealed secrets of the Seraglio. At least we may suppose that nobody's conscience was violated if a pretty woman was occasionally dropped into the Bosphorus, and there was the authority of custom for the strangling of all the children of the sisters of the Sultan, so that the succession might not be em-

barrassed. In this court is the *cage*, a room accessible only by
a window, where the royal children were shut up to keep them
from conspiracy against the throne; and there Sultan Abdul
Aziz spent some years of his life.

We went from the treasure-room to the ancient and large
Church of St. Irene, which is now the arsenal of the Seraglio, and
become, one might say, a church militant. The nave and aisles
are stacked with arms, the walls, the holy apse, the pillars, are
cased in guns, swords, pistols, and armor, arranged in fanciful
patterns, and with an ingenuity I have seen nowhere else. Here
are preserved battle-flags and famous trophies, an armlet of Tamerlane, a sword of Scanderbeg, and other pieces of cold, pliant
steel that have a reputation for many murders. There is no way
so sure to universal celebrity as wholesale murder. Adjoining
the arsenal is a museum of Greek and Roman antiquities of the
city, all in Turkish disorder; the Cyprus Collections, sent by
General di Cesnola, are flung upon shelves or lie in heaps unarranged, and most of the cases containing them had not been
opened. Near this is an interesting museum of Turkish costumes
for the past five hundred years, — rows on rows of ghastly wax
figures clad in the garments of the dead. All of them are ugly,
many of them are comical in their exaggeration. The costumes
of the Janizaries attract most attention, perhaps from the dislike with which we regard those cruel mercenaries, who deposed
and decapitated sultans at their will, and partly because many
of the dresses seem more fit for harlequins or eunuchs of the
harem than for soldiers.

When the Church of Santa Sophia, the House of Divine Wisdom, was finished, and Justinian entered it, accompanied only by
the patriarch, and ran from the porticos to the pulpit with outstretched arms, crying, "Solomon, I have surpassed thee!" it
was doubtless the most magnificently decorated temple that had
ever stood upon the earth. The exterior was as far removed in
simple grandeur as it was in time from the still matchless Doric
temples of Athens and of Pæstum, or from the ornate and lordly
piles of Ba'albek; but the interior surpassed in splendor almost
the conception of man. The pagan temples of antiquity had

been despoiled, the quarries of the known world had been ransacked for marbles of various hues and textures to enrich it; and the gold, the silver, the precious stones, employed in its decoration, surpassed in measure the barbaric ostentation of the Temple at Jerusalem. Among its forest of columns, one recognized the starred syenite from the First Cataract of the Nile; the white marble of Phrygia, striped with rose; the green of Laconia, and the blue of Libya; the black Celtic, white-veined, and the white Bosphorus, black-veined; polished shafts which had supported the roof of the Temple of the Delian Apollo, others which had beheld the worship of Diana at Ephesus and of Pallas Athene on the Acropolis, and, yet more ancient, those that had served in the mysterious edifices of Osiris and Isis; while, more conspicuous and beautiful than all, were the eight columns of porphyry, which, transported by Aurelian from the Temple of the Sun at Heliopolis to Rome, the pious Marina had received as her dowry and dedicated to the most magnificent building ever reared to the worship of the True God, and fitly dominating the shores of Europe and Asia.

One reads of doors of cedar, amber, and ivory; of hundreds of sacred vessels of pure gold, of exquisitely wrought golden candelabra, and crosses of an hundred pounds' weight each; of a score of books of the Evangelists, the gold covers of which weighed twenty pounds; of golden lilies and golden trumpets; of forty-two thousand chalice-cloths embroidered with pearls and jewels; and of the great altar, for which gold was too cheap a material, a mass of the most precious and costly stones imbedded in gold and silver. We may recall also the arches and the clear spaces of the walls inlaid with marbles and covered with brilliant mosaics. It was Justinian's wish to pave the floor with plates of gold, but, restrained by the fear of the avarice of his successors, he laid it in variegated marbles, which run in waving lines, imitating the flowing of rivers from the four corners to the vestibules. But the wonder of the edifice was the dome, one hundred and seven feet in span, hanging in the air one hundred and eighty feet above the pavement. The aerial lightness of its position is increased by the two half-domes of equal span and the nine cupolas which surround it.

More than one volume has been exclusively devoted to a description of the Mosque of St. Sophia, and less than a volume
would not suffice. But the traveller will not see the ancient
glories. If he expects anything approaching the exterior richness and grandeur of the cathedrals of Europe, or the colossal
proportions of St. Peter's at Rome, or the inexhaustible wealth
of the interior of St. Mark's at Venice, he will be disappointed.
The area of St. Peter's exceeds that of the grand Piazza of St.
Mark, while St. Sophia is only two hundred and thirty-five feet
broad by three hundred and fifty feet long; and while the Church
of St. Mark has been accumulating spoils of plunder and of piety
for centuries, the Church of the Divine Wisdom has been ransacked by repeated pillages and reduced to the puritan plainness
of the Moslem worship.

Exceedingly impressive, however, is the first view of the interior; we stood silent with wonder and delight in the presence
of the noble columns, the bold soaring arches, the dome in the
sky. The temple is flooded with light, perhaps it is too bright;
the old mosaics and paintings must have softened it; and we
found very offensive the Arabic inscriptions on the four great
arches, written in characters ten yards long. They are the names
of companions of the Prophet, but they look like sign-boards.
Another disagreeable impression is produced by the position of the
Mihrab, or prayer-niche; as this must be in the direction of
Mecca, it is placed at one side of the apse, and everything in the
mosque is forced to conform to it. Thus everything is askew;
the pulpits are set at hateful angles, and the stripes of the rugs
on the floor all run diagonally across. When one attempts to
walk from the entrance, pulled one way by the architectural plan,
and the other by the religious diversion of it, he has a sensation
of being intoxicated.

Gone from this temple are the sacred relics which edified the
believers of former ages, such as the trumpets that blew down
Jericho and planks from the Ark of Noah, but the Moslems have
prodigies to replace them. The most curious of these is the
sweating marble column, which emits a dampness that cures diseases. I inserted my hand in a cavity which has been dug in it,

and certainly experienced a clammy sensation. It is said to sweat
most early in the morning. I had the curiosity to ascend the
gallery to see the seat of the courtesan and Empress Theodora,
daughter of the keeper of the bears of the circus, — a public and
venal pantomimist, who, after satisfying the immoral curiosity of
her contemporaries in many cities, illustrated the throne of the
Cæsars by her talents, her intrigues, and her devotion. The fondness of Justinian has preserved her initials in the capitals of the
columns, the imperial eagle marks the screen that hid her seat,
and the curious traveller may see her name carved on the balustrade where she sat.

To the ancient building the Moslems have added the minarets
at the four corners and the enormous crescent on the dome, the
gilding of which cost fifty thousand ducats, and the shining of
which, a golden moon in the day, is visible at the distance of a
hundred miles. The crescent, adopted by the Osmanli upon the
conquest of Jerusalem, was the emblem of Byzantium before the
Christian era. There is no spot in Constantinople more flooded
with historical associations, or more interesting to the student of
the history of the Eastern Empire, than the site of St. Sophia.
Here arose the church of the same name erected by Constantine ;
it was twice burned, once by the party of St. John Chrysostom,
and once in a tumult of the factions of the Hippodrome. I
should like to have seen some of the pageants that took place here.
After reposing in their graves for three centuries, the bodies of
St. Andrew, St. Luke, and St. Timothy were transported hither.
Fifty years after it was honored by a still more illustrious presence ; the ashes of the prophet Samuel, deposited in a golden
vase covered with a silken veil, left their resting-place in Palestine for the banks of the Bosphorus. The highways from the
hills of Judæa to the gates of Constantinople were filled by an
uninterrupted procession, who testified their enthusiasm and joy,
and the Emperor Arcadius himself, attended by the most illustrious of the clergy and the Senate, advanced to receive his illustrious guest, and conducted the holy remains to this magnificent
but insecure place of repose. It was here that Gregory Nazian-
zen was by force installed upon the Episcopal throne by Theodo-

sius. The city was fanatically Arian. Theodosius proclaimed the Nicene creed, and ordered the primate to deliver the cathedral and all the churches to the orthodox, who were few in number, but strong in the presence of Gregory. This extraordinary man had set up an orthodox pulpit in a private house; he had been mobbed by a motley crowd which issued from the Cathedral of St. Sophia, " common beggars who had forfeited their claim to pity, monks who had the appearance of goats or satyrs, and women more horrible than so many Jezebels"; he had his triumph when Theodosius led him by the hand through the streets — filled with a multitude crowding pavement, roofs, and windows, and venting their rage, grief, astonishment, and despair — into the church, which was held by soldiers, though the prelate confessed that the city had the appearance of a town stormed by barbarians. It was here that Eutropius, the eunuch, when his career of rapacity exceeded even the toleration of Arcadius, sought sanctuary, and was protected by John Chrysostom, archbishop, who owed his ecclesiastical dignity to the late sexless favorite. And it was up this very nave that Mohammed II., the conqueror, spurred his horse through a crowd of fugitives, dismounted at the foot of the altar, cried, " There is no God but God, and Mohammed is his prophet!" and let loose his soldiery upon the priests, virgins, and promiscuous multitude who had sought shelter here.

I should only weary you with unintelligible details in attempting a description of other mosques which we visited. They are all somewhat alike, though varying in degrees of splendor. There is that of Sultan Ahmed, on the site of the Hippodrome, distinguished as the only one in the empire that has six minarets, — the state mosque of the Sultan, whence the Mecca pilgrimages proceed and where the great festivals are held. From a distance it is one of the most conspicuous and poetically beautiful objects in the city. And there is the Mosque of Suleiman the Magnificent, a copy of St. Sophia and excelling it in harmonious grandeur, — indeed, it is called the finest mosque in the empire. Its forecourt measures a thousand paces, and the enclosure contains, besides the mosque and the tomb of the founder, many founda-

tions of charity and of learning, — three schools for the young,
besides one for the reading of the Koran and one of medicine,
four academies for the four Moslem sects, a hospital, a kitchen
for the poor, a library, a fountain, a resting-place for travellers,
and a house of refuge for strangers.   From it one enjoys a magnificent view of the Golden Horn, the Bosphorus, and the piled-
up city opposite.   When we entered the mosque hundreds of
worshippers were at prayer, bowing their turbans towards Mecca
in silent unison.   The throng soon broke up into groups of from
ten to forty, which seated themselves in circles on the floor for
the reading of the Koran.   The shoes were heaped in the centre
of each circle, the chief reader squatted at a low desk on one side,
and all read together in a loud voice, creating an extraordinary
vocal tumult.   It was like a Sunday school in fancy dress.

Stamboul is a very interesting place to those who have a taste
for gorgeous sepulchres, and I do not know any such pleasant
residences of the dead as the *turbehs*, or tombs of the imperial
family.   Usually attached to the mosques, but sometimes standing apart, they are elegant edifices, such as might be suitable for
the living; in their airy, light, and stately chambers the occupants are deprived of no splendor to which they were accustomed
in life.   One of the most beautiful of these *turbehs*, that of Sultan
Mahmood II., I mistook for a fountain; it is a domed, circular
building of white marble, with Corinthian pilasters, and lighted
by seven large windows with gilded grating.   Within, in a cheerful, carpeted apartment, are the biers of the sultan, his valideh
sultana, and five daughters, covered with cloths of velvet, richly
embroidered, upon which are thrown the most superb India
shawls; the principal sarcophagi are surrounded by railings of
mother-of-pearl; massive silver candlesticks and Koran-stands,
upon which are beautiful manuscripts of the Koran, are disposed
about the room, and at the head of the Sultan's bier is a fez with
a plume and aigrette of diamonds.   In the court of Santa Sophia
you may see the beautiful mausoleum of Selim II., who reposes beside the Lady of Light; and not far from it the *turbeh* containing
the remains of Mohammed III., surrounded by the biers of seventeen brothers whom he murdered.   It is pleasant to see brothers

united and in peace at last. I found something pathetic in other
like apartments where families were gathered together, sultans and
sultanas in the midst of little span-long biers of sons and daughters, incipient sultans and sultanas, who were never permitted by
state policy, if I may be allowed the expression, to hatch. Strangled in their golden cradles, perhaps, these innocents! Worth-
less little bodies, mocked by the splendor of their interments.
One could not but feel a little respect for what might have been
a " Sublime Porte " or a Light of the Seraglio.

The Imperial Palace, the Church of Santa Sophia, the Hippodrome, — these are the triangle of Byzantine history, the trinity
of tyranny, religion, and faction. The Circus of Constantinople,
like that on the banks of the Tiber, was the arena for the exhibition of games, races, spectacles, and triumphs; like that, it was
the arena of a licentious democracy, but the most disorderly mob
of Rome never attained the power or equalled the vices of the
murderous and incendiary factions of Byzantium. The harmless
colors that at first only distinguished the ignoble drivers in the
chariot races became the badges of parties, which claimed the
protection and enjoyed the favor of emperors and prelates; and
the *blue* and the *green* factions not only more than once involved
the city in conflagration and blood, but carried discord and frenzy
into all the provinces. Although they respected no human or
divine law, they affected religious zeal for one or another Christian
sect or dogma; the " blues " long espoused the orthodox cause,
and enjoyed the partiality of Justinian. The dissolute youth of
Constantinople, wearing the livery of the factions, possessed the
city at night, and abandoned themselves to any deed of violence
that fancy or revenge suggested; neither the sanctity of the church,
nor the peace of the private house, nor the innocence of youth,
nor the chastity of matron or maid, was safe from these assassins
and ravishers. It was in one of their seditious outbreaks that
the palace and Santa Sophia were delivered to the flames.

The oblong ground of the Hippodrome is still an open place,
although a portion of the ground is covered by the Mosque of
Ahmed. But the traveller will find there few relics of this historical arena; nothing of the marble seats and galleries that sur-

rounded it. The curious may look at the Egyptian obelisk of
syenite, at the crumbling pyramid which was the turning goal of
the chariots ; and he may find more food for reflection in the
bronze spiral column, formed by the twinings of three serpents
whose heads have been knocked off. It deserves to be housed
and cared for. There is no doubt of its venerable antiquity ; it
was seen by Thucydides and Herodotus in the Temple of Delphi,
where its three branching heads formed a tripod upon which
rested the dish of gold which the Greeks captured among the
spoils of the battle of Platæa. The column is not more than
fifteen feet high ; it has stood here since the time of Constantine.

This is the most famous square of Constantinople, yet in its
present unromantic aspect it is difficult to reanimate its interest.
It is said that its statues of marble and bronze once excelled the
living population of the city. In its arena emperors, whose vices
have alone saved their names to a conspicuous contempt, sought
the popular applause by driving in the chariot races, or stripped
themselves for the sports with wild beasts, proud to remind the
spectators of the exploits of Caligula and Heliogabalus. Here,
in the reign of Anastasius, the "green" faction, entering the
place with concealed daggers, interrupted a solemn festival and
assassinated three thousand of the "blues." This place was in
the first quarter of this century the exercise and parade ground of
the Janizaries, until they were destroyed. Let us do justice to
the Turks. In two memorable instances they exhibited a nerve
which the Roman emperors lacked, who never had either the firm-
ness or the courage to extirpate the Prætorian Guards. The Janizaries set up, deposed, murdered sultans, as the Guards did
Emperors ; and the Mamelukes of Egypt imitated their predeces-
sors at Rome. Mahmood II. in Constantinople, and Mohammed
Ali in Cairo, had the courage to extinguish these enemies of
Turkish sovereignty.

In this neighborhood are several ancient monuments ; the
Burnt Column, a blackened shaft of porphyry ; the column called
Historical; and that of Theodosius, — I shall not fatigue you with
further mention of them. Not far from the Hippodrome we descended into the reservoir called A Thousand and One Columns ;

I suppose this number is made up by counting one as three, for each column consists of three superimposed shafts. It is only partially excavated. We found a number of Jews occupying these subterranean colonnades, engaged in twisting silk, the even temperature of the cellar being favorable to this work.

As if we had come out of a day in another age, we walked down through the streets of the artificers of brass and ivory and leather, to the floating bridge, and crossed in a golden sunset, in which the minarets and domes of the mosque of Mohammed II. appeared like some aerial creation in the yellow sky.

XXVI.

SAUNTERINGS ABOUT CONSTANTINOPLE.

DURING the day steamers leave the Galata bridge every half-hour for the villages and palaces along the Bosphorus ; there is a large fleet of them, probably thirty, but they are always crowded, like the ferry-boats that ply the waters of New York Bay.

We took our first sail on the Bosphorus one afternoon toward sunset, ascending as far as Bebek, where we had been invited to spend the night by Dr. Washburne, the President of Roberts College. I shall not soon forget the animation of the harbor, crowded with shipping, amid which the steamers and caïques were darting about like shuttles, the first impression made by the palaces and ravishingly lovely shores of this winding artery between two seas. Seven promontories from Asia and seven promontories from Europe project into the stream, creating as many corresponding bays ; but the villages are more numerous than bays and promontories together, for there are over forty in the fourteen miles from the Sea of Marmora to the Black Sea ; on the shores is an almost unbroken line of buildings, many of them palaces of marble ; the heights are crowned with cottages and luxurious villas, and abodes of taste and wealth peep out along the slopes. If you say that we seem to be sailing in the street of a city, I can only answer that it is not so ; nature is still supreme here, and the visible doweress of the scene. These lovely hills rising on both sides, these gracious curves are hers, as are these groves and gardens of fruits and flowers, these vines

13*

and the abundant green that sometimes conceals and always softens the work of man.

Before we reached the Sultan's palace at Beshiktash, our
steamer made a *détour* to the east bank, outside of the grim iron-
clads that lie before the imperial residence. No steamers are
permitted to approach nearer, lest the smoke should soil the
sparkling white marble of the palace, or their clamor and dangerous freight of men should disturb the serenity of the harem.
The palace, which is a beautiful building, stretches for some distance along the water, with its gardens and conservatories, and
seems to be a very comfortable home for a man who has no more
ready money than the Sultan.

We landed at Bebek and climbed the steep hill, on whose slope
nightingales were singing in the forest, just in time to see the
sunset. Roberts College occupies the most commanding situation on the strait, and I do not know any view that surpasses in
varied beauty that to be enjoyed from it. I shall make myself
comprehended by many when I say that it strongly reminded me
of the Hudson at West Point; if nature could be suspected of
copying herself, I should say that she had the one in mind when
she made the other. At that point the Hudson resembles the
Bosphorus, but it wants the palaces, the Vale of the Heavenly
Water into which we looked from this height, and some charming
mediæval towers, walls, and castles.

The towers and walls belong to the fortress built in 1451 by
Mohammed II., and are now fallen into that decrepitude in
which I like best to see all fortresses. But this was interesting before it was a ruin. It stands just above the college, at
Roomeli Hissar, where the Bosphorus is narrowest, — not more
than half a mile broad, — and with the opposite fortress of
Anatolia could perfectly close the stream. Two years before the
capture of the city, Mohammed built this fort, and gave it the
most peculiar form of any fortress existing. His idea was that
the towers and the circuit of the walls should spell the name of
the Prophet, and consequently his own. As we looked down upon
it, my friend read for me this singular piece of caligraphy, but I
could understand it no further than the tower which stands for

the Arabic ring in the first letter. It was at this place that Darius threw a bridge across the Bosphorus, and there is a tradition of a stone seat which he occupied here while his Asiatics passed into Europe.

So far as I know, there is no other stream in the world upon which the wealth of palaces and the beauty of gardens may be so advantageously displayed. So far as I know, there is no other place where nature and art have so combined to produce an enchanting prospect. As the situation and appearance of Constantinople are unequalled, so the Bosphorus is unique.

Whatever may be the political changes of the Turkish Empire, I do not believe that this pleasing picture will be destroyed; rather let us expect to see it more lovely in the rapidly developing taste of a new era of letters and refinement. It was a wise forethought that planted the American College just here. It is just where it should be to mould the new order of things. I saw among its two hundred pupils scholars of all creeds and races, who will carry from here living ideas to every part of the empire, and I learned to respect that thirst for knowledge and ability to acquire it which exist in the neighboring European provinces. If impatient men could wait the process of education, the growth of schools, and the development of capacity now already most promising, the Eastern question might be solved by the appearance on the scene in less than a score of years, of a stalwart and intelligent people, who would not only be able to grasp Constantinople, but to administer upon the decaying Turkish Empire as the Osmanli administered upon the Greek.

On Friday the great business of everybody is to see the Sultan go to pray; and the eagerness with which foreigners crowd to the spectacle must convince the Turks that we enjoy few religious privileges at home. It is not known beforehand, even to the inmates of the palace, to what mosque the Sultan will go, nor whether he will make a street progress on horseback, or embark upon the water, for the chosen place of prayer. Before twelve o'clock we took carriage and drove down the hill, past the parade-ground and the artillery barracks to the rear of the palace of Beshiktash; crowds on foot and in carriages were streaming

in that direction; regiments of troops were drifting down the
slopes and emptying into the avenue that leads between the palace
and the plantation of gardens; colors were unfurled, drums
beaten, trumpets called from barrack and guard-house; gorgeous
officers on caparisoned horses, with equally gaudy attendants,
cantered to the rendezvous; and all the air was full of the expectation of a great event. At the great square of the palace we
waited amid an intense throng; four or five lines of carriages
stretched for a mile along; troops were in marching rank along
the avenue and disposed in hollow square on the place; the palace gates were closed, and everybody looked anxiously toward the
high and gilded portal from which it was said the announcement
of the Sultan's intention would be made. From time to time our
curiosity was fed by the arrival of a splendid pasha, who dismounted and walked about; and at intervals a gilded personage
emerged from the palace court and raised our expectation on tip-
toe. We send our dragoman to interrogate the most awful dig-
nities, especially some superb beings in yellow silk and gold, but
they know nothing of the Sultan's mind. At the last moment
he might, on horseback, issue from the gate with a brilliant
throng, or he might depart in his caïque by the water front. In
either case there would be a rush and a scramble to see and to
accompany him. More regiments were arriving, bands were
playing, superb officers galloping up and down; carriages, gilded
with the arms of foreign embassies, or filled with Turkish ladies,
pressed forward to the great gate, which still gave no sign. I
have never seen such a religious excitement. For myself, I found
some compensation in the usual Oriental crowd and unconscious
picturesqueness : swart Africans in garments of yellow, sellers of
sherbet clinking their glasses, venders of faint sweetmeats walking about with trays and tripods, and the shifting kaleidoscope of
races, colors, and graceful attitudes.

Suddenly, I do not know how, or from what quarter, the feeling
— for I could not call it information — was diffused that the successor of the Prophet would pray at the mosque in Ortakeui, and
that he would go by caïque; and we all scampered up the road, a
mile or two, racing carriages, troops and foot men, in eager outset,

in order to arrive before the pious man. The mosque stands upon the Bosphorus, where its broad marble steps and pillared front and dome occupy as conspicuous a position as the Dogana at Venice. We secured a standing-place on the dock close to the landing, but outside the iron railing, and waited. A cordon of troops in blue regimentals with red facings was drawn around the streets in the rear of the mosque, and two companies of soldiers in white had stacked their guns on the marble landing, and were lounging about in front of the building.

The scene on the Bosphorus was as gay as a flower-garden. The water was covered with graceful caïques and painted barges and every sort of craft, mean and splendid, that could be propelled by oars or sails. A dozen men-of-war were decked with flags from keel to maintop; on every yard, and from bowsprit to stern, stood a line of sailors sharply defined against the blue sky. At one o'clock a cannon announced that the superior devotee had entered his caïque, and then from every vessel of war in the harbor salute answered salute in thunder that awoke the echoes of two continents; until on all the broad water lay a thick battle-smoke, through which we could distinguish only the tops of the masts, and the dim hulks spouting fire.

In the midst of this earthquake of piety, there was a cry, "He comes, he comes!" The soldiers grasped their arms and drew a line each side of the landing, and the officials of the mosque arranged themselves on the steps. Upon the water, advancing with the speed of race-horses, we saw two splendid gilded caïques, the one containing the Sultan, the other his attendants. At the moment, a light carriage with two bay horses, unattended, dashed up to the side door, and there descended from it and entered the mosque the imperial heir, the son of the late Sultan and the nephew of the present, a slender, pale youth of apparently twenty-five or thirty years. We turn (not knowing how soon he is to become Sultan Murad V.) our eyes to him only for a moment, for the Sultan's caïque comes with imperious haste, with the rush as it were of victory, — an hundred feet long, narrow, rising at the stern like the Venetian Bucentaur, carved and gilded like the golden chariot in which Alexander entered Babylon, — propelled by fifty-two long sweeps, rising and falling in unison with the bending backs of twenty-six black rowers, clad in white and with naked feet. The Sultan is throned in the high stern, hung with silk, on silken cushions, under a splendid canopy on the top of which glisten his arms and a blazing sun. The Sultan, who is clad in the uniform of a general, steps quickly out, walks up the steps over a carpet spread for his royal feet, — the soldiers saluting, everybody with arms crossed bending the body, — and disappears in the mosque. The second caïque lands immediately, and the imperial ministers step from it and follow their master.

At the side entrance an immense closed baggage-wagon, drawn by four horses and said to contain the sacred wardrobe, was then unlocked and unloaded, and out of it came trunks, boxes, carpet-bags, as if the imperial visitor had come to stay a week. After a half-hour of prayer he came out, his uniform concealed under his overcoat, got quickly into a plain carriage, drawn by four magnificent gray horses, and drove rapidly away, attended by a dozen outriders. His heir followed in the carriage in which he came. We had a good view of the chief of Islam. He was a tall, stout man, with a full gray beard, and on the whole a good face and figure. All this parade is weekly enacted over one man going to pray. It is, after all, more simple than the pageantry that often attends the public devotion of the vicegerent of Christ in St. Peter's.

Upon our return we stopped at the *tekkeb*, in Pera, to see the performance of the Turning Darwishes. I do not know that I have anything to add to the many animated descriptions which have been written of it. It is not far from the Little Field of the Dead, and all about the building are tombs of the faithful, in which were crowds of people enjoying that peculiar Oriental pleasure, graveyard festivity. The mosque is pleasant, and has a polished dancing-floor, surrounded by a gallery supported on columns. I thought it would be a good place for a "hop." Everybody has seen a picture of the darwishes, with closed eyes, outstretched arms, and long gowns inflated at the bottom like an old-fashioned churn, turning smoothly round upon their toes, a dozen or twenty of them revolving without collision. The mo-

tion is certainly poetic and pleasing, and the plaintive fluting of
the Arab *nay* adds I know not what of pathos to the exercise.　I
think this dance might advantageously be substituted in Western
salons for the German, for it is graceful and perfectly moral.

Constantinople is a city of the dead as much as of the living, and one encounters everywhere tombs and cemeteries senti-
nelled by the mournful dark-green cypress.　On our way to take
boat for the Sweet Waters of Europe we descended through the
neglected Little Field of the Dead.　It is on a steep acclivity, and
the stones stand and lean thickly there, each surmounted by a
turban in fashion at the period of the occupant's death, and with
inscription neatly carved.　That "every man has his date" strikes
Abd-el-Atti as a remarkable fact.　The ground is netted by hap-
hazard paths, and the careless living tread the graves with thoughtless feet, as if the rights of the dead to their scanty bit of soil
were no longer respected.　We said to the boatman that this did
not seem well.　There was a weary touch of philosophy in his
reply : " Ah, master, the world grows old ! "

It is the fashion for the world to go on Friday to the Sweet
Waters of Europe, the inlet of the Golden Horn, flowing down
between two ranges of hills.　This vale, which is almost as celebrated in poetry as that of the Heavenly Water on the Asiatic
shore, is resorted to by thousands, in hundreds of carriages from
Pera, in thousands of caïques and barges.　On the water, the
excursion is a festival of the people, of strangers, of adventurers
of both sexes; the more fashionable though not moral part of
society, who have equipages to display, go by land.　We chose
the water, and selected a large four-oared caïque, in the bottom
of which we seated ourselves, after a dozen narrow escapes from
upsetting the tottlish craft, and rowed away, with the grave Abd-
el-Atti balanced behind and under bonds to preserve his exact
equilibrium.

All the city seems to be upon the water; the stream is alive
with the slender, swift caïques; family parties, rollicking mid-
shipmen from some foreign vessel, solitary beauties reclining in
selfish loveliness, grave fat Turks, in stupid enjoyment.　No
voyage could be gayer than this through the shipping, with the

multitudinous houses of the city rising on either hand. As we
advance, the shore is lined with people, mostly ladies in gay
holiday apparel, squatting along the stream; as on a spring day
in Paris, those who cannot afford carriages line the avenues to
the Bois de Boulogne to watch the passing pageant. The stream
grows more narrow, at length winds in graceful turns, and finally
is only a few yards wide, and the banks are retained by masonry.
The vale narrows also, and the hills draw near. The water-way
is choked with gayly painted caïques, full of laughing beauties
and reckless pleasure-seekers, and the reader of Egyptian history
might think himself in a saturnalia of the revel-makers in the
ancient *fête* of Bubastis on the Nile. The women are clad in
soft silks, — blue, red, pink, yellow, and gray, — some of them
with their faces tied up as if they were victims of toothache,
others wearing the gauze veils, which enhance without concealing
charms; and the color and beauty that nature has denied to many
are imitated by paint and enamel.

We land and walk on. Singers and players on curious instruments sit along the bank and in groups under the trees, and fill
the festive air with the plaintive and untrained Oriental music.
The variety of costumes is infinite; here we meet all that is gay
and fantastic in Europe and Asia. The navigation ends at the
white marble palace and mosque which we now see shining amid
the trees, fresh with May foliage. Booths and tents, green and
white, are erected everywhere, and there are many groups of
gypsies and fortune-tellers. The olive-complexioned, black-eyed,
long-haired women, who trade in the secrets of the Orient and
the vices of the Occident, do a thriving business with those curious of the future, or fascinated by the mysterious beauty of the
soothsayers. Besides the bands of music, there are solitary bag-
pipers whose instrument is a skin, with a pipe for a mouthpiece
and another at the opposite end having graduated holes for fingering; and I noticed with pleasure that the fingering and the
music continued long after the musician had ceased to blow into
the inflated skin. Nothing was wanting to the most brilliant
scene; ladies in bright groups on gay rugs and mats, children
weaving head-dresses from leaves and rushes, crowds of carriages,

fine horses and gallant horsemen, sellers of refreshments balancing great trays on their heads, and bearing tripod stools, and all degrees of the most cosmopolitan capital enjoying the charming spring holiday.

In the palace grounds dozens of peacocks were sunning themselves, and the Judas-trees were in full pink bloom. Above the palace the river flows in walled banks, and before it reaches it tumbles over an artificial fall of rocks, and sweeps round the garden in a graceful curve. Beyond the palace, also on the bank of the stream, is a grove of superb trees and a greensward; here a military band plays, and this is the fashionable meeting-place of carriages, where hundreds were circling round and round in the imitated etiquette of Hyde Park.

We came down at sunset, racing swiftly among the returning caïques, passing and passed by laughing boatsful, whose gay hangings trailed in the stream, as in a pageant on the Grand Canal of Venice, and watching with the interest of the philosopher only, the light boat of beauty and frailty pursued by the youthful caïque of inexperience and desire. The hour contributed to make the scene one of magical beauty. To our right lay the dark cypresses of the vast cemetery of Eyoub (or Ayub) and the shining mosque where, at their inauguration, the Osmanli Sultans are still girt with the sword of their founder. At this spot, in the first siege of Constantinople by the Arabs, fell, amid thirty thousand Moslems, slain outside the Golden Gate, the Aboo Ayub, or Job, one of the last companions of the Prophet. He was one of the immortal auxiliaries; he had fought at Beder and Obud side by side with Abubeker, and he had the honor to be one of the first assailants of the Christian capital, which Mohammed had predicted that his followers should one day possess. The site of his grave, forgotten for seven centuries, was revealed to the conqueror of the city by a fortunate vision, and the spot was commemorated by a mosque, and a gathering congregation of the dead.

Clouds had collected in the west, and the heavy smoke of innumerable steamers lay dark upon the Bosphorus. But as we came down, the sun broke out and gave us one of those effects of

T

which nature is sparing. On the heights of Stamboul, a dozen
minarets, only half distinct, were touched by the gold rays; the
windows of both cities, piled above each other, blazed in it; the
smooth river and the swift caïques were gilded by it; and behind us, domes and spires, and the tapering shafts of the Muezzin,
the bases hid by the mist, rose into the heaven of the golden sunset and appeared like mansions, and most unsubstantial ones, in
the sky. And ever the light caïques flew over the rosy water in a
chase of pleasure, in a motion that satisfied the utmost longing
for repose, while the enchantment of heaven seemed to have
dropped upon the earth.

"The world has lost its gloss for us,
    Since we went boating on the Bosphorus."

Constantinople enjoys or suffers the changeable weather appropriate to its cosmopolitan inhabitants and situation, and we
waited for a day suitable to cross to Scutari and obtain the view
from Boolgoorloo. We finally accepted one of alternate clouds
and sunshine. The connection between the European city and its
great suburb is maintained by frequent ferry-steamers, and I believe that no other mile-passage in the world can offer the traveller
a scene more animated or views so varied and magnificent. Near
the landing at Scutari stands a beacon-tower ninety feet high,
erected upon a rock; it has the name of the Maiden's Tower, but
I do not know why, unless by courtesy to one of the mistresses
of Sultan Mohammed, who is said to have been shut up in it.
Scutari, — pronounced with the accent on the first syllable, a corruption of the Turkish name *Uskudar*, — the site of the old Greek
and Persian Chrysopolis, is a town sprawling over seven hills, has
plenty of mosques, baths, and cemeteries, — the three Oriental
luxuries,   but little to detain the traveller, already familiar with
Eastern towns of the sort. The spot has been in all ages an
arriving and starting point for Asiatic couriers, caravans, and
armies; here the earliest Greek sea-robbers hauled up their ven-
turous barks; here Xenophon rested after his campaign against
Cyrus; here the Roman and then the Byzantine emperors had
their hunting-palaces; here for a long time the Persians menaced
and wrung tribute from the city they could not capture.

We took a carriage and ascended through the city to the mountain of Boolgoorloo. On the slopes above the town are orchards
and vineyards and pretty villas. The last ten minutes of the
climb was accomplished on foot, and when we stood upon the
summit the world was at our feet. I do not know any other view
that embraces so much and such variety. The swelling top was
carpeted with grass, sprinkled with spring flowers, and here and
there a spreading pine offered a place of shade and repose. Behind us continued range on range the hills of the peninsula ; to
the south the eye explored Asia Minor, the ancient Bithynia and
Mysia, until it rested on the monstrous snowy summits of Olympus, which rears itself beyond Broussa, city famed for its gauzy
silk and the first capital of the Osman dynasty. There stretches
the blue Sea of Marmora, bearing lightly on the surface the nine
enchanting Princes' Islands, whose equable climate and fertile soil
have obtained for them the epithet of the Isles of the Blest. Opposite, Stamboul rises out of the water on every side ; in the distance a city of domes and pinnacles and glass, the dark-green
spires of cypress tempering its brilliant lustre ; there the Golden
Horn and its thronged bridges and its countless masts and steamers' funnels ; Galata and Pera, also lifted up into nobility, and
all their shabby details lost, and the Bosphorus, its hills, marble
palaces, mosques, and gardens, on either side. I do not know any
scene that approaches this in beauty except the Bay of Naples,
and the charm of that is so different from this that no comparison
is forced upon the mind. The Bay of New York has many of the
elements of this charming prospect, on the map. But Constantinople and its environs can be seen from many points in one
view, while one would need to ascend a balloon to comprehend in
like manner the capital of the Western world. It is the situation
of Constantinople, lifted up into a conspicuousness that permits
no one of its single splendors to be lost in the general view, that
makes it in appearance the unrivalled empress of cities.

In the foreground lay Scutari, and in a broad sweep the heavy
mass of cypress forest that covers the great cemetery of the Turks,
which they are said to prefer to Eyoub, under the prophetic impression that they will one day be driven out of Europe. The

precaution seems idle.   If in the loss of Constantinople the Osmanli sultans still maintain the supremacy of Islam, the Moslem
capital could not be on these shores, and the caliphate in its mi-
grations might again be established on the Nile, on the Euphrates,
or in the plains of Guta on the Abana.   The iron-clads that lie
in the Bosphorus, the long guns of a dozen fortresses that command every foot of the city and shore, forbid that these contiguous
coasts should fly hostile flags.

   We drove down to and through this famous cemetery in one
direction and another.   In its beauty I was disappointed.   It is
a dense and gloomy cypress forest ; as a place of sepulture, without the architectural pretensions of Père-la-Chaise, and only less
attractive than that.   Its dark recesses are crowded with grave-
stones, slender at the bottom and swelling at the top, painted in
lively colors, — green, red, and gray, a necessary relief to the
sombre woods, — having inscriptions in gilt and red letters, and
leaning at all angles, as if they had fallen out in a quarrel over
night.   The graves of the men are distinguished by stones crowned
with turbans, or with tarbooshes painted red, — an imitation, in
short, of whatever head-dress the owner wore when alive, so that
perhaps his acquaintances can recognize his tomb without reading
his name.   Some of the more ancient have the form of a mould
of Charlotte Russe.   I saw more than one set jauntily on one side,
which gave the monument a rakish air, singularly *débonnaire* for
a tombstone.

   In contrast to this vast assembly of the faithful is the pretty
English cemetery, dedicated to the fallen in the Crimean war, —
a well-kept flower-garden, which lies close to the Bosphorus on a
point opposite the old Seraglio.   We sat down on the sea-wall in
this quiet spot, where the sun falls lovingly and the undisturbed
birds sing, and looked long at the shifting, busy panorama of a
world that does not disturb this repose ; and then walked about
the garden, noting the headstones of soldiers, — this one killed
at Alma, that at Inkermann, another at Balaklava, and the tall,
graceless granite monument to eight thousand nameless dead ;
nameless here, but not in many a home and many a heart, any more
than the undistinguished thousands who sleep at Gettysburg **or**
on a hundred other patriot fields.

Near by is the great hospital which Florence Nightingale controlled, and in her memory we asked permission to enter its wards and visit its garden. After some delay this was granted, but the Turkish official said that the hospital was for men, that there was no woman there, and as for Miss Nightingale, he had never heard of her. But we persevered and finally found an officer who led us to the room she occupied, — a large apartment now filled with the beds of the sick, and, like every other part of the establishment, neat and orderly. But our curiosity to see where the philanthropist had labored was an enigma to the Turkish officials to the last. They insisted at first that we must be relations of Miss Nightingale, — a supposition which I saw that Abd-el-Atti, who always seeks the advantage of distinction, was inclined to favor. But we said no. Well, perhaps it was natural that Englishmen should indulge in the sentiment that moved us. But we were not Englishmen, we were Americans, — they gave it up entirely. The superintendent of the hospital, a courtly and elderly bey, who had fought in the Crimean war, and whom our dragoman, dipping his hand to the ground, saluted with the most profound Egyptian obeisance, insisted upon serving us coffee in the garden by the fountain of gold-fish, and we spent an hour of quiet there.

On Sunday at about the hour that the good people in America were beginning to think what they should wear to church, we walked down to the service in the English Memorial Church, on the brow of the hill in Pera, a pointed Gothic building of a rich and pleasing interior. Only once or twice in many months had we been in a Christian church, and it was, at least, interesting to contrast its simple forms with the elaborate Greek ritual and the endless repetitions of the Moslem prayers. A choir of boys intoned or chanted a portion of the service, with marked ability, and wholly relieved the audience of the necessity of making responses. The clergymen executed the reading so successfully that we could only now and then catch a word. The service, so far as we were concerned, might as well have been in Turkish; and yet it was not altogether lost on us. We could distinguish occasionally the Lord's Prayer, and the name of Queen Victoria, and we caught some of the Commandments as they whisked past us. We knew also when we were in the Litany, from the regular cadence of the boys' responses. But as the entertainment seemed to be for the benefit of the clergymen and boys, I did not feel like intruding beyond the office of a spectator, and I soon found myself reflecting whether a machine could not be invented that should produce the same effect of sound, which was all that the congregation enjoyed.

Rome has been until recently less tolerant of the Protestant faith than Constantinople; and it was an inspiration of reciprocity to build here a church in memory of the Christian soldiers who fell in the crusade to establish the Moslem rule in European Turkey.

Of the various views about Constantinople we always pronounced that best which we saw last, and at the time we said that those from Seraglio Point, from Boolgoorloo, and from Roberts College were crowned by that from Giant's Grave Mountain, a noble height on the Asiatic side of the Bosphorus near the Black Sea.

One charming morning, we ascended the strait in a steamboat that calls at the landings on the eastern shore. The Bosphorus, if you will have it in a phrase, is a river of lapis lazuli lined with marble palaces. As we saw it that morning, its sloping gardens, terraces, trees, and vines in the tender bloom of spring, all the extravagance of the Oriental poets in praise of it was justified, and it was easy to believe the nature-romance with which the earliest adventurers had clothed it. There, at Beshiktash, Jason landed to rest his weary sailors on the voyage to Colchis; and above there at Koroö Chesmeh stood a laurel-tree which Medea planted on the return of the Argonauts. Tradition has placed near it, on the point, the site of a less attractive object, the pillar upon which Simeon Stylites spent forty years of a life which was just forty years too long; but I do not know by what authority, for I believe that the perch of the Syrian hermit was near Antioch, where his noble position edified thousands of Christians, who enjoyed their piety in contemplating his, and took their pleasures in the groves of Daphne.

Our steamer was, at this moment, a craft more dangerous to

mankind than an iron-clad; it was a sort of floating harem; we sat upon the awning-covered upper deck; the greater part of the lower deck was jealously curtained off and filled with Turkish ladies. Among them we recognized a little flock of a couple of dozen, the harem of Mustapha Pasha, the uncle of the Khedive of Egypt. They left the boat at his palace in Chenguel Keuy, and we saw them, in silk gowns of white, red, blue, and yellow, streaming across the flower-garden into the marble portal, — a pretty picture. The pasha was transferring his household to the country for the summer, and we imagined that the imprisoned troop entered these blooming May gardens with the elation of freedom, which might, however, be more perfect if eunuchs did not watch every gate and foot of the garden wall. I suppose, however, that few of them would be willing to exchange their lives of idle luxury for the misery and chance of their former condition, and it is said that the maids of the so-called Christian Georgia hear with envy of the good fortune of their sisters, who have brought good prices in the Turkish capital.

When the harem disappeared we found some consolation in a tall Croat, who strutted up and down the deck in front of us, that we might sicken with envy of his splendid costume. He wore tight trousers of blue cloth, baggy in the rear but fitting the legs like a glove, and terminating over the shoes in a quilled inverted funnel; a brilliant scarf of Syrian silk in loose folds about his loins; a vest stiff with gold-embroidery; a scarlet jacket decked with gold-lace, and on his head a red fez. This is the costly dress of a Croatian gardener, who displays all his wealth to make a holiday spectacle of himself.

We sailed close to the village of Kandili and the promontory under which and upon which it lies, a site which exhausts the capacity of the loveliness of nature and the skill of art. From the villas on its height one commands, by a shifted glance, the Euxine and the Marmora, and whatever is most lovely in the prospect of two continents; the purity of the air is said to equal the charm of the view. Above this promontory opens the valley down which flows the river Geuksoo (sky-water), and at the north of it stands a white marble kiosk of the Sultan, the most beauti-

ful architectural creation on the strait. Near it, shaded by great
trees, is a handsome fountain ; beyond the green turf in the tree-
decked vale which pierces the hill were groups of holiday-makers
in gay attire. I do not know if this Valley of the Heavenly
Water is the loveliest in the East, but it is said that its charms
of meadow, shade, sweet water, and scented flowers are a substantial foretaste of the paradise of the true believer. But it is
in vain to catalogue the charming villages, the fresh beauties of
nature and art to which each revolution of the paddle-wheel
carried us. We thought we should be content with a summer
residence of the Khedive, on the European side below the lovely
bay of Terapea, with its vast hillside of gardens and orchards
and the long line of palaces on the water. Fanned by the invigorating breezes from the Black Sea, its summer climate must
be perfect.

We landed at Beicos, and, in default of any conveyance, walked
up through the straggling village, along the shore, to a verdant,
shady meadow, sweet with clover and wild-flowers. This is in
the valley of Hun-Kiar Iskelesi, a favorite residence of the sultans ; here on a projecting rocky point is a reddish palace built
and given to the Sultan by the Khedive. The meadow, in which
we were, is behind a palace of old Mohammed Ali, and it is now
used as a pasture for the Sultan's horses, dozens of which were
tethered and feeding in the lush grass and clover. The tents
of their attendants were pitched on the plain, and groups of
Turkish ladies were picnicking under the large sycamores. It was
a charming rural scene. I made the silent acquaintance of an old
man, in a white turban and flowing robes, who sat in the grass
knitting and watching his one white lamb feed ; probably knitting
the fleece of his lamb of the year before.

We were in search of an *araba* and team to take us up the
mountain ; one stood in the meadow which we could hire, but
oxen were wanting, and we despatched a Greek boy in search
of the animals. The Turkish ladies of fashion delight in the
araba when they ride into the country, greatly preferring it to the
horse or donkey, or to any other carriage. It is a long cart of
four wheels, without springs, but it is as stately in appearance as

the band-wagon of a circus; its sloping side-boards and even the platform in front are elaborately carved and gilded. While we waited the motions of the boy, who joined to himself two others even more prone to go astray than himself, an officer of the royal stables invited us to take seats under the shade of his tent and served us with coffee. After an hour the boy returned with two lean steers. The rude, hooped top of the araba was spread with a purple cloth, a thick bedquilt covered the bottom, and by the aid of a ladder we climbed into the ark and sat or lay as we could best stow ourselves. A boy led the steers by a rope, another walked at the side gently goading them with a stick, and we rumbled along slowly through the brilliant meadows. It became evident after a time that we were not ascending the mountain, but going into the heart of the country; the cart was stopped and the wild driver was interrogated. I never saw a human being so totally devoid of a conscience. We had hired him to take us up to Giant's Grave Mountain. He was deliberately cheating us out of it. At first he insisted that he was going in the right direction, but upon the application of the dragoman's fingers to his ear, he pleaded that the mountain road was bad and that it was just as well for us to visit the Sultan's farm up the valley. We had come seven thousand miles to see the view from the mountain, but this boy had not the least scruple in depriving us of it. We turned about and entered a charming glen, thoroughly New England in its character, set with small trees and shrubs and carpeted with a turf of short sweet grass. One needs to be some months in the Orient to appreciate the delight experienced by the sight of genuine turf.

As we ascended, the road, gullied by the spring torrents, at last became impassable for wheels, and we were obliged to abandon the araba and perform the last half-mile of the journey on foot. The sightly summit of the mountain is nearly six hundred feet above the water. There, in a lovely grove, we found a coffee-house and a mosque and the Giant's Grave, which the Moslems call the grave of Joshua. It is a flower-planted enclosure, seventy feet long and seven wide, ample for any hero; the railing about it is tagged with bits of cloth which pious devotees have tied

14

there in the expectation that their diseases, perhaps their sins, will vanish with the airing of these shreds. From the minaret is a wonderful view, — the entire length of the Bosphorus, with all its windings and lovely bays enlivened with white sails, ships at anchor, and darting steamers, rich in villages, ancient castles, and forts; a great portion of Asia Minor, with the snow peaks of Olympus; on the south, the Islands of the Blest and the Sea of Marmora; on the north, the Cyanean rocks and the wide sweep of the Euxine, blue as heaven and dotted with a hundred white sails, overlooked by the ruin of a Genoese castle, at the entrance of the Bosphorus, built on the site of a temple of Jupiter, and the spot where the Argonauts halted before they ventured among the Symplegades; and immediately below, Terapea and the deep bay of Buyukdereh, the summer resort of the foreign residents of Constantinople, a paradise of palaces and gardens, of vales and stately plane-trees, and the entrance to the interior village of Belgrade, with its sacred forest unprofaned as yet by the axe.

The Cyanean rocks which Jason and his mariners regarded as floating islands, or sentient monsters, vanishing and reappearing, are harmlessly anchored now, and do not appear at all formidable, though they disappear now as of old when the fierce Euxine rolls in its storm waves. For a long time and with insatiable curiosity we followed with the eye the line of the coast of the Pontus Euxinus, once as thickly set with towns as the Riviera of Italy, — cities of Ionian, Dorian, and Athenian colonies, who followed the Phœnicians and perhaps the Egyptians, — in the vain hope of extending our vision to Trebizond, to the sea fortress of Petra, renowned for its defence by the soldiers of Chosroes against the arms of Justinian, and, further, to the banks of the Phasis, to Colchis, whose fabulous wealth tempted Jason and his sea-robbers. The waters of this land were so impregnated with particles of gold that fleeces of sheep were used to strain out the yellow metal. Its palaces shone with gold and silver, and you might expect in its gardens the fruit of the Hesperides. In the vales of the Caucasus, we are taught, our race has attained its most perfect form; in other days its men were as renowned for strength and valor as its women were for beauty, — the one could not be permanently subdued, the others conquered, even in their slavery. Early converts to the Christian faith, they never adopted its morals nor comprehended its metaphysics; and perhaps a more dissolute and venal society does not exist than that whose business for centuries has been the raising of maids for the Turkish harems. And the miserable, though willing, victims are said to possess not even beauty, until after a training in luxury by the slave-dealers.

We made our way, not without difficulty, down the rough, bush-grown hillside, invaded a new Turkish fortification, and at length found a place where we could descend the precipitous bank and summon a boat to ferry us across to Buyukdereh. This was not easy to obtain; but finally an aged Greek boatman appeared with a caïque as aged and decayed as himself. The chances seemed to be that it could make the voyage, and we all packed ourselves into it, sitting on the bottom and filling it completely. There was little margin of boat above the water, and any sudden motion would have reduced that to nothing. We looked wise and sat still, while the old Greek pulled feebly and praised the excellence of his craft. On the opposite slope our attention was called to a pretty cottage, and a Constantinople lady, who was of the party, began to tell us the story of its occupant. So dramatic and exciting did it become that we forgot entirely the peril of our frail and overloaded boat. The story finished as we drew up to the landing, which we instantly comprehended we had not reached a moment too soon. For when we arose our clothes were soaked; we were sitting in water, which was rapidly filling the boat, and would have swamped it in five minutes. The landing-place of Buyukdereh, the bay, the hills and villas, reminded us of Lake Como, and the quay and streets were rather Italian than Oriental. The most soaked of the voyagers stood outside the railing of the pretty garden of the café to dry in the sun, while the others sat inside, under the vines, and passed out to the unfortunates, through the iron bars, tiny cups of coffee, and fed them with rahot-al-lacoom and other delicious sweetmeats, until the arrival of the steamer. The ride down was lovely; the sun made the barracks and palaces on the east shore a blaze of diamonds; and the minarets seen through the steamer's smoke which, transfused with the rosy light, overhung the city, had a phantasmagorical aspect.

Constantinople shares with many other cities the reputation of being the most dissolute in the world. The traveller is not required to decide the rival claims of this sort of pre-eminence, which are eagerly put forward; he may better, in each city, acquiesce in the complaisant assumption of the inhabitants. But when he is required to see in the moral state of the Eastern capital signs of its speedy decay, and the near extinction of the Othman rule, he takes a leaf out of history and reflects. It is true, no doubt, that the Turks are enfeebled by luxury and sensuality, and have, to a great extent, lost those virile qualities which gave to their ancestors the dominion of so many kingdoms in Asia, Africa, and Europe; in short, that the race is sinking into an incapacity to propagate itself in the world. If one believes what he hears, the morals of society could not be worse. The women, so many of whom have been bought in the market, or are daughters of slaves, are educated only for pleasure; and a great proportion of the male population are adventurers from all lands, with few domestic ties. The very relaxation of the surveillance of the harem (the necessary prelude to the emancipation of woman) opens the door to opportunity, and gives freer play to feminine intrigue. One hears, indeed, that even the inmates of the royal harem find means of clandestine intercourse with the foreigners of Pera. The history of the Northern and Western occupation of the East has been, for fifteen centuries, only a repetition of yielding to the seductive influences of a luxurious climate and to soft and pleasing invitation.

But, heighten as we may the true and immoral picture of social life in Constantinople, I doubt if it is so loose and unrestrained as it was for centuries under the Greek Emperors; I doubt if the imbecility, the luxurious effeminacy of the Turks has sunk to the level of the Byzantine Empire; and when we are asked to expect in the decay of to-day a speedy dissolution, we remember that for a period of over a thousand years, from the partition of the Roman Empire between the two sons of Theodosius to the capture of Constantinople by Mohammed II., the empire subsisted in a state of premature and perpetual decay. These Oriental dynasties are a long time in dying, and we cannot measure their decrepitude by the standards of Occidental morality.

The trade and the commerce of the city are largely in the hands of foreigners ; but it has nearly always been so, since the days of the merchants and manufacturers of Pisa, Genoa, and Venice. We might draw an inference of Turkish insecurity from the implacable hatred of the so-called Greek subjects, if the latter were not in the discord of a thousand years of anarchy and servitude. The history of the islands of the Eastern Mediterranean has been a succession of Turkish avarice and rapacity, horrible Greek revenge and Turkish wholesale devastation and massacre, repeated over and over again ; but there appears as yet no power able either to expel the Turks or unite the Greeks. That the leaven of change is working in the Levant is evident to the most superficial observation, and one sees everywhere the introduction of Western civilization, of business habits, and, above all, of schools. However indifferent the Osmanlis are to education, they are not insensible to European opinion ; and in reckoning up their bad qualities, we ought not to forget that they have set some portions of Christendom a lesson of religious toleration, — both in Constantinople and Jerusalem the Christians were allowed a freedom of worship in their own churches which was not permitted to Protestants within the sacred walls of Pontifical Rome.

One who would paint the manners or the morals of Constantinople might adorn his theme with many anecdotes, characteristic of a condition of society which is foreign to our experience. I select one which has the merit of being literally true. You who believe that modern romance exists only in tales of fiction, listen to the story of a beauty of Constantinople, the vicissitudes of whose life equal in variety if not in importance those of Theodora and Athenais. For obvious reasons, I shall mention no names.

There lives now on the banks of the Bosphorus an English physician, who, at the entreaty of Lord Byron, went to Greece in 1824 as a volunteer surgeon in the war of independence; he arrived only in time to see the poet expire at Missolonghi. In the course of the war, he was taken prisoner by the Egyptian troops, who in their great need of surgeons kept him actively employed in his profession. He did not regain his freedom until after the war, and then only on condition that he should reside in Constantinople as one of the physicians of the Sultan, Mohammed II.

We may suppose that the Oriental life was not unpleasant, nor the position irksome to him, for he soon so far yielded to the temptations of the capital as to fall in love with a very pretty face which he saw daily in a bay-window of the street he traversed on the way to the Seraglio. Acquaintance, which sometimes precedes love, in this case followed it; the doctor declared his passion and was accepted by the willing maid. But an Oriental bay-window is the opportunity of the world, and the doctor, becoming convinced that his affianced was a desperate flirt, and yielding to the entreaties of his friends, broke off the engagement and left her free, in her eyry, to continue her observations upon mankind. This, however, did not suit the plans of the lovely and fickle girl. One morning, shortly after, he was summoned to see two Turkish ladies who awaited him in his office; when he appeared, the young girl (for it was she) and her mother threw aside their disguise, and declared that they would not leave the house until the doctor married the daughter, for the rupture of the engagement had rendered it impossible to procure any other husband. Whether her own beauty or the terrible aspect of the mother prevailed, I do not know, but the English chaplain was sent for; he refused to perform the ceremony, and a Greek priest was found who married them.

This marriage, which took the appearance of duress, might have been happy if the compelling party to it had left her fondness of adventure and variety at the wedding threshold; but her constancy was only assumed, like the Turkish veil, for an occasion; lovers were not wanting, and after the birth of three children, two sons and a daughter, she deserted her husband and went to live with a young Turk, who has since held high office in the government of the Sultan. It was in her character of Madame Mehemet Pasha that she wrote (or one of her sons wrote for

her) a book well known in the West, entitled "Thirty Years in
a Harem." But her intriguing spirit was not extinct even in a
Turkish harem; she attempted to palm off upon the pasha, as
her own, a child that she had bought; her device was detected by
one of the palace eunuchs, and at the same time her amour with
a Greek of the city came to light. The eunuch incurred her dis-
pleasure for his officiousness, and she had him strangled and
thrown into the Bosphorus. Some say that the resolute woman
even assisted with her own hands. For these breaches of decorum,
however, she paid dear; the pasha banished her to Kutayah, with
orders to the guard who attended her to poison her on the way;
but she so won upon the affection of the officer that he let her
escape at Broussa. There her beauty, if not her piety, recommended her to an Imam of one of the mosques, and she married
him and seems for a time to have led a quiet life; at any rate,
nothing further was heard of her until just before the famous
cholera season, when news came of the death of her husband, the
Moslem priest, and that she was living in extreme poverty, all her
beauty gone forever, and consequently her ability to procure another husband.

The pasha, Mehemet, lived in a beautiful palace on the eastern
shore of the Bosphorus, near Kandili. During the great cholera
epidemic of 1865, the pasha was taken ill. One day there appeared at the gate an unknown woman, who said that she had
come to cure the pasha; no one knew her, but she spoke with
authority, and was admitted. It was our adventuress. She
nursed the pasha with the most tender care and watchful skill, so
that he recovered; and, in gratitude for the preservation of his
life, he permitted her and her daughter to remain in the palace.
For some time they were contented with the luxury of such a
home, but one day — it was the evening of Wednesday — neither
mother nor daughter was to be found; and upon examination it
was discovered that a large collection of precious stones and some
ready money had disappeared with them. They had departed on
the French steamer, in order to transfer their talents to the fields
of Europe. The fate of the daughter I do not know; for some
time she and her mother were conspicuous in the dissipation of

Paris life ; subsequently the mother lived with a son in London, and, since I heard her story in Constantinople, she has died in London in misery and want.

The further history of the doctor and his family may detain our curiosity for a moment. When his wife left him for the arms of the pasha, he experienced so much difficulty in finding any one in Constantinople to take care of his children that he determined to send them to Scotland to be educated, and intrusted them, for that purpose, to a friend who was returning to England. They went by way of Rome. It happened that the mother and sister of the doctor had some time before that come to Rome, for the sake of health, and had there warmly embraced the Roman Catholic faith. Of course the three children were taken to see their grandmother and aunt, and the latter, concerned for their eternal welfare, diverted them from their journey, and immured the boys in a monastery and the girl in a convent. The father, when he heard of this abduction, expressed indignation, but, having at that time only such religious faith as may be floating in the Oriental air and common to all, he made no vigorous effort to recover his children. Indeed, he consoled himself, in the fashion of the country, by marrying again ; this time a Greek lady, who died, leaving two boys. The doctor was successful in transporting the offspring of his second marriage to Scotland, where they were educated ; and they returned to do him honor, — one of them as the eloquent and devoted pastor of a Protestant church in Pera, and the other as a physician in the employment of the government.

After the death of his second wife, the doctor — I can but tell the story as I heard it — became a changed man, and — married again : this time a Swiss lady, of lovely Christian character. In his changed condition, he began to feel anxious to recover his children from the grasp of Rome. He wrote for information, but his sister refused to tell where they were, and his search could discover no trace of them. At length the father obtained leave of absence from the Seraglio, and armed with an autograph letter from Abdul Aziz to Pius IX., he went to Rome. The Pope gave him an order for the restoration of his children. He drove first to the convent to see his daughter. In place of the little girl

whom he had years ago parted with, he found a young lady of extraordinary beauty, and a devoted Romanist. At first she refused
to go with him, and it was only upon his promise to allow her
perfect liberty of conscience, and never to interfere with any of
the observances of her church, that she consented. Not daring
to lose sight of her, he waited for her to pack her trunk, and then,
putting her into a carriage, drove to the monastery where he heard,
after many inquiries, that his boys were confined. The monk who
admitted him denied that they were there, and endeavored to lock
him into the waiting-room while he went to call the Superior.
But the doctor anticipated his movements, and as soon as the
monk was out of sight, started to explore the house. By good
luck the first door he opened led into a chamber where a sick boy
was lying on a bed. The doctor believed that he recognized one
of his sons; a few questions satisfied him that he was right. "I
am your father," he said to the astonished lad, "run quickly and
call your brother and come with me." Monastic discipline had
not so many attractions for the boys as convent life for the girl,
and the child ran with alacrity and brought his brother, just as
the abbot and a score of monks appeared upon the scene. As the
celerity of the doctor had given no opportunity to conceal the boys,
opposition to the order of the Pope was useless, and the father
hastened to the gate where he had left the carriage. Meantime
the aunt had heard of the rescue, and followed the girl from the
convent; she implored her, by tears and prayers, to reverse her
decision. The doctor cut short the scene by shoving his sons into
the carriage and driving rapidly away. Nor did he trust them
long in Rome.

The subsequent career of the boys is not dwelt on with pleasure.
One of them enlisted in the Turkish army, married a Turkish
wife, and, after some years, deserted her, and ran away to England.
His wife was taken into a pasha's family, who offered to adopt
her only child, a boy of four years; but the mother preferred to
bring him to his grandfather. None of the family had seen her,
but she established her identity, and begged that her child might
be adopted by a good man, which she knew his grandfather to be,
and receive a Christian training. The doctor, therefore, adopted

the grandchild, which had come to him in such a strange way, and the mother shortly after died.

The daughter, whose acquired accomplishments matched her inherited beauty, married, in time, a Venetian Count of wealth ; and the idler in Venice may see on the Grand Canal, among those mouldy edifices that could reveal so many romances, their sumptuous palace, and learn, if he cares to learn, that it is the home of a family happy in the enjoyment of most felicitous fortune. In the gossip with which the best Italian society sometimes amuses itself, he might hear that the Countess was the daughter of a slave of the Sultan's harem. I have given, however, the true version of the romantic story ; but I am ignorant of the social condition or the race of the mother of the heroine of so many adventures. She may have been born in the Caucasus.

XXVII.

FROM THE GOLDEN HORN TO THE ACROPOLIS.

OUR last day in Constantinople was a bright invitation for us to remain forever. We could have departed without regret in a rain-storm, but it was not so easy to resolve to look our last upon this shining city and marvellous landscape under the blue sky of May. Early in the morning we climbed up the Genoese Tower in Galata and saw the hundred crescents of Stamboul sparkle in the sun, the Golden Horn and the Bosphorus, shifting panoramas of trade and pleasure, the Propontis with its purple islands, and the azure and snowy mountains of Asia. This massive tower is now a fire-signal station, and night and day watchmen look out from its battlemented gallery; the Seraskier Tower opposite in Stamboul, and another on the heights of the Asiatic shore, keep the same watch over the inflammable city. The guard requested us not to open our parasols upon the gallery for fear they would be hailed as fire-signals.

The day was spent in last visits to the bazaars, in packing and leave-takings, and the passage of the custom-house, for the government encourages trade by an export as well as an import duty. I did not see any of the officials, but Abd-el-Atti, who had charge of shipping our baggage, reported that the eyes of the customs inspector were each just the size of a five-franc piece. Chief among our regrets at setting our faces toward Europe was the necessity of parting with Abd-el-Atti and Ahmed; the former had been our faithful dragoman and daily companion for five months, and we had not yet exhausted his adventures nor his stores of Oriental humor; and we could not expect to find elsewhere a

character like Ahmed, a person so shrewd and obliging, and of
such amusing vivacity.   At four o'clock we embarked upon an
Italian steamer for Salonica and Athens, a four days' voyage.   At
the last moment Abd-el-Atti would have gone with us upon the
least encouragement, but we had no further need of dragoman or
interpreter, and the old man sadly descended the ladder to his
boat.   I can see him yet, his red fez in the stern of the caïque,
waving his large silk handkerchief, and slowly rowing back to
Pera, — a melancholy figure.

As we steamed out of the harbor we enjoyed the view we had
missed on entering : the Seraglio Point where blind old Dandolo
ran his galley aground and leaped on shore to the assault; the
shore of Chalcedon ; the seven towers and the old wall behind
Stamboul, which Persians, Arabs, Scythians, and Latins have
stormed ; the long sweeping coast and its minarets; the Princes'
Islands and Mt. Olympus, — all this in a setting sun was superb ;
and we said, "There is not its equal in the world."   And the
evening was more magnificent, — a moon nearly full, a sweet and
rosy light on the smooth water, which was at first azure blue, and
then pearly gray and glowing like an amethyst.

Smoothly sailing all night, we came at sunrise to the entrance
of the Dardanelles, and stopped for a couple of hours at Chanak
Kalessi, before the guns of the Castle of Asia.   The wide-awake
traders immediately swarmed on board with their barbarous pottery, and with trays of cooked fish, onions, and bread for the deck
passengers.   The latter were mostly Greeks, and men in the costume which one sees still in the islands and the Asiatic coasts,
but very seldom on the Grecian mainland ; it consists of baggy
trousers, close at the ankles, a shawl about the waist, an embroidered jacket usually of sober color, and, the most prized part
of their possessions, an arsenal of pistols and knives in huge
leathern holsters, with a heavy leathern flap, worn in front.   Most
of them wore a small red fez, the hair cut close in front and falling long behind the ears.   They are light in complexion, not tall,
rather stout, and without beauty.   Though their dress is picturesque in plan, it is usually very dirty, ragged, and, the last confession of poverty, patched.   They were all armed like pirates;

and when we stopped a cracking fusillade along the deck suggested a mutiny; but it was only a precautionary measure of the captain, who compelled them to discharge their pistols into the water and then took them from them.

Passing out of the strait we saw the Rabbit Islands and Tenedos, and caught a glimpse of the Plain of Troy about as misty as its mythic history; and then turned west between Imbros and Lemnos, on whose bold eastern rock once blazed one of the signal-fires which telegraphed the fall of Troy to Clytemnestra. The first women of Lemnos were altogether beautiful, but they had some peculiarities which did not recommend them to their contemporaries, and indeed their husbands were accustomed occasionally to hoist sail and bask in the smiles of the damsels of the Thracian coast. The Lemnian women, to avoid any legal difficulties, such as arise nowadays when a woman asserts her right to slay her partner, killed all their husbands, and set up an Amazonian state which they maintained with pride and splendor, permitting no man to set foot on the island. In time this absolute freedom became a little tedious, and when the Argonauts came that way, the women advanced to meet the heroes with garlands, and brought them wine and food. This conduct pleased the Argonauts, who made Lemnos their headquarters and celebrated there many a festive combat. Their descendants, the Minyæ, were afterwards overcome by the Pelasgians, from Attica, who, remembering with regret the beautiful girls of their home, returned and brought back with them the willing and the lovely. But the children of the Attic women took on airs over their superior birth, which the Pelasgian women resented, and the latter finally removed all cause of dispute by murdering all the mothers of Attica and their offspring. These events gave the ladies of Lemnos a formidable reputation in the ancient world, and furnish an illustration of what society would be without the refining and temperate influence of man.

To the northward lifted itself the bare back of Samothrace, and beyond the dim outline of Thasos, ancient gold-island, the home of the poet Archilochus, one of the few Grecian islands which still retains something of its pristine luxuriance of vegetation, where the songs of innumerable nightingales invite to its deep, flowery valleys. Beyond Thasos is the Thracian coast and Mt. Pangaus, and at the foot of it Philippi, the Macedonian town where republican Rome fought its last battle, where Cassius leaned upon his sword-point, believing everything lost. Brutus transported the body of his comrade to Thasos and raised for him a funeral pyre; and twenty days later, on the same field, met again that spectre of death which had summoned him to Philippi. It was only eleven years after this victory of the Imperial power that a greater triumph was won at Philippi, when Paul and Silas, cast into prison, sang praises unto God at midnight, and an earthquake shook the house and opened the prison doors.

In the afternoon we came in sight of snowy Mt. Athos, an almost perpendicular limestone rock, rising nearly six thousand four hundred feet out of the sea. The slender promontory which this magnificent mountain terminates is forty miles long and has only an average breadth of four miles. The ancient canal of Xerxes quite severed it from the mainland. The peninsula, level at the canal, is a jagged stretch of mountains (seamed by chasms), which rise a thousand, two thousand, four thousand feet, and at last front the sea with the sublime peak of Athos, the site of the most conspicuous beacon-fire of Agamemnon. The entire promontory is, and has been since the time of Constantine, ecclesiastic ground; every mountain and valley has its convent; besides the twenty great monasteries are many pious retreats. All the sects of the Greek church are here represented; the communities pay a tribute to the Sultan, but the government is in the hands of four presidents, chosen by the synod, which holds weekly sessions and takes the presidents, yearly, from the monasteries in rotation. Since their foundation these religious houses have maintained against Christians and Saracens an almost complete independence, and preserved in their primitive simplicity the manners and usages of the earliest foundations. Here, as nowhere else in Europe or Asia, can one behold the architecture, the dress, the habits of the Middle Ages. The good devotees have been able to keep themselves thus in the darkness and simplicity of the past by a rigorous exclusion of the sex always impatient of monotony, to which all the changes of the world are due. No woman, from the beginning till now, has ever been permitted to set foot on the peninsula. Nor is this all; no female animal is suffered on the holy mountain, not even a hen. I suppose, though I do not know, that the monks have an inspector of eggs, whose inherited instincts of aversion to the feminine gender enable him to detect and reject all those in which lurk the dangerous sex. Few of the monks eat meat, half the days of the year are fast days, they practise occasionally abstinence from food for two or three days, reducing their pulses to the feeblest beating, and subduing their bodies to a point that destroys their value even as spiritual tabernacles. The united community is permitted to keep a guard of fifty Christian soldiers, and the only Moslem on the island is the solitary Turkish officer who represents the Sultan; his position cannot be one generally coveted by the Turks, since the society of women is absolutely denied him. The libraries of Mt. Athos are full of unarranged manuscripts, which are probably mainly filled with the theologic rubbish of the controversial ages, and can scarcely be expected to yield again anything so valuable as the Tischendorf Scriptures.

At sunset we were close under Mt. Athos, and could distinguish the buildings of the Laura Convent, amid the woods beneath the frowning cliff. And now was produced the apparition of a sunset, with this towering mountain cone for a centre-piece, that surpassed all our experience and imagination. The sea was like satin for smoothness, absolutely waveless, and shone with the colors of changeable silk, blue, green, pink, and amethyst. Heavy clouds gathered about the sun, and from behind them he exhibited burning spectacles, magnificent fireworks, vast shadow-pictures, scarlet cities, and gigantic figures stalking across the sky. From one crater of embers he shot up a fan-like flame that spread to the zenith and was reflected on the water. His rays lay along the sea in pink, and the water had the sheen of iridescent glass. The whole sea for leagues was like this; even Lemnos and Samothrace lay in a dim pink and purple light in the east. There were vast clouds in huge walls, with towers and battlements, and in all fantastic shapes, — one a gigantic cat with a preternatural

tail), a cat of doom four degrees long. All this was piled about
Mt. Athos, with its sharp summit of snow, its dark sides of
rock.

It is a pity that the sounding and somewhat sacred name of
Thessalonica has been abbreviated to Salonica; it might better
have reverted to its ancient name of Therma, which distinguished the Macedonian capital up to the time of Alexander. In
the early morning we were lying before the city, and were told
that we should stay till midnight, waiting for the mail. From
whence a mail was expected I do not know; the traveller who
sails these seas with a cargo of ancient history resents in these
classic localities such attempts to imitate modern fashions. Were
the Dardanians or the Mesians to send us letters in a leathern
bag? We were prepared for a summons from Calo-John, at the
head of his wild barbarians, to surrender the city; and we should
have liked to see Boniface, Marquis of Montferrat and King of
Thessalonica, issue from the fortress above the town, the shields
and lances of his little band of knights shining in the sun, and
answer in person the insolent demand. We were prepared to see
the troop return, having left the head of Boniface in the possession
of Calo-John; and if our captain had told us that the steamer would
wait to attend the funeral of the Bulgarian chief himself, which
occurred not long after the encounter with Boniface, we should
have thought it natural.

The city lies on a fine bay, and presents an attractive appearance from the harbor, rising up the hill in the form of an amphitheatre. On all sides, except the sea, ancient walls surround it,
fortified at the angles by large round towers and crowned in the
centre, on the hill, by a respectable citadel. I suppose that portions of these walls are of Hellenic and perhaps Pelasgic date, but
the most are probably of the time of the Latin crusaders' occupation, patched and repaired by Saracens and Turks. We had come
to Thessalonica on St. Paul's account, not expecting to see much
that would excite us, and we were not disappointed. When we
went ashore we found ourselves in a city of perhaps sixty thousand inhabitants, commonplace in aspect, although its bazaars are
well filled with European goods, and a fair display of Oriental

stuffs and antiquities, and animated by considerable briskness of
trade. I presume there are more Jews here than there were in
Paul's time, but Turks and Greeks, in nearly equal numbers, form
the bulk of the population.

In modern Salonica there is not much respect for pagan antiquities, and one sees only the usual fragments of columns and
sculptures worked into walls or incorporated in Christian churches.
But those curious in early Byzantine architecture will find more
to interest them here than in any place in the world except Constantinople. We spent the day wandering about the city, under
the guidance of a young Jew, who was without either prejudices
or information. On our way to the Mosque of St. Sophia, we
passed through the quarter of the Jews, which is much cleaner
than is usual with them. These are the descendants of Spanish
Jews, who were expelled by Isabella, and they still retain, in a
corrupt form, the language of Spain. In the doors and windows
were many pretty Jewesses ; banishment and vicissitude appear to
agree with this elastic race, for in all the countries of Europe
Jewish women develop more beauty in form and feature than in
Palestine. We saw here and in other parts of the city a novel
head-dress, which may commend itself to America in the revolutions of fashion. A great mass of hair, real or assumed, was
gathered into a long slender green bag, which hung down the
back and was terminated by a heavy fringe of silver. Otherwise,
the dress of the Jewish women does not differ much from that of
the men ; the latter wear a fez or turban, and a tunic which reaches
to the ankles, and is bound about the waist by a gay sash or
shawl.

The Mosque of St. Sophia, once a church, and copied in its
proportions and style from its namesake in Constantinople, is retired, in a delightful court, shaded by gigantic trees and cheered
by a fountain. So peaceful a spot we had not seen in many a
day ; birds sang in the trees without disturbing the calm of the
meditative pilgrim. In the portico and also in the interior are
noble columns of marble and verd-antique, and in the dome is a
wonderfully quaint mosaic of the Transfiguration. We were shown
also a magnificent pulpit of the latter beautiful stone cut from a

solid block, in which it is said St. Paul preached. As the Apostle, according to his custom, reasoned with the people out of the Scriptures in a synagogue, and this church was not built for centuries after his visit, the statement needs confirmation; but pious ingenuity suggests that the pulpit stood in a subterranean church underneath this. I should like to believe that Paul sanctified this very spot with his presence; but there is little in its quiet seclusion to remind one of him who had the reputation when he was in Thessalonica of one of those who turn the world upside down. Paul had a great affection for the brethren of this city, in spite of his rough usage here, for he mingles few reproaches in his fervent commendations of their faith, and comforts them with the assurance of a speedy release from the troubles of this world, and the certainty that while they are yet alive they will be caught up into the clouds to meet the Lord in the air. Happily the Apostle could not pierce the future and see the dissensions, the schisms, the corruptions and calamities of the Church in the succeeding centuries, nor know that near this spot, in the Imperial Hippodrome, the sedition of the citizens would one day be punished by the massacre of ninety thousand, — one of the few acts of inhumanity which stains the clemency and the great name of Theodosius. And it would have passed even the belief of the Apostle to the Gentiles could he have foreseen that, in eighteen centuries, this pulpit would be exhibited to curious strangers from a distant part of the globe, of which he never heard, where the doctrines of Paul are the bulwark of the Church and the stamina of the government, by a descendant of Abraham who confessed that he did not know who Paul was.

The oldest church in the city is now the Mosque of St. George, built about the year 400, if indeed it was not transformed from a heathen temple; its form is that of the Roman Pantheon. The dome was once covered with splendid mosaics; enough remains of the architectural designs, the brilliant peacocks and bright blue birds, to show what the ancient beauty was, but the walls of the mosque are white and barn-like. Religions inherit each other's edifices in the East without shame, and we found in the Mosque of Eske Djuma the remains of a temple of Venus, and columns of ancient Grecian work worthy of the best days of Athens. The most perfect basilica is now the Mosque of St. Demetrius (a name sacred to the Greeks), which contains his tomb. It is a five-aisled basilica ; about the gallery, over the pillars of the centre aisle, are some fine mosaics of marble, beautiful in design and color. The Moslems have spoiled the exquisite capitals of the pillars by painting them, and have destroyed the effect of the aisles by twisting the pulpit and prayer-niche away from the apse, in the direction of Mecca. We noticed, however, a relaxation of bigotry at all these mosques : we were permitted to enter without taking off our shoes ; and, besides the figures of Christian art left in the mosaics, we saw some Moslem pictures, among them rude paintings of the holy city Mecca.

On our way to the citadel we stopped to look at the Arch of Constantine before the Gate of Cassander, — a shabby ruin, with four courses of defaced figures, carved in marble, and representing the battles and triumphs of a Roman general. Fortunately for the reader we did not visit all the thirty-seven churches of the city ; but we made the acquaintance in a Greek church, which is adorned with quaint Byzantine paintings, of St. Palema, who lies in public repose, in a coffin of exquisite silver filigree-work, while his skull is enclosed in solid silver and set with rubies and emeralds. This may please St. Palema, but death is never so ghastly as when it is adorned with jewelry that becomes cheap in its presence.

The view from the citadel, which embraces the Gulf of Salonica and Mt. Olympus, the veritable heaven of the Grecian pantheon, and Mt. Ossa and Mt. Pelion, piercing the blue with their snow-summits, is grand enough to repay the ascent ; and there is a noble walk along the wall above the town. In making my roundabout way through modern streets, back to the bazaars, I encountered a number of negro women, pure Africans, who had the air and carriage of the aristocracy of the place ; they rejoiced in the gay attire which the natives of the South love, and their fine figures and independent bearing did not speak of servitude.

This Thessalonica was doubtless a healthful and attractive place

at the time Cicero chose to pass a portion of his exile here, but it
has now a bad reputation for malaria, which extends to all the
gulf, — the malaria seems everywhere to have been one of the
consequences of the fall of the Roman Empire. The handbook
recommends the locality for its good "shooting"; but if there is
any part of the Old World that needs rest from arms, I think it is
this highway of ancient and modern conquerors and invaders.

In the evening, when the lights of the town and the shore were
reflected in the water, and a full moon hung in the sky, we did
not regret our delay. The gay Thessalonians, ignorant of the
Epistles, were rowing about the harbor, circling round and round
the steamer, beating the darabouka drum, and singing in that
nasal whine which passes for music all over the East. And, indeed, on such a night it is not without its effect upon a sentimental mind.

At early light of a cloudless morning we were going easily
down the Gulf of Therma or Salonica, having upon our right the
Pierian plain; and I tried to distinguish the two mounds which
mark the place of the great battle near Pydna, one hundred and
sixty-eight years before Christ, between Æmilius Paulus and King
Perseus, which gave Macedonia to the Roman Empire. Beyond,
almost ten thousand feet in the air, towered Olympus, upon whose
"broad" summit Homer displays the ethereal palaces and inaccessible abode of the Grecian gods. Shaggy forests still clothe
its sides, but snow now, and for the greater part of the year,
covers the wide surface of the height, which is a sterile, light-
colored rock. The gods did not want snow to cool the nectar at
their banquets. This is the very centre of the mythologic world;
there between Olympus and Ossa is the Vale of Tempe, where
the Peneus, breaking through a narrow gorge fringed with the
sacred laurel, reaches the gulf, south of ancient Heracleum. Into
this charming but secluded retreat the gods and goddesses, weary
of the icy air, or the Pumblechookian deportment of the court
of Olympian Jove, descended to pass the sunny hours with the
youths and maidens of mortal mould; through this defile marks
of chariot-wheels still attest the passages of armies which flowed
either way, in invasion or retreat; and here Pompey, after a ride

of forty miles from the fatal field of Pharsalia, quenched his thirst. Did the Greeks really believe that the gods dwelt on this mountain in clouds and snow ? Did Baldwin II. believe that he sold, and Louis IX. of France that he bought, for ten thousand marks of silver, at Constantinople, in the thirteenth century, the veritable *crown of thorns* that the Saviour wore in the judgment-hall of Pilate ?

At six o'clock the Cape of Posilio was on our left, we were sinking Olympus in the white haze of morning, Ossa, in its huge silver bulk, was near us, and Pelion stretched its long white back below. The sharp cone of Ossa might well ride upon the extended back of Pelion, and it seems a pity that the Titans did not succeed in their attempt. We were leaving, and looking our last on the Thracian coasts, once rimmed from Mt. Athos to the Bosphorus with a wreath of prosperous cities. What must once have been the splendor of the Ægean Sea and its islands, when every island was the seat of a vigorous state, and every harbor the site of a commercial town which sent forth adventurous galleys upon any errand of trade or conquest ! Since the fall of Constantinople, these coasts and islands have been stripped and neglected by Turkish avarice and improvidence, and perhaps their naked aspect is attributable more to the last owners than to all the preceding possessors ; it remained for the Turk to exhaust Nature herself, and to accomplish that ruin, that destruction of peoples, which certainly not the Athenian, the Roman, or the Macedonian accomplished, to destroy that which survived the contemptible Byzantines and escaped the net of the pillaging Christian crusaders. Yet it needs only repose, the confidence of the protection of industry, and a spirit of toleration, which the Greeks must learn as well as the Turks, that the traveller in the beginning of the next century may behold in the Archipelago the paradise of the world.

We sailed along by the peninsula of Magnesia, which separates the Ægean from the Bay of Pagasæus, and hinders us from seeing the plains of Thessaly, where were trained the famous cavalry, the perfect union of horse and man that gave rise to the fable of centaurs ; the same conception of double prowess which our own early settlers exaggerated in the notion that the Kentuckian was half horse and half alligator. Just before we entered the group of lovely Sporades, we looked down the long narrow inlet to the Bay of Maliacus and saw the sharp snow-peaks of Mt. Œta, at the foot of which are the marsh and hot springs of Thermopylæ. We passed between Skiathos and Skopelos, — steep, rocky islands, well wooded and enlivened with villages perched on the hillsides, and both draped in lovely color. In the strait between Skiathos and Magnesia the Greek vessels made a stand against the Persians until the defeat at Thermopylæ compelled a retreat to Salamis. The monks of the Middle Ages, who had an eye for a fertile land, covered the little island with monasteries, of which one only now remains. Its few inhabitants are chiefly sailors, and to-day it would be wholly without fame were it not for the beauty of its women. Skopelos, which is larger, has a population of over six thousand, — industrious people who cultivate the olive and produce a good red wine, that they export in their own vessels.

Nearly all day we sailed outside and along Eubœa; and the snow dusting its high peaks and lonely ravines was a not unwelcome sight, for the day was warm, oppressively so even at sea. All the elements lay in a languid truce. Before it was hidden by Skopelos, Mt. Athos again asserted its lordship over these seas, more gigantic than when we were close to it, the sun striking the snow on its face (it might be the Whiteface of the Adirondacks, except that it is piled up more like the Matterhorn), while the base, bathed in a silver light, was indistinguishable from the silver water out of which it rose. The islands were all purple, the shores silver, and the sea around us deeply azure. What delicious color!

Perhaps it was better to coast along the Eubœan land and among the Sporades, clothed in our minds with the historic hues which the atmosphere reproduced to our senses, than to break the dream by landing, to find only broken fragments where cities once were, and a handful of fishermen or shepherds the only inheritors of the homes of heroes. We should find nothing on Ikos, except rabbits and a hundred or two of fishers, perhaps not even the grave of Peleus, the father of Achilles; and the dozen little rocky islets near, which some giant in sportive mood may have tossed into the waves, would altogether scarcely keep from famine a small flock of industrious sheep. Skyros, however, has not forgotten its ancient fertility; the well-watered valleys, over-looked by bold mountains and rocky peaks (upon one of which stood "the lofty Skyros" of Homer's song) still bear corn and wine, the fig and the olive, the orange and the lemon, as in the days when Achilles, in woman's apparel, was hidden among the maidens in the gardens of King Lycomedes. The mountains are clothed with oaks, beeches, firs, and plane-trees. Athens had a peculiar affection for Skyros, for it was there that Cymon found the bones of Theseus, and transported them thence to the temple of the hero, where they were deposited with splendid obsequies, Æschylus and Sophocles adding to the festivities the friendly rivalry of a dramatic contest. In those days everything was for the state and nothing for the man; and naturally — such is the fruit of self-abnegation — the state was made immortal by the genius of its men.

Of the three proud flagstaffs erected in front of St. Mark's, one, for a long time, bore the banner of Eubœa, or Negropont, symbol of the Venetian sovereignty for nearly three centuries over this island, which for four centuries thereafter was to be cursed by the ascendency of the crescent. From the outer shore one can form little notion of the extraordinary fertility of this land, and we almost regretted that a rough sea had not driven us to take the inner passage, by Bœotia and through the narrow Euripus, where the Venetian-built town and the Lion of St. Mark occupy and guard the site of ancient Chalkis. The Turks made the name of Negropont odious to the world, but with the res-toration of the Grecian nationality the ancient name is restored, and slowly, Eubœa, spoiled by the Persians, trampled by Mace-donians and Romans, neglected by Justinian (the depopulator of the Eastern Empire), drained by the Venetians, blighted by the Osmanlis, is beginning to attract the attention of capital and travel, by its unequalled fertility and its almost unequalled scenery.

Romance, mythology, and history start out of the waves on either hand; at twilight we were entering the Cyclades, and beginning to feel the yet enduring influence of a superstition which so mingled itself with the supremest art and culture, that after two thousand years its unreal creations are nearly as mighty as ever in the realms of poetry and imagination. These islands are still under the spell of genius, and we cannot, if we would, view them except through the medium of poetic history. I suppose that the island of Andros, which is cultivated largely by Albanians, an Illyrian race, having nothing in common with the ancient Ionians, would little interest us; if we cared to taste its wine, it would be because it was once famous throughout Greece, and if we visited the ruins of its chief city, it would be to recall an anecdote of Herodotus: when Themistocles besieged the town and demanded tribute, because the Andrians had been compelled to join the fleet of Xerxes at Salamis, and threatened them with the two mighty deities of Athens, Persuasion and Necessity, the spirited islanders replied that they were protected by two churlish gods, Poverty and Inability.

It was eleven o'clock at night when we sailed between Keos and Helena, the latter a long barren strip that never seems to have been inhabited at all, except from the tradition that Helen once landed there; but Keos and its old town of Iulis was the home of legends and poets, and famous for its code of laws, one of which tended to banish sickness and old age from its precincts, by a provision that every man above sixty should end his life by poison. Its ancient people had a reputation for purity and sobriety, which was probably due to the hegira of the nymphs, who were frightened away to the mainland by a roaring lion. The colossal image of the lion is still to be seen in marble near the ruins of the old city. The island of the Cyclades, which we should have liked most to tread, but did not see, is Delos, the holy, the religious and political centre of the Greek confederation, the birthplace of Apollo and Artemis, the seat of the oracle, second only to that of Delphi, the diminutive and now almost deserted rock, shaken and sunken by repeated earthquakes, once crowned with one of the most magnificent temples of antiquity, the spot of pilgrimage, the arena of games and mystic dances and poetic contests, and of the joyous and solemn festivities of the Delian Apollo.

We were too late to see, though we sat long on deck and watched for it by the aid of a full moon, the white Doric columns of the temple of Minerva on Sunium, which are visible by daylight a long distance at sea. The ancient mariners, who came from Delos or from a more adventurous voyage into the Ægean, beheld here, at the portals of Attica, the temple of its tutelary deity, a welcome and a beacon ; and as they shifted their sails to round the cape, they might have seen the shining helmet of the goddess herself, — the lofty statue of Minerva Promachus on the Acropolis.

XXVIII.

ATHENS.

IN the thought of the least classical reader, Attica occupies a space almost as large as the rest of the world. He hopes that it will broaden on his sight as it does in his imagination, although he knows that it is only two thirds as large as the little State of Rhode Island. But however reason may modify enthusiasm, the diminutive scale on which everything is drawn is certain to disappoint the first view of the reality. Who, he asks, has made this little copy of the great Athenian picture?

When we came upon deck early in the morning, the steamer lay in the land-locked harbor of the peninsula of Piræus. It is a round, deep, pretty harbor; several merchant and small vessels lay there, a Greek and an Austrian steamer, and a war-vessel, and the scene did not lack a look of prosperous animation. About the port clusters a well-to-do village of some ten thousand inhabitants, many of whom dwell in handsome houses. It might be an American town; it is too new to be European. There, at the entrance of the harbor, on a low projecting rock, are some ruins of columns, said to mark the tomb of Themistocles; sometimes the water nearly covers the rock. There could be no more fitting resting-place for the great commander than this, in sight of the strait of Salamis, and washed by the waves that tossed the broken and flying fleet of Xerxes. Beyond is the Bay of Phalerum, the more ancient seaport of the little state. And there — how small it seems! — is the plain of Athens, enclosed by Hymettus, Pentelicus, and Parnes. This rocky peninsula of Piræus, which embraced three small harbors, was fortified by Themistocles with strong walls that extended, in parallel lines, five miles to Athens. Between them ran the great carriage-road, and I suppose the whole distance was a street of gardens and houses.

A grave *commissionnaire*, — I do not know but he would call himself an embassy, — from one of the hotels of Athens, came off and quietly took charge of us. On our way to the shore with our luggage, a customs officer joined us and took a seat in the boat. For this polite attention on the part of the government our plenipotentiary sent by the officer (who did not open the trunks) three francs to the treasury; but I do not know if it ever reached its destination. We shunned the ignoble opportunity of entering the classic city by rail, and were soon whirling along the level and dusty road which follows the course of the ancient Long Wall. Even at this early hour the day had become very warm, and the shade of the poplar-trees, which line the road nearly all the way, was grateful. The fertile fields had yet the freshness of spring, and were gay with scarlet poppies; the vines were thrifty. The near landscape was Italian in character: there was little peculiar in the costumes of the people whom we met walking beside their market-wagons or saw laboring in the gardens; turbans, fezes, flowing garments of white and blue and yellow, all had vanished, and we felt that we were out of the Orient and about to enter a modern city. At a half-way inn, where we stopped to water the horses, there was an hostler in the Albanian, or as it is called, the Grecian national, costume, wearing the *fustanella* and the short jacket; but the stiff white petticoat was rumpled and soiled, and I fancied he was somewhat ashamed of the half-womanly attire, and shrank from inspection, like an actor in harlequin dress, surprised by daylight outside the theatre.

This sheepish remnant of the picturesque could not preserve for us any illusions; the roses blooming by the wayside we knew; the birds singing in the fields we had heard before; the *commissionnaire* persisted in pointing out the evidences of improvement. But we burned with a secret fever; we were impatient even of the grateful avenue of trees that hid what we at every moment expected to see. I do not envy him who without agitation approaches for the first time, and feels that he is about to look upon the Acropolis! There are three supreme sensations, not twice to be experienced, for the traveller: when he is about to behold the ancient seats of art, of discipline, of religion, — Athens, Rome, Jerusalem. But it is not possible for the reality to equal the expectation. "There!" cried the *commissionnaire*, "is the Acropolis!" A small oblong hill lifting itself some three hundred and fifty feet above the city, its sides upheld by walls, its top shining with marble, an isolated fortress in appearance! The bulk of the city lies to the north of the Acropolis, and grows round to the east of it along the valley of the Ilissus.

In five minutes more we had caught a glimpse of the new excavations of the Keramicus, the ancient cemetery, and of the old walls on our left, and were driving up the straight broad Hermes Street towards the palace. Midway in the centre of the street is an ancient Byzantine church, which we pass round. Hermes Street is intersected by Æolus Street; these two cut the city like a Greek cross, and all other streets flow into them. The shops along the way are European, the people in the streets are European in dress, the *cafés*, the tables in front of hotels and restaurants, with their groups of loungers, suggest Paris by reminding one of Brussels. Athens, built of white stone, not yet mellowed by age, is new, bright, clean, cheerful; the broad streets are in the uninteresting style of the new part of Munich, and due to the same Bavarian influence. If Ludwig I. did not succeed in making Munich look like Athens, Otho was more fortunate in giving Athens a resemblance to Munich. And we were almost ashamed to confess how pleasant it appeared, after our long experience of the tumble-down Orient.

We alighted at our hotel on the palace place, ascended steps decked with flowering plants, and entered cool apartments looking upon the square, which is surrounded with handsome buildings, planted with native and exotic trees, and laid out in walks and beds of flowers. To the right rises the plain façade of the royal residence, having behind it a magnificent garden, where the pine rustles to the palm, and a thousand statues revive the dead mythology; beyond rises the singular cone of Lycabettus. Commendable foresight is planting the principal streets with trees, the shade of which is much needed in the long, dry, and parching summer.

From the side windows we looked also over the roofs to the Acropolis, which we were impatient and yet feared to approach. For myself, I felt like deferring the decisive moment, playing with my imagination, lingering about among things I did not greatly care for, whetting impatience and desire by restraining them, and postponing yet a little the realization of the dream of so many years, — to stand at the centre of the world's thought, at the spring of its ideal of beauty. While my companions rested from the fatigue of our sea voyage, I went into the street and walked southward towards the Ilissus. The air was bright and sparkling, the sky deep blue like that of Egypt, the hills sharp and clear in every outline, and startlingly near; the long reach of Hymettus wears ever a purple robe, which nature has given it in place of its pine forests. Travellers from Constantinople complained of the heat : but I found it inspiring ; the air had no languor in it ; this was the very joyous Athens I had hoped to see.

When you take up the favorite uncut periodical of the month, you like to skirmish about the advertisements and tease yourself with dipping in here and there before you plunge into the serial novel. It was absurd, but my first visit in Athens was to the building of the Quadrennial Exposition of the Industry and Art of Greece, — a long, painted wooden structure, decked with flags, and called, I need not say, the Olympium. To enter this imitation of a country fair at home, was the rudest shock one could give to the sentiment of antiquity, and perhaps a dangerous experiment, however strong in the mind might be the subtone of Acropolis. The Greek gentleman who accompanied me said that the exhibition was a great improvement over the one four years before. It was, in fact, a very hopeful sign of the prosperity of the new state ; there was a good display of cereals and fruits, of silk and of jewelry, and various work in gold and silver, — the latter all from Corfu ; but from the specimens of the fine arts, in painting and sculpture, I think the ancient Greeks have not much to fear or to hope from the modern ; and the books, in printing and binding, were rude enough. But the specimens from the

mines and quarries of Greece could not be excelled elsewhere;
the hundred varieties of exquisite marbles detained us long; there
were some polished blocks, lovely in color, and you might almost
say in design, that you would like to frame and hang as pictures on the wall.   Another sign of the decadence of the national
costume, perhaps more significant than its disappearance in the
streets, was its exhibition here upon lay figures. I saw a countryman who wore it sneaking round one of these figures, and regarding it with the curiosity of a savage who for the first time sees
himself in a mirror. Since the revolution the Albanian has been
adopted as the Grecian costume, in default of anything more
characteristic, and perhaps because it would puzzle one to say of
what race the person calling himself a modern Greek is. But the
ridiculous *fustanella* is nearly discarded; it is both inconvenient
and costly; to make one of the proper fulness requires forty
yards of cotton cloth; this is gathered at the waist, and hangs in
broad pleats to the knees, and it is starched so stiffly that it stands
out like a half-open Chinese umbrella. As the garment cannot
be worn when it is the least soiled, and must be done up and
starched two or three times a week, the wearer finds it an expensive habit; and in the whole outfit — the jacket and sleeves
may be a reminiscence of defensive armor — he has the appearance of a *landsknecht* above and a ballet-girl below.

Nearly as rare in the streets as this dress are the drooping red
caps with tassels of blue. The women of Athens whom we
saw would not take a premium anywhere for beauty; but we
noticed here and there one who wore upon her dark locks the
long hanging red fez and gold tassel, who might have attracted
the eye of a roving poet, and been passed down to the next age
as the Maid of Athens. The Athenian men of the present are a
fine race ; we were constantly surprised by noble forms and intelligent faces. That they are Greek in feature or expression, as we
know the Greek from coins and statuary, we could not say. Perhaps it was only the ancient Lacedemonian rivalry that prompted
the remark of a gentleman in Athens, who was born in Sparta,
that there is not a drop of the ancient Athenian blood in Athens.
There are some patrician families in the city who claim this hon-

orable descent, but it is probable that Athens is less Greek than
any other town in the kingdom; and that if there remain any
Hellenic descendants they must be sought in remote districts of
the Morea. If we trusted ourselves to decide by types of face,
we should say that the present inhabitants of Athens were of
Northern origin, and that their relation to the Greeks was no
stronger than that of Englishmen to the ancient Britons. That
the people who now inhabit Attica and the Peloponnesus are
descendants of the Greeks whom the Romans conquered, I suppose no one can successfully claim; that they are all from the
Slavonians, who so long held and almost exclusively occupied the
Greek mainland, it is equally difficult to prove. All we know is,
that the Greek language has survived the Byzantine anarchy, the
Slavonic conquest, the Frank occupation; and that the nimble
wit, the acquisitiveness and inquisitiveness, the cunning and craft
of the modern Greek, seem to be the perversion of the nobler
and yet not altogether dissimilar qualities which made the ancient
Greeks the leaders of the human race. And those who ascribe
the character of a people to climate and geographical position
may expect to see the mongrel inheritors of the ancient soil
moulded, by the enduring influences of nature, into homogeneity,
and reproduce in a measure a copy of that splendid civilization
of whose ruins they are now unappreciative possessors.

Beyond the temporary Olympium, the eye is caught by the Arch
of Hadrian, and fascinated by the towering Corinthian columns of
the Olympicum or Temple of Jupiter. Against the background
of Hymettus and the blue sky stood fourteen of these beautiful
columns, all that remain of the original one hundred and twenty-
four, but enough to give us an impression of what was one of the
most stately buildings of antiquity. This temple, which was begun
by Pisistratus, was not finished till Hadrian's time, or until the
worship of Jupiter had become cold and sceptical. The columns
stand upon a terrace overlooking the bed of the Ilissus; there
coffee is served, and there we more than once sat at sundown, and
saw the vast columns turn from rose to gray in the fading light.

Athens, like every other city of Europe in this age of science
and Christianity, was full of soldiers; we saw squads of them

drilling here and there, their uniforms sprinkled the streets and the *cafés*, and their regimental bands enlivened the town. The Greeks, like all the rest of us, are beating their pruning-hooks into spears and preparing for the millennium. If there was not much that is peculiar to interest us in wandering about among the shops, and the so-called, but unroofed and not real, bazaars, there was much to astonish us in the size and growth of a city of over fifty thousand inhabitants, in forty years, from the heap of ruins and ashes which the Turks left it. When the venerable American missionaries, Dr. Hill and his wife, came to the city, they were obliged to find shelter in a portion of a ruined tower, and they began their labors literally in a field of smoking desolation. The only attractive shops are those of the antiquity dealers, the collectors of coins, vases, statuettes, and *figurines*. Of course the extraordinary demand for these most exquisite mementos of a race of artists has created a host of imitations, and set an extravagant and fictitious price upon most of the articles, a price which the professor who lets you have a specimen as a favor, or the dealer who calmly assumes that he has gathered the last relics of antiquity, mentions with equal equanimity. I looked in the face of a handsome graybeard, who asked me two thousand francs for a silver coin, which he said was a Solon, to see if there was any guile in his eye; but there was not. I cannot but hope that this race which has learned to look honest will some time become so.

Late in the afternoon we walked around the south side of the Acropolis, past the ruins of theatres that strew its side, and ascended by the carriage-road to the only entrance, at the southwest end of the hill, towards the Piræus. We pass through a gate pierced in the side wall, and come to the front of the Propylæa, the noblest gateway ever built. At the risk of offending the travelled, I shall try in a paragraph to put the untravelled reader in possession of the main features of this glorious spot.

The Acropolis is an irregular oblong hill, the somewhat uneven summit of which is about eleven hundred feet long by four hundred and fifty feet broad at its widest. The hill is steep on all sides, and its final spring is perpendicular rock, in places a hundred and fifty feet high. It is lowest at the southwest end, where it dips down, and, by a rocky neck, joins the Areopagus, or Mars Hill. Across this end is built the Propylæa, high with reference to the surrounding country, and commanding the view, but low enough not to hide from a little distance the buildings on the summit. This building, which is of the Doric order, and of pure Pentelic marble, was the pride of the Athenians. Its entire front is about one hundred and seventy feet; this includes the central portico (pierced with five entrances, the centre one for carriages) and the forward projecting north and south wings. In the north wing was the picture-gallery; the south wing was never completed to correspond, but the balance is preserved by the little Temple of the Wingless Victory, which from its ruins has been restored to its original form and beauty. The Propylæa is approached by broad flights of marble steps, which were defended by fortifications on the slope of the hill. The distant reader may form a little conception of the original splendor of this gateway from its cost, which was nearly two and a half millions of dollars, and by remembering that it was built under the direction of Pericles at a time when the cost of a building represented its real value, and not the profits of city officials and contractors.

Passing slowly between the columns, and with many a backward glance over the historic landscape, lingering yet lest we should abruptly break the spell, we came into the area. Straight before us, up the red rock, ran the carriage-road, seamed across with chisel-marks to prevent the horses' hoofs from slipping, and worn in deep ruts by heavy chariot-wheels. In the field before us a mass of broken marble; on the right the creamy columns of the Parthenon; on the left the irregular but beautiful Ionic Erechtheum. The reader sees that the entrance was contrived so that the beholder's first view of the Parthenon should be at the angle which best exhibits its exquisite proportions.

We were alone. The soldier detailed to watch that we did not carry off any of the columns sat down upon a broken fragment by the entrance, and let us wander at our will. I am not sure that I would, if I could, have the temples restored. There is an indescribable pathos in these fragments of columns and architraves

15 *

and walls, in these broken sculptures and marred inscriptions, which time has softened to the loveliest tints, and in these tottering buildings, which no human skill, if it could restore the pristine beauty, could reanimate with the Greek idealism.

And yet, as we sat upon the western steps of the temple dedicated to Pallas Athene, I could imagine what this area was, say in the August days of the great Panathenaic festival, when the gorgeous procession, which I saw filing along the Via Sacra, returning from Eleusis, swept up these broad steps, garlanded with flowers and singing the hymn to the protecting goddess. This platform was not then a desolate stone heap, but peopled with almost living statues in bronze and marble, the creations of the genius of Phidias, of Praxiteles, of Lycius, of Cleœtas, of Myron; there, between the two great temples, but overtopping them both, stood the bronze figure of Minerva Promachus, cast by Phidias out of the spoils of Marathon, whose glittering helmet and spearpoint gladdened the returning mariner when far at sea, and defied the distant watcher on the Acropolis of Corinth. First in the procession come the sacrificial oxen, and then follow in order a band of virgins, the quadriga, each drawn by four noble steeds, the *élite* of the Athenian youth on horseback, magistrates, daughters of noble citizens bearing vases and pateræ, men carrying trays of offerings, flute-players and the chorus singers. They pass around to the entrance of the Parthenon, which is toward the east, and those who are permitted enter the *naos* and come into the presence of the gold-ivory statue of Minerva. The undraped portions of this statue show the ivory; the drapery was of solid gold, made so that it could be removed in time of danger from a public enemy. The golden plates weighed ten thousand pounds. This work of Phidias, since it was celebrated as the perfection of art by the best judges of art, must have been as exquisite in its details as it was harmonious in its proportions; but no artist of our day would dare to attempt to construct a statue in that manner. In its right, outstretched hand it held a statue of Victory, four cubits high; and although it was erected nearly five hundred years before the Christian era, we are curious to notice the already decided influence of Egyptian ideas in the figure of the sphinx surmounting the helmet of the goddess.

The sun was setting behind the island of Salamis. There was a rosy glow on the bay of Phalerum, on the sea to the south, on the side of Hymettus, on the yellow columns of the Parthenon, on the Temple of the Wingless Victory, and on the faces of the ever-youthful Caryatides in the portico of the Erechtheum, who stand reverently facing the Parthenon, worshipping now only the vacant pedestal of Athene the Protector. What overpowering associations throng the mind as one looks off upon the crooked strait of Salamis, down upon the bare rock of the Areopagus; upon the Pnyx and the *bema*, where we know Demosthenes, Solon, Themistocles, Pericles, Aristides, were wont to address the populace who crowded up from this valley, the Agora, the tumultuous market-place, to listen; upon the Museum Hill, crowned by the monument of Philopappus, pierced by grottos, one of which tradition calls the prison of Socrates, — the whole history of Athens is in a nutshell! Yet if one were predetermined to despise this mite of a republic in the compass of a quart measure, he could not do it here. A little of Cæsar's dust outweighs the world. We are not imposed upon by names. It was, it could only have been, in comparison with modern naval engagements, a petty fight in the narrow limits of that strait, and yet neither the Persian soldiers who watched it from the Acropolis and in terror saw the ships of Xerxes flying down the bay, nor the Athenians, who had abandoned their citadel and trusted their all to the "wooden walls" of their ships, could have imagined that the result was laden with such consequences. It gives us pause to think what course all subsequent history would have taken, what would be the present complexion of the Christian system itself, if on that day Asiatic barbarism had rendered impossible the subsequent development of Grecian art and philosophy.

We waited on the Acropolis for the night and the starlight and the thousand lights in the city spread below, but we did not stay for the slow coming of the midnight moon over Hymettus.

On Sunday morning we worshipped with the Greeks in the beautiful Russian church; the interior is small but rich, and is like a private parlor; there are no seats, and the worshippers stand or kneel, while gilded and painted figures of saints and

angels encompass them. The ceremony is simple, but impressive.
The priests are in gorgeous robes of blue and silver; choir-boys
sing soprano, and the bass, as it always is in Russian churches,
is magnificent. A lady, tall, elegant, superb, in black faced and
trimmed with a stuff of gold, sweeps up to the desks, kisses the
books and the crucifix, and then stands one side crossing herself.
We are most of us mortal, and all, however rich in apparel, poor
sinners one day in the week. No one of the worshippers carries a
prayer-book. There is reading behind the screen, and presently
the priests bring out the elements of communion and exhibit
them, the one carrying the bread in a silver vessel on his head,
and the other the wine. The central doors are then closed on
the mysterious consecration. At the end of the service the holy
elements are brought out, the communicants press up, kiss the
cross, take a piece of bread, and then turn and salute their
friends, and break up in a cheerful clatter of talk. In contrast
to this, we attended afterwards the little meeting, in an upper
chamber, of the Greek converts of the American Mission, and
listened to a sermon in Greek which inculcated the religion of
New England, — a gospel which, with the aid of schools, makes
slow but hopeful progress in the city of the unknown God.

The longer one remains in Athens the more he will be impressed with two things : the one is the perfection of the old art
and civilization, and what must have been the vivacious, joyous
life of the ancient Athenians, in a climate so vital, when this
plain was a garden, and these beautiful hills were clad with
forests, and the whispers of the pine answered the murmurs of
the sea; the other is the revival of letters and architecture and
culture, visible from day to day, in a progress as astonishing as
can be seen in any Occidental city. I cannot undertake to describe, not even to mention, the many noble buildings, either
built or in construction, from the quarries of Pentelicus, — the
University, the Academy, the new Olympium, — all the voluntary
contributions of wealthy Greeks, most of them merchants in foreign
cities, whose highest ambition seems to be to restore Athens to
something of its former splendor. It is a point of honor with
every Greek, in whatever foreign city he may live and die, to leave

something in his last will for the adornment or education of the
city of his patriotic devotion. In this, if in nothing else, they
resemble the ancient patriots who thought no sacrifice too costly
for the republic. Among the ruins we find no palaces, no sign
that the richest citizen used his wealth in ostentatious private
mansions. Although some of the Greek merchants now build
for themselves elegant villas, the next generation will see the
evidences of their wealth rather in the public buildings they have
erected. In this little city the University has eighty professors
and over twelve hundred students, gathered from all parts of
Greece ; there are in the city forty lady teachers with eight hundred female pupils; and besides these there are two gymnasiums
and several graded schools. Professors and teachers are well
paid, and the schools are free, even to the use of books. The
means flow from the same liberality, that of the Greek merchants,
who are continually leaving money for new educational foundations. There is but one shadow upon this hopeful picture, and
that is the bigotry of the Greek church, to which the government
yields. I do not now speak of the former persecutions suffered
by the Protestant missionaries, but recently the schools for girls
opened by Protestants, and which have been of the highest service
in the education of women, have been obliged to close or else
" conform " to the Greek religion and admit priestly teachers.
At the time of our visit, one of the best of them, that of Miss
Kyle of New York, was only tolerated from week to week under
perpetual warnings, and liable at any moment to be suppressed
by the police. This narrow policy is a disgrace to the government, and if it is continued must incline the world to hope that
the Greeks will never displace the Moslems in Constantinople.

In the front of the University stands a very good statue of the
scholar-patriot Korais, and in the library we saw the busts of other
distinguished natives and foreigners. The library, which is every
day enriched by private gifts, boasts already over one hundred
and thirty thousand volumes. As we walked through the rooms,
the director said that the University had no bust of an American,
though it had often been promised one. I suggested one of
Lincoln. No, he wanted Washington ; he said he cared to have

no other. I did not tell him that Washington was one of the heroes of our mythic period, that we had filled up a tolerably large pantheon since then, and that a century in America was as good as a thousand years in Byzantium. But I fell into something of a historic revery over the apparent fact that America is as yet to Greece nothing but the land of Washington, and I rather liked the old-fashioned notion, and felt sure that there must be somewhere in the United States an antiquated and rich patriot who remembered Washington and would like to send a marble portrait of our one great man to the University of Athens.

XXIX

ELEUSIS, PLATO'S ACADEME, ETC.

THERE was a nightingale who sang and sobbed all night in the garden before the hotel, and only ceased her plaintive reminiscence of Athenian song and sorrow with the red dawn. But this is a sad world of contrasts. Called upon the balcony at midnight by her wild notes, I saw, — how can I ever say it ? — upon the balcony below, a white figure advance, and with a tragic movement of haste, if not of rage, draw his garment of the night over his head and shake it out over the public square ; and I knew — for the kingdom of knowledge comes by experience as well as by observation — that the lively flea was as wakeful in Greece as the nightingale.

In the morning the north-wind arose, — it seems to blow constantly from Bœotia at this time of the year, — but the day was bright and sparkling, and we took carriage for Eleusis. It might have been such a morning — for the ancient Athenians always anticipated the dawn in their festivals — that the Panathenaic processions moved along this very Via Sacra to celebrate the Mysteries of Ceres at Eleusis. All the hills stood in clear outline, — long Pentelicus and the wavy lines of Parnes and Corydallus ; we drove over the lovely and fertile plain, amid the olive-orchards of the Kephissus, and up the stony slope to the narrowing Pass of Daphne, a defile in Mt. Ægaleos ; but we sought in vain the laurel grove, or a single specimen of that tree whose twisted trunk and outstretched arms express the struggle of vanishing humanity. Passing on our right the Chapel of St. Elias, on a commanding eminence, and traversing the level plateau of the rocky gorge, we alighted at the Monastery of Daphne, whose half-ruined cloister and chapel occupy the site of a temple of Apollo. We sat for half an hour in its quiet, walled churchyard, carpeted with poppies and tender flowers of spring, amid the remains of old columns and fragments of white marble, sparkling amid the green grass and blue violets, and looked upon the blue bay of Eleusis and Salamis, and the heights of Megara beyond. Surely nature has a tenderness for such a spot; and I fancied that even the old dame who unlocked for us the chapel and its cheap treasures showed us with some interest, in a carving here and a capital there, the relics of a former religion, and perhaps mingled with her adoration of the Virgin and the *bambino* a lurking regard for Venus and Apollo. A mile beyond, at the foot of a rocky precipice, are pointed out the foundations of a temple of Venus, where the handbook assured us doves had been found carved in white marble; none were left, however, for us, and we contented ourselves with reading on the rock *Phile Aphrodite*, and making a vain effort to recall life to this sterile region.

Enchanting was the view as we drove down the opening pass to the bay, which spreads out a broad sheet, completely landlocked by the irregular bulk of Salamis Island. When we emerged through the defile we turned away from the narrow strait where the battle was fought, and from the " rocky brow " on which Xerxes sat, a crowned spectator of his ruin, and swept around the circular shore, past the Rheiti, or salt-springs, — clear, greenish pools, — and over the level Thriasian Plain. The bay of Eleusis, guarded by the lofty amphitheatre of mountains, the curving sweep of Ægaleos and Kithæron, and by Salamis, is like a lovely lake, and if anywhere on earth there could be peace, you would say it would be on its sunny and secluded shores. Salamis appears only a bare and rocky island, but the vine still flourishes in the scant soil, and from its wild-flowers the descendants of the Attic bees make honey as famous as that of two thousand years ago.

Across the bay, upon a jutting rocky point, above which rises the crown of its Acropolis, lies the straggling, miserable village of Eleusis. Our first note of approach to it was an ancient pavement, and a few indistinguishable fragments of walls and columns. In a shallow stream which ran over the stones the women of the town were washing clothes; and throngs of girls were filling their pails of brass at an old well, as of old at the same place did the daughters of Keleos. Shriller tones and laughter mingled with their incessant chatter as we approached, and we thought, — perhaps it was imagination, — a little wild defiance and dislike. I had noticed already in Athens, and again here, the extraordinary rapidity with which the Greeks in conversation exchange words; I think they are the fastest talkers in the world. And the Greek has a hard, sharp, ringing, metallic sound; it is staccato. You can see how easily Aristophanes imitated the brittle-brattle of frogs. I have heard two women whose rapid, incessant cackle sounded exactly like the conversation of hens. The sculptor need not go further than these nut-brown maids for classic forms; the rounded limbs, the generous bust, the symmetrical waist, which fashion has not made an hour-glass to mark the flight of time and health. The mothers of heroes were of this mould; although I will not say that some of them were not a trifle stout for grace, and that their well-formed faces would not have been improved by the interior light of a little culture. Their simple dress was a white, short chemise, that left the legs bare, a heavy and worked tunic, like that worn by men, and a colored kerchief tied about the head. Many of the men of the village wore the *fustanella* and the full Albanian costume.

The Temple of Ceres lies at the foot of the hill; only a little portion of its vast extent has been relieved of the superincumbent, accumulated soil, and in fact its excavation is difficult, because the village is built over the greater part of it. What we saw was only a confused heap of marble, some pieces finely carved, arches, capitals, and shattered columns. The Greek government, which is earnestly caring for the remains of antiquity and diligently collecting everything for the National Museum, down to broken toes and fingers, has stationed a keeper over the ruins; and he showed us, in a wooden shanty, the interesting fragments of statues which had been found in the excavation. I coveted a little hand, plump, with tapering fingers, which the conservator

permitted us to hold, — a slight but a most suggestive memento
of the breeding and beauty of the lady who was the sculptor's
model; and it did not so much seem a dead hand stretched out
to us from the past, as a living thing which returned our furtive
pressure.

We climbed up the hill where the fortress of the Acropolis
stood, and where there is now a little chapel. Every Grecian city
seems to have had its Acropolis, the first nucleus of the rude tribe
which it fortified against incursion, and the subsequent site of
temples to the gods. The traveller will find these steep hills,
rising out of plains, everywhere from Ephesus to Argos, and will
almost conclude that Nature had consciously adapted herself to
the wants of the aboriginal occupants. It is well worth ascending this summit to get the fine view of plain and bay, of Mt. Ke-
rata and its double peaks, and the road that pierces the pass of
Kithæron, and leads to the field of Platæa and the remains of
Thebes.

In a little wine-shop, near the ruins, protected from the wind
and the importunate swarms of children, we ate our lunch, and
tried to impress ourselves with the knowledge that Æschylus was
born in Eleusis; and to imagine the nature of the Eleusinian
mysteries, the concealed representations by which the ancients
attempted to symbolize, in the myths of Ceres and Proserpine,
the primal forces of nature, perhaps the dim suggestions of immortality, — a secret not to be shared by the vulgar, — borrowed
from the deep wisdom of the Egyptians.

The children of Eleusis deserve more space than I can afford
them, since they devoted their entire time to our annoyance.
They are handsome rascals, and there were enough of them, if
they had been sufficiently clothed, to form a large Sunday school.
When we sat down in the ruins and tried to meditate on Ceres,
they swarmed about us, capering and yelling incessantly, and
when I made a charge upon them they scattered over the rocks
and saluted us with stones. But I find that at this distance I
have nothing against them; I recall only their beauty and vivacity, and if they were the worst children that ever tormented
travellers, I reflect, yes, but they were Greeks, and the gods loved

their grandmothers. One slender, liquid-eyed, slim-shanked girl offered me a silver coin. I saw that it was a beautiful Athenian piece of the time of Pericles, and after some bargaining I bought it of her for a reasonable price. But as we moved away to our carriage, I was followed by the men and women of the settlement, who demanded it back. They looked murder and talked Greek. I inquired how much they wanted. Fifty francs! But that is twice as much as it is worth in Athens; and the coin was surrendered. All through the country, the peasants have a most exaggerated notion of the value of anything antique.

We returned through the pass of Daphne and by the site of the academic grove of Plato, though olive-groves and gardens of pomegranates in scarlet bloom, quinces, roses, and jasmines, the air sweet and delightful. Perhaps nowhere else can the traveller so enter into the pure spirit of Attic thought and feeling as among these scattered remains that scholars have agreed to call the ruins of Plato's Academe. We turned through a lane into the garden of a farm-house, watered by a branch rivulet of the Kephissus. What we saw was not much, — some marble columns under a lovely cypress-grove, some fragments of antique carving built into a wall; but we saw it as it were privately and with a feeling of the presence of the mighty shade. And then, under a row of young plane-trees, by the meagre stream, we reclined on ripe wheat-straw, in full sight of the Acropolis, — perhaps the most poetic view of that magnetic hill. So Plato saw it as he strolled along this bank and listened to the wisdom of his master, Socrates, or, pacing the colonnade of the Academe, meditated the republic. Here indeed Aristotle, who was born the year that Plato died, may have lain and woven that subtle web of metaphysics which no subsequent system of thought or religion has been able to disregard. The centuries-old wind blew strong and fresh through the trees, and the scent of flowers and odorous shrubs, the murmur of the leaves, the unchanged blue vault of heaven, the near hill of the sacred Colonus, celebrated by Sophocles as the scene of the death of Œdipus, all conspired to flood us with the poetic past. What intimations of immortality do we need, since the spell of genius is so deathless?

After dinner we laboriously, by a zigzag path, climbed the sharp cone of Lycabettus, whose six hundred and fifty feet of height commands the whole region. The rock summit has just room enough for a tiny chapel, called of St. George, and a narrow platform in front, where we sat in the shelter of the building and feasted upon the prospect. At sunset it is a marvellous view, — all Athens and its plain, the bays, Salamis and the strait of the battle, Acro-Corinth; Megara, Hymettus, Penteli-cus, Kithæron.

When, in descending, we had nearly reached the foot on the west side, we heard the violent ringing of a bell high above us, and, turning about, saw what seemed to be a chapel under the northwest edge of the rock upon which we had lately stood. Bandits in laced leggings and embroidered jackets, chattering girls in short skirts and gay kerchiefs, were descending the wandering path, and the clamor of the bell piqued our curiosity to turn and ascend. When we reached our goal, the affair seemed to be pretty much all bell, and nobody but a boy in the lusty exuber-ance of youth could have made so much noise by the swinging of a single clapper. In a niche or rather cleft in the rock was a pent-roofed bell-tower, and a boy, whose piety seemed inspired by the Devil, was hauling the rope and sending the sonorous metal over and over on its axis. In front of the bell is a narrow ter-race, sufficient, however, to support three fig-trees, under which were tables and benches, and upon the low terrace-wall were planted half a dozen large and differently colored national ban-ners. A hole in the rock was utilized as a fireplace, and from a pot over the coals came the fumes of coffee. Upon this perch of a terrace people sat sipping coffee and looking down upon the city, whose evening lights were just beginning to twinkle here and there. Behind the belfry is a chapel, perhaps ten feet by twelve, partly a natural grotto and partly built of rough stones ; it was brilliantly lighted with tapers, and hung with quaint pictures. At the entrance, which is a door cut in the rock, stood a Greek priest and an official in uniform selling wax-tapers, and raking in the *leptas* of the devout. We threw down some coppers, de-clined the tapers, and walked in. The adytum of the priest was wholly in the solid rock. There seemed to be no service; but the women and children stood and crossed themselves, and passionately kissed the poor pictures on the walls. Yet there was nothing exclusive or pharisaic in the worshippers, for priest and people showed us friendly faces, and cordially returned our greetings. The whole rock quivered with the clang of the bell, for the boy at the rope leaped at his task, and with ever-increasing fury summoned the sinful world below to prayer. Young ladies with their gallants came and went; and whenever there was any slacking of stragglers up the hillside the bell clamored more importunately.

As dusk crept on, torches were set along the wall of the terrace, and as we went down the hill they shone on the red and blue flags and the white belfry, and illuminated the black mass of overhanging rock with a red glow. There is time for religion in out-of-the-way places here, and it is rendered picturesque, and even easy and enjoyable, by the aid of coffee and charming scenery. When we reached the level of the town, the lights still glowed high up in the recess of the rocks, girls were laughing and chattering as they stumbled down the steep, and the wild bell still rang. How easy it is to be good in Greece!

One day we stole a march on Marathon, and shared the glory of those who say they have seen it, without incurring the fatigue of a journey there. We ascended Mt. Pentelicus. Hymettus and Pentelicus are about the same height, — thirty-five hundred feet, — but the latter, ten miles to the northeast of Athens, commands every foot of the Attic territory; if one should sit on its summit and read a history of the little state, he would need no map. We were away at half past five in the morning, in order to anticipate if possible the rising of the daily wind. As we ascended, we had on our left, at the foot of the mountain, the village of Kephisia, now, as in the days of Herodes Atticus, the summer resort of wealthy Athenians, who find in its fountains, the sources of the Kephissus, and in its groves relief from the heat and glare of the scorched Athenian plain. Half-way we halted at a monastery, left our carriage, and the ladies mounted horses. There is a handsome church here, and the situation is picturesque and commands a wide view of the plain and the rugged north

slope of Hymettus, but I could not learn that the monastery was
in an active state; it is only a hive of drones which consumes the
honey produced by the working-bees from the wild thyme of the
neighboring mountain.   The place, however, is a great resort of
parties of pleasure, who picnic under the grove of magnificent
forest-trees, and once a year the king and queen come hither to
see the youths and maidens dance on the greensward.

Up to the highest quarries the road is steep, and strewn with
broken marble, and after that there is an hour's scramble through
bushes and over a rocky path.   We rested in a large grotto near
the principal of the ancient quarries; it was the sleeping-place
of the workmen, subsequently a Christian church, and then, and
not long ago, a haunt and home of brigands.   Here we found a
party of four fellows, half clad in sheep-skins, playing cards, who
seemed to be waiting our arrival; but they were entirely civil,
and I presume were only shepherds, whatever they may have been
formerly.   From these quarries was hewn the marble for the
Temple of Theseus, the Parthenon, the Propylæa, the theatres, and
other public buildings, to which age has now given a soft and
creamy tone; the Pentelic marble must have been too brilliant
for the eye, and its dazzling lustre was no doubt softened by the
judicious use of color.   Fragments which we broke off had the
sparkle and crystalline grain of loaf-sugar, and if they were placed
upon the table one would unhesitatingly take them to sweeten his
tea.   The whole mountain-side is overgrown with laurel, and
we found wild-flowers all the way to the summit.   Amid the
rocks of the higher slopes, little shepherd-boys, carrying the traditional crooks, were guarding flocks of black and white goats,
and, invariably as we passed, these animals scampered off and
perched themselves upon sharp rocks in a photographic *pose*.

Early as we were, the wind had risen before us, and when we
reached the bare back of the summit it blew so strongly that we
could with difficulty keep our feet, and gladly took refuge in a
sort of stone corral, which had been a camp and lookout of brigands.   From this commanding point they spied both their victims and pursuers.   Our guide went into the details of the
capture of the party of Englishmen who spent a night here, and

pointed out to us the several hiding-places in the surrounding country to which they were successively dragged. But my attention was not upon this exploit. We looked almost directly down upon Marathon. There is the bay and the curving sandy shore where the Persian galleys landed; here upon a spur, jutting out from the hill, the Athenians formed before they encountered the host in the plain, and there — alas! it was hidden by a hill — is the mound where the one hundred and ninety-two Athenian dead are buried. It is only a small field, perhaps six miles along the shore and a mile and a half deep, and there is a considerable marsh on the north and a small one at the south end. The victory at so little cost, of ten thousand over a hundred thousand, is partially explained by the nature of the ground; the Persians had not room enough to manœuvre, and must have been thrown into confusion on the skirts of the northern swamp, and if over six thousand of them were slain, they must have been killed on the shore in the panic of their embarkation. But still the shore is broad, level, and firm, and the Greeks must have been convinced that the gods themselves terrified the hearts of the barbarians, and enabled them to discomfit a host which had chosen this plain as the most feasible in all Attica for the action of cavalry.

A sea-haze lay upon the strait of Euripus and upon Eubœa, and nearly hid from our sight the forms of the Cyclades; but away in the northwest were snow peaks, which the guide said were the heights of Parnassus above Delphi. In the world there can be few prospects so magnificent as this, and none more inspiring to the imagination. No one can properly appreciate the Greek literature or art who has not looked upon the Greek nature which seems to have inspired both.

Nothing now remains of the monuments and temples which the pride and piety of the Athenians erected upon the field of Marathon. The visitor at the Arsenal of Venice remembers the clumsy lion which is said to have stood on this plain, and in the Temple of Theseus, at Athens, he may see a slab which was found in this meadow; on it is cut in very low relief the figure of a soldier, but if the work is Greek the style of treatment is Assyrian.

The Temple of Theseus, which occupies an elevation above the
city and west of the Areopagus, is the best-preserved monument
of Grecian antiquity, and if it were the only one, Athens would
still be worthy of a pilgrimage from the ends of the earth. Behind it is a level esplanade, used as a drill-ground, upon one side
of which have been gathered some relics of ancient buildings and
sculptures ; seated there in au ancient marble chair, we never
wearied of studying the beautiful proportions of this temple, which
scarcely suffers by comparison with the Parthenon or that at
Pæstum. In its construction the same subtle secret of curved
lines and inclined verticals was known, a secret which increases
its apparent size and satisfies the eye with harmony.

While we were in Athens the antiquarians were excited by the
daily discoveries in the excavations at the Keramicus (the field
where the Athenian potters worked). Through the portion of this
district outside the gate Dipylum ran two streets, which were
lined with tombs; one ran to the Academe, the other was the sacred
way to Eleusis. The excavations have disclosed many tombs and
lovely groups of funereal sculpture, some of which are *in situ*, but
many have been removed to the new Museum. The favorite device is the seated figure of the one about to die, who in this position of dignity takes leave of those most loved ; perhaps it is a
wife, a husband, a lovely daughter, a handsome boy, who calmly
awaits the inevitable moment, while the relatives fondly look or
half avert their sorrowful faces. In all sculpture I know nothing
so touching as these family farewells. I obtained from them a
new impression of the Greek dignity and tenderness, of the simplicity and nobility of their domestic life.

The Museum, which was unarranged, is chiefly one of fragments, but what I saw there and elsewhere scattered about the
town gave me a finer conception of the spirit of the ancient art
than all the more perfect remains in Europe put together ; and it
seems to me that nowhere except in Athens is it possible to attain
a comprehension of its depth and loveliness. Something, I know,
is due to the *genius loci*, but you come to the knowledge that the
entire life, even the commonest, was pervaded by something that
has gone from modern art. In the Museum we saw a lovely

statue of Isis, a noble one of Patroclus, fine ones of athletes, and also, showing the intercourse with Egypt, several figures holding the sacred *sistrum*, and one of Rameses II. But it is the humbler and funereal art that gives one a new conception of the Greek grace, tenderness, and sensibility. I have spoken of the sweet dignity, the high-born grace, that accepted death with lofty resignation, and yet not with stoical indifference, of some of the sepulchral groups. There was even more poetry in some that are simpler. Upon one slab was carved a figure, pensive, alone, wrapping his drapery about him and stepping into the silent land, on that awful journey that admits of no companion. On another, which was also without inscription, a solitary figure sat in one corner; he had removed helmet and shield, and placed them on the ground behind him; a line upon the stone indicated the boundary of the invisible world, and, with a sad contemplation, the eyes of the soldier were fixed upon that unknown region into which he was about to descend.

Scarcely a day passed that we did not ascend the Acropolis; and again and again we traversed the Areopagus, the Pnyx, the Museum hills. From the valley of the Agora stone steps lead up the Areopagus to a bench cut in the rock. Upon this open summit the Areopagite Council held, in the open air, its solemn sessions; here it sat, it is said, at night and in the dark, that no face of witness or criminal, or gesture of advocate, should influence the justice of its decisions. Dedicated to divine justice, it was the most sacred and awful place in Athens; in a cavern underneath it was the sanctuary of the dread Erinnyes, the avenging Furies, whom a later superstition represented with snakes twisted in their hair; whatever the gay frivolity of the city, this spot was silent, and respected as the dread seat of judicature of the highest causes of religion or of politics. To us Mars Hill is chiefly associated with the name of St. Paul; and I do not suppose it matters much whether he spoke to the men of Athens in this sacred place or, as is more probable, from a point farther down the hill, now occupied by a little chapel, where he would be nearer to the multitude of the market-place. It does not matter; it was on the Areopagus, and in the centre of temples and a thousand statues that

16

bespoke the highest civilization of the pagan world, that Paul proclaimed the truth, which man's egotism continually forgets, that in temples made with hands the Deity does not dwell.

From this height, on the side of the Museum Hill, we see the grotto that has been dignified with the title of the "prison of Socrates," but upon slight grounds. When the philosopher was condemned, the annual sacred ship which was sent with thank-offerings to Delos was still absent, and until its return no execution was permitted in Athens. Every day the soldiers who guarded Socrates ascended this hill, and went round the point to see if the expected vessel was in sight; and it is for their convenience that some antiquarian designated this grotto as the prison. The delay of the ship gave us his last immortal discourse.

We went one evening by the Temple of Jupiter, along the Ilissus, to the old Stadium. This classic stream, the Ilissus, is a gully, with steep banks and a stony bottom, and apparently never wet except immediately after a rain. You would think by the flattery it received from the ancient Athenians that it was larger than the Mississippi. The Panathenaic Stadium, as it is called, because its chief use was in the celebration of the games of the great quadrennial festival, was by nature and art exceedingly well adapted to chariot races and other contests. Open at the end, where a bridge crossed the Ilissus, it extended a hundred feet broad six hundred and fifty feet into the hill, upon the three sloping sides of which, in seats of marble, could be accommodated fifty thousand spectators. Here the Greek youth contended for the prizes in the chariot race, and the more barbarous Roman emperors amused a degenerate people with the sight of a thousand wild beasts hunted and slain in a single celebration.

The Stadium has been lately re-excavated, and at the time of our visit the citizens were erecting some cheap benches at one end, and preparing, in a feeble way, for what it pleases them to call the Olympic Games, which were to be inaugurated the following Sunday. The place must inevitably dwarf the performance, and comparison render it ridiculous. The committee-men may seem to themselves Olympic heroes, and they had the earnest air of trying to make themselves believe that they were really

reviving the ancient glory of Greece, or that they could bring it
back by calling a horse-race and the wrestling of some awkward
peasants an "Olympiad." The revival could be, as we afterwards
learned it was, only a sickly and laughable affair. The life of a
nation is only preserved in progress, not in attempts to make dead
forms live again. It is difficult to have chariot races or dramatic
contests without chariots or poets, and I suppose the modern
imitation would scarcely be saved from ludicrousness, even if the
herald should proclaim that now a Patroclus and now an Aristophanes was about to enter the arena. The modern occupants
of Athens seem to be deceiving themselves a little with names and
shadows. In the genuine effort to revive in its purity the Greek
language, and to inspire a love of art and literature, the Western
traveller will wholly sympathize. In the growth of a liberal commercial spirit he will see still more hope of a new and enduring
Greek state. But a puerile imitation of a society and a religion
which cannot possibly have a resurrection excites only a sad
smile. There is no more pitiful sight than a man who has lost
his ideals, unless it be a nation which has lost its ideals. So long
as the body of the American people hold fast to the simple and
primitive conception of a republican society, — to the ideals of a
century ago, — the nation can survive, as England did, a period
of political corruption. There never was, not under Themistocles
nor under Scanderbeg, a more glorious struggle for independence
than that which the battle of Navarino virtually terminated. The
world had a right to expect from the victors a new and vigorous
national life, not a pale and sentimental copy of a splendid original, which is now as impossible of revival as the Roman Empire.
To do the practical and money-getting Greeks justice, I could not
learn that they took a deep interest in the "Olympiad"; nor that
the inhabitants of ancient Sparta were jealous of the re-institution
of the national games in Athens, since, they say, there are no
longer any Athenians to be jealous of.

The ancient Athenians were an early people; they liked the
dewy freshness of the morning; they gave the first hours of the
day to the market and to public affairs, and the rising sun often
greeted the orators on the *bema,* and an audience on the terrace

below. We had seen the Acropolis in almost every aspect, but I thought that one might perhaps catch more of its ancient spirit at sunrise than at any other hour.

It is four o'clock when my companion and I descend into the silent street and take our way to the ancient citadel by the shortest and steepest path. Dawn is just breaking in pink, and the half-moon is in the sky. The sleepy guard unbolts the gate and admits us, but does not care to follow; and we pass the Propylæa and have the whole field to ourselves. There is a great hush as we come into the silent presence of the gray Parthenon; the shades of night are still in its columns. We take our station on a broken pillar, so that we can enjoy a three-quarters view of the east front. As the light strengthens we have a pink sky for background to the temple, and the smooth bay of Phalerum is like a piece of the sky dropped down. Very gradually the light breaks on the Parthenon, and in its glowing awakening it is like a sentient thing, throwing shadows from its columns and kindling more and more; the lion gargoyles on the corners of the pediment have a life which we had not noticed before. There is now a pink tint on the fragments of columns lying at the side; there is a reddish hue on the plain about Piræus; the strait of Salamis is green, but growing blue; Phalerum is taking an iridescent sheen; I can see, beyond the Gulf of Ægina, the distant height of Acro-Corinth.

The city is still in heavy shadow, even the Temple of Theseus does not relax from its sombreness. But the light mounts; it catches the top of the white columns of the Propylæa, it shines on the cornice of the Erechtheum, and creeps down in blushes upon the faces of the Caryatides, which seem to bow yet in worship of the long-since-departed Pallas Athene. The bugles of the soldiers called to drill on the Thesean esplanade float up to us; they are really bugle-notes summoning the statues and the old Panathenaic cavalcades on the friezes to life and morning action. The day advances, the red sun commanding the hill and flooding it with light, and the buildings glowing more and more in it, but yet casting shadows. A hawk sweeps around from the north and hangs poised on motionless wings over the building just as the sun touches it. We climb to the top of the western pediment for the wide sweep of view. The world has already got wind of day, and is putting off its nightcaps and opening its doors. As we descend we peer about for a bit of marble as a memento of our visit; but Lord Elgin has left little for the kleptomaniac to carry away.

At this hour the Athenians ought to be assembling on the Pnyx to hear Demosthenes, who should be already on the *bema ;* but the *bema* has no orator, and the terrace is empty. We might perhaps see an early representation at the theatre of Dionysus, into which we can cast a stone from this wall. We pass the gate, scramble along the ragged hillside, — the dumping-ground of the excavators on the Acropolis, — and stand above the highest seats of the Amphitheatre. No one has come. The white marble chairs in the front row — carved with the names of the priests of Bacchus and reserved for them — wait, and even the seats not reserved are empty. There is no white-clad chorus manœuvring on the paved orchestra about the altar; the stage is broken in, and the crouching figures that supported it are the only sign of life. One would like to have sat upon these benches, that look on the sea, and listened to a chorus from the Antigone this morning. One would like to have witnessed that scene when Aristophanes, on this stage, mimicked and ridiculed Socrates, and the philosopher, rising from his undistinguished seat high up among the people, replied.

XXX.

THROUGH THE GULF OF CORINTH.

WITH deep reluctance we tore ourselves from the fascinations of Athens very early one morning. After these things, says the Christian's guide, Paul departed from Athens and came to Corinth. Our departure was in the same direction. We had no choice of time, for the only steamer leaves on Sunday morning, and, besides, our going then removed us from the temptation of the Olympic games. At half past five we were on board the little Greek steamer at the Piræus.

We sailed along Salamis. It was a morning of clouds; but Ægina (once mistress of these seas, and the hated rival of Athens) and the Peloponnesus were robed in graceful garments that, like the veils of the Circassian girls, did not conceal their forms. In four hours we landed at Kalamaki, which is merely a station for the transfer of passengers across the Isthmus. Six miles south on the coast we had a glimpse of Cenchreæ, which is famous as the place where Paul, still under the bonds of Jewish superstition, having accomplished his vow, shaved his head. The neck of limestone rock, which connects the Peloponnesus with the mainland, is ten miles long, and not more than four miles broad from Kalamaki to Lutraki on the Gulf of Corinth, and as it is not, at its highest elevation, over a hundred feet above the sea, the project of piercing it with a canal, which was often entertained and actually begun by Nero, does not seem preposterous. The traveller over it to-day will see some remains of the line of fortification, the Isthmian Wall, which served in turn Greeks, Macedonians, Saracens, Latin Crusaders, and Slavonic settlers; and fragments of the ancient buildings of the Isthmian Sanctuary, where the Pau-hellenic festivals were celebrated.

The drive across was exceedingly pleasant. The Isthmus is seamed with ravines and ridges, picturesque with rocks which running vines drape and age has colored, and variegated with corn-fields. We enjoyed on either hand the splendid mountain forms ; on the north white Helicon and Parnassus ; on the south the nearly two-thousand-feet wall-crowned height of Acro-Corinth and the broken snowy hills of the Morea.

Familiar as we were with the atlas, we had not until now any adequate conception how much indented the Grecian mainland and islands are, nor how broken into peaks, narrow valleys, and long serrated summits are the contours. When we appreciate, by actual sight, the multitude of islands that compose Greece, how subject to tempests its seas are, how difficult is communication between the villages of the mainland, or even those on the same island, we understand the naturalness of the ancient divisions and strifes ; and we see the physical obstacles to the creation of a feeling of unity in the present callow kingdom. And one hears with no surprise that Corfu wishes herself back under English protection.

We drove through the cluster of white houses on the bay, which is now called Corinth, and saw at three miles' distance the site of the old city and the Acropolis beyond it. Earthquakes and malaria have not been more lenient to the ancient town than was Roman vengeance, and of the capital which was to Greece in luxury what Athens was in wit, only a few columns and sinking walls remain. Even the voluptuousness of Corinth is a tale of two thousand years ago, and the name might long ago have sunk with the fortunes of the city, but for the long residence there of a poor tent-maker, in whom no proud citizen of that day, of all those who " sat down to eat and drink and rose up to play," would have recognized the chief creator of its fame.

Our little Greek steamer was crowded excessively, and mainly with Greeks going to Patras and Zante, who noisily talked poli-tics and business in a manner that savored more of New England than of the land of Solon and Plato. For the first time in a

travel of many months we met families together, gentlemen with
their wives and children, and saw the evidences of a happy home-
life. It is everything in favor of the Greeks that they have preserved the idea of home, and cherish, as the centre of all good and
strength, domestic purity.

At dinner there was an undisguised rush for seats at the table,
and the strongest men got them. We looked down through the
skylights and beheld the valiant Greeks flourishing their knives,
attacking, while expecting soup, the caviare and pickles, and
thrusting the naked blades into their mouths without fear. The
knife seems seldom to hurt the Greek, whose display of deadly
weapons is mainly for show. There are dozens of stout swarthy
fellows on board, in petticoats and quilted leggings, with each
a belly full of weapons, — the protruding leathern pouch contains
a couple of pistols, a cheese-knife, cartridges, and pipes and
tobacco.

The sail through the Gulf of Corinth is one to be enjoyed and
remembered, but the reader shall not be wearied with a catalogue
of names. What is it to him that we felt the presence of Delphi,
that we had Parnassus on our right, and Mt. Panachaicum, lifting
itself higher than Mt. Washington, on our left, the Locrian coast
on one side, and the range of Arcadia on the other? The strait
narrowed as we came at evening near Patras, and between the
opposite forts of Rheum and Antirheum it is no broader than the
Bosphorus; it was already dusky when we peered into the Bay
of Lepanto, which is not, however, the site of the battle of that
name in which the natural son of the pretty innkeeper of Ratisbon
rendered such a signal service to Christendom. Patras, a thriving
new city, which inherits the name but not the site of the ancient,
lies open in the narrow strait, subject to the high wind which
always blows through the passage, and is usually a dangerous landing. All the time that we lay there in the dark we thought a
tempest was prevailing, but the clamor subsided when we moved
into the open sea. Of Patras we saw nothing except a circle of
lights on the shore a mile long, a procession of colored torches
which illumined for an instant the façade of the city hall, and
some rockets which went up in honor of a local patriot who had

returned on our boat from Athens. And we had not even a glimpse of Missolonghi, which we passed in the night.

At daylight we are at Zante, anchored in its eastward-looking harbor opposite the Peloponnesian coast. The town is most charmingly situated, and gives one an. impression of wealth and elegance. Old Zacynthus was renowned for its hospitality before the days of the Athenian and Spartan wars, and — such is the tenacity with which traits are perpetuated amid a thousand changes — its present wealthy and enterprising merchant-farmers, whose villas are scattered about the slopes, enjoy a reputation for the same delightful gift. The gentlemen are distinguished among the Ionians for their fondness of country life and convivial gayety. Early as it was, the town welcomed us with its most gracious offerings of flowers and fruit; for the pedlers who swarmed on board brought nothing less poetical than handfuls of dewy roses, carnations, heliotrope, freshly cut mignonette, baskets of yellow oranges, and bottles of red wine. The wine, of which the Zante passengers had boasted, was very good, and the oranges, solid, juicy, sweet, the best I have ever eaten, except, perhaps, some grown in a fortunate year in Florida. Sharp hills rise behind the town, and, beyond, a most fertile valley broadens out to the sea. Almost all the land is given up to the culture of the currant-vine, the grapes of *Corinth*, for in the transfer of the chief cultivation of this profitable fruit from Corinth to Zante, the name went with the dwarf vines. On the hillsides, as we sailed away, we observed innumerable terraces, broad, flat, and hard like threshing-floors, and learned that they were the drying-grounds of the ripe currants.

We were all day among the Ionian Islands, and were able to see all of them except Cythera, off Cape Malea, esteemed for its honey and its magnificent temple to the foam-born Venus. They lay in such a light as the reader of Homer likes to think of them. We sailed past them as in a dream, not caring to distinguish history from fable. It was off the little Echinades, near the coast, by the mouth of the Achelous, that Don John, three hundred years ago, broke the European onset of the Ottoman arms; it was nearly a dear victory for Christendom, for among the severely

16 *   x

wounded was Cervantes, and Don Quixote had not yet been written. But this battle is not more real to us than the story of
Ulysses and Penelope which the rocky surface of Ithaca recalls.
And as we lingered along the shores of Cephalonia and Leucadia,
it was not of any Cæsar or Byzantine emperor or Norman chieftain
that we thought, but of the poet whose verses will outlast all their
renown. Leucadia still harbors, it is said, the breed of wolves
that, perhaps, of all the inhabitants of these islands preserve in
purity the Hellenic blood. We sailed close to the long promontory, " Leucadia's far-projecting rock of woe," and saw, if any one
may see, the very precipice from which Sappho, leaping, quenched
in brine the amatory flames of a heart that sixty years of song
and trouble had not cooled.

Through the strait of Actium we looked upon the smooth inland sea of Ambracia, while our steamer churned along the very
waters that saw the flight of the purple sails of Cleopatra, whom
the enamored Antony followed and left the world to Augustus.
The world was a small affair then, when its possession could be
decided on a bit of water where, as Byron says, two frigates could
hardly manœuvre. These historical empires were fleeting shows
at the best, not to be compared to the permanent conquests and
empire of the mind. The voyager from the Bosphorus to Corfu
feels that it is not any Alexander or Cæsar, Chagan or Caliph, but
Homer, who rules over the innumerable islands and sunny main-
lands of Greece.

It was deep twilight when we passed the barren rock of Anti-
paxos, and the mountain in the sea called Paxos. There is no
island in all these seas that has not its legend; that connected
with Paxos, and recorded by Plutarch, I am tempted to trans-
cribe from the handbook, in the quaint language in which it is
quoted, for it expresses not only the spirit of this wild coast, but
also our own passage out of the domain of mythology into the
sunlight of Christian countries: " Here, about the time that
our Lord suffered his most bitter passion, certain persons sailing from Italy to Cyprus at night heard a voice calling aloud,
Thamus! Thamus! who giving ear to the cry was bidden (for
he was pilot of the ship), when he came near to Pelodes to tell

that the great god Pan was dead, which he doubting to do, yet
for that when he came to Pelodes there was such a calm of wind
that the ship stood still in the sea unmoored, he was forced to
cry aloud that Pan was dead ; wherewithal there were such piteous outcries and dreadful shricking as hath not been the like.
By which Pan, of some is understood the great Sathanas, whose
kingdom was at that time by Christ conquered, and the gates of
hell broken up; for at that time all oracles surceased, and en-
chanted spirits that were wont to delude the people henceforth
held their peace."

It was ten o'clock at night when we reached Corfu, and sailed
in under the starlight by the frowning hill of the fortress, gliding
spectrally among the shipping, with steam shut off, and at a signal given by the bowsman letting go the anchor in front of the
old battery.

Corfu, in the opinion of Napoleon, enjoys the most beautiful
situation in the world. Its loveliness is in no danger of being
overpraised. Shut in by the Albanian coast opposite, the town
appears to lie upon a lake, surrounded by the noblest hills and
decorated with a tropical vegetation. Very picturesque in its
moss-grown rock is the half-dismantled old double fortress, which
the English, in surrendering to the weak Greek state, endeavored
to render as weak as possible. It and a part of the town occupy
a bold promontory ; the remainder of the city lies around a little
bay formed by this promontory and Quarantine Island. The
more we see of the charming situation, and become familiar with
the delicious mountain outlines, we regret that we can tarry but
a day, and almost envy those who make it a winter home. The
interior of the city itself, when we ascend the height and walk in
the palace square, appears bright and cheerful, but retains something of the dull and decorous aspect of an English garrison
town. In the shops the traveller does not find much to interest
him, except the high prices of all antiquities. We drove five
miles into the country, to the conical hill and garden of Gasturi,
whose mistress gathered for us flowers and let us pluck from the
trees the ripe and rather tasteless *nespoli*. From this summit is
an extraordinary prospect of blue sea, mountains, snowy summits,

the town, and the island, broken into sharp peaks and most luxuriant valleys and hillsides. Ancient, gnarled olive-trees abound,
thousands of acres of grapevines were in sight, the hedges were
the prickly-pear cactus, and groves of walnuts and most vigorous
fig-trees interspersed the landscape. There was even here and
there a palm. A lovely land, most poetical in its contours.

The Italian steamer for Brindisi was crowded with passengers.
On the forward deck was a picturesque horde of Albanian gypsies.
The captain said that he counted eighty, without the small ones,
which, to avoid the payment of fare, were done up in handkerchiefs and carried in bags like kittens. The men, in broad, short
breeches and the jackets of their country, were stout and fine
fellows physically. The women, wearing no marked costume, but
clad in any rags of dresses that may have been begged or stolen,
were strikingly wild in appearance, and if it is true that the
women of a race best preserve the primeval traits, these preserve,
in their swarthy complexions, burning black eyes, and jet black
hair, the characteristics of some savage Oriental tribe. The hair
in front was woven into big braids, which were stiff with coins
and other barbarous ornaments in silver. A few among them
might be called handsome, since their profiles were classic; but
it was a wild beauty which woman sometimes shares with the
panther. They slept about the deck amidst their luggage, one
family usually crawling into a single sack. In the morning there
were nests of them all about, and, as they crawled forth, especially
as the little ones swarmed out, it was difficult to believe that the
number of passengers had not been miraculously increased in the
night. The women carry the fortune of the family on their heads;
certainly their raiment, which drapes but does not conceal their
forms, would scarcely have a value in the rag-market of Naples.
I bought of one of them a silver ornament, cutting it from the
woman's hair, but I observed that her husband appropriated the
money.

It was like entering a new world of order and civilization, next
morning, to sail through the vast outer harbor of Brindisi into
the inner one, and lie, for the first time in the Mediterranean, at
a dock. The gypsies made a more picturesque landing than the

other passengers, trudging away with their bags, tags, rags, and
tent-poles, the women and children lugging their share. It was
almost touching to see their care for the heaps of rubbish which
constitute all their worldly possessions. They come like locusts
to plunder sunny Italy; on a pretence of seeking work in the
fields, they will spend the summer in the open air, gaining health
and living, as-their betters like to live, upon the labor of others.

Brindisi has a beautiful Roman column, near it the house where
Virgil is said to have died, and an ancient fortress, which is half
crumbling walls and half dwelling-houses, and is surrounded, like
the city wall, by a moat, now converted into a vegetable garden.
As I was peacefully walking along the rampart, intending to surround the town, a soldier motioned me back, as if it had been
time of war. I offered to stroll over the drawbridge into the
mouldy fortress. A soldier objected. As I turned away, he
changed his mind, and offered to show me the interior. But it
was now my turn to decline; and I told him that, the idle impulse passed, I would rather not go in. Of all human works I
care the least for fortresses, except to look at from the outside;
it is not worth while to enter one except by storming it or stroll-
ing in, and when one must ask permission the charm is gone. You
get sick to death almost of these soldier-folk who start up and
bar your way with a bayonet wherever you seek to walk in Europe. No, soldier; I like the view from the wall of the moat,
and the great fields of ripe wheat waving in the sweet north-wind,
but I don't care for you or your fortress.

Brindisi is clean, but dull. Yet it was characteristically Italian
that I should encounter in the Duomo square a smart, smooth-
tongued charlatan, who sold gold chains at a franc each, — which
did not seem to be dear; and a jolly, almost hilarious cripple,
who, having no use of his shrunken legs, had mounted himself on
a wooden bottom, like a cheese-box, and, by the aid of his hands,
went about as lively as a centipede.

I stepped into the cathedral; a service was droning on, with
few listeners. On one side of the altar was a hideous, soiled
wax image of the dead Christ. Over the altar, in the central
place of worship, was a flaring figure of the Virgin, clad in the

latest mode of French millinery, and underneath it was the legend, *Viva Maria.* This was the salutation of our return to a Christian land : Christ is dead ; the Virgin lives !

Here our journey, which began on the other coast of Italy in November, ends in June. In ascending the Nile to the Second Cataract, and making the circuit of the Levant, we have seen a considerable portion of the Moslem Empire and of the nascent Greek kingdom, which aspires, at least in Europe, to displace it. We have seen both in a transition period, as marked as any since the Saracens trampled out the last remnants of the always sickly Greek Empire. The prospect is hopeful, although the picture of social and political life is far from agreeable. But for myself, now that we are out of the Orient and away from all its squalor and cheap magnificence, I turn again to it with a longing which I cannot explain ; it is still the land of the imagination.

INDEX.

THE END.